Literal Madness

Other books by Kathy Acker
published by Grove Press

GREAT EXPECTATIONS
BLOOD AND GUTS IN HIGH SCHOOL
DON QUIXOTE

Literal Madness:

KATHY GOES TO HAITI
MY DEATH MY LIFE
BY PIER PAOLO PASOLINI
and
FLORIDA

Three Novels by
KATHY ACKER

GROVE PRESS
New York

Published by Grove Press, Inc.
920 Broadway
New York, N.Y. 10010

Kathy Goes to Haiti was first
published by Rumor Publications in 1978,
and *My Death My Life by Pier Paolo Pasolini* was first published
by Pan Books, Ltd., London, in 1984.

Library of Congress Cataloging-in-Publication Data
Acker, Kathy, 1948–
Literal madness.
Contents: Kathy goes to Haiti—My death, my life,
by Pier Paolo Pasolini—Florida.
I. Title.
PS3551.C44L5   1988   813'.54   87-14860
ISBN 0-8021-0001-5
Designed by Irving Perkins Associates

Manufactured in the United States of America
First Edition 1988

10 9 8 7 6 5 4 3 2 1

CONTENTS

KATHY GOES TO HAITI

FIRST DAYS IN PORT-AU-PRINCE

KATHY is a middle-class, though she has no money, American white girl, twenty-nine years of age, no lovers and no prospects of money, who doesn't believe in anyone or anything. One summer she goes down to Haiti. She steps out of the American Airlines plane and on to the cement runway, her first example of Haitian soil. She's scared to death because she doesn't know anybody, she doesn't know where to go in Haiti, and she can't speak the language.

Kathy has her small duffel bag strapped to her shoulder and is going through Customs. The Customs man asks Kathy where she's going to stay in Port-au-Prince. "I don't know," Kathy replies. "Most tourists stay at the _____ or the _____ " The Customs man says two indistinguishable names. "Oh," says Kathy. "I'm sure you'll be very comfortable there. We just want to make sure that you know where you're going." "Thank you," says Kathy. "I'll be sure to take your advice."

Kathy takes up her bag and continues traveling through the airport. A man comes over to her.

"Would you like a taxi?"

"No, thank you. I prefer to travel more cheaply."

"Do you know anyone in Port-au-Prince?"

"No."

"You'll have to take a taxi to get into the city."

"OK I'll take a taxi."

The man introduces Kathy to another man. The second man is fat. Kathy and the fat man shake hands.

"OK," she says. "Where's the taxi?"

"It's outside."

Kathy and the fat man walk out of the Jean-Claude Duvalier airport to a small parking lot. The light from a big white sun is beating down on the cement. The man opens the door of a light blue Plymouth.

"This is a nice car."

"I decorated it myself."

Kathy and the fat man climb into the car.

The fat man starts the car.

Everywhere she sees the combinations of things she's never seen before. The land is very flat and dry. Shoeless women with huge baskets balanced on their heads walk on the sides of the road. Sometimes these women walk past small brick and cement motel and cocktail lounges. Nothing surrounds these motel and cocktail lounges. There are no trees. No brush. Suddenly there's a bridge and a huge cement bank which is tall enough to look like an American bank. It says THE BANK OF NOVA SCOTIA.

"Where am I going?" the driver asks the woman.

"I don't know. I've never been to Haiti before I know nothing about Haiti. I guess to a hotel."

"Which hotel?"

"I don't know. Which one do you recommend? I don't have much money."

"It all depends on how much you want to spend. How much do you want to spend?"

"I don't have any idea. It depends on how much I have to spend. Do you understand?"

"Do you want to spend twelve a night? Fifteen? Twenty? You can spend as much as you want."

"Twelve, fifteen would be OK. I'd like to get cheaper. I want a bathroom."

"Do you want a pool? Most Americans like a pool."

"I don't care much about a pool. You know what I'd really love? I'd love to be next to the ocean. Can I go swimming in the ocean?"

"Not around here."

"I mean can I find a place that's near the ocean?"

"I know a place you'll like. It won't cost you much."

"Is it near the ocean?"

"It's right on the ocean."

"Oh goody. I'm so happy. This is the first time I've ever been out of New York. Everything is so strange to me." She watches the children in torn dresses, the men in cut-off sandals shirtless lead the yoked cows and mules. The doorless stores set on wooden platforms. "How much will it cost for you to take me there?"

"That depends."

"What does it depend on?"

"Do you like me?"

"Yes."

"I'll take you for nothing. You'll be my girlfriend."

"I don't know."

"Why not?"

"I don't want to stay in Port-au-Prince more than one night. I want to go to Jacmel."

"To be my girlfriend you'll have to stay in Port-au-Prince a week. I can tell. You're going to like it in Port-au-Prince a lot."

"I don't know. I don't think I'm going to stay here."

"Do you speak French?"

"A little."

"Speak French."

From now on Kathy speaks only French in Port-au-Prince. Her French stinks.

"I'll stay in Port-au-Prince two days."

"A week."

"We're arguing already."

The fat man smiles. His right hand covers her left hand. Kathy and the taxi-driver hold hands.

Haiti is a mountainous country. Mountains rise from the seacoasts and cover most of the inland part of the country. There are almost no roads in Haiti and many of the people who live inland have not and cannot leave the acres that are their village of birth. The city of Port-au-Prince lies between the beginning of the mountains and the ocean. Because hot winds sweep dust and then pollution down from the mountains into the lower lands and because the heat collects in the lower regions, the rich Port-au-Prince inhabitants—the tourists and the Haitian multimillionaires—live in the mountains: at the edge of Port-au-Prince in the suburb of Petionville and even farther west into the mountains. Port-au-Prince is a city that descends. One moves from the mansions hidden in the mountainous luxuriant foliage down to the tourist hotels and government offices of the wide city streets down, as it gets hotter and hotter, to the block-large markets, the Iron Market, where all the Haitians buy their necessities, down to the slums where shacks are piled on shacks, where twenty people live in one room, down to the edge of the water, the docks, where there are no breezes, only hot dust, and where the United States Navy waits a mile away in the ocean.

This is what Kathy sees: First paper-thin paper-like-wall shacks on thin wooden platforms. Walls are dirty pink, dirty pale green, dirty tan. Some of these shacks are stores because they have no doors and bear signs like EPICERIE and BOUTIQUE DE PARIS. There are more and more people everywhere. Soon there's at least one person per square foot. Men and women and girls and boys and babies sit and argue and sell and buy and stand around and eat and walk. No animals in sight. A few thin mangy green-leafed trees. The shacks move closer and closer together until they form a solid row that walls in the road. So there's this road with lots of cars running up and down it and long eight-feet-high paper strips on each side of it. The paper strips contain small paper doors. As they grow larger, the paper strips separate from each other and become individual buildings. Partly rotting two-and three-story houses surrounded by weeds and high concrete white fences. Larger semi-decaying mansions. Some of the buildings are stone and there are one or two rectangular cement office buildings. The buildings lie far apart from each other. The roads are wide. All the people here are walking. Some of the people wear clothes which aren't torn. There's a park. To the left and right of the road there are quasi-triangular ten-acre sections of low-cut grass, trimmed hedges, and here and there small circles of red flowers in the low-cut grass. To the right, below the grass, there's another few acres of plain dirt. Across the road from the dirt, still descending, there're a strip of joined yellow concrete houses which form a fence around a large dirt square.

"That's the army barracks," the taxi-driver says. The light blue Plymouth keeps moving. "To your left's a mausoleum."

On the left, the park continues. Low-cut grass and occasional small white and yellow flowers surround white steps and the large white building the white steps lead up to. Below the park there's a huge oval strip of land. A black metal fence surrounds this strip. Within the fence is a huge totally clean whiter-than-the-sun mansion. The mansion looks like an American government mansion. White white steps lead up to the mansion. There are no trees. There are no people. The shacks begin again and all the people walk and sit and talk and carry baskets and have dogs and quarrel. The road's a hard dirt road. It winds around, goes up and down, basically it moves north-south. There's dust everywhere. Dust on the road, dust in the air, dust on the skin, dust on the straw and wood shacks. The distance is a light tan haze. The shacks are light tan and grey. They're about two feet apart from each other. Dogs and chickens run from the shacks into the street. The sides of the road are ruts. Women and a few children walk in these ruts. There are almost no men. The women wear brightly colored scarves around their heads and closefitting dresses or blouses and skirts ending at their knees. Some of the dresses and skirts are torn. Sometimes they wear aprons over their skirts. The road's flat and runs directly north and south. On the right the dry land rises and on the left it slopes down and can't be seen again. Eight-feet-high paper walls line the road. There are so many men and women walking in front of the walls, there's a closer wall of black flesh. Cars pass on top of each other. Honk.

Honk. The people thin out. To the right, on the sloping dirt's a small cement house. The sign on the wood fence that surrounds this house says MARIE'S VOODOO. NIGHTLY. There are lots of similar houses surrounded by fences that are nightclubs and voodoo places. The sun is hot and bright. There are fewer and fewer houses. Just a long strip of road and more trees.

Kathy hasn't seen any white people.

The light blue Plymouth pulls into a driveway. On one side of the driveway there's a white stucco rectangular building. The other side is a patio: a round thatched roof reaches upward to a point over a raised cement floor. There are about ten rough wood chairs and tables and then a clear space around the jukebox which says WURLITZER.

"You stay in the car," the taxi-driver says to his new girlfriend. "I'm going to talk to somebody."

When the fat man returns to the taxicab, he tells Kathy she can stay here for nine dollars a night. That includes two meals a day. Kathy thinks that's cheap. "Is this a motel or your friend's house?" she asks the taxi-driver.

"A motel. Lots of tourists stay here."

The proprietor of the motel, a tall elegant Haitian who speaks French rather than Creole walks with the taxi-driver and the girl through the rubble and stones in back of the white building. From the rubble a hill made up of stone pebbles and a bit of dirt rises sharply upward toward inland Haiti. The sun beats down on the broken glass and rubbish under the girl's feet. Small white concrete rooms stick together and form the two rows of buildings behind the large white building. The last room is about a foot from the paved highway.

"How long will you be staying here?"

"I don't know. Probably three days."

"She'll be staying longer," the taxi-driver says.

"No, I won't."

"Well, we can have this room fixed up for you tomorrow." The proprietor shows Kathy the last room, a ten foot by eight foot room containing a rocking chair and a large window. The room has no floor.

"I like the room," the girl says. "I like the rocking chair."

"You also have your own bathroom here and you can come and leave without anyone bothering you."

The proprietor, the taxi-driver, and the girl walk around the building, through the hot rubble, to the first row of stuck-together rooms. The proprietor opens the door of the first room on the right. The room is ten feet by seven feet, has a cot, a small window, a table with a fan on it, and a straw mat. It looks like a cell.

"You can take this room for tonight. The other will be ready tomorrow."

"This is fine. This is perfect. I'm very happy." The taxi-driver goes to bring the girl her bag. The proprietor leaves. The taxi-driver brings the girl her bag and she starts unpacking.

"I'm going to go swimming. That's what I want to do most of all. I haven't been swimming in two years." The taxi-driver leaves the girl alone.

There's a knocking at the door.

"Who's there?"

"It's Sammy."

Kathy opens the door and sees the taxi-driver.

"I went to the car to get my bathing suit." He walks into the room. "Close the door."

Kathy closes the door and puts her arms around him and hugs him. He kisses her. Their tongues touch. Their tongues touch for a long time.

"Put on your suit. I'll put mine on," says the taxi-driver. She watches the taxi-driver and takes off her blue shirt. Her blue jeans. She's taking off her underpants. The taxi-driver walks into the bathroom. He comes back wearing a tiny yellow and orange flower bikini. His stomach sticks out over the bikini.

"Would you like a drink?"

"Sure."

A tall rather handsome young man's leaning against a stone wall. On the top of the stone wall's a bottle of rum, a tin bowl of ice, and two plastic cups. He pours rum into one of the cups and hands it to Kathy.

The taxi-driver puts his arm around Kathy. A small girl in a green bathing suit leans against the handsome young man's front.

"Where are you from?" the handsome man asks Kathy.

"I'm from New York City."

"Oh. How old are you?"

"I'm twenty-nine."

"I'm twenty-four. Sammy is twenty-nine."

"You are my age," she says to the fat man. "How old are you?" she asks the girl.

"Twenty-two."

"Uh."

Sammy and the two other people talk for a while in Creole.

"I want to talk to you," the handsome man says to Kathy and takes her hand in his.

"Is something the matter?"

"My brother tells me he loves you very much. There is a great deal of love in his heart for you. He says to me that he's very glad he has met you."

"Uh. That's nice."

"When are you going to get married?"

"Married? Wait a minute. Who's your brother?"

"Sammy. He's your driver."

"But we were just holding hands. You know. I don't even know him. Even if I did know him, I don't want to get married."

"Maybe you're married already."

"No, I'm not married."

"You're not going to marry him? He tells me he loves you very much."

"I don't want to get married. No. No way."

The handsome man leads Kathy to the right, on to the empty porch of a deserted white stucco house. "I want to talk to you very openly. I want you to tell me the truth. My brother says he feels a lot of love for you in his heart. Do you love him?"

"I don't love him or don't not love him. I don't know your brother."

"I want you to understand. My brother has been very lonely. He has had no girlfriend for a long time. His girlfriend left him and went away to the north last year. He needs to go with someone. Are you going with anyone?"

"No."

"Then he'll go with you. And we'll see what happens."

"I'm not staying. I'm going away tomorrow."

"Why? You could stay here for awhile."

"I want to go to Jacmel."

"Do you have some friends in Jacmel?"

"No. I just want to go to Jacmel."

"You could stay here for a few days and we could see what happens."

"No. I'm going to go to Jacmel."

"You like my brother?"

"Yes. Your brother seems like a nice person."

"When you go away, you'll write my brother?"

"Look. You have to tell me what's going on. I don't want to hurt your brother. You understand? I don't want to do anything to hurt anyone. I'm in a foreign land and I don't know quite how to act, what the customs are here. In my country people take a long time to get married. They have to know each other very well."

"My brother's alone and you are alone."

"I don't want to do anything to hurt your brother. I think he's a nice person, but I want to be free. I know it's hard being lonely so I don't want to do anything to hurt him. I don't know what to do in this situation."

"You like him?"

"I think he's a nice person."

"When you go away, you'll write him?"

"Yes. I'll write him some letters."

"You'll write him, he'll answer, maybe you'll fall in love. That'll be good."

They walk back to the other two people. Everyone but Kathy drinks some more rum. The three Haitians talk to each other. "I'm going swimming," says the white girl.

At a break in the concrete wall some rough stone steps lead down to the ocean. Kathy walks down the rough steps and into the ocean. Swims out in the cold gray wetness. Gray and gray-green with late sun looking more like a sheath of white diamond light than a fiery ball. Through tiny gray waves on the surface of this moving shifting air. Outward as far as she wants to go. Lays on her back and kicks water into the air. A three-seat wood rowboat moves by her. To her left's a small dirt beach. Skinny kids play on the beach. Time is slow here. The taxi-driver swims out to her. She swims to the stone steps. The rowboat turns around and comes to the stone steps. The man in the rowboat gives Sammy's younger brother a heavy straw bag. The younger brother's sitting on the steps. He opens the ugly black, white, and gray shells. Gives half a shell to the white girl. Remembers. Give her a slice of lime. She squeezes the lime over the oyster and swallows. He gives half a shell to Sammy. Sammy doesn't like to eat these things. He eats a few oysters. He and the white girl eat three rounds of tiny oysters. The girl goes back to swimming. She returns and they eat two more rounds of oysters. The man hands the straw bag and twenty cents to the fisherman. The rowboat goes back into the ocean. The air's turning gray and cold. The ocean's warmer and warmer. The white girl rises out of the water and shivers.

"Why don't you eat now?" the taxi-driver tells the white girl.

"Are you going to eat?"

"I'll eat."

The taxi-driver puts his arm around the girl and kisses her neck. The motel proprietor appears.

"We have chicken tonight. Is that OK?"

The fat man says something in Creole.

"That's fine," says the girl. "I'm starving." The girl turns to the handsome man and his girlfriend. "Aren't you going to eat?"

They look at her.

"I don't want to eat if you're not going to eat."

"We'll eat later."

A young girl places a large plate containing fried plantains, tomatoes, lettuce, and half-a-chicken roasted dry in front of Kathy. Kathy turns to the fat man. "Aren't you going to eat?"

"I'll help you eat." The fat man cuts up the chicken and places pieces of chicken in Kathy's mouth. When he's not putting pieces of chicken in her mouth, he's placing slobbering kisses on her neck. She finishes her dinner.

It's too dark outside to see the three Haitians and the white girl sitting on the patio under the thatched roof. To the left ten teenagers dance to American music on the jukebox.

"We'll go dancing tonight," the fat man tells Kathy. "I want to please you."

"I'd love to go dancing."

He orders a bottle of rum and pours a glass of rum for Kathy. The three Haitians talk to each other and drink rum. Kathy can't speak Creole.

"Come here," the fat man whispers. She leans her head on his shoulder. "It'll cost us to go dancing."

"How much?"

"Ten dollars."

"Ten dollars? That's ridiculous. I can't afford to pay that much money."

"We have to pay to get in and then we have to drink rum. It costs."

"OK." She gives the fat man ten dollars.

"Drink your rum."

She doesn't drink any rum. The three Haitians talk desultorily. "I'm too tired," she says. "I'm sorry. We'll go dancing tomorrow night. I want to go to my room."

"You don't want to go dancing? I thought you wanted to dance."

"Tomorrow night. I'm too tired now."

"I'll go to your room with you."

The fat man keeps his arm closely around Kathy. They say goodnight to his younger brother and the girl.

"I'm kind of weird," Kathy says to him as they step into her room.

"Close the door."

She closes the door. "I like to sleep alone. I mean, I like to be with guys, but I never spend the whole night with anyone."

"I understand."

She smiles. "That's wonderful. I mean, I know I'm weird." She turns around and kisses the guy as passionately as she can since she doesn't feel anything. He leads her to the bed, lays her down, and kisses her lightly. He doesn't want to take her clothes off, he just wants to kiss her slowly and lightly. She can't stand this. She reaches into his bathing suit and finds a long, thin cock. He doesn't react. After a while she takes her hand out of the bathing suit.

"In Haiti time is very very slow," the taxi-driver says.

The girl sighs. The man and the girl kiss some more. They take off their bathing suits. The girl leans down and gently places the man's cock in her mouth. It gets semi-hard. She turns her hand around the cock and opens and closes her hand. Her tongue moves fast up and down along the ridge of the head. Her mouth opens and closes. Softly. The cock is long and hard. She presses and rubs and licks. Nothing else happens no matter what she does.

"Since we're not going dancing, why don't you give me the money back?"

"No. I bought you rum."

"I didn't ask you for rum. And the rum couldn't have cost ten dollars."

"I don't want to give you the money."

"It's my money."

"Do you really need it?"

"OK. Keep it."

The girl and the man go back to kissing. Kathy grabs the man's cock. As soon as it's hard, she sticks it in her cunt. She pulls away, reaches for her purse, opens a blue plastic case, and sticks her diaphragm in her. "What's that?" asks the man.

"A diaphragm."

"I don't like it."

"I have to use it. I can't afford to get pregnant."

"I don't like it." The man refuses to fuck the girl. She takes her diaphragm out. She's scared he's going to hit her. They kiss for a while. "I'm going to drink," says the man. "Do you mind?"

"Do you get violent when you're drunk?"

"What do you mean?"

"Do you smash chairs and beat up people?"

"No."

"Why should I mind?"

"I'm going to go now."

"Where are you going?"

"I'm going to drink."

Kathy locks the door of her cell after the man and starts to meditate.

There's a knocking at the door. "Put this on the table," the taxi-driver tells Kathy as he enters the room. "I brought it for you."

"I don't like rum." She puts the bottle on the table.

"C'mon baby. Do you like me?"

She puts her lips up to his.

"Oh. Mon amour. Mon amour."

They take off their clothes and lie in the hot room on the narrow cot. She tries to put his cock in her cunt. It's too soft. She touches him and tries to put the cock in again. It's still too soft.

"I can't fuck you cause of that thing."

"The diaphragm."

"I don't like it." He turns her around and sticks his cock in her ass. Kathy's so happy to get laid at last she immediately comes. "Mon amour. Mon amour," says the man. "Je t'aime. Je t'aime. Do you know what that means?"

"Yes."

"Mon amour. Mon amour." The man comes. They sit in the middle of the bed and stare at the door. "I'm very tired," she says. "I'd like to go to sleep." The man looks at his watch and keeps sitting on the bed.

Around eleven o'clock the man tells her he loves her, she's his girlfriend, and leaves. Kathy can't sleep cause it's hot and the bed is strange.

It's hot and dry. Kathy sits on the patio porch, doing nothing. There's no one around. After a while some young boys show up. They sit down by her and stare at her. The white girl walks into the large building of the motel to get a beer. A boy who's sixteen, older than the boys outside, asks her where's she from.

"New York City."

"I have a relative in New York City."

She goes back outside. The fat man drives his light blue Plymouth into the driveway. He gets out of the car. When he puts his arm around Kathy, she shies away. He asks her when he should pick her up. She tells him she wants to be alone today. He should pick her up at six. He tells her he's very jealous and he'll be by at six. She kisses his cheek. Eight or nine young boys are sitting on the patio, talking, drinking beer, smoking. The girl walks across the black highway to the concrete wall.

The tall thin sixteen-year-old boy who was sitting inside the large motel building walks up to her.

"Are you a student?"

"No. I'm not."

"Do you have any babies?"

"No."

"You don't have any babies? Why not?"

"I never wanted any babies."

"Are you married?"

"No."

"Why don't you marry me?"

"What?"

"You could marry me and stay in Haiti."

"I don't want to get married. I like being alone."

"Don't you like Haiti?"

"Yes. It's beautiful here. Everything is very slow here. There's no tension."

"There is no time in Haiti. No one has to do anything here."

"Yes," says Kathy. "That's true."

They watch the green ocean for awhile. Another young boy walks up to Kathy and the tall thin boy. "This is Kathy," the tall thin boy says. "She's from New York City."

"Hello," says the shorter boy. "How long have you been here?"

"A day."

"You act like you've been here longer."

Kathy smiles.

"How long are you going to stay here?"

"I don't know," says Kathy. She smiles. "I'll be in Haiti for a month, two months. I'm going to Jacmel today."

"Today? How are you going today?"

"The motel proprietor told I don't know who the jeep to stop by the motel for me. The jeep'll come by about four o'clock."

"Why are you going to Jacmel?"

"Friends of mine told me it was very beautiful. They told me to stay at Pension Kraft."

"Don't go there. You won't like it there. Nothing ever happens in Jacmel. Stay in Port-au-Prince." He puts his hand over her hand.

"The car's coming for me today. Since I found a ride I have to go."

"No. You'll stay with me tonight. In Port-au-Prince. I'll take you to the bus tomorrow."

"I want to go to Jacmel today."

"Please. If you don't stay with me, I'll become very sick." The boy sings to her a Haitian rock-n-roll song. "You'll stay with me tonight." His brown eyes look pleading into hers.

"I'm going swimming now. It's too hot." Kathy swims in the cold green waters. The boys walk away. She sits on one of the lowest concrete steps. Every now and then the waves fall over this step. She swims some more. A man's sitting on the concrete wall that connects to the porch of the deserted house. Kathy gets out of the ocean and sits on another part of the wall.

"It's hot, isn't it?" the older man says.

"Yes," says the girl.

A strange boy walks up to Kathy. "Hello." He takes off his shirt. A friend of his joins him.

"Hello," says Kathy.

"Where are you from?" the first boy asks Kathy.

"New York City."

The boy's friend jumps up and sits down on the concrete wall. A copy of *Les Freres Karamazov* lies in his hand.

"Oh. Dostoyevsky. He's one of my favorite authors." She's happy she can talk about books.

"We're reading him in school."

"What school do you go to?"

"I study biology at the college."

"Oh," says Kathy. "Are these your notes?" She's looking at a small pink notebook.

"These are my biology notes. I'm studying to be a doctor."

"Can I look at them?"

"Sure."

Kathy looks at the green and red pen drawings of plants. Some of them look familiar.

"Why did you come to Haiti?" asks the medical student.

"I don't know. I wanted to. For the last two years I've wanted to come to Haiti."

"That's not that long."

"I guess not."

"You are very beautiful."

"Thank you."

"It's not usual for a young beautiful girl to travel alone."

"I'm not that young. I'm twenty-nine."

"You're not twenty-nine. I don't believe it."

"I am twenty-nine."

"You're younger than that. You're about twenty-two or twenty-three. Do you have a boyfriend?"

"No."

"You don't have a boyfriend. How can that be? You don't like love?"

"Well, I have several boyfriends. Kind of. Back in the States. You know how it is."

"When I come to the United States to study, I'll come visit you. Give me your name and address."

"OK."

"Tonight we'll go dancing together."

"We can't go dancing. I'm going to Jacmel at four o'clock."

"Do you have any babies?" the first boy asks.

"No."

"You've never had any babies?"

"Never."

"That's very strange. How come?"

"A woman can't have babies in New York City unless she's got money or a husband. Everything's too expensive in New York City."

"Do you want a baby?"

"Yes. Sometimes. When I can afford it."

"I'd like to have a baby with you."

"I can't have your baby. I don't know you."

"That way you'd get to know me. We'd have a beautiful baby."

"We can't have a baby." A dark blue car honks. "I'm going to Jacmel today." The car honks again. Kathy turns around. A hand's waving from the car. She walks over to the car.

"Hello. How are you this morning?" asks the taxi-driver's brother.

"This is Kathy." The brother introduces her to three gorgeous men. "This is Robert. Malcolm. Henri. You'n Sammy're going dancing with us tonight. Right?"

"Yeah. Sammy already dropped by this morning to see me. He's going to pick me up around six."

"I'll see you then. How'd you and my brother get along last night?"

"OK. He tells me he loves me, but I don't know him."

"I'll see you at six. Stay good until then."

"I'll try, but it'll be hard."

"Are those your friends in the car?" the medical student's friend asks the girl.

"He's the brother of the guy who drove me yesterday from the airport to the motel."

"Is he your husband?"

"Oh. I see what you mean by 'husband.' "

"Is he your husband?"

"No. I don't have a husband."

"Listen. You don't understand how things are in Haiti. Women in Haiti don't go around alone."

"What about the women who aren't married? Are there any woman who aren't married?"

"They live with their families."

"It's not like that in the United States."

"You can't go to Jacmel alone. You have to have a boyfriend."

"But I don't want a boyfriend. I want to be alone."

"If you don't go with a boyfriend, the driver of the jeep'll become your boyfriend."

"You mean he'll rape me?"

"No. No. There's no violence in Haiti. Anybody can do any-thing they want in Haiti."

"What'm I supposed to do?"

"I'll be your boyfriend in Jacmel."

"But you're in Port-au-Prince."

"I'll go to Jacmel with you. You'll stay over at my house tonight and we'll go together tomorrow."

"I want to go to Jacmel today."

"It's no good today. I'll put my name and address in Port-au-Prince in your book and you'll come to my house in Port-au-Prince this afternoon. Around four o'clock. I'll take you to the museum and all the art galleries. Are you interested in Haitian art?"

"Yes."

The boy writes his name and address on the first page of *Desolation Angels*. "You take a tap-tap and tell the driver to let you off here. I'll see you at four o'clock and tomorrow we'll go to Jacmel."

"At four o'clock. I'm going in swimming now." She walks down the concrete steps, across the sharp stones about two feet below the water, and dives. No one's around the concrete wall and the white porch. She gets out of the water and sits on the highest stone step. A strange thin boy walks up to her.

"Do you go swimming here a lot?"

"This is my first time. I just got to Port-au-Prince."

"How do you like Port-au-Prince?"

"I don't know." She sighs. "There are too many men here. They're always following me around."

The thin boy's silent.

"Are there very few women in Haiti? Am I acting in a funny way?"

"There are more women in Haiti than men. The women usually chase the men. But it's unusual for someone so young and beautiful to be alone. Everyone's curious about you."

"Oh. But they all want me to be their girlfriend."

"Don't you have a boyfriend?"

"No. I like being alone."

"I'll be your boyfriend if you want."

The medical student and his friend walk up to Kathy and the thin boy. She nods hello to them and turns back to the thin boy. "I like you very much but I don't want a boyfriend."

"She's going to Jacmel with me," says the medical student's friend.

"Well," she says, "I don't know."

"You're coming to my house today at four o'clock and we'll go to Jacmel tomorrow."

"Why're you going to Jacmel?" the thin boy questions her. "There's nothing in Jacmel."

"Friends of mine back in New York City told me I should stay at this pension in Jacmel. They said it's very beautiful there."

"Why don't you stay in Port-au-Prince?" the thin boy says. "You can stay with me."

"I don't want to stay in Port-au-Prince. I want to go somewhere where I can be alone. In New York City everything's always crazy and I want somewhere it's not crazy. Where it's very peaceful."

"You should go to Cap Haitian."

"Where's Cap Haitian?"

"It's up north. It's a tourist city. You'd like it there."

"I don't want to be a tourist. I just want to go somewhere where I can lie on a beach and not be hassled."

"I'm from Cap Haitian," the thin boy says. "I love it there. I love Port-au-Prince. This is also my homeland but even more I love Cap Haitian. It's very very peaceful there and very small. You can walk anywhere. No one will bother you. It's not big and noisy like Port-au-Prince. If you want nightlife, you stay in Port-au-Prince."

"I don't want nightlife. I got all the nightlife I wanted in New York."

"You should stay at L'Ouverture pension."

"I stayed there when I was in Cap Haitian," says the medical student's friend. "That's a really good place."

"Is it like the motel here?" asks Kathy. "I feel like I'm staying in a dumpy prison."

"Which motel?"

"The one right across the street."

"No no. L'Ouverture is really nice. Everyone who goes to Cap Haitian stays there. All the Haitians stay there."

"That's true," says the medical student's friend.

"I think I'll go to Jacmel and then to Cap Haitian."

"Where are you going now?"

"I'm going to the motel to see whether the jeep that's going to Jacmel came yet."

"I thought you were going to come to my house today and go to Jacmel with me tomorrow," says the medical student's friend.

"I really want to go to Jacmel today. I already had the motel proprietor send someone just so I could get this ride. I'll meet you in Jacmel tomorrow."

"The car won't come today," says the medical student's friend.

"Why do you say that?"

"It won't."

"Well, if it doesn't come, I'll go to your house at four o'clock and then we'll go to Jacmel tomorrow. Either way I'll see you in Jacmel tomorrow. OK?"

"No problem."

The thin boy grabs her arm. "If you leave me like this, I'm going to die."

"C'mon," says Kathy. "That's not true."

"It is true." The boy cries. "I love you."

"I'm just going to the motel," says Kathy. "I'm not leaving yet."

"You'll be at the motel?"

"I'll be at the motel."

"OK. I'll join you there."

The sun's at its hottest. Against the stucco white wall by the highway a woman sits by a small black pig. Another woman peels a mango for a young boy. Across the highway everything's white. White motel walls. White cement underneath. The patio's crowded. Women with full short torn skirts and homemade bandanas, huge baskets filled with clean laundry, walk in the ruts.

"Has the jeep that goes to Jacmel come by yet?"

"No."

There are men everywhere. Men talk to men. Ten-year-old men. Forty-year-old men. Most of all twenty-year-old men. Men lounge around and do nothing. Men drink rum and coke. Men play the jukebox. Kathy sits down at an empty table on the patio.

"Would you like to join us?"

Kathy says no, then yes. She sits next to a semi-gray-haired man and a short-haired robust woman.

"My name's Walter," says the man. He pours her some rum.

"Mine's Kathy. What's your name?"

"I'm Marguerite."

The thin boy who was talking to Kathy asks her to dance. She dances with him. A slightly older and heavier boy cuts in. The older boy holds Kathy close and grinds his cock against her. The medical student and his friend show up. Kathy walks away from the older boy to the medical student.

"You're still here? I thought you were going to Jacmel."

"The jeep hasn't shown up. I guess it isn't going to come."

Seven boys crowd around Kathy. One of them sticks his hand under her bathing suit top and strokes her breast. She walks back to Walter and Marguerite.

"Walter's my boyfriend," says Marguerite. "I spend the days with him and the nights with my husband."

"Does your husband know about this?"

"My husband and Walter are best friends. It's wonderful. I like everything to be out in the open. You know, in Haiti a woman has to be married."

"What do you mean?"

"If a woman's married, she can do anything she wants. She's protected. If she's not married, no man'll respect her."

"You're the first woman here I've been able to talk with. I'm confused about what's happening. How do the women in Haiti act? Everyone here tells me that women never go anywhere alone. Is that true? Am I going to be unable to travel here?"

"That's not true. There are career women here." Marguerite laughs. "But there is a problem in Haiti. A woman has no freedom unless she's married. She needs a man who'll take care of her. Then she can do anything. I have a man who takes care of me, my husband, and then I have as many boyfriends as I want. I don't love my husband."

"But I don't want a husband."

"You need to have a man who'll protect you. So men will respect you. The men here don't respect you."

"You're too young for this place," Walter says to Kathy. "How d'you get here?"

"The driver brought me here from the airport. I didn't know where I was going."

"You know what?" says Marguerite. "Tonight Walter and I'll take you back to my place. You'll eat dinner with us. I want you to understand: I don't know if you'll like it: my place is very small, but you can stay at my place. Did your driver take you around Port-au-Prince?"

"I haven't been anywhere. Just here."

"Tomorrow we'll go around Port-au-Prince and you'll see how beautiful my city is. I want you to have a good impression of my city. Would you like that?"

"That would be incredibly wonderful. I'm very happy now."

The taxi-driver and his brother sit down at the table. Everyone says hello. Sammy tries to put his arm around Kathy, and Kathy moves away.

"I don't want to be your girlfriend."

"OK. No problem."

The Haitians talk Creole to each other. Sammy asks Kathy where she's going. She's going to Marguerite's house.

The sky's growing dark. A $6,000 light tan car. Almost all consumer goods are imports from the US. If a Haitian wants to produce cars or TV's in Haiti, he has to make the items in Haiti, export them to the US, import them to Haiti. That's the only way the Haitian government can make the luxury taxes they so desperately need. Light tan leather seats.

"Sammy told us he's your boyfriend. You have to be back by six o'clock so you can go dancing with him."

"He's not my boyfriend. Sure we kissed a little and you know but that doesn't make him my boyfriend. He's crazy. He picks me up at the airport yesterday, he's my driver, and takes me to this godforsaken motel. I don't even know how to get out of it and get back to Port-au-Prince. Then he tells me I can't speak to any other men cause he's very jealous. Then he asks me if I want to go dancing. 'OK,' I tell him, 'sure.' He asks me for ten bucks. We don't go dancing, but he keeps the ten bucks. Some boyfriend."

"I want to explain something to you. Sammy's a driver. I know all the drivers in this town and they're all the same. They only see money. Tourists to them, first of all, mean money."

"Then you understand. I don't see why I have to keep the date with him tonight. When I left the motel just now, I told him he wasn't my boyfriend. He acts like he doesn't hear. I don't want to make trouble, understand; I'm in a foreign country."

"When Sammy was your driver, did he take you on a tour of Port-au-Prince?"

"Huh? No . . . He just drove straight to the motel. As far as I can tell cause I don't know the place."

"He should have taken you on a tour. Sammy's an evil man. All he cares about is money. Most Haitians are gentle and good. I want you to see the other side of Haiti."

The gray sky turns purples. Layers of roses and lavenders. Top layers of blues and dark purples. Everything in front of the sky has become forms of dark blues and black. The sky is dark blue. Now and then there are tiny lights. Carrefour, the town or stretch of land and swamp on the ocean between the motel and Port-au-Prince. Paper walls are black. Black shapes pass each other in front of these black walls.

The air's hot. The drums are beating.

"If you want, you can stay at my house for as long as you're in Port-au-Prince," Marguerite says to the white girl.

"I'd love to stay at your house. But I'm going to Jacmel tomorrow morning."

"Why are you going to Jacmel? If you want to go somewhere,

you should go to Cap Haitian. Cap Haitian is my hometown.
It's the most beautiful place in Haiti. The people there are all
gentle and good. No one will harm you there. Sometimes the
people in Port-au-Prince are no good."

"If you want," Walter says, "I can drive you there. I'm a driver
for tourists." He shows Kathy his card.

"How far is it to Cap Haitian?"

"Six hours. Four hours."

"How much will you charge me?"

"I don't charge you anything. I don't want your money. I do
it for friendship."

"Walter will take care of you. He'll be very good to you."

"I don't understand. Why will you do this? Are you going to
Cap Haitian on your own?"

"No. I'll drive you there and then I'll come back. It won't take
me long."

"Will I have to be your girlfriend?"

"Well. Yes."

"But Marguerite's your girlfriend. I don't want to come between
you and Marguerite."

"It's OK," says Marguerite.

"No. I'll go to Cap Haitian by plane."

"You don't have to be my girlfriend. We'll just see what happens."

Port-au-Prince is a mass of decaying white and yellow houses.
The sky grows blacker and blacker. The black road between Port-
au-Prince and the motel stretches out into the blackness. Trees,
walls, huts are indistinct shapes. Walter, Marguerite, and Kathy
are drinking rum on the motel patio. Walter's wearing pale yellow
pants and a pale yellow shirt.

"I dressed up especially for you. Because you're my girl."

"Oh," says Kathy. She's extremely tired since she hasn't slept
in two days. "I'm going to sleep."

"I'll pick you up early tomorrow morning and take you all
around Port-au-Prince so you can see how beautiful my city is.

I want you to go home with a good impression of Haiti. Then you stay at my house and the next day you can go to Jacmel."

"That'd be great," says Kathy, "goodnight." She locks herself in her cell and immediately falls asleep.

The small black-and-white goats bleat. The rooster crows, stops, crows again. Footsteps outside the window. Sound of water dripping on the rubble. Outside there's no one except for two young girls short tight skirts with slips showing under skirts T-shirts and bras plastic sandals who're cleaning up last night's debris. One girl disappears into the large room. The other girl sweeps the patio, straightens the chairs, sweeps the cement driveway, sweeps the rocks on the sides of the driveway. Men without shirts leading two yoked oxen or two yoked mules start to walk down the road south to the market.

Kathy, Marguerite, and Marguerite's husband climb into the tan Buick.

"Did you pay your bill?"

"Yes." Actually Kathy didn't pay for the last night.

"I've got to be at work at eight o'clock," says Marguerite. "But I don't have to stay. You'll go to my house now, and I'll come back for you at nine o'clock and I'll take you around Port-au-Prince. When are you going to Jacmel?"

"I think I'm going to Cap Haitian today."

"I thought you were going to Jacmel."

"I changed my mind. You made Cap Haitian sound so terrific. I can do whatever I want."

"Are you going with Walter?"

"No. Walter wants me to be his girlfriend and I'm just not attracted to him."

"Does he know this?"

"Yes. We discussed it last night."

"We'll go around Port-au-Prince today and then I'll take you to the airport. You know what I'll do for you because you're alone and you don't know anyone in Cap Haitian? I want you to be happy. Cap Haitian is my hometown: I love Port-au-Prince, but

I love Cap Haitian most of all. It's the most beautiful place in
Haiti. I'll write a note for you to Api. He's a driver there so he'll
take you around. He'll respect you."

"He won't want to fuck me?"

"No. That's why I tell you about him. He's what-do-you-call-
it? a lesbian."

"A homosexual."

"Yes. I'll write you a note introducing you to him."

The Buick swerves up a thin winding street in the center of
Port-au-Prince and stops in front of a wooden fence. Beyond the
fence there's an old decaying mansion. Soil mixed with inches
of grass, a few stone steps, then a dark room containing a cut-
tingboard and a sink. This must be the kitchen. There seems to
be no ceiling. To the left, up a huge staircase half of whose stairs
are missing. Huge wide open windows with gray shutters. Lots
of light. No air and what air there is, is hot. A wide white and
gray hall. Five rooms all of whose doors are open or broken lie
off this hall. Different kinds of beds, curtains, cabinets fill each
room. Each room contains a different family. Half-dressed men
and women lounge around.

Kathy and Marguerite are lying on a huge double bed in the
corner of one of these rooms. Over the bed there's a large open
shuttered window. The window frame's falling down. The room
contains three beds and one huge wooden antique cabinet dom-
inating the middle of the room. Hand-hung ropes and large pieces
of silver cloth separate the beds. There's almost no visible floor.
A table covered with a red-and-white checkered cloth situated
against the door wall holds all the dishes silverware bottles of
gingerale different kinds of cola mineral water and beer. A dressing table against the wall between the double bed and one of the
cots holds lots of makeup bottles and a bottle of Barbancourt rum.
Kathy has her clothes on; Marguerite wears a bra and underpants.
Kathy and Marguerite hold hands. Marguerite's sister and her
child sit on the cot behind the dressing table. A male cousin sits
in a wood chair by the double bed. Another young woman's

standing. Everyone's watching "Hogan's Heroes" on TV. Another boy's sleeping on the cot in back of the cabinet. Three
families who are all interrelated live in this room. A program in
French about a Haitian woman who murders her child comes
on the TV.

"What's your life like? Are you able to do what you want?"

"I have a good life. I don't have to work too much: I only go
to work three days a week I only work in the mornings. I only
want to work as much as I have to. I would rather do what I
want and be poor, than work."

"I'm the same way. Work's the worst thing that can happen
to someone."

"I don't live this way all the time. In Cap Haitian I have a big
beautiful house. But here I don't want to spend all my money
on rent. It's too expensive here. I'd rather spend my money on
other things."

"Do you have many girlfriends?"

"A woman can't have girlfriends. Not the way things are in
Haiti. I tell you something. I have a good husband who protects
me. If I have a girlfriend, immediately she steals my husband or
my boyfriend. I've never really had a girlfriend."

"That's terrible. Is that the way things are for all Haitian women?"

"There's some influx of American ideas, some of the women
are starting to have careers, but I tell you, things are very slow.
Women still don't have their freedom here. I tell you something.
If I ever stop being married, I'm not going to get married again.
I want my freedom."

The sun coming through the window is growing hotter and
hotter. There's no breeze. Children run in and out of the room.
The two women drink rum, beer and lay around. Then they go
to the airport. The airport contains hundreds and hundreds of
people. Kathy gives Marguerite a fan and some money for the
taxis. Marguerite gives Kathy the letter for Api the driver. They
drink some more beer.

LOVE AT FIRST SIGHT

I<small>T's</small> rapidly turning dark. The winds are blowing. Water hits the stone wall and leaps straight up into the air, thirty feet. Forty feet. Behind the stone wall there's a black road behind that a high white stucco wall. Stucco wall, overgrown garden, terrace.

There are musicians playing in the dark night.

Kathy looks up and sees a good-looking man.

"Gee, he must be an American. He looks like an American. And he's not even looking at me, much less chasing after me like all the Haitian men. I haven't spoken English in four days and I haven't talked to any man like a friend cause all the men here think about is sex and marriage and I'm confused and I want to ask someone what's going on, but I can't walk over to a strange man. I'd be picking him up."

Breezes blow through the coconut trees and musicians wiggle their long-cock hips.

The white girl walks over to the man. "Are you an American?"

"No," he says in a thick Southern accent.

He has light brown curly hair. His nose and his face are as fat and snub as a beautiful hard red cock. "Oh, I'm sorry. I didn't mean to interrupt you. I just haven't seen an American in four days, much less anyone who speaks English."

"Sit down anyway. Take a load off your feet."

"I don't want to interrupt you. I just thought . . . Are you sure it's OK?" She doesn't want the man to think she's trying to pick him up.

"My name's Gerard. What's yours?"

"Kathy. How come you've got a Southern accent?"

He takes off his light brown-tinted glasses. "I went to school in the States. In Nashville."

"Did you like it there?"

"It was real nice. The people there were all nice, real friendly."

"Just like here. But I get confused. Listen. I mean you're the first person I've been able to talk with, you know, really talk with in the last four days and I don't understand what's going on. There's been nobody I've been able to ask."

"Where have you been?"

"Port-au-Prince. I just got to the Cap a few hours ago."

"You can ask me anything you want. I'm just a nice, friendly person."

"I don't understand what the relations are between men and women in this country."

"What don't you understand?"

"Are the men desperately horny all the time?"

"There are lots more women than men in Haiti. I think that can hardly be true."

"Well why are these men following me all the time? I don't understand. When I was in Port-au-Prince, all the time, these guys would follow me. At least twenty guys. I could never be alone. Every time I went somewhere, there was another guy. The first day I was in Port-au-Prince, I got seven marriage proposals, not to mention the other propositions. I don't even know anyone."

"Well, I'm not going to ask you to marry me."

"Thank God."

"I'm going to get married myself. In September."

"That's wonderful. Who to?"

"I don't know yet."

"Oh. How the hell can you get married if you don't know who to?"

"I work in the mountains. I only come down here on the

weekend. And when I finally get down here, I'm so goddamn tired all I can do is grab a book I fall asleep before I know it. I don't have the time to go looking for a girl. I'm real lonely. I want to come off that goddamn mountain and find someone waiting for me. I want a hot meal cause I'm sick of eating out of cans and I want someone in my bed."

"I see your point. I wouldn't mind shacking up with someone myself, I don't know, I like my freedom. It's hard to find someone I can bear to stay with for a while."

A young Fidel Castro in a filthy Donald Duck T-shirt walks past Gerard and Kathy. "Hey Roger, don't go away. Sit down at the table with us. This here is Kathy. She just came to the Cap today."

Fidel Castro doesn't say hello to Kathy. "We were talking about you getting married," she says to Gerard.

"Oh yeah I'm getting married in September. All I need to do is find the girl. But I tell you, girls are scarce around here."

"I thought you said there are more Haitian women than men."

"Sure there are, but they're dogs. Most of them you can't even look at. Either they're after you all the time cause they're so desperate for men, or they're the type their mothers keep them at home and won't let them dance closer than two feet to a man and watch every little thing they do."

"Oh brother," says Fidel Castro. "Women. When I was in school in Florida, I was involved with this woman. Or rather she was involved with me. She was my teacher."

" 'I remember when I was a teacher,' " she says, " 'Jesus Christ I couldn't keep my hands off those young boys. They were so cute. I knew I shouldn't, being a teacher and all that ethics or something but I couldn't resist.' "

"She chased me all over the place. Oh brother. First she wants me to stay after class. Says I need help with my work or something. I know what she wants. I stay after class and she's always pulling up her skirt or shoving her breasts in my face or something."

"Was she pretty?"

"She was alright. She was, I don't know how to say it, too sweet. She was all over the place. She was a big woman, her blonde hair tied up in a bun, but she acted like she was real small and cute. All the time she was too sweet."

"I know the type. Blabblabblabblabblab. All over the place." The girl's hands wave in the air. "I don't like women like that. You can't trust them."

"I don't like sweet women either. One time I take her out. Boy, was that a mistake. Immediately, she's all over me. Dancing real close to me laying her head on my shoulder."

"So did you sleep with her?"

"Yeah but I didn't want to have anything to do with her after that. She wore all this stuff in her hair you know? I didn't really like her. Then she was after me even more. She said she'd make trouble for me if I didn't see her again."

"Why didn't you tell her to go to hell?"

"She knew I was smoking in the bathroom during class. You know, pot."

"Yeah."

"She threatened to tell the principal about me. I had to be very careful because I'm a foreigner."

"But everybody smokes in college."

"This was high school."

"High school! Oh my God. Now I understand."

"But she was so hot for me, you know, she couldn't do anything. Finally, she'd do anything for me."

"Well, I hope you got As out of it."

"I did."

Kathy and Gerard laugh.

"Do you take a lot of drugs?" Roger asks Kathy.

"No," Kathy says. "Certainly not as many as my friends take. I'm pretty puritanical. I never buy pot though I take it if someone offers it to me. Well, you know. The only drugs I like are psychedelics. I used to take a lot of acid, well, not a lot, not like some people would take it, every fucking day, that was really crazy, I took it about once a month for a year, when I was in college. I just stopped. Now and then I still take some peyote and psilocybin. I mean I use them. Oh I love opium. Opium's my one big habit. I've never eaten it goddamnit I hear it's wonderful I've only smoked it. It's not expensive but it's real impossible to get. So you can't get hooked on it, cause it really only comes through once a year."

"Everyone in America takes drugs," says Roger, "that's why Americans are so crazy. Drugs are ruining everything about America."

"It's true," Kathy says. "Not psychedelics or shit like that, but those damn pills. Everyone pops them. When I first went to California, the first thing I saw was a newspaper article saying that nine-year-old kids were shooting stuff into the undersides of their tongues."

"Oh brother. California. Everyone there is somewhere else. When I first rode in there, I saw a sign saying THE GRASS IS FREE. I don't like it there everyone's too much in the clouds."

"I like San Francisco. I lived there for two years. The people are real gentle and open. Just like the people here. LA's a horror show."

"The people in San Francisco take those new things, what are they?"

"Quaaludes?"

"Yeah, Quaaludes. The kids here are even beginning to take them: reds, whites, Quaaludes. Here it's worse because the Haitians don't know anything about drugs. They don't know what they're doing. Like Ally, Henry's son. He takes everything he can put his hands on and he keeps wanting more. He's acting hyper and strung-out."

"If he doesn't know about drugs, he could end up poisoning himself. Like he could take downs on top of liquor."

"What's worse here is that if you get caught, even if you get caught just smoking a joint, oh brother, that's it for you. A year in jail or maybe a lifetime. The jails here are deathpits. So everyone's very cool. You don't talk about drugs."

Gerard, Roger, and Kathy leave Pension L'Ouverture and go

to the Imperial. The Imperial is a small motel and cocktail lounge with food in the outskirts of Cap Haitian. Stretch of road over flat empty soil, a semicircle of white stucco rooms, flat empty land until the mountains begin. The center room is the cocktail lounge, a dark red-light room full of empty tables covered with white cloths, a New York City 1950s cocktail lounge.

"Where's your wife?" Gerard asks Roger.

"You're married?"

"I'm married," Roger says. "Oh brother."

"What's your wife like?"

"If you're interested, I can show you pictures of her."

"She's very pretty. I like her better with the short hair."

"That's what she had when I first met her in Oklahoma. But she's let it grow since then."

"You should have seen him," Gerard says, "when he was getting married. He comes to me and says, 'Gerard, what'm I supposed to do with her? I can't treat her like any other girl.' I say, 'Roger, buddy, look. Marriage is very simple. You come home from the wedding, you know, and you're madly in love, you can't keep your hands off each other, and you don't. Well, you calm down from that a little, maybe you drink a little, you talk a little, it's your wedding night, you know, so you do it three, four times. You fall asleep. Then maybe, about two o'clock in the morning, you're both a little nervous, you don't really know each other, you wake up and you're surprised: you feel a warm body next to you and you're not used to feeling a warm body next to you. So you feel around a little, you know, just to check out who's next to you and before you know it, you're doing it again. Then about four in the morning, maybe one of you has a bad dream. You know, all that champagne and wedding cake and crap you've eaten in the past day, it's probable that one of you's going to have a bad dream. There's a scream; both of you wake up; one of you's going to have to comfort the other. You do it again.' "

"And the next day you get divorced," says Kathy. "How else can you handle all that fucking?"

" 'Well you wake up around five cause you have to go to work and you kiss sweetie goodbye. But she's so sorry to see you go, she doesn't want to see you go and after all, she's your wife, you've got to help her out. You do it again. Now about twelve o'clock you come home for your lunch. You've got to have lunch. Your wife's been waiting for you all day; she's been worried about you; you're so happy to see her you've missed her so much you can't help yourselves you just do it again.' "

"I should have listened to you. I never would have gotten married."

" 'Then about two o'clock, well, you're getting a little nervous. You know you're wondering what she's doing all alone in that big house. So you decide to take a little peek, just to be sure she's not with some other man. You go home and take a little peek, and there she is, her dress pulled up over her legs, her hand up there, well you just have to help her out. She loves you so much.' "

"I don't even want to fuck that much. I wouldn't have the time to do anything else."

"I agree," says Roger.

Kathy and Roger stare at each other.

"No. You've got to realize what marriage is. 'Well, about five o'clock you get home and you're exhausted. Just plumb tired. You just open that door and fall down on that soft bed. She comes over to you and rubs your feet and your calves and the insides of your knees and your thighs and by the time she goes up a little farther, you just can't help yourself. After all, she's been sitting in the house all day, alone, just waiting for your return. Then she serves you this hot meal and you feel terrific. All your energy returns. So you look at this woman you've married who's doing everything possible to make you feel terrific and you grab her, just to show how much you love her. You do it again. By now it's dark and the stars are shining, it's time to go to bed. So it begins all over again.' "

"So that's what your marriage's like," the girl says to Roger.

"I never see my wife. She stays shut up in the house and does what I tell her to do."

"You're weird, Roger."

Roger reacts as if she said something horrible. "I'm just an ordinary person. I'm like anyone else. It's bad to be unlike everybody else. You stick out and people pick on you. My goal in life is to be an ordinary person. That's why I wear these filthy clothes."

"I used to think I was a freak all the time, but I don't think so anymore."

Next stop: three huge bronze statues overlook the deserted road. Roger's huge white truck clambers to a halt.

"Can you see that bronze thing through the trees?"

"No," says Kathy. "Yes. I can see it. Who is it?"

"Toussaint L'Ouverture. There are some others with him, but I don't know who they are."

"What happened to him? Did he die in battle?"

"The French took him prisoner and brought him back to France. They imprisoned him in the Jura Mountains because they knew his body couldn't adjust to the cold. He spent a winter in an unheated cell—he had never before known the cold—without blankets, no doctor, so by the end of the winter he died."

Gerard leaves to buy some beers.

Kathy and Roger sit in the silence and don't speak to each other and don't look at each other.

Gerard gives them two beers and leaves.

Kathy and Roger sit in the silence and don't speak to each other and don't look at each other.

"Don't look at me like that," Roger says.

"How'm I looking at you?"

"I don't know. You're looking at me strangely. You're making me unable to drink my beer."

"That's funny. This guy I uh knew in New York used to tell me I looked at him strangely. I never knew I was doing anything. I guess there's something in the way I look."

The two of them don't speak.

"I'm not looking at you now, so drink your beer."

They don't speak.

"Hey folks," Gerard says, "I've brought us all some cigarettes."

They stop in front of a place where they can dance.

The first room of The Fish contains a small bar and a low black couch. A Jimi Hendrix poster, a hippy fuck poster, a Black Satan female poster, a Janis Joplin poster, words such as REVO-LUTION and LOVE written in orange and green day-glo cover the walls of this room.

The next room is empty and dark.

The third room is black. Low black couches hug the walls of this room. A few indistinguishable couples sit and lie on the couches.

"Let's dance," Roger says.

They walk into the next room.

"How do Haitians dance?" Kathy asks.

Roger puts his arms around Kathy and holds her body lightly against his. His thighs move slightly from side to side. Sometimes his feet move slightly. She tries to follow him. It feels easy to her.

"This is how my friends in New York dance." She pulls away from him and leaps on her toes and turns in circles. "This is what we do at parties."

Roger pulls her to him. They move together so that inch by inch they're slowly traversing the floor, their genitals are lightly grinding against each other.

The jukebox plays another song. This one's an old American rock tune. His face falls so that his lips brush across Kathy's forehead.

"You're so small," Roger says.

"I know."

She lifts her face and his lips touch her lips. Kathy thinks they both feel slightly embarrassed.

"You're not dancing like a Haitian."

"Oh. How do Haitians dance?"

"You're twisting too much to one side. We move from side to side. Like this."

"I see. Like this. The weight's mainly in your knees."

"Let's go back."

They go back to the other room and sit down next to each other on the couch. For a while they don't touch. Roger takes Kathy's left hand in his right hand.

"I don't understand what's happening."

"I don't either."

"I mean, I . . . I mean, I . . . Where did Gerard go to?"

"He's in the front room. I think he's with a girlfriend."

They're both silent for a long time.

"You're very shy."

"Yes. I am. How do you know that? Most people don't realize that."

"I don't know. It's obvious. I'm very shy too."

"I'm just like everybody else."

"You keep saying that," she says. "Why? You're obviously not."

"You're too smart."

Gerard appears. "Do you want to dance?" he asks the girl.

"Well," she hesitates, "OK."

Gerard and Kathy walk into the next room. He puts his arms around her and holds her lightly against him. His left leg falls between her thighs so that as they dance, her cunt and inner thighs rub against his leg. Her body gets hot. She moves away from him and starts dancing American style. Gerard pulls Kathy close to him. The music stops. He wants to dance another dance, but she says no.

They walk back to the couches and sit down next to Roger. Nobody says anything. Nobody does anything.

"Let's dance."

As soon as they get to the dance floor, Roger's and Kathy's arms slide around each other's bodies. They kiss and their tongues enter each other's mouth. They remain this way for several minutes. Hot spasms are shooting up and down Kathy's spine. She's scared because she feels so turned on. She moves her face down and to the side so that her face sleeps in the hollow of Roger's chest under his head and in from his armpit. His muscled arms hold her tightly enough that she feels protected. Roger and Kathy alternately kiss and dance with Kathy's head under Roger's head. Roger and Kathy, as far as they know, are the only people left in the bar. They keep on dancing.

"Let's go," Roger tells Kathy.

Roger and Kathy walk by the high white pension wall. Across the street, the ocean.

They sit down on the grass and begin to kiss.

"What do you want to do?" Roger asks.

"What do y'mean, 'what do I want to do'?"

"What do you want to do?" He smiles.

Kathy kisses Roger.

"Well, what do you want to do?"

Kathy buries her head to the side in Roger's lap and giggles. "For God's sakes Roger you know what . . ." She can't finish her statement.

"I want you to be sure."

"Good God I am sure."

Roger and Kathy kiss for a while.

"Look at that couple over there," says Roger. "They're really in love. They're quarreling. Oh brother. Once two people who are really in love start quarreling, they can't turn back. Their love's starting to end."

"That isn't always true. I think for love to last you have to learn to survive the quarrels. I mean it's possible to survive the quarrels, but you have to be real smart and know how to compromise. I don't know. I've never had any love that lasted."

"I know. Once two people start quarreling, that's it. There's no way they can patch it up. Things just keep getting worse and worse."

"Is that the way it is between you and your wife?"

Roger and Kathy start walking back on the sidewalk to Kathy's pension.

"We don't get along." Silence. "My wife. Oh brother. We don't understand each other at all. I like to go out at night and boogie, and she doesn't go out of the house at all. You know most people in this town don't even know I'm married."

"Well, there's no reason you and she have to do the same things."

"She keeps trying to leave me. Last year she went back to the United States three times to visit her parents. She said she was homesick. And I had to give her a thousand dollars plus plane fare every time she went."

"It must be hard for an American girl to adjust to the life here. Haitian women live real differently than American women."

"We almost got divorced. The last time she went back to the States she wanted to leave me for good. We had the papers signed and everything. She's calling me up collect every day in Haiti always bothering me and crying oh brother. So just as we're about to sign the final papers she tells the American ambassador to Haiti she doesn't want to do it and he tells my lawyer. My lawyer stops everything. So we're still married."

Kathy opens the white door and walks in. She turns around and sees Roger about six inches away from her. They kiss passionately. Tongues slither down throats. Roger pushes Kathy they topple on the bed.

"Draw your curtains."

Kathy tries to draw the curtains and fails.

Kathy lies down next to Roger so their faces are only a few inches apart. Kathy and Roger look at each other for a long time. They reach out to each other and Roger moves down on her.

They start doing the same things at the same time without thinking about it.

Roger kisses Kathy's lips and eyes. His tongue sticks up her nostrils. His hand reaches down, under her halter, and rubs her nipples.

"Do you ever come from this?" Roger asks.

"From what?"

"From having your titties played with?"

"Once I did."

Roger bends his head, lifts the halter, and places his mouth on the brown aureole. While he licks and sucks this nipple, his hand rubs the other breast.

Kathy's so open she can't believe it.

Roger and Kathy take off their clothes. They're glad to get their clothes off cause now they can touch each other all over.

They lie on their sides so all of their front presses, and rub, and slip, shove against each other. They're constantly kissing.

Roger's upper legs thrust down between Kathy's thighs so that Roger's lying partially on top of Kathy. Kathy's dying to fuck.

Kathy's in agony. She knows this is going to be a good fuck. Roger rubs his cock-head up and down Kathy's clit and the skin around her clit. Kathy knows that Roger's playing with her but she's too hot to care.

She opens her legs wider and thrusts upward. The right part of her body rises higher than her left. Roger moves slightly backward so the back part of his cock rubs roughly against the skin at the back of Kathy's cunt. Then he moves forward so he's lying fully on top of Kathy. Kathy wants to come so badly she's thrusting and shoving and bouncing too much every which way.

Roger and Kathy roll to their sides and Kathy's left leg bends so her knee's near Roger's face. He's using his hands to push her back and forth. Kathy swings her left leg over Roger's thigh so his cock presses against the back and left side of her cunt. They begin to fuck a little bit faster.

Kathy's about to come.

Roger slips on top of Kathy. He continues fucking at the same pace. Kathy feels spasms run up and down his cock and at the same time she feels all her muscles relax, a force like a warm fire an exploding bomb and all the wants in the world, these three things together rise up her cunt muscles and then slowly into her whole body. She shakes and relaxes in Roger's arms.

"That fuck was good, but it wasn't as terrific as the buildup had promised. I've got to try harder the second time so that the fuck'll be as good as we've kind of promised each other."

He slides down her body with his face upraised so she watches his large brown eyes. When his face reaches her cunt, he stops and his fingers open her nether lips.

"You don't have to do that."

"I love to suck women. Sometimes I come in my pants when I'm sucking a woman I like it so much."

Roger opens Kathy's lips and sticks his tongue into her. Kathy wants to tell Roger he's hurting her, but she doesn't because she's scared she'll hurt his feelings and he'll stop sucking her. She tries to relax to him and open herself up to him. "If Roger likes to suck, I don't have to worry about making myself come as soon as possible. I must taste terrible cause of the dysentery."

Kathy feels Roger's tongue move up to the extra-sensitive spot where her cunt lips meet. Roger's tonguing hurts and makes Kathy feel good. The hurt increases the pleasure. The hurt disappears. Kathy feels the beginning of the rising that always comes when she relaxes.

Kathy's amazed that the rising's beginning so fast. All of her cunt skin begins to tingle. The trick is your cunt membrane has to get more and more sensitive but not so fast that you tense up cause the more you relax the more you feel. You want to feel everything. Roger touches Kathy's clit with his tongue and her clit swells. The tingling increases strength and speed. Then Roger blows on her cunt so Kathy feels almost nothing. Instantaneously she wants him to touch her even harder. By the time his tongue returns to her clit, her clit feels like a three inch long raw desirous nerve.

"Follow Roger's tongue, follow Roger's tongue. Don't let the feeling carry you away. Don't go too fast."

The vibrations move around Kathy's cunt like a snake. Are what Roger's doing. As the vibrations run up and down, they grow fiercer and sharper so at the extreme there are these peaks of fire, tiny explosions everywhere, and nothing.

Kathy's cunt is silent, ready, nothing. Roger's tongue is the explosions, the fires, the desire. The explosions the fires the desire come faster and harder they become simultaneous and infinite.

Roger's tongue draws Kathy out of herself, makes her quiver, and puts her back, slightly changed, into herself.

"Oh my God," Kathy says. She's in love with Roger.

Roger rises up and sticks his cock in Kathy. As soon as he moves back and forth about three times, she comes. She spreads her legs as wide as possible. She feels like she's ready for anything. He continues moving his cock slowly back and forth in her cunt. Her cunt is sensitive to feel his cock. She can feel every inch of that cock it's going into her.

He pulls out of her so that only his cock-head is lying in her cunt. He presses and rubs the upper ridge of his cock back and forth past the tight uterine opening.

Kathy can't come again because Roger's cock isn't in her. She's desperate. She begins to flex her cunt muscles. Soft. Tight. Around and around. Soft. Tight. He sticks his cock back in her and begins to fuck her good and hard. She comes again. She keeps on tensing her cunt muscles.

They're both a little crazy. They roll around so she's sitting on top of him.

She leans down over him so her breasts dangle in his eyes. His hands hold her breasts for dear life. Her clit catches against the edge of the bones above his cock. She arches her back so his cock razes the sides of her cunt. She bends back as far as she can, now she can move freely, and

Roger and Kathy begin fucking like maniacs. They crash against each other. They throw themselves against each other as hard as they can. They rub their genitals against each other like they're trying to grind each other to bits. They're too out of it to do anything but want more. Kathy comes again but she hardly knows what she's doing any more. The cheap pension double bed is bumping against the back wall and banging in time to the fucking movements. Roger rolls over Kathy so he's partially on his side and partially over Kathy. His hands hold Kathy's thighs. He moves his cock in and out of Kathy and his thighs up and down on Kathy steadily and hard. Kathy comes so much she no longer knows what coming means. Roger's body stops moving. Only his cock moves. Kathy's cunt clearly feels his cock grow smaller and larger like an accordion and hot liquid shooting out of the end of his cock.

"I get crazy when I come too much."

"I thought women could come indefinitely."

"I can't. When I come too hard and too much, I can't stop anymore. My body gets out of control. I shiver and shake and go crazy cause I'm so oversensitive."

"Do you fuck a lot of men?"

"No. Not a lot. I'm alone, you know, and I've got to get laid. I've changed a lot in the past few years though. I used to fuck around all the time just fuck anyone. I can't do that. I guess fucking's getting too important to me or too serious. I can only fuck people I really go for now, and I only go for about three or four different men a year. And sometimes these men don't go for me."

"The only person I've slept with since I started living with my wife," Roger says, "was this French teacher. She was staying here at L'Ouverture. And she really wanted it oh boy. She came after me."

"But you fucked her?"

"I spent the night with her. But it didn't mean anything."

"What do you do when you go out at night?"

"I drink so much you wouldn't believe it. Last month I really drank too much."

"That's no good. Why don't you take your wife out now and then?"

"She doesn't want to go. She wants to stay shut up in the house. You know she doesn't even like to fuck. She won't let me do anything to her but fuck her how-do-you-call-it?"

"Missionary style?"

"Yes. She's from Kansas and she's very young. She stays all alone in that house and never sees anyone."

"I'd love to meet her. I'd love to be able to talk to an American who's been in Haiti for a while."

"Why don't you come to Le Roi tomorrow?"

"What's Le Roi?"

"It's where all of us live. Betty, me, my two brothers and their families. It's one of my father's factories."

"What does your father do?"

"Oh, he's into lots of things. He's got lumber rubber sugar cocoa and coffee factories and plantations. He owns Cap Haitian."

"Oh."

"Last year the government tried to arrest him cause they wanted to take over his money. They sent some troops up here to arrest him. All the people around here stood up for my father and protected him. My father's nice to his peasants so the peasants'll protect him. The troops had to go back to Port-au-Prince. All of us are always in danger of being arrested."

"That's why Gerard said you're 'retired.' "

"I'm not retired. I work at the factory as hard as Gerard works on the mountain. But I earn much more for my work than he does for his and he resents that. Everyone in this town knows who I am and resents me cause I'm my father's son."

"Everyone watches what you do. You have no privacy."

"Whatever I'm doing, I have to be very careful. I live out in the country where no one can spy on me. Sometimes I can relax out there."

He gets up to go to the bathroom. Kathy hears him piss. "Come here."

She walks into the bathroom and sees him sitting on the toilet.

"Sit on me."

She sits down slowly, her back facing him. His cock slides up her asshole. His hands grab her tits.

She wonders if he's still going to the bathroom. "Shit and piss," she thinks to herself, "Fuck and suck what and not."

Everything's everything else. Kathy's crouching behind the window, watching the gray cat stalk someone she can't see. "Let's go to bed," Roger says.

He takes Kathy's hand and leads her to the bed.

Lays her back down on the bed. "This bed makes too much noise."

"It's just a lousy bed."

"Let's move it away from the wall."

"Do I have to get up?"

"No." He pulls the bed away from the wall so the wood head-board doesn't bang against the wall and lies down. His head is on Kathy's cunt. He sticks his tongue in Kathy's cunt and licks. Then he raises his head. His dark brown beard hairs are rubbing the lighter brown wet cunt hairs. Roger's beard hairs are partly white from sucking Kathy.

She moans.

"Now do you like my beard?" Roger asks.

"I always liked your beard."

"But now you see why my beard's so special."

"Oh shit." Kathy's heat's rising. She's about to come again. Roger doesn't want her to come again from his tongue. He rises over Kathy and sticks his cock into her cunt.

Kathy doesn't exactly know what's happening. Roger and Kathy fuck and then stop fuck and then stop fuck and then stop. They're actually fucking slowly and in a steady rhythm. Kathy's cunt is so sore that Kathy comes whenever Roger's cock is inside her. Yet they're fucking slowly enough that she's not becoming hysterical. Fucking is not fucking and not fucking is fucking. No one can tell who's coming or who's not coming. No one knows and forgets anything.

"Will you really come to Le Roi tomorrow?"

"I said I would," laughing.

"What haven't you done in bed?"

"I don't know. If I knew, I'd do it. Oh, I've never really gotten tied up and beaten or tied up and beaten someone, though I've thought about it a lot. Have you?"

"Oh yes. I once went with a girl the only way she could get off was if I tied her up and hit her. Otherwise she didn't want it, no way. I tied her wrists behind her back. I hit her hard. When she was ready she'd be writhing and shaking and then she'd want it so bad."

"You didn't like it?"

"It was OK. I didn't care for it that much. Did you ever ass fuck?"

"Jesus Christ we were ass fucking when we were on the toilet. Couldn't you tell?"

"I was so hot, all I could think about was getting my own. I don't even know if you've been coming."

"I've been coming enough. I'm satisfied."

"I want to fuck you up the ass when I know it."

"I like to fuck women. I don't do it much anymore though I used to."

"I like when women make love with women."

"Have you ever made it with a man?"

"I wouldn't let a man near me. I know what I want," Roger says.

"What do you want?"

"Are you really going to come to Le Roi?"

"I said I was going to. Jesus Christ, I'm here cause I want to see as much of Haiti as possible."

"I'd love to have you make love to my wife. That's why I want you to come to Le Roi."

"Waaiit a minute. I don't go for women all that much and I definitely only go for women I want. I don't even know Betty. I'd like to meet Betty cause she's an American and cause she sounds pretty damn lonely, but that's it."

"Maybe you and her will get something together. I want to find a woman who'll make love to my wife. That's what Betty needs."

"Roger, even if Betty and I do do anything, that's between me and Betty. It's none of your business. What goes on between you and Betty doesn't concern me. Jesus Christ I don't even know Betty yet."

"I don't believe you're going to come to Le Roi tomorrow."

"How do I get to Le Roi?"

"Everyone in town knows where Le Roi is. You can ask anyone. There's a bridge and there's a big red chimney. The big red chimney's Le Roi."

"On the way to the airport?"

"Yes."

"I guess I'll find it."

"What time will you come?"

"About one o'clock."

"I'll wait for you. My father's rebuilding the factory. He has three new rum tanks. I'll show you the rum tanks, and then I'll take you in to meet Betty."

"Are you sure it'll be OK with Betty? I don't know if she wants to meet me."

"The only way Betty ever meets people is when I introduce them to her."

Roger and Kathy look at each other. Their lips meet. Roger sticks his cock into Kathy's overfucked cunt. Roger comes. Kathy feels every inch of his cock spasm back and forth as clearly as she sees the white ceiling above her. Roger's orgasm makes Kathy hot.

They stop fucking. Roger's cock is hard again. Roger wets his finger and sticks it into Kathy's ass. His finger moves around easily. He sloshes some saliva on the asshole and eases his cock into Kathy's ass. Kathy doesn't feel any pain at all.

Roger's moving his cock back and forth rapidly. Kathy's coming like a maniac. All of her ass and intestinal muscles are shaking. "Oh oh oh," Kathy cries. Kathy stops coming. Roger's still shaking away. Kathy feels a little pain. Kathy and Roger both come again.

THE MYSTERES

THE Mysteres are a family of mulatto robber barons. The grandfather of the present M. Mystere made and lost a million dollars. The grandfather's son made a million and lost a million two times and then went crazy. The present M. Mystere started out life with this heritage and nothing else. Like his grandfather and father, he made and lost a million. Presently he is working on his second million or, at this point, multimillion.

M. Mystere or le Mystere, nobody in town calls him anything else probably nobody even knows his first name, has a wife, three sons, and a daughter. The three sons are married and the oldest two have children. The daughter, although twenty-seven years old, is a virgin. The three sons work for their father and, like the daughter, live where their father tells them to live. The youngest son's name is Roger.

Of the several lumber, cocoa, coffee, rum and bottling plantations and factories le Mystere owns, Le Roi is his baby. He is currently rebuilding Le Roi. The decaying wood scarecrow building with its rusted metal ceiling, old dead machines surrounded by dust, is abandoned. Giant new brick cylinders filled with new rum rise into the sky. Sweating men construct massive orange metal frames. There are no more buildings here. Only metal skeletons, huge machines, and dust.

Like the American robber barons of early this century, le Mystere wants to depend on no one but himself. All the profits he makes are immediately turned into new business. His baby, Le

Roi, was built and is being rebuilt from cash, the cash profits which his other factories and plantations made last year. Le Roi is part of a giant rum concern, a concern which will rival Barbancourt, a Haitian rum monopoly which so far has no competitor. Rum is one of Haiti's main products. If the rum concern succeeds, by this spring as soon as the rum's distributed for the first time, le Mystere will make three million dollars above costs. And then more.

The sugar grows and the rum is aged at Le Roi. Miles and miles of sugar cane, tall strong green plants, lie mixed with weeds. Machines that extract a syrup from the sugar cane. Machines for fermenting and flavoring the syrup. The pride of Le Roi is the three giant red brick tanks which hold the syrup plus at least sixty per cent water for the fermentation period. In Haiti it's hard to get decent machines, the government tries to get everything, so these tanks might explode at any second. The cheap raw white rum can be packaged almost immediately. Le Mystere's cheapest rum is aging a year. His most expensive rum has already aged three years. When all this rum is ready, in March, it will be shipped to le Mystere's bottling factory in Port-au-Prince, bottled, and there exported and distributed throughout Haiti.

The road to Le Roi, after it leaves the bridge and the overhead arch announcing the town of Cap Haitian, under which women in torn filthy short skirts sit and stand beside their baskets filled with mangoes of all varieties, plantains, figs or bananas, breadfruit, meat-filled pastries, dried fish, whole fishes, canaps, cashews, sit and stand and talk in the dust, the road curves around a small bay and then reaches straight, like an extended arm, into the Haitian countryside. At this point the road's mostly though badly paved. Deep ruts line both sides of the road. Men leading mules or women in the same short full skirts with huge filled straw baskets balanced on their heads every now and then walk in the deep ruts. A truck filled with rocks or bananas and people packed together like rocks or bananas sitting on top of the rocks or bananas passes them by.

To the sides of the road, the country is flat and the soil is dry. Bare earth now and then covered with low-lying bush. At first there are no houses. Then a few rectangular thatch houses lie a few feet away from the road. There's usually a mango or some kind of palm tree next to each of these huts.

The road gets dustier and dustier. It passes by the small Cap Haitian airport. Twice a day for twenty minutes a six-seater plane lands here. Otherwise the airport's empty. Now the bush at the sides of the road is thicker and there are more trees. There's more green. But one can still see the dry dusty brown through the areas of shiny light and darkening greens.

Weeds rise up everywhere. Birds and crickets are making noise. The endless sun. The weeds and trees are becoming a tangle. About ten minutes inland from the airport, it's necessary to turn off the almost-paved road on to a path of dirt and stones to get to Le Roi. There are no signs on the road. As is true everywhere in Haiti, you have to know what you're doing. Or not care what you're doing.

Here the weeds and sparsely-leafed trees and tall grasses and small wild yellow flowers choke the dirt path. Tangle. The car gets through slowly. Finally it stops.

"I drove down to L'Ouverture to pick you up at eleven o'clock but you weren't there."

The girl looks around and sees a small black man walking toward her. "Oh shit. I was out playing with the little beggar boys. We sat in the park."

"Yeah, they told me that."

"I wish I had known you were going to pick me up. I could hardly find this place and the taxi-driver charged me a fortune."

"How much did he charge you?"

"Six bucks."

"Shee-it." Kathy and Roger hold hands. "First, I'm going to show you my factory. This part of my father's business is the part that's mine."

"I'd like to see it. I want to see as much of Haiti as possible."

"This is the new factory. The old wood structure over there is where the factory used to be. That was no good. It used to leak a lot. We've got to get all this up by the beginning of September cause that's when the sugar cane comes in."

"Will you be able to do it by then?"

"It'll have to be finished. That's how things are around here. We work as hard as we have to and, then, when we don't have to work, sometimes we don't work at all. My father works all the time; he never thinks about anything but his work. Oh brother. He's sharp too. If you say or do one thing wrong, he'll remember it, and three days later he'll ask you why you said or did exactly what you said or did. He remembers every little detail where you don't remember anything. He doesn't care about nobody."

"Does he do anything besides work?"

"Sometimes he reads a book at night. My mother and he live quietly. They hardly see anyone."

"Huh. What's your mother like?"

"My mother? She's just a mother."

"Oh. What are these?"

"That's sugar cane. Haven't you seen sugar cane before?"

"No."

"Here. Eat one." Roger hands her the top part of the sugar cane stalk, a thick woody cylinder. She gnaws at it. "Sometimes about six o'clock when nobody's here, I come here and sit down. I just sit down. I love it here. This is my home. I sit here against this white wall and watch the plants. This is the only time I really rest. No one bothers me here."

A slim bearded man walks up to them. "Hello."

"Kathy, this is my older brother Nicolas. Nicolas, Kathy."

"Hello."

"Nicolas is the chemist of the family. He went to college for two years in the States." She sits down against the white wall of the building that holds the rum tanks. "I'm going back to work now and you wait here. I'll come get you when I'm finished. Are you going to be OK?"

"I like being alone."

She stares at the orange metal skeletons, the welding equipment, the half-naked workers, huge yellow tractors plastered against a solid wall of green. A few minutes later he returns.

"Will you be OK here?"

"Of course I'll be alright." To her left's the small empty dirt field that's the end of the road and a low white fence. The stucco fence surrounds a huge pink rectangular building. To her right are miles and miles of sugar cane plants. Flat land as far as the eye can see. Clear light blue sky. Burning white sun.

When her ass starts to hurt, she moves to her right and back, into the sugar cane plants. Lies down among the tall rough green plants. The sun can only reach small sections of her body. Thousands of different kinds of insects crawl over her. Wasps the size of bumblebees and small red ants large red ants and small black ants and thin-bodied fliers translucent green wings and grasshoppers and big black beetles. When the ants start crawling under her clothes, into her nostrils, and biting her, she moves back to the concrete step in front of the white building.

At first, she can't see anything. She sees men climbing up the orange shafts and men hammering men sticking stakes in the ground men wiping their hands on their dark pants. She sees Roger on top of a big yellow tractor. He's circling the tractor around the periphery of welding, hammering, and building. He doesn't see her. He sees her and waves.

Five minutes later he stops the tractor and walks over to her. Sweat runs down his face and arms. Muscles cover his body. "Come on. I'm ready."

"You can't be ready. It's only early afternoon. Go back and work."

"I want to take time off now. I can take off when I want. I'm going to take you in to meet Betty. I'll have a beer, and then I'll come back here."

They're walking.

"Does Betty live in that pink house over there?"

"Yes. She never leaves the house. Her skin's allergic to the sun down here so she can't go out of the house during the day unless she's totally covered up. All this summer she kept begging me to buy her an air-conditioner. 'Roger,' she kept saying, 'I can't live without an air-conditioner. I've got to have an air-conditioner.' Finally I gave in and bought her this air-conditioner that was designed to air-condition a factory. She made me put the air-conditioner in the bedroom and now she stays in the bedroom all the time."

"But it's not even hot here."

"Betty's very delicate. She can't take the heat."

They walk in silence for a while. "I feel upset," Kathy says to herself. "Every time this year I fucked someone I liked, I fell in love. I'd want to see the person again in the next few days. Every time I wanted this, the guy'd start hating me. Either he wouldn't see me or he'd kick me in the guts. I spent all my time trying to figure out if everyone who fucked me hated me. I knew I was obsessing. I hated myself. I decided I was going to get rid of all my thoughts. No more love. I don't love anyone I fuck with and no one loves me. And I thought I had succeeded Jesus Christ I've been so proud of myself. So here I am again. I want to tell Roger I love him. That's insane. I want to tell him I love him and I can't. Does he love me? I know he doesn't care about me I'm a cunt he hates me. He hates me cause I love him. Jesus Christ I'm going to cry. I've got to tell him I love him and I absolutely must not. I have to control myself or I'll never be able to do anything."

They've reached the archway in the white wall. A few feet away're the steps of the pink house.

"Roger I think I'm falling in love with you." She starts crying.

"I think about it too."

She can't say anything. Her tears dry.

"C'mon. We've got to see Betty. Betty!" he yells at a large barred window. Kathy follows him as he walks through a small white door, up some narrow steps, through a large stainless steel kitchen, through a hall, into an empty white room. The only things in this room are two pushed-together beds and a large air-conditioner. "Kathy, this is Betty."

Betty's skinny and there's no blood in her face. She looks like she has no blood. She's not albino. Even though her hair is so blonde it's almost white, it's dingy. Straggly. She looks as if she's been totally permanently frightened. Otherwise she's pretty in a midwestern American way. Her eyes are pale pale blue. She's wearing an obviously new dark cotton dress which chokes her neck, droops at her waist and ruffles again and again around her nonexistent hips. She doesn't want to look at Kathy.

"Hello, Betty. Do you uh have a bathroom?"

"Of course," says Roger. He points to the left.

A huge clean bathroom with a bathtub and a shower. Kathy throws herself on the toilet as wave after wave of dysentery hits her. Shit pours out of her.

"Roger, why don't you get some lunch? You haven't eaten lunch today."

"I don't want any."

"But I've kept it in the oven waiting for you. It's probably burnt to a crisp by now."

"I'm not hungry."

"You have to eat, Roger. You can't work all day and not eat. If you're not going to eat, you have to get back to work. You can't take off from work like this. You know what your father said."

"I can stop working whenever I want to."

Kathy gets off the toilet, though she doesn't want to, and walks back to the bedroom. "I've been traveling through Haiti for the past week and I haven't seen any Americans much less spoken English the whole time. It's a treat for me to meet an American here."

"There are lots of Americans in Haiti."

She sits down on the bed next to Betty. "There are? I haven't met any. Last night I met Gerard. You know Gerard. He introduced me to Roger and Roger invited me to visit you two. I thought it'd be nice to talk with you cause you're an American who's lived in Haiti for a while. I hope I'm not disturbing you."

"You're not disturbing me. I don't do anything. I don't like Haiti very much. I don't go out of the house much and now that I don't have a car . . ."

"What happened to your car?"

Roger's watching the two women. "It's getting fixed," he says to Kathy. "It just takes a while."

"It's been broken for two weeks now and Roger won't get it fixed."

"You see how she is," Roger says to his girlfriend.

"It must be lonely here," Kathy says to Betty. "Why don't you get a small cycle or a motorbike so at least you can get into town?"

"What I really want is a horse. I've always adored horses. I was really scared of them when I was younger, but even then I couldn't stay away from them. I know I'm not scared anymore. If I had a horse, I could go anywhere around here."

"Why don't you get a horse?"

"She doesn't know how to ride," says Roger.

"You know Roger, if I had a horse, I could keep it here real cheap. It wouldn't cost anything. We could feed the horse the scrap sugar cane plants. We could stable the horse right here in the yard. I know your father wouldn't mind."

He doesn't reply.

"And there are horse-trails all over the country."

"We've talked about this before. There are no horses around here."

"I know where I could get a horse. Mr. Palero's bringing two palominos here from Port-au-Prince. Even if I couldn't buy one, I know he'd let me stable one here."

"She talks all the time about horses," he says. "If she tried riding one, she'd get so scared, she'd run away yelling 'Eek, eek.' "

"I would not Roger. I know I wouldn't be scared now."

"Why don't you try riding one of the horses I saw out there?"

asks Kathy. "You would get more confident and then you could get a bigger horse."

"What horses are you talking about?"

"Weren't those horses I saw," she asks Roger, "when we were walking from the factory to this house?"

"Oh, those old things," Betty says. "They're not really horses, they're like mules."

"If they're so old, they'd be good to learn to ride on. They wouldn't hurt you."

"I don't want to," says Betty.

"Betty's crazy about animals. She wanted to bring her dog here from the United States the last time she was in the United States, but I wouldn't let her do it. It would cost a fortune. She really loves that dog. Betty, show Kathy pictures of your dog."

"I'd love to see them."

"No. They're boring."

"It's too bad you can't ship your dog here. I know how you feel. Every time I've had a pet, it's killed me, not killed me but you know what I mean, to abandon it. You always have to leave a pet and it hurts so much, I'm scared to have a pet again. I think pets are babies."

"We couldn't bring the dog into Haiti. You can't bring anything into Haiti. It's like being in prison here. When I first moved here my mother sent me a carton of books, just some old books I had at home, and it cost me seventy-five dollars to take these books out of the post office."

"Seventy-five dollars?"

"The government calls it the luxury tax. Whenever anyone takes anything in or out of Haiti, that person has to pay a huge luxury tax. It's one of the only ways the Haitian government makes money."

"She keeps going back to her parents in the United States. Last year she went back to the United States three times. And then when she's back there the last time, she wanted to return here with her dog."

"He's really a beautiful dog. You should see him. He's so big he's as big as Roger but he wouldn't hurt anybody. You should see him around people he doesn't like. He never growls. He just goes 'rrrrrrr.' Low and steady. The people take one look at him and run. He's never even bitten anyone. Once he bit the postman. He's really very gentle. Would you like to see pictures of him?"

"I'd love to."

Betty shows Kathy a picture of a huge mutt standing in front of an empty rectangular wood-frame house. Bare flat soil surrounds the mutt and the house.

"He's a really beautiful dog," Kathy says to Betty. "Why don't you get another kind of pet here? One you don't have to import. You won't feel so bad and you can see your dog when you go back home."

"I once kept a cat here, but Roger kicked him out of the house. Roger says animals don't belong in a house."

"Animals don't belong in a house," he says. "Animals belong outside a house. That's how things are in Haiti."

"He doesn't understand. In Kansas we have animals running around all over the place."

"I love animals. When I had cats, I slept with them every night. Pickle Paul, that was the male one's name, used to place his back against me and just rub into me. Then he'd look up at me with his big blue eyes and take his paw and put it on my hand. His paw pushed my hand to his nipple. He loved having his nipples rubbed. That's what he liked most in the world. Lizzie, she was his sister and wife, would sit on things and claim them. She especially loved leather. She was incredibly beautiful: green eyes lined in black, black tongue, a calico. In San Francisco I had these wonderful parakeets."

"The only pets I really like are dogs."

"I don't want Betty to have any pets. Animals belong outside the house. There are lots of animals outside the house she can play with."

Kathy can't answer because she's about to shit in her pants.

She barely makes it to the toilet when the gook starts flowing out of her. She looks down and sees a beautiful calico long-hair cat skin. "Shit. What's this?"

"What are you talking about?"

"This cat."

"Oh," Betty replies, "that's a cat."

"You mean I'm stepping on your pet cat? Did he die naturally?"

"We killed him," Roger says.

"You killed him? Oh. I'm not being sentimental or anything isn't it weird to kill your pet and stick him in the toilet?"

"Do you want a beer?" Betty asks her husband.

"No."

"Well, at least take something to eat. Your lunch is still in the oven. You've got to eat your lunch."

"I told you. I'm not hungry. Ask Kathy if she wants a beer."

"That cat wasn't a pet," she yells to Kathy. "It was just a stray cat."

"I thought it was your pet. I got scared for a moment. I thought you were horrible people."

Roger's girlfriend is lying down on the huge double bed. His wife's sitting upright, almost touching her. He watches the two women.

"Ask Kathy if she wants a beer."

"Do you want a beer?"

"No. Yes, I'll split one with you if you want."

"I'll also have a beer," says Roger.

"Roger, go down to the kitchen and get two beers."

"I don't want to move. You go down."

"I don't want to move either. Please, Roger, do me a favor."

"I'll go get the beers," says the girlfriend. "I love to walk. You two have to stop fighting."

Roger goes to get the beers.

The girlfriend and the wife are alone in the huge air-conditioned bedroom. They feel embarrassed.

"Would you like to see the rest of our house?"

"I'd love to."

Through a narrow gray hall to the kitchen. All the latest stainless steel tools and no food. One can of peaches. The refrigerator holds sixteen packages of Kraft cream cheese. The servants do all the work. Down the stairs. Through the narrow white door. Mowed green lawns. Through another white door. A long empty dark gray hall. The doors stuck in the walls of this hall are closed. Turn right. The same gray hall. Turn left. The same gray hall only light gray. "Roger's brother Nicolas and his family live here. We're not allowed to enter." Turn left again. A shorter light gray hall. Ends in a huge light yellow room. The yellow makes you want to puke. Two Holiday Inn chairs one Holiday Inn couch in the center of this room. White polyester curtains cover the windows. Turn left. This part of the yellow room's empty. The yellow room ends. Through a light yellow door. A long dark gray hall. A darker gray room just big enough to contain an ironing board and a maid. A narrow white door. Green lawn. Through the other white door. Up the steps. The modern kitchen. Two long light gray halls.

"You've got a really nice house. How come all the doors are locked?"

"Roger's brothers' wives don't want us coming into their parts of the house. They're scared something might get stolen."

"Jesus Christ. What are these women like?"

"Nicolas, he's the second oldest, is married to a Chinese girl. The oldest brother married a Haitian girl. They're both real pretty. They don't pay much attention to me. They act like typical upper-class Haitian women, you know, they go out every day and buy clothes, they have servants who do everything for them and they don't do anything for themselves, even though they were born real poor. I'm not like that. I don't get along with them."

"So you're here alone most of the time?"

"I don't go out of the house anymore. I like to read. I read a lot. It's really hard to get books in Haiti. There's nowhere to buy books and the only person I can get them from is papa."

"Papa?"

"Peter. The old guy at L'Ouverture."

"I haven't met him."

"He's probably still down in Port-au-Prince. You'll meet him when he comes back. Everyone knows papa."

"That's horrible that you can't get hold of books. I'd die if I couldn't get hold of the books I wanted to read. Much less any books." She turns around and sees a pile of dusty paperbacks lying in the corner. "What books do you have here?"

"Have you ever read John Fowles' book?"

"That one? I've never read any of John Fowles' books. I hear he's a good writer."

"You should read him. He's a great writer. You know what book I like the best? You must have read it. *Future Shock*. I think that book really says what's happening."

"I know everyone was reading it last year."

"I think that guy what's his name?"

"Toffler."

"Toffler puts his finger on it when he says the world's going to end."

"Uh."

"Have you read any E. Eddison? I love his writing."

"Do you know any books about Haiti? About what's happening now?"

"No. I like to read books about imaginary places. Do you? You know who else I think's a great writer? Irving Wallace."

"I don't know. I just like to read. What's this book about?"

"Oh, Thurber. That's just a funny book. Do you want to borrow it?"

"I've got enough to read. You can have the Dostoyevsky book I'm reading when I'm finished if you want it. What do you do when you're not reading?"

"Sometimes Roger takes me out. Last Saturday night he took me to the voodoo dances in the country. They hold them every Saturday night."

"Oh wow what are those like? I want to go to them."

"They're nothing special. I didn't see anything exciting happen like they say happens like people breathing fire and walking over hot coals. I didn't even see anyone go into a trance. Roger and I might not have stayed there long enough to see the good part. We got there around eleven o'clock. There were some women turning in circles. That was all. They turned in circles for a long time. At the end just before we left, it wasn't the end of the ceremony, this man started to stick needles into his skin. Maybe he was in a trance. I don't know. I didn't like it. He stuck these long needles into his skin, all over his body and then he went around the perimeter of the circle and asked other people to stick needles into him."

"Did he ask you?"

"Yes. I couldn't do it. I wanted to vomit. I felt I was watching him torture himself."

"Maybe he wasn't torturing himself. Maybe he was using the pain to bring himself, I don't know how to explain it, into a new consciousness."

"Right after he asked me to stick needles into him, Roger and I left. I didn't feel good."

"I think I'd like it. What was Roger's reaction?"

"Roger didn't like it. Roger has trouble with that stuff."

"What do you mean?"

Betty looks through the bars over the air-conditioner, out the window. "Roger's great-grandfather, grandfather Mystere, made a fortune and lost it. His son, Roger's grandfather, made his fortune, lost that, made a second fortune and lost it. After he lost his second fortune, he went crazy. Roger's father felt he had to make money. He made a million dollars and, like his father and grandfather, lost that million. Now he's working on his second fortune. He's very scared he's going to lose the money he now has. All he does is work. All he cares about is work. All the money he makes goes back into the business. He has no real money. He doesn't want to depend on banks or on other partners. Whenever he does work like the rebuilding he's doing at Le Roi now, it's all done out of cash. He has to keep expanding the business, cause if he loses this money, he thinks he'll go crazy like his father did. Roger's father is a very powerful man."

"I still don't understand why he's scared of going crazy."

"Roger's uncle went to some business school and came back and started working. He was doing OK but he wasn't making a lot of money. He kept working harder and harder. He didn't take a vacation for two years, not one day off, and then he started working nights. Finally one month he tried to go without sleep. He sees things and he gets very nervous if anyone's even around him with a pencil. They keep him locked up in their house in Port-au-Prince. He says he needs peace and quiet. He sits in an empty cool white room. The doctor says if he gets constant peace and rest, he might be OK in a year or two. No one wants to talk about him."

"Maybe he just got overworked and overstrained. That doesn't mean there's insanity in the family. Rich people often go crazy, but they're so rich, the other rich people protect them."

"Roger's sister lives with her parents. She never leaves the house unless they tell her to. She's twenty-seven. She's sick all the time: she has these special allergies. The only thing she likes to do is eat. She eats all the time. She can cook anything you ask her to cook: Spanish, Chinese, American. You'd really like her. Two years ago she got this incurable liver disease so she's not allowed to eat anymore."

"She doesn't sound so crazy. Does she fuck?"

"She's never had any boyfriends."

"Never? Jesus Christ I didn't think there was a virgin in Haiti. Except for the zero to three year olds. She must be a case. What are Roger's brothers like?"

"I don't see them much. The oldest one runs the lumber plant. Nicolas is the chemist, he went to some college in the States for two years. He likes to tell people what to do. I see their wives more, but I don't like them. They're very mean to me. I'm pretty lonely here."

"You and Roger should have a house of your own."

"Roger's his father's right-hand man. Roger has to go wherever his father tells him to. Sometimes we live here and sometimes we live in Port-au-Prince."

"But couldn't you live somewhere else besides right here in this building when you're in Cap Haitian?"

"Roger says he's going to build us a house with the money that comes in from the rum factory this spring. His father expects to net a few million immediately which he's going to split among his sons to avoid taxes. I don't know if Roger'll build a house. He loves living here."

"It must be hard for you. Do you have anyone you can talk to around here?"

"There's this girl named Suzy. She lives in the hills in the back of Mont Joli pension. Do you know where Mont Joli is?"

"Yes."

"She and her boyfriend came here from Port-au-Prince three years ago when there were no roads. They rode on horseback through the inland mountains and swamps. They met tribes in the mountains who had never seen white men before. I don't see her anymore cause I don't have a car."

"I'd love to meet her."

"You'd really like her. She does macramé. Her house is incredibly beautiful. It's covered with macramé and weaving. She and her boyfriend and Oliver run a pottery factory just outside of town. Roger and I used to visit them all the time but lately we've stopped. I don't see them anymore. If I could borrow Nicolas' car one day, we could visit them."

"I'd like that. I'd love to find out more about their trip through the inland. You should get your car fixed."

"Roger says it takes a long time. It's hard to get machine parts in Haiti."

"Then why don't you buy yourself a small scooter or motor-bike? You have enough money to do that."

"Roger says they're dangerous. He doesn't want me to ride a

bicycle cause the natives might bother me because of who we are."

"Roger's crazy. Nobody's going to hurt you. I go everywhere around here night and day by myself and nobody even bothers me. Everyone thinks I'm crazy cause I'm always alone they're real curious, but so what? You've got to do what you want."

"Roger doesn't even want me to walk through the town. He says there are a lot of poor people around and I might get syphilis."

"How are you going to get syphilis?"

"Most of those poor people have large sores. If I touch one of them or one of them grabs me, I might brush against the sore and pick up his germs. That's how I'd get syphilis."

"You can't get syphilis by touching someone. You can only get it by fucking. Oh you can get syphilis of the mouth, but even that has to be genital contact. I know."

"Roger says I'll get syphilis if I walk through the poor parts of town."

"Then Roger doesn't know. It's absolutely impossible for you to get syphilis if you don't fuck."

"Well, I might pick up some other germs. Those people are crowded closely together."

"What are you going to do with your life?"

"I had a job at Mont Joli pension earlier this year. I really liked that job. I was working from nine to twelve five days a week and earning fifty dollars a week."

"That's a lot of money here."

"The maids at L'Ouverture work twelve hours a day every day and earn thirty dollars a month. They're allowed to eat rice once a day. That's high pay for Haiti."

"So why aren't you working now?"

"The people at Mont Joli told me to leave. They were able to get the woman they wanted who had lots and lots of experience. I couldn't keep the job anyway cause I had to follow Roger down to Port-au-Prince."

"You could hold down a job. When Roger goes to Port-au-Prince, you could stay here."

"I don't get along with Roger's brothers' wives. I don't want to stay here alone."

"Then you could stay in town at L'Ouverture. You've got to have your own life."

"It doesn't matter. I lost the job at Mont Joli and there are no other jobs in Cap Haitian."

"But you don't need money. Roger's rich. You could teach some of the beggar kids how to read, you could help the doctors, there are thousands of things that need to be done in this town."

"If I mix with the poor kids, I might get syphilis." Betty looks through the bars over the air-conditioner, out the window.

"Roger says you do art. You're very good. Do you have anything around I could see?"

"Do you really want to see my work?"

"Sure."

Betty walks into a large empty boiling-hot room. She moves part of a wall, climbs up on a chair, and starts piling huge boxes, hidden behind the sliding wall, on the floor. Box after box. "I'm not really good. I took art in school and all the teachers said I was their best student, but I haven't shown anyone my work in two years." She lugs a thin tan portfolio out of the back of the closet, steps over the piles of cartons, and opens it up. "This is a Japanese print I did. I drew some of it myself, traced some pictures I found, cut out some things."

"This is my favorite."

"This is just an abstract color thing. I was starting to use colors."

"The rest are just drawings. I like to draw. These are drawings of Roger."

"This is a drawing of a cat."

"These are two self-portraits. I don't like the rest of the drawings. I can't work anymore cause I can't get the right kind of pencils and paper down here."

"Why don't you show these to some Haitian artist as long as you're down here? There are lots of terrific artists in Haiti. You could show your work and maybe you could study with someone.

That'd be terrific: you'd get all this off your hands you'd be able to learn you'd meet people."

"We don't know any Haitian artists."

"There's a real famous one who lives right in Cap Haitian. His name begins with U. What the hell is it? Just go and introduce yourself to him. You can't lose. Lots of artists take on students. Even if the artist isn't that great you're studying with, you still learn a whole lot about how an artist creates."

"I don't think I'm into art that much anymore. I want a job like the one I had at Mont Joli."

"You've got to do something. You're as pale as a ghost."

"That's cause I can't go out into the sun. I'm allergic to the Haitian sun. I'm allergic to most Haitian foods."

"Betty's very very delicate," Roger says. Both the women turn around.

"Roger, why don't you get some lunch? You haven't eaten lunch today."

"I don't want any."

"But I've kept it in the oven waiting for you. It's probably burnt to a crisp by now."

"I'm not hungry."

"At least change your pants. Those pants are filthy. We should throw them away."

"I'm comfortable in these pants." Roger turns to his girlfriend. "She always wants me to wear clothes that make me feel uncomfortable. She doesn't understand that I'm a workman. I want to dress like a workman."

"I'm going out to the garden," she replies.

"You should try a canap," says Betty. "Those little round green fruits on that tree. I don't know if they're ripe yet. They make you high."

"I'm going to try a canap."

The garden between the back of the pink rectangular house and the part of the white wall which faces the factory part of Le Roi, unlike the smooth green lawn in front of the pink house, is wild and overgrown. Some of the grass is short; some, long. Grass mingles with dirt. Occasional patches of dirt and strips of dirt hide in the welter of grass or hug the white stucco wall. Three small black-and-white goats nibble at the grass and weeds. A wood picnic bench and a half-rotting wood picnic table. Behind and on both sides of this table grow two gnarled-branched trees. A low round wood platform surrounds one of the tree trunks.

Kathy leaps on this platform. She's able to stick her foot into a depression between the tree's two main branches. But she's not tall enough to get her right leg up there. Shit. She brings her left leg back down. She's standing on the platform. She jumps up her hands grab a thick low branch her feet hit the trunk monkey-style and stick. Her arms pull her legs up into the depression. She kneels, stands upright in the depression.

Wants to climb upward but can't reach any of the branches.

Tries to crawl out on a wood stick, part of a square wood frame for hanging laundry or just plain hanging, that's sticking out of the tree trunk. The entire wood frame starts shaking.

Slowly climbs out of the hunchback tree, and steps off the wood platform down to the grass. Thick weeds everywhere rose bushes with dark heavy open roses a stone fountain that has no water. Sky is white light. Heating beating down except for one cool breeze slithers in and out of the heat like a little lizard. Blue blue sky. The garden's incredibly beautiful and silent. Goats are munching by the hunchback tree. Tries to pet the goats, but they don't want anything to do with her.

Sees some beautiful large white flowers. Walks over to the beautiful large white flowers. Beyond the flowers there's a chicken coop. A wood frame, a wood shelf, and lots of chicken wire form the square coop. Three roosters and six hens run around inside the coop and two hens run around outside. "You see what I mean about Betty. She's still a baby."

"She's very unhappy," Kathy says to Roger. "She can't stay shut up here. She has to be doing some kind of work."

"You can't do anything with her. You can't tell her anything.

If you try to say anything, she says 'Just leave me alone.' She's like a child and you can't tell her what the world's like. Now do you see why I act the way I do? Now do you see what I'm up against?"

"She's very scared, Roger. She's so scared she almost can't function any more. She doesn't have any blood in her. No one has to be as pale as she is. It's unhealthy. You've got to let her get a job or at least have transportation so she can get out of here now and then."

"She had a job. She couldn't keep it."

Kathy sees her standing almost next to her and Roger. "Shut up," she whispers to Roger.

"Now do you see what I'm up against? I'll never be able to leave her."

"We'll talk about this later, Roger. Shut up." She walks over to Betty. "This is a beautiful garden."

Betty doesn't reply.

"This is a beautiful garden."

"I don't like it."

"You're just in it too much. You can't see it anymore. After being in a city for two years, this place is paradise."

"I guess so."

"Do you ever come here and play with the chickens and the goats?"

"I don't like chickens. I think they're horrible."

"I like chickens," says Roger.

"I play with the goats sometimes. This one's my favorite. Isn't he beautiful?" Exactly half of the little goat's face is white and half is black.

"He is beautiful. Look at that goat there. He's got a gray spot. Can I pet him?"

"Sure you can. He's tied to the tree."

"I don't want to torture him. That's no way to love an animal."

"Look. The servants are bringing the cows in for the night."

"Cows!"

"I used to wrestle that one when I was a kid. He was a mean one. I would win though."

"Jesus, he's huge. How the hell could you wrestle with him?"

"Not the brown one. The one with the black stripe over his eye behind him."

"He's smaller. You must love him."

"I do."

"Do you still wrestle him?"

Roger walks over to the bull and makes faces. The bull ignores him. "Not anymore. Why don't you go inside now? You're getting too much sun and you're going to get sick."

"OK."

"Roger," says Betty, "stop it. You're treating her like you're her father."

"It's OK." Kathy smiles at Roger.

The three people walk around to the front of the house where the grass is short. Roger and his wife go inside the house while Kathy stays on the lawn. She dances and knows that Roger's watching her.

She goes through one of the white doors. She finds herself in a light gray hall. At the end of the hall a maid's ironing in a small gray room. She walks down this hall and turns left down a white hall. All the doors in this hall have huge brass bolts bolted shut. At the end of this hall's a large empty living room, the yellow room she had seen before. The door from the living room to the front lawn's bolted. The servant who's cleaning the living room stares at her. She turns back down the white hall. The maid who's ironing stares at her and doesn't reply to her hello. She walks through the white door to the green-gray lawn. She tries another white door. She walks up the narrow white steps into Betty's and Roger's kitchen. "I got lost."

"We were wondering where you were," Roger says to Kathy.

"I want to go soon. I want to get back to the pension for dinner."

"You can get a ride back with my father's engineer. He'll be leaving about now. I'll ride into town with you. I'll go see where he is." Roger goes back downstairs.

The two women follow him. "I loved being able to meet you," Kathy says to Betty. "Why don't you visit me at the pension and we can go swimming and sunbathing together?"

"Roger'll have to drive me there. I have no other way of getting there."

"Come visit me. I can give you the books I've finished reading so you'll have some new books to read."

"OK. I'll come tomorrow or the next day. You're getting a bad burn. Here's some good suntan oil and here are some Haitian matches."

"Oh, they're beautiful."

"The engineer's waiting," says Roger.

Roger's girlfriend climbs into a huge gray jeep. "Aren't you going to come with me, Roger? I thought you were going into town with me."

"I'm not going tonight. I'll see you tomorrow night."

She wanted to fuck all day, and now she's not going to be able to. "Goodbye Roger."

Roger throws her a kiss.

PASSIONS

OUR past comes back and hooks you. Your insane search for affection because your mother didn't want you, disliked you, and she wouldn't tell you who your father was. You kept looking for someone to turn to. You kept looking for a home. Your need gathers. Passion collects. You're in it now, baby . . . passions, just as they are . . .

You're going to bang your head against that wall again. No affection. You. Where are you going to find love? How can you run away from yourself? Last year you banged your head against a wall so hard you were sure it had to break, but it didn't. The only difference this time is you know you can't break down that wall. You're going to hit your head so hard against it this time, you're going to bust in your head. What a pleasure it'll be when your head breaks . . .

You've got to get love. You've lost your sense of propriety. Your social so-called graces. You're running around a cunt without a head. You could fuck anybody anytime any place you don't give a damn who the person is except you really don't want to get murdered any number of people except when the sex situations happen you have this idea lingering from the past maybe you shouldn't fuck so much and so openly other people are looking down on you other people are thinking you're shit. People misunderstand why you act the ways you do so they might harm you. You've already gotten beaten up once even though you kind of liked it. You've got to use your intellect to keep you in line, no insane sexual behavior no pleading and groveling for love, you don't know the difference between friends and strangers, cause if you don't use your arbitrary, it feels arbitrary, intellect to keep you in line, you're going to go too far out, you're beyond the limits of decent human behavior, pleading and groveling on the ground, every time you get a bit a scrap of love wanting twice as much more more, you've got to have more cause you know no one could love you cause no one's ever loved you, and home is secure love you've got to get enough love all the love in the world to make it secure. You step on the people you meet. You use them for your insane desires. You don't know the difference between friends and strangers and you're unable to give anyone, especially the people who say they want to fuck you, ordinary human affection. You're beyond the bounds of being human. You're inhuman. You're now out of control and you're showing only the slightest pretense that it's otherwise. "I love you," Roger says to Kathy. "I love you so much I think I'm going to die."

Someday there'll have to be a new world. A new kind of woman. Or a new world for women because the world we perceive, what we perceive, causes our characteristics. In that future time a woman will be a strong warrior: free, stern, proud, able to control her own destiny, able to kick anyone in the guts, able to punch out any goddamn son-of-a-bitch who tells her he loves her she's the most beautiful thing on earth she's the greatest artist going fucks her beats her up a little then refuses to talk to her, and able to fuck (love and get love) as much as she wants. In that future time the woman will be beautiful and be the hottest number whose eyes breathe fire, who works hard, who's honest and blunt, who demands total honesty. Greta Garbo in *Queen Christina*. Meanwhile things stink, Kathy thinks to herself. I have to be two different people if I want to be a woman. I'm me: I'm lonely I'm miserable I'm crazy I'm hard and tough I work so much I'm determined to see reality I don't compromise I use people especially men to get money to keep surviving I juggle reality (thoughts of reality) I feel sorry for myself I love to hurt myself and to get hurt etc. i.e., I'm a person like any goddamn man's a person. I have to make my way in this world like any man makes his way and I'm as tough as any man. I earned that respect. But unlike most other goddamn men, I don't want a woman. I tried wanting women but it was no go. I want a man. I want to be a woman to a man. I'm usually not a woman so it's a little weird. Two types of men come on to me. One type thinks I'm a little sweetheart cause I'm small, pretty, and I'm shy. As soon as he talks to me he finds out I'm a brassy maniacal Jew. I have to keep acting out the shy baby number to keep this one. The second type knows I'm loud hard together. He wants to fuck me cause he wants someone who won't jellyfish all over him. This type is butch. I love butch men. The minute he says "I love you" boom I'm a woman. I'm creaming all over him. So to keep this type I have to act out the tough role. Not too tough cause everyone wants affection even though he doesn't want to give any. This is all so cold and academic. I'm in constant pain cause I want a lover and I don't have a lover. I don't know how anymore. I can't be polite I can barely manage to mutter "Let's fuck." Most of the time when I want to fuck, I stumble over to the guy and stare at him. Real feminine. I can't tell anyone how lonely I am and I can't show any feeling. Just this blunt shit. I don't show any feeling and then when the tough guy leaves me call him up and say "Please take me back, please tell me why you're leaving me, are you leaving me? I don't understand what reality is, please I'll do anything become anyone please I need love." The guy who wants me to be the tough girl he desires and expects and who has his own goddamn problems, panics and leaves I'm alone all the time I want to throw everything out the windows I want to bust up the windows the jibberjabbers are getting me again and mad whirling energy I've got to get away from myself I've got to get away from myself. "I love you too."

He rolls over Kathy and rubs his naked body against hers and the cold floor. "I've never told any girl before I love her. Not like this. I feel scared."

"I don't understand what's happening."

Roger rolls on top of her and lays his throbbing cock in her cunt. The moment she feels him enter her, she moans and cries out. She loves to have his cock in her.

They don't move. She moves the muscles of her vaginal walls very softly. No other part of her body moves. They go crazy and tear at each other, naked, on that cold motel floor, abdomen battering abdomen, hands grab at shoulders bite, bite hard through the skin, they're wild beasts, they find the rhythm. Fast strong hard steady rhythm. Boom boom boom. Bone at the base of the cock smashes against bone immediately above the clit.

"I don't know how I'm going to exist when you're not in Haiti. I can't stand being away from you for even a day right now."

"Shh. Roger."

"I don't want to know you. I don't want you to go away. I know you're going to go away and leave me."

"I'm here right now. Shh, baby. I have to go away, but I won't be going away for a long time, and then, if I want, I can come back here in a month. We don't need to talk about this now."

"Will you come back? I don't think you'll come back. Everyone always goes away and leaves me."

"If you want me to, I'll come back. I love Haiti. New York is hell you don't know how horrible it is. I hate living there. I just have to be there sometimes cause at this point that's the only place I can get money for my writing. I'm not rich: if I don't make money I'm going to die. I don't have to be in New York all the time. I can be here whenever you want."

"I love you too much. It's no good. Will you really come back to Haiti?"

"Would, would you want me to come back?"

"I hate you because you're going to leave." He pulls his dripping cock out of her.

"Roger, oh Roger, look Roger this is totally ridiculous because I'm not going to be leaving for two months, but I'll discuss it anyway. I'm not the one who's married. You are. I can do whatever I want."

"She doesn't matter. I tell you already: I try to get away from her, but she won't let me go. I don't know what to do."

"I know I know. But look, as it stands right now, between your work and your wife, I hardly get to see you. You know this' true."

"You're right." He lays his curly-haired head on her cunt.

"I'm the one who's on shaky ground. This is your country and you've got a wife. I'll stay here for you, darling, but I want to know you want me."

His tongue's lapping the insides of her cunt lips. Liquid drips out of her. His cock grows hard. For a moment he stops.

"Don't stop," she moans. "I'm about to come."

"How do I know you'll come back to Haiti? I'll wait around for you, already I dream of you every night last night I lay on my bed I thought of fucking you and I masturbated."

"Didn't you fuck Betty?"

"No, I never fuck Betty anymore. I don't like to. I masturbated as I saw your body and then I fell asleep and dreamt all night about you, I was always with you . . ."

You don't want to steal, but you don't know how to get along if you don't steal. You make seven dollars a night you work an average of two to three nights a week. However you can always borrow money from a guy you used to fuck who still loves you, he may have gotten wise and doesn't anymore, or you can make a porn film. Even if you don't need the money, you get off on stealing. You steal from your friends; if they every caught you, you'd be out. Totally out. You get off on the danger. The only guy you keep fucking is a guy who doesn't give a shit whether you live or die, who tells you he loves you only when you decide to stop fucking him, and who beats you up when you have sex.

You wonder why you're getting sick all the time . . .

Writing these things down doesn't alleviate your suffering. You don't want to steal. You steal. There's a sharp constant pain in you running from ovary to ovary. When this pain hits you, you think you're going to die. You're a stupid bitch. At least half your thoughts are about the men you've fucked or want to fuck: you're desperate for affection, you don't want any affection because you're selfish and egotistical and insecure, so you get sick. For the past year you've had a lousy medical history: four abortions, four PID attacks, five flu cases, one breast cancer (now almost gone). Maybe you're in a bind.

"I want to buy you a yacht," Roger murmurs. "What color yacht do you want?"

"What do you mean?"

Roger's sperm's dripping out of her cunt. His hand cups and presses her left breast. "When you come back to Haiti, there'll be a yacht waiting for you. What color do you like?"

"Roger, when I'm in the United States, sometimes I don't even have enough money to buy food. I don't even know what I'd do with a yacht. Sure, I'd like a yacht. If you really want to help me out, you can help pay for the ticket so I can come back to Haiti to see you."

"How much did it cost you to come here?"

"Two hundred and forty dollars round trip. If I stay more than three weeks, which I'm going to, I'll have to plunk down another hundred dollars. Three hundred and forty dollars."

"That's not any money. I spend more than that amount of money on my bar drinking every month."

"It's a lot of money to me."

"If I send you a ticket, will you come back to me?"

"I said I would."

"I want you to tell me again."

They're lying on the cold floor and looking up at the white ceiling. "You work for your father and you're going to keep working for him. You have to do what your father tells you. Plus you're married. As it is I only get to see you once every few days."

"You're not going to come back to Haiti. I'm never going to see you again."

"I'm trying to be straight Roger. It's silly for me to spend all this money to come see you and never get to see you. I want to come back to Haiti when I'll be able to spend a lot of time with you. As it is I spend most of my time daydreaming about you sucking my cunt."

"Do you like that?"

"I love it."

"I'm going to do it now." Their flesh's so wet, it squeaks as it separates, recloses, she moans her nerves are sprung up like thousands of open wounds. He wiggles two fingers up her asshole.

About a minute later she starts to come.

"I can't stop shaking."

"I want to get rid of Betty and marry you."

"Oh my God Roger not again. I can't take anymore. I'm so sore the moment you touch me I come. I just want you more and more. I'm going to go crazy."

"I'm coming too. I'm going to come inside you."

Roger looks into Kathy's eyes while his cock grows larger and harder.

His right hand strokes her tenderized cunt. "I'm going to be with you all the time from now on."

"You can't be with me all the time. I have to go back to the States now and then cause that's where my money is. I have a career. I couldn't stand staying in Haiti all the time. There's not enough for me to do here. For me, the women here live in prison."

"People can't stay together the way we are. This isn't going to last."

"Does that make you sad? Roger, this is right now. You're tormenting yourself with your thoughts. You've got lots of money, or you're going to have lots of money, so you can do exactly what you want. Don't be a fool. You're not going to find another American woman so easily who can stand the life down here, being cooped up all the time. Keep Betty, I mean if you want to I don't know what you want. Betty's not so bad. She's a little scared, but all you have to do is treat her gently. She could use some gentle treatment. You don't have to love her. She adores you, and she'll stick with you, and that's the main thing if you want to have kids. Then you can fall in love with whoever you want. You've got enough money. You can keep as many mistresses as you want buy them all houses. As long as you're fortunate enough to be rich, fuck, why don't you set things up exactly the way you want them?

"I'm going to build a mansion near Gonaives, in the inland, where I'll be all alone. No one will ever be allowed to come there. I won't have any mistresses, nothing. I won't let any of my family in. I'm going to build tennis courts and swimming pools and a golf course."

"Golf? Golf's disgusting."

"Golf's my favorite sport. I learned to play golf in the United States when I went to this school for ambassadors' kids. I'm going to let you come there."

"I'll come if you have some books there."

"No. I don't like to read."

"Don't your parents ever read?"

"Sometimes my father picks up a book after work's over. He doesn't care what he reads."

"You've got to have some books for me. Otherwise I'll go crazy and I won't be able to stay there."

"You'll play golf with me and tennis. I'll have the tennis courts for you."

"I could stay there at least half the year and then hit New York for the height of the art season. I have to be in New York sometime during the art season."

Maybe your body will forget about being fucked. You forget about being fucked. For a moment. Tra la la la la la la. A layer of not caring if you're fucked over desperate to get fucked.

But it seems so weird to get fucked. This huge red hard object pointed at you. You're supposed to do something with it? It's warm. It moves when you touch it. The rest of the skin is cold and clammy and it smells and it's too close to you. Go away.

Go away. I don't want the ground pulled out from under my feet. I don't want to lose consciousness.

I'm nauseous. I know what this territory's like. I've been here before. Terror horror the red means. I can sit it out. I know my own strength.

All around me buildings are crumbling strange vibrations are going about people are so miserable they're doing everything they can to escape everything. I should tell them the only thing I know: there's no fire escape.

He sinks his cock into her and pulls it back and forth. The membrane inside her cunt sticks to his cock.

"I don't want you to come back to Haiti."

"You don't?"

"In September we'll harvest the sugar cane. After that, I'll take my vacation. You'll take my vacation with me. You're going to go to Puerto Rico."

"OK. I don't care where I go."

"You'll stay with me in my hotel and we'll do everything together. We'll go out drinking and gambling and eating all the expensive food. The only thing is you can't get upset when I go with other women."

"I don't care if you go with other women. It's so hard these days for a man and woman to stay together for more than two days, jealousy's the least of all the problems. I don't get jealous anymore. But I don't want to be left alone in some strange hotel room for days. I have to have the same freedom you have."

"What do you mean?"

"If you fuck around, I fuck around."

"I don't like that."

"Tough shitty. I'm not the kind of woman you can keep locked up in a hotel room. If you want that kind of woman, you can get anyone. I'm as tough as you are."

"I like that. You can do what you want as long as I don't find out about it. If I find out about it . . . watch out. I beat you up."

"I like being beat up."

"You do?" He smiles. His eyes are soft and gentle. "When I send you a ticket, you come down there."

"You'll have to send me a round-trip ticket. I don't trust you and I don't want to get stuck without any money in some god-forsaken hotel room."

He smiles again. "I shouldn't love you. I love you too much."

"Roger . . . There's something I don't understand." Her big brown eyes look up at him.

"What?"

"Not exactly 'don't understand.' I think I'm in a bit of trouble. You know Ally's always bugging me to sleep with him."

"Ally's always trying to compete with me. He knows damn well you're going with me."

"I don't know if I should tell you this. Yesterday afternoon I was smoking with Duval and that nice Spanish sailor, I was totally stoned and the Spanish guy left the room. I didn't know he was going to leave the room. Duval wanted to fuck me. I told him I couldn't cause I was going with you."

"Duval told me he didn't have any more grass. Where did he get that grass from?"

"I was real stoned. Duval didn't listen to me: he grabbed me and almost raped me. When I got the chance, I pushed him away and ran out of the room. I think he's very angry. You know how close he and Ally are and how they talk. I hope there isn't any trouble."

"Did he kiss you?"

"Yeah, he kissed me. So what? That isn't the point."

"Did you like him kissing you?"

"Look, Roger, I'm scared. Last night there was this knocking on my door. Not on the front door to the room which is always locked, on the back door. I was asleep the knocking woke me up I couldn't tell what was happening I thought it was you. I yelled, 'Qui est la?' Someone said, I think, 'Alfred.' I don't know: I was asleep. I don't know any Alfred. I said 'Go away.' Then the doorknob started turning. He was trying to break in. The doorknob turned for about ten minutes. I freaked. I mean in New York City women get raped all the time. I didn't think. I screamed. I ran to the front door, opened it, saw that little twerp who runs around the motel. He looked at me like I was crazy. I slammed the door in his face. I was really scared. Scared out of my mind. I didn't know what to do. Finally I was able to get to sleep. Who do you think it was?"

"It was Ally. He has the hots for you and he's pissed because you're fucking me and not him. He usually gets all the women who come here. You better watch out he doesn't rape you. Now that you've kissed Duval, you're fair game."

"I didn't kiss Duval because I wanted to. I was stoned and he grabbed me. I got out of there as soon as I could."

"You let him kiss you. C'mon. Put your clothes on. Let's go."

"But Roger, what can I do? I'm really scared."

Disgusting putrid horror-face no one wants to fuck you you make a fool of yourself you always make a fool of yourself everyone's always laughing at you everywhere you go you don't belong anywhere nowhere nowhere you're worse than a bum cause a bum can take care of himself he can stand sleeping on the streetcorners at night he can travel from place to place without worrying about his five thousand books how he's going to drag the right dresses with him you can't do anything for yourself you're a demented abortion on God's earth you don't do anything useful you hate to work all of you is one mass of squirming and totally disgusting worms that squirm against each other hate each other.

Gotta run. Gotta get out. Gotta get moving. Get out. Escape. Escape. Burst open. Stop. Get the fuck out of here anyway I can. Dig my way out. Break all these goddamn windows. Bust the world open. Beat up everyone until someone pounds me into a pulp. Stick more razor blades in my wrists. Fuck up my life. Destroy.

I want to go home, mommy. I thought this was a passion, but

it's not. Emotions are like thoughts. They come and go. They're not me. I can play at being in one, being one, but it's not me, it's just playing, and after a while it makes me sick. I don't know what to do anymore, mommy. Mommy mommy mommy mommy mommy mommy mommy mommy mommy mommy mommy mommy mommy mommy mommy mommy mommy mommy mommy mommy

Middle finger of left hand presses down cunt lips above clit. See hand with ring. See bluejean jumpsuit and scarf twisted black yellow red blue orange. Have to stop to say colors. Don't stop when see. Feel finger pressing down lips. Lips feel. I feel. I can see. Mind (perceptions, thoughts, emotions) swirling. I can perceive mind swirling.

You can't rely on those passions . . . you don't know where to go . . .

The gray sportscar races down the boulevard, the main road in Cap Haitian, which separates the ocean and the houses.

"Is something the matter? Are you angry with me?"

"I'm not angry about nothing."

She thinks for a minute. "You are angry. I don't know what I did wrong."

"I said 'I'm not angry.' "

"Why are you acting so queer? You won't notice me or nothing. You must be upset."

The sportscar moves faster and faster. "Where do you want to go?"

"I don't know anything about this place. Where do you want to go?"

"Where do you want me to take you?"

"Is it Duval? Are you angry cause that thing happened with Duval?"

The car races around the poor people who are walking.

"It wasn't my fault that thing happened with Duval. He grabbed me. I didn't know what to do. I was scared if I fought back, he'd murder me. I don't know karate: I have to use my wits. I got away as soon as I could. Nothing happened Roger. I didn't even take my clothes off."

"Did he touch your titty?"

"His hand might have brushed it when we were struggling."

"I see. You're in a lot of trouble. He's going to tell Ally he's had you and Ally's going to tell everyone. That's how those two are. All the men are going to want you to go with them."

"Is everyone in this town crazy?" She starts to cry. "Duval attacked me. I didn't want him to attack me. If one guy attacks me, does that mean every guy here has the right to attack me?"

"He wouldn't have attacked you if you didn't want him to. You liked it when he touched your breast. Did he touch it nicely?"

"No, he didn't touch it nicely. Do you want me to go with Duval?"

"I don't care what you do."

"Goddamnit. I was smoking and I was stoned. Totally stoned. When I get stoned, I get horny and also, when I have great sex and I've been having the best sex with you I've ever had, I'm horny all the time. I can't help it. That's the way I am. I just don't know what I'm doing sometimes and I get turned on. But I didn't want to sleep with Duval I'm sleeping with you. I even told Duval I couldn't sleep with him cause I'm sleeping with you. I can't handle two boyfriends." She puts her hand on his hard cock. "All I want is you."

"What did Duval say when you told him that?"

"He said all the girls here have more than one boyfriend."

"He's lying to you. Duval, Ally, and I are a threesome and sometimes we trade girls around, but those girls aren't worth anything. You can do what you want. I don't want to tell you to do anything."

Her hand rubs his cock through his pants material. "I've slept with a lot of men. I just don't want another man right now. I couldn't see another man right now if he stood naked in front of me and raped me. You're satisfying me completely."

"You like me?"

"I love you. I don't give a shit about Duval or anybody. You're happy now? I love it when you're happy."

"I love you too much."

"Roger, this is serious. Do you think it was Ally who tried to break into my room? If it was Ally and Duval tells him what happened today."

"Unzip my pants and put your hand on my cock. I love that. I love when a girl sucks me in the car. I know Ally. He's going crazy from all the drugs he's been taking. When he hears Duval had you today, he's going to rape you."

"What am I going to do?"

"Suck my cock. Lean down and put your mouth around my cock."

She leans down and places her mouth around his distended cock.

The car pulls up in front of a small white building. A woman leans against the wood bar in the large empty room of a brothel that has Dominican Republic girls. The woman's wearing a bright green dress. When Roger and Kathy walk into the room, the woman walks over to Kathy and smiles at her.

Roger tells one of the girls to bring him some cigarettes. When she returns with the cigarettes, he refuses to pay her. The girls think Kathy's Roger's wife because she's white. They crowd around her and giggle. Heat flashes through her body. She walks over to Roger and sits next to him.

The gray car speeds down the empty road away from Cap Haitian. "Do you realize you're a very powerful person here? You're going to get more powerful as you get older and older. It's not only that you're rich: everyone here knows who you are and looks up to you. Everybody knows every little thing you do."

"I know this."

"I'm not being clear what I mean to say . . . Do you realize most of the people here are poor?"

"I think about it."

"It's not just that they're poor. There are a lot of poor people in the world. These people don't have a chance to be anything else. Your father's business is going to come to you and you're going to have a chance to do something for these people. If nothing else, you're an example for these people."

"I've told you that. That's why I live out in the country. There nobody can see me. Even the servants we have out there take advantage of us, they spy on us, and they steal everything. Last week one of our workers stole two black cows. My father dismissed him."

"Maybe he was hungry. You've got to think about who you are. That's what I'm trying to say. These people follow you. If you have love in your heart and live for other people, these people will have love in their hearts. I know I'm sounding soppy, but it's what I believe."

"That's why I don't hang around with Ally and Duval anymore. We three used to be like one person, I told you this, we split our women and shared our dope. But now I'm a man. They're still boys. I have a lot of responsibilities. The only men I can talk to are thirty and forty years old."

"You have to show people who act like babies the way. In one way you're lucky cause you were born rich, you have every opportunity anyone could want, but in another way it's really hard for you: you can't be a private person. You have to think in terms of other people."

"I have no friends. Everyone in this town will do anything I say. Except for Gerard. No one can tell Gerard what to do. He doesn't take shit from anybody."

"Gerard is your friend."

"No. He envies me. You remember when he was saying I'm 'retired'? He's jealous because I earn four times as much when I do half the work he does. All he wants is to get rich and he's not going to."

"Isn't there anyone you talk to? You know, really talk to?"

"I don't have any friends. I'm going to build the castle; I told you about the castle. As soon as I get rid of Betty. I don't want her living in it. I'm going to build this huge mansion in the middle of Haiti, surrounded by tennis courts, swimming pools, and a golf course. Do you like to play tennis?"

"No."

"I'm going to have only older women there."

"What do you mean by 'older'?"

"They can't be younger than fifty. I like older women cause they act like nursemaids. They'll take care of me. They might all have to be dumb. I'll have a few huge dogs who'll stay outside and I'll have the best stereo system money can buy plus all the records I can get. I like listening to records. That's all I'll have."

"You can't cut yourself off like that from the world. It might work for a while, but then something bad'll happen to you and you'll have no way to deal with your suffering. Even if nothing bad happens to you your whole life, you're going to die and you're going to have to deal with your dying."

"I told you. I'm going to have lots of old women there who'll take care of me. I won't even fuck them."

"Jesus Christ. What about all the people here who are suffering and starving all the time? Haiti's the poorest country in the world. There are almost no roads. Most of the people can't read. The rivers are polluted. There're almost no hospitals. How can you totally forget about everyone?"

"Did you like it when Duval put his hand on your titty?"

"Jesus Christ, Roger."

"You know what I think? I think you like Duval. I think you're going to make love with him."

"Don't be ridiculous. I thought we got through all that. I love you."

While they're arguing, Roger stops the car at The Imperial. They get out of the car and walk into a disgusting room. No fan, and the heat's so thick it's solid.

"Why d'you want to come here, Roger? This room's repulsive." Clear plastic covers the bed mattress.

"Back at L'Ouverture, I saw Ally following us. He's trying to stop us from being together."

His huge cock rushes into her. He's too rough and he hurts

her. Maybe all the interest has gone out of our sex, she says to
herself. Do I love him? Maybe I don't love him. It was just sexual
it's amazing how strong sex is you forget about it when you're
not having it good sex is everything. I guess I don't love Roger
anymore. Do I love him? Do I love him? His fingers're stroking
the slimy puffed cunt lips. "Oh Roger oh Roger. That delicately.
That is so good." His fingers keep stroking the red lips in the
same way. His fingers are stroking the red lips in the same way.
Thoughts endless thoughts it's Roger's fingers who are stroking
my cunt lips it's Roger's fingers who are stroking my cunt lips I
am those fingers I am the tips of those fingers I've found a man
who loves me and is taking care of me this black man really loves
me and he's a man the main thing he's a man his chest is broad
he looks like a macho pig he's a businessman he's going to watch
out for me and give me everything I've ever wanted I don't care
if he has nothing to do with my life except sex sex is so important.
I'm coming oh thank God I'm coming, she thinks to herself, as
his cock plunges back and forth inside her, I needed to come so
badly I was so scared I wasn't going to come I need him so much,
clinging to his huge brown chest rivulets of sweat running between their bodies his cock plunges back and forth inside her,
I'll never be horny again I'll never be horny again. Desire takes
over. Dreams ideas . . . everything awakens. Your body is the
most beautiful thing I've ever known and your touch satisfies all
the longings I've ever had. I need to feel and see your body to
keep on living. I can't live without you because you're so incredibly beautiful and I know you love me. I'm beginning to
believe that I'll give up everything for you, because, so far, in
spite of my blossoming career and endless need to break all limits,
my life has been nothing.

    "Are you going to leave me? I know you're going to leave me
for another man."

    "Stop it. Think for a moment. Your mind's driving you crazy.
I don't want anyone else. I don't even think of any other man.
Am I acting like I want another boyfriend?"

"I'm realistic. I know you're going to meet another man and fall in love with him. You're going to forget about me."

"Oh shit I've started bleeding. At least I'm not pregnant."

"I don't like it when woman are on the rag. I make Betty use only tampax. She has to change them every hour and flush them down the toilet. I won't go near her until she's clean again. It disgusts me. You know what my sister once did to me when I was a young boy? I got into bed and there were all her used rags."

"Well. You can stay away from me if you want."

"I don't want you to leave me. That's all I think about. If it's not Duval, it's someone else. All the boys are after you."

"I'm going to tell you something about myself, I'm really a very private person I don't discuss this with anybody. How do I explain this? I spend most of my time doing this uh work, Zen. I'm trying to find out who I am, my mind is basically occupied with this. That's where my mind is. I go with one guy, OK I love to love and I love to fuck, but there's no spaces in my life for a lot of sex."

"What do you do when you do this Zen? Do you go to a temple and bow before the Buddha?"

"No. I sit in front of a wall and stare at the wall." Kathy stares at herself in the mirror to see if she's getting fat. She isn't.

"I can't continue seeing you if you're a Buddhist."

"Why not?"

"Buddhists don't like to fuck or get drunk or do any of the things I like to do."

"I'm not that kind of Buddhist. I just do this weird kind of thing so I won't be selfish all the time and so I can find out who I am. I'm not even sure I'm a Buddhist. At the Zen Center I go to back home Jerry and Robert and I, those are two people in the Zen Center, couldn't decide if we were Buddhists or not. What I do doesn't concern you."

"If you do it too much, it won't make you stop fucking me?"

She laughs and throws her arms around his neck. "Roger I couldn't stand to stop fucking you."

"I can't help it. I don't want you to go away from me."

Arm in arm they walk through the night. Into the Imperial restaurant-and-cocktail lounge. It's midnight when most of the poor Haitians are asleep. They order their dinner.

"It's very hard for me to live here because everyone here watches me and knows what I'm doing. I ignore all of them I do what I want. I always do exactly what I want. But I have to be careful. You know if someone insults me, if someone wants to kill me, I can't do anything."

The lights in the restaurant are red. The walls are brown and the waiters are black and white.

"Who would want to kill you?"

"I have my enemies. People resent me. People think I'm hurting them. Just because of who I am. I don't do anything bad. Last year this kid waited outside the Poisson. When I came out, he punched me in the face. I couldn't do anything because if I do, everyone'll blame me and say it's my fault. I had to get my friends to beat up the kid the next day. I tell you a story why it's dangerous for me to go around town alone. Last year a cop stopped me and wanted to see my identification. I didn't want to show him nothing. He didn't want to give in to me. He said he was going to take me in. I warned him."

"Didn't he know who you were?"

"He was with a lot of his buddies and he couldn't lose face. I still refused to show him ID. When he was about to put his handcuffs on me, I showed him some ID. The next day my henchmen beat him up. He died."

"You killed a cop? Just cause he was acting like a punk?"

"You don't understand what it's like for me. You see this scar?"

"Yes."

"One time, when I was in school in Arizona, this girl she's crazy for me. I don't want anything to do with her."

"You fucked her?"

"I fucked her a few times. It wasn't anything special. I tell her I'm not going to see her again. She doesn't say anything. The next day I walk out of the cafeteria there she is. She has a knife and goes for my throat. The next thing I know, I wake up in the hospital. I find out she's been calling and calling to see if I'm still alive. Then she comes to see me and tells me she loves me madly won't I please let her take care of me. Oh brother."

"Sounds like a classical situation."

"This one girl here, she tells me she's been to a voodoo doctor who's done a work so I have to fall in love with her. But I tell her I don't believe in that stuff. Women are always falling in love with me."

"Have you ever loved a woman?"

"I had this mistress once I paid her a lot of money. She cheated on me and I didn't know at the time oh brother. She took all the money I gave her. Then she got pregnant with my child and had an abortion without asking me if she could have one."

"Roger, I love you."

A black-and-white waiter brings them their food: a whole fried fish surrounded by fried plantains, salads, sauces, lobster, and some other food Roger tells him to take away.

"I have things hard. I want to be like everyone else, but no one will let me. When I was staying in New York City, every day I got mugged. That's where I got this bump on my head. This man beat the hell out of me cause he said I'm a black man. I couldn't fight back."

"Jesus Christ."

"I don't like New York City. The white people hate us there. I'd lose my life if I lived in New York City. Here, when white people visit my father, they treat my father and the rest of us with a lot of respect. People like, what's that really good brandy?"

"Courvoisier?"

"No."

"Martell?"

"Yes. Those people, and the people who own Grand Marnier, important people: they all visit my father and bring us fabulous presents. Sometimes I date their daughters."

"Have you killed anyone else?"

"I've never killed anyone. I have some friends who protect me when I need it. It's good. This way no one can find me doing anything wrong and no one bothers me because they all know I'm protected. I don't have any more trouble."

"But don't you care about the people who are less powerful than you?"

"I can't do anything out in the open, none of us can, cause the government's always trying to get us. That's why when I first met you I said it's not good to talk openly about dope. You remember? If anyone caught me with even a joint on me, the government would use that against my father. They already tried to arrest my father directly, but they couldn't do that cause my father's workers stood up for him. Now they're trying to get at my father through us."

She starts crying over her fried fish, fried plantains, salad, and beer.

"Why are you crying? Is something the matter with the food? I'll have them take it back." This makes her cry louder and louder. A strange forty-year-old man walks over to the table. "I'll do anything for you. I love you."

"Hello, Roger."

"Wait a second Lewis. Kathy, please tell me. What's the matter? I don't want to see you crying."

"We'll talk about it later," she says through her tears. "Uh hello. My name is Kathy." She sticks out her hand at the strange man.

"Kathy, this is my uncle Lewis."

He shakes her hand and smiles at Roger. "How are things going at the factory? I hear your family's going down to Port-au-Prince."

"Yes. We'll be going next week. My father has to take care of that lumber business and see about Carlos. I'm going to take Kathy with me."

"That's terrific." He slaps Roger's back. "I see they got my lobster in today."

"This was your shipment. It's not any good I'm not going to eat any more of it. Waiter, take this away. They use bad fish here and they don't know how to cook."

"That lobster came from Port-au-Prince by truck in this heat. There's no way it could still be good. You should know you can't eat lobster around here. You should get the fish they catch right here."

"I saw Carol yesterday. He was drinking champagne. I guess he's doing well."

"Easy come, easy go. I'm doing pretty well myself. How are the rum tanks coming along?"

"I'm worried about the pressure-gauger. I think that gauger we're setting up might blow on us, and then we'd be sunk. That new French engineer isn't any good. I'm going to have papa come up and check it out as soon as I can do it behind my father's back. Papa's a smart one; he knows every goddamn thing there is to know about machinery."

"Maybe I'll come up and take a look at it myself. Are you going to be around tomorrow?"

"I'm working every day now. I'm working my ass off."

"Well, I've got to get going now."

"It was nice having met you," Kathy says as she sticks her hand out at him.

"You're a beautiful young lady. Make Roger happy."

"I'll see you tomorrow," Roger says and his uncle slaps him on the back.

"What a nice man. Waah. Waah. Roger how could you kill someone?"

"Two more beers, please. What are you talking about? I've never killed anyone."

"Well you said you have these henchmen and they kill people for you. For no reason at all. That cop was just trying to save his face. He probably didn't want to be outpowered by a kid in front of his friends. And he lost his life. It's not that you kill people. That's not that important. It's much more. Waah. Waah.

All the poverty and misery and all the suffering. You suffer so much. You don't understand."

"I understand what you're saying. Let's go."

"Don't you have to pay?"

"No. They know who I am."

They walk outside and the stars are moving and the winds are moving in and out of the stars and the moon moves in an even arc the clouds moving in front of the stars in front of and behind the moon, moving faster than the moon, irregularly: the night sky is a grouping of second-to-second changing light and heat and moving substances. Everything moving and changing and pulsating and they call this "death" and they call this "alive."

The ocean is a black still mass, a black monster hiding under his own death, and the town is absolutely still. A dead mass of houses and shacks and slums piled together, jumbled, shackled, no reason at all, just there. The faraway mountains lead slowly down, flatter and flatter land, to the rich houses the rich houses look way down on the poor houses. To the left of the poor houses a secret police shark chute swings down to the sea. This is death. Stillness. The slight ocean rises hit a stone wall, leap up in the air five to thirty feet high. Suddenly white and movement you-never-know-where. Don't hear anything. Hear the water slap the stones. Winds hit the coconut tree leaves. Hear nothing. Sudden violent unsuspected movement everywhere.

Break all speed records. Keep going. You're the gray sportscar and you're moving. I'm the richest prick in town. Poor people don't need arms and legs. I'm the richest prick in town. I wanna go out farther. I wanna get more fucked up. I want to go out there right now. Me go way me me. Moving as fast as the car winds. Grab the cock and up the energy. Anything to up the energy. Get right out there. The faster I go the faster the stars go maybe we'll all stop moving.

"I love it when you touch my cock. Why don't you suck it?"

"Roger, I know it's none of my business but you can't treat the poor people like animals."

"How do I treat them like animals?"

"You don't even realize. Like when you ordered that whore to bring you cigarettes and she even bought them for you and asked you for the money, you wouldn't give her the money."

"I never carry money on me. Everyone knows that. If they want money, they can go to my father and he'll pay them."

"These are poor people. They can't afford to pay for your cigarettes."

"My brother goes out drinking with our workers just so he can order them around. He has lots of girlfriends." The gray sportscar races up and down the long black boulevard. There are no other cars. It reaches the end of the boulevard, circles around Pension L'Ouverture, and heads back down the boulevard. Each time the car goes back, its speed increases.

"The main thing is to have love in your heart. That's what I'm trying to do. If you can love, nothing else matters. If you loved everyone Roger, there'd be a revolution in this town."

"I've never been in love with a woman."

"You haven't? Wow. Last year I fell in love for the first time. I just went crazy. I'd do anything for the guy. He didn't care about me at all. I learned what it was like to really feel for someone."

"I don't like it."

"What?"

"This is no good. You're going to fall in love with another man."

"I should have never told you about that incident with Duval. I love you Roger. I don't love anyone else. I don't want to love anyone else."

"You're going to go back to New York and fall in love with another man."

"No I'm not. I know exactly what my life's like in New York. I can tell you exactly. I spend most of my time at the Zen Center. I don't have much time left over. I see this one guy, the one I told you about, who doesn't give a shit about me. He's just hooked on fucking me. He doesn't give a shit about me. But I can't stop seeing him and I can't see anyone else cause I'm so crazy about him. I'm not going to fall in love with anyone but you."

"Why doesn't this guy fall in love with you? I know he's gonna start to love you when you get back to New York."

"No way. The people I hang around with in New York don't love each other. Not this way."

"You're going to fuck someone else while you're here. You can't have just one boyfriend."

"Do you want me to fuck someone else?"

"I'd hate it." The car goes faster and faster. "I believe what you're telling me, that you don't want to sleep with anyone else. But the flesh is stronger than the spirit."

"Not in my case."

"Tomorrow I'm going to leave Le Roi at lunchtime so I can see you. Then I'll leave you and I'll return in the evening. We'll spend the whole evening together fucking."

"I'd love that."

"And we'll spend all Saturday together. Saturday night I'm going to take you to the voodoo dances. I remember what I've promised you."

The car keeps going around and around the boulevard. The fastest and the only car on the road. It's almost dawn.

THE CHILDREN

B OATS out on the sea. Dense dark clouds with openings in clouds. Look like lands. Lands are serrated areas of bright reds and bright pinks. The water's dark green-blue and calm.

The sea reflects all the light that's in the sky. Uncountable tiny yellow-white quasi-circles moving toward the shore are the color and luminosity of light. At the horizon in the center of the sea is this luminosity. Here the sea is lighter than the sky. The sky is a uniform blue so pale it's almost yellow. To the right some small fluffy clouds are almost disappearing into the paleness. The ocean grows greener. A few whitecaps. A small wooden fishing-boat moves across the sea from right to left. The boat is pale green and both the fisherman who stands in the back of the boat moving the boat with a long pole and the fisherman who crouches down in front of the boat are black. The boat's rim is red.

The roosters are crowing their lungs out and small goats are pissing on the sand and dry dust which covers everything and the pigs are rooting in the sand for whatever garbage the rising waves are leaving behind and white and red hens are scampering up the thin branches of the canap trees.

A group of eleven-year-old boys are sitting on a curb. Alex has two toothpicks, one long and one short, legs from rickets or polio and for the last two days has been running a fever. Kathy walks out of the pension.

"Did you bring me my food?"

"I couldn't get much out. They're watching me. I brought you the white bread. I'm sorry, Alex."

He turns away from her.

"Let's go for a walk," she says to Fritz who always has clean clothes. Fritz and Alex are her two closest friends.

Fritz, Alex, Kathy, and Tony the head of the gang and older walk along the stone wall. Tony puts his arm around Kathy. Alex refuses to talk to her and throws a stone at her. She turns around, pissed. "Why'd you throw a stone at me?" He throws another stone at her: "I want you to die." She's so upset, she starts to cry. All the boys refuse to talk to her. Finally Fritz explains to her that when someone wants to fight her, she has to fight back. Otherwise: everyone will lose his respect for her. If Alex tells her he wants to kill her, she has to tell Alex she's going to kill him. Then they can both forget anything happened. "I'm going to kill you if you give me any more trouble," she says to Alex. He smiles, and runs up to her, and holds her hands. There are tears in his eyes. They're walking back along the stone wall to the dusty white street curb. Fritz tells her she has to fight kung-fu. He demonstrates.

Kathy walks away from the pension. A little red-hair boy asks the white girl if she saw Mrs. Betty this morning. "Sure I saw Betty. She was at the breakfast table talking to papa when I came down for breakfast this morning. I didn't get to speak to her cause I had to run to the bank. I like Betty."

"You know why Mrs. Betty was there?"

"No. Why was she there?"

"We don't have to tell you. You know why she was there," says Fritz.

"She was there because she was talking to papa. Betty and papa are good friends."

"I think she was there for another reason."

"Are you talking about me and Roger? Betty knows all about that."

"I think Mrs. Betty's one very smart lady. She does something," the red-head boy says.

"What's Betty doing?"

"You'll find out what she does."

"I don't have any idea what you're talking about. Fritz, what's this boy talking about?"

"Don't you worry. I'll take care of you. Anyone who brings any trouble to you will have to fight me."

"I'm not worried about anything. I just want to know what's going on."

"Don't you worry. Mrs. Betty won't be able to do anything to you."

"What's Betty going to do to me? Betty and I are friends."

All the boys look at her with pity.

"Where were you last night?" Alex asks. "Did you have good eat?"

"I didn't go anywhere last night. You guys know that. You were watching my room all night. I was waiting for Roger, I had a date with him, but he never showed up."

"I think you ate well last night. I think Gerard came to visit you. You like Gerard?"

"Did any of you see Roger last night?"

"I saw him go into the Poisson," the red-head says. "He was alone."

"That's weird. Why would he go into the Poisson and not see me? I don't think Roger loves me anymore."

"Don't you listen to that little red-haired guy," Fritz says. "He makes you bad. Mr. Mystere didn't go into the Poisson last night."

"Why're you lying to me?" she asks the red-hair guy.

"I'm not lying. I saw the Mystere go into the Poisson."

"Did any of you see Roger today?"

"Nobody's seen Mr. Mystere for the past two days. Don't listen to that little guy. He just wants to cause trouble. All the time he tries to cause trouble."

"I'm gonna beat him up for you," says Alex.

"No. Don't do any fighting. I feel really upset."

"I think Mr. Mystere makes you bad."

"It's not Roger's fault. He just doesn't love me anymore."

"Don't you worry about nothing. If Mr. Mystere makes you bad, I fight him for you."

"I feel good now. You're making me feel happy."

"Mrs. Betty's my friend," the red-hair boy says. "She's very kind to me."

"I like Betty too. I think she's a great person."

"I saw Mrs. Betty talking to papa. She's going to make trouble for you."

"What kind of trouble can Betty make for me? I'm an American."

"Last year," Alex says, "Mrs. Betty was talking to a girlfriend of hers. As soon as Mrs. Betty turns her back, Mr. Mystere starts kissing the girl."

"That's tacky."

"Mrs. Betty sees what's happening. She's no dope. She goes up to the girl and says, 'That's my husband you're kissing. You have no right to kiss him.' She slaps the girl."

"What'd the girl do?"

"Mrs. Betty takes care of herself. She knows Mr. Mystere has to do what his parents say. She gets Mr. Mystere's father to keep him in line."

"That's true. Roger absolutely worships his father and does everything his father says."

"This morning," the red-head boy says, "I talked to Mrs. Betty."

Just then a completely and highly unusually clean blue-green jeep drives up in front of the curb. This car doesn't even have a spot on it. The white girl lackadaisically watches the jeep stop.

Three men get out of the jeep. They're as clean as the jeep. They're wearing blue pin-striped starched and pressed shirts, stiff white pants, thin brown leather belts, real brown leather polished shoes, and black sunglasses. Their bodies are thin and their hair is less than an inch long.

The white girl looks around and sees the boys running away. The three men stand over her. She looks up at them and doesn't say anything. She feels too dazed and lightheaded from the boiling hot sun to stand up.

After a while of staring, she asks them in her lousy French if they want anything. They don't reply. They just keep staring at her. She sighs and sinks down against the white stucco wall. The morning sun's getting hotter and hotter. After a while, they get back into the jeep.

As soon as the blue-green jeep drives away, the beggar boys return to the curb. Kathy's shaking. "Who were those men?"

"Oh, they were the police."

"The secret police?"

"Yes. The police," Fritz says. He's wearing a short-sleeve khaki shirt and has his hands in his pockets.

"What . . . what did they want with me?"

"I don't know. You must have been bad."

"Look, you've got to tell me about the secret police here. I've heard they kill people whenever they want to. Do they always do this to tourists? They stood over me and didn't say anything."

"No. They usually don't go near the tourists."

"Then why me? Have I been doing something wrong?"

"You must have been."

"What've I been doing?"

"I don't know."

"Why'd all of you run away when the police came? Why didn't you tell me who they are?"

"If the police catch us talking to you, they'll arrest us. They'll think we're bothering you. We had to run away. They won't arrest you because you're an American."

"Then why were they standing over me and staring at me like that? I don't like cops I'm really scared of them. You've got to tell me exactly what's happening. I don't understand what's happening."

"Don't you worry," Fritz sticks his hands in his pockets and spreads his legs, "about nothing. I'll fight those big men for you if they give you trouble."

"You're not going to fight those men. Don't be ridiculous."

"You shouldn't worry about nothing. In Haiti there are no problems." All the boys nod in agreement.

"I just want to know what's going on. I want to know if I've been doing something wrong."

Alex says, "You have a lot of evil thoughts."

"You mean I'm evil?"

"Yes. You're going to have to go to church to get rid of the evil."

"I don't want to go to church. I go to my own kind of church. Every day I sit by myself and pray. My kind of religion doesn't have a church and a priest."

"Alex is right," Fritz says. "You're a Haitian now and you have to behave like a Haitian. You run around with too many men."

"I do not. You know the only man I see is Roger. Am I supposed to go without a boyfriend?"

"You see Gerard and lots of other men. Last night you let some man into your room. All of us saw you."

"That's not true and you know it. I spent all last night sitting around and waiting for Roger. I love Roger. I don't love anybody else."

"Then why," the oldest and biggest boy asks, "when I asked you last night to take a little walk with me, you said you were too busy?"

"I was busy. I had a date with Roger, but he never showed up."

"You said you were busy and now you say you didn't eat last night. I think you're lying."

"I think you have a lot of bad in you," Fritz adds.

"You're all being ridiculous. I want to know about those cops. I hate cops. They ruin everything. What did they want with me?"

"You shouldn't see Mr. Mystere. He has a wife."

"I know he has a wife. I don't want to be in love with someone who's married. Do you think I can choose who I fall in love with?"

"Mrs. Betty's a nice lady," Fritz says, "she's always kind to us. She's not going to like the something you're doing with her husband."

"I'm only going to be here a few weeks I'm leaving. I don't want to break up Roger's and Betty's marriage. I think their marriage is terrific. Betty knows all about me and Roger and it's OK."

"Mrs. Betty's not going to like it when she hears Roger spends his nights in your room. Mrs. Betty's a very jealous woman."

"I don't want to hurt Betty and I don't want to break up her marriage. What'm I supposed to do: make myself stop being in love? I can't do that. Do you understand?"

"I understand," Fritz says. His bare foot kicks a pebble.

"Mrs. Betty's my friend," the red-headed boy says. "This morning I talked to her."

"Why don't you go with me the way you go with the Mystere?" asks Tony. "You have to give me comfort."

"Oh Tony."

"I want to know why not."

"You're too young. I'm twenty-nine years old and you're only twelve."

"In Haiti there is no age. I'm a man like the Mystere."

The white girl's silent for a moment. She feels ashamed. "You're right, Tony."

"The Mystere give you good suck? I give good suck. I have many girlfriends. Ask anyone. I have girlfriends who are older than you. There's one of my girlfriends. She's twenty-five years old. All the time she's after me. 'Tony Tony give me a kiss please just one kiss.' "

I don't believe you, she thinks to herself. She sees a tall, strangely thin woman high-high cheekbones and glittering eyes walk up to Tony and throw her arms around him while the woman kisses Tony, she stares at the white girl with her glittering eyes and Tony says, "You see . . ." The woman holds out a bunch of tiny purple-pink flowers toward the white girl Tony puts his arms around both of them, "I have two girlfriends." "No," the white girl says. The woman kisses Alex twice. "I'm number one," says Tony. The woman places two sprigs of the purple-pink flowers in the white girl's hair.

A nineteen-year-old boy is trying to teach the white girl how to read the Creole of a Jesus magazine. They're slowly translating into English a prayer to Jesus. "Tonight," Tony says to the white girl, "there's going to be a mist over the ocean."

OUR FATHER WHO ART IN HEAVEN

"This mist is called laughter."

HALLOWED BE THY NAME

"If you see this mist, you sleep all the time."

THY KINGDOM IS COMING

"Don't look. Don't look," the kids yell and turn her face away from the glittering eyes of the woman. The woman's standing an inch away from her. "Don't look at her." The woman reaches for her hand. "Don't let her touch you." The woman's hand's holding her hand. "Why?" she asks, "what's the matter?"

JESUS IS COMING JESUS YOU ARE
OUR SAVIOR ONLY YOU CAN UNITE
US ONLY YOU BRING US COMFORT

The women are standing an inch away from each other and staring at each other.

The nineteen-year-old boy explodes. "Don't touch her. Don't let her get near you. She has nothing to do with Jesus. She's trying to stop me."

"She wants a something from you," Fritz says. "She's a bad woman. She's going to do something to you. She's going to make the mist come and you're going to get very sick." She sees the woman's eyes glitter and glitter more.

The woman descends on the nineteen-year-old boy. "I don't care about you I do what I want. You can't stop me."

"I can't, but my father can. My father's a captain. You know who he is. He's a captain so you better watch your step. You know what I'm talking about." The woman with glittering eyes turns around and runs away.

All the little boys have their arms around the white girl. They're all touching her.

"Mrs. Betty's going to make trouble for you. Mrs. Betty's a smart lady. She's going to make plenty hot water for you with Mr. Mystere's father. You better watch your step," the red-head boy warns Kathy.

"How do you know Betty's going to make trouble for me?"

"She say so to me. She say she going to cause you a lot of trouble."

"She said she was going to cause me a lot of trouble? What's she going to do?"

"Don't you believe him," Fritz says. "He tells lies all the time."

"How can he say something like this if it isn't true? Doesn't he know what he's doing?"

"Don't you worry yourself. You get lots of thoughts in your head and you become bad."

"Listen Fritz. Sometimes it's necessary that people talk things out. Just to get them straight. All I want to know is what Betty said. I know what's going on and it's all OK. I just want to know what Betty said."

"Mrs. Betty said you're in a lot of hot water," the red-head says.

"How do you know this? Did Betty say it to you?"

"It's our job to know everything," Fritz says. All the boys agree.

"Then Betty didn't say this directly to you?"

"Don't you listen to him. Come with me." Fritz takes her to a corner of the curb. All the children follow him. The corner ends in burning white sun, burning white dust covers the sky and makes the concrete dirt sand and wood burn like heated car metal. This burning white dust leads straight ahead to the ocean. Thin women are sitting rocking babies and fanning coal fires and pounding something in straw baskets and talking to each other and the maids on the pension are handwashing laundry spreading it out in the sun to dry and preparing food for the night's dinner to the left of the white dust, facing the green ocean, a filthy sandy beach curves outward into the reefs and upward into low rocky hills. The women sit on the edge of this beach. The land is very flat and the women and houses are almost invisible. Small black pigs, goats, chickens, and some mangy dogs run around the women. Tall flashy men elegant shirts walk up and down the sidewalk to the right of the burning dust. A few bare-chested rolled-up pants men are trying to clear the small beach for the tourists by moving the heavier rocks from the sand to the more distant reefs. There are no old people because all the old people are dead. It's the middle of the day. "You know what somebody tells me about you?"

"No."

"This somebody says you do your something with Mr. Mystere because he gives you money."

"That's ridiculous."

"This somebody also says you do a something with lots of men for money."

"Do you mean I'm a prostitute?"

"You do your something with lots of men for money."

"Look: You know I go only with Roger, and no one else. How can I be a prostitute? I do something with Roger, but does that make me a prostitute? Do you think I shouldn't do anything with anyone?"

"We know about your something with Mr. Mystere. It's OK. You also go with other men for money."

"What the fuck are you talking about? That's a totally horrible disgusting thing to say. It's horrible to call a woman a prostitute. You know who I am. I'm your friend. How can you think such things about me? You must be crazy."

"I'm not crazy," says Fritz who's offended.

"I'm not crazy," says another boy.

"Then whoever told you this is lying."

"The somebody who said it to us doesn't tell lies," Fritz says.

"Who said I'm a prostitute?"

"You know who. That little boy, Tommy."

"I don't know who you're talking about."

"That little boy who's always running around the pension with a radio in his ear. He's the owner's nephew. He sees men going into your room every night. He says you're staying at the pension so you can get lots of money from the rich tourists."

"I don't even know this little boy. I mean I know him by sight, but I've never even said two words to him." She thinks for a moment. "He's got some weird thing in his head about me cause he always avoids me. I'm going to tell you something. If I really was a prostitute, I wouldn't be staying at L'Ouverture cause it's not possible for a prostitute to make any money at L'Ouverture. The tourists who come here aren't rich enough, you know they're the plane tourists rather than the boat tourists, and there isn't a quick enough overturn of tourists. And L'Ouverture isn't cheap. A prostitute would starve to death here."

"Then why does he say you take money from men?"

"I don't know. How the hell should I know?"

"There must be something in what he says." All the other boys agree with Fritz. "There's no smoke without fire."

"That's true," Alex adds, "there's no smoke without fire."

"You don't believe anything I'm saying."

"I believe you. I think you do a something with lots of men."

"The only person I do a something with is Roger. You know that. Have you ever seen another man go into my room?"

"No."

"You're watching my room all the time. I know all of you are. You know I never let anyone besides Roger in my room. So why do you believe whatever some little guy says about me rather than what I say about me? You don't even like him and I'm your friend."

"I don't believe Tommy and I don't believe you. I don't think nothing."

"How can you think nothing? You tell me this horrible vicious thing people are saying about me, you say you believe it, and then when I prove that it's false, you say the whole thing doesn't matter. It matters to me. I don't want people saying horrible false things about me. I'm in a foreign country. I don't know what's going on here if I get in trouble I don't know anyone I can run to."

"Nobody says horrible things about you. Lots of women are prostitutes."

"I'm not a prostitute."

"If you say you're not a prostitute, I believe you."

"I swear on anything you consider holy, the holiest thing you know, I'm not a prostitute."

"How much money do you make from men?" the red-head asks.

"Haven't you been listening to anything I've been saying?"

"How much do you charge each man?"

"I'm getting out of here."

Papa and Kathy are sitting on the dining-room terrace that overlooks the ocean. Papa is a seventy-six-year-old American perhaps ex-CIA ex-sailor. "Papa, the tontons macoute just stopped me. They got out of the jeep and stared at me then they drove away. What do you think they wanted?"

"You better watch out for those guys. People disappear around here."

"Do you really think I might be in trouble? They didn't say anything."

"As far as I know, I repeat, as far as I know, they don't bother Americans unless they think you're trying to overthrow their government. Then they don't even give you a trial. Now if you were a Haitian, you might be in hot water. Now I don't know anything for sure."

"Do you think there's going to be a revolution here? The people in this country are so poor. All those boys out there are going to starve this fall cause of the drought."

"There's not going to be a revolution here. There can't be.

These government blacks have the country sewn up. No one can get into this country to start a revolution. Cuba's on one side America's on the other side both of them are dying to grab the one resource that's left in this country: cheap labor, and Baby Doc's not letting either of them stick their noses in the door. Why just last year this boat, just a rowboat, comes over here from Cuba. This happens every so often here. Cuba's just around the next bend. The rowboat's heading toward this beach down here, right around that little hill." Papa points to the left, to a small piece of land that juts out into the ocean. "No one knows exactly what happened. We saw the whole damn army come out of the woodwork. The colonel and all his men in full uniforms, guns loaded, stood on this beach, ready to shoot. They covered the whole beach front. Got a few fisherman. The colonel and his men were waiting for that rowboat to touch the beach. How they knew that rowboat was coming, I'll never know. They know things around here. No one knows who was in that rowboat, how many men, what happened to them. Those men disappeared. You don't put men on trial for political crimes in a country like this. Why there used to be this real nice fellow, a big guy, came around here every now and then to sell some fish. A real nice guy. He didn't show up for a few days one time so I asked around. You know? If anyone knows what happened to him? No one knows anything. Finally I asked Raoul and Raoul tells me it's not good to ask questions. Just keep your mouth shut. You know that guy just disappeared."

"But what about back in the hills, papa? I heard there are guerrilla groups who work in the country."

"Who're you kidding? First of all, these people are," he whispers, "Voodooists. They'll tell you they're not, but they are, every last one of them. They're not going to fight Baby Doc, honey, cause they know he's Papa Loi."

"He is. He's got all the power."

"That's right. If he's got so much power, he must be Head Voodoo Man. These people aren't stupid. Plus the voodoo men, you know each village has a head voodoo man. The head voodoo man isn't the chief; he's equal to the chief. He's the doctor. Everyone comes to him with their problems. 'Doctor, my boyfriend's disappeared.' 'Doctor, someone's poisoned my dog.' So this voodoo man knows everything. There's nothing that can happen in the village that he doesn't know. And the voodoo man goes and tells the sheriff, or whoever's the big government guy in the district, what's happening in the village. And the government guy goes and tells the big government guys in Port-au-Prince."

"Do you think things will ever get better here?" She looks at the beggar boys who are sitting on the low ocean wall, the blue-green ocean, the men working on the beach, the goats, chickens, pigs, dogs, and sand.

"Well, sure, things are already better here. Used to be when a tourist ship'd come into the harbor, its captain would radio to the cops, 'Please put away your guns so the tourists won't see them.' They didn't want to scare the tourists cause it was bad for the tourist trade. Why there were shootings all over the place. The tontons macoute, you hardly see them anymore."

"I saw them. They scared the shit out of me. The boys knew what was going on and ran away. I sat in front of those cops and stared at them like a stupid dog."

"They used to be all over the place. And with guns. After all, they didn't pull any guns on you. I had a run-in with them once. About five years ago. We had to go from Cap Haitian to Port-au-Prince. In those days the only way you could make a trip like that was in a good jeep. And you had to stop at every police station to show your police pass and make a report. We stop at one station and goddamnit that army man can't read. He looks at our papers and he can't read a damn word. He's got his gun on us the whole time. You know you don't go to jail in Haiti for political crimes. You just disappear. Finally we persuade him to drive with us to the next village where there's a man who can read. That son-of-a-bitch cop gets in the truck with us, cocks his gun, and sticks his gun in our backs the whole way to the next village. And at that time I was in the employ of the Haitian government. These police don't work for money, you know. They're in love with their jobs. The regular cops in Port-au-Prince, the ones in yellow shirts, get paid like regular cops, but these guys don't get anything. Of course they take whatever they want from whoever they want."

"Papa, Roger told me he gives Betty a thousand a month above expenses. Do you think that's true?"

"Roger was lying. My God, he doesn't even have a thousand a month for himself. His father has money, but that doesn't mean he has money. You know what I'm talking about: your parents are the same way. That father keeps all the money for himself. That way he can control the boys. He doesn't let those boys have a penny. Why just last year all three boys, you know they're all married, go to him and ask for some money. 'We're all married, father, we've got wives and kids: we need some money now, etc.' So he buys them all cars."

"Why don't they tell him to go to hell? Jesus Christ, in the States no kid would put up with that kind of shit from his parents. Especially a kid who's over twenty-one."

"For heaven's sake those kids know the guy has money. They're just waiting around for the good stuff; hanging on to daddy until daddy decides to cough up. He's never going to cough up you know."

"So Roger's always going to be controlled by daddy?"

"Of course he is. Do you know how much that father has stored up? Why just that one rum tank: that's going to gross a half-million this year. Sure he has expenses, but what are those? Haitian labor's cheaper than slavery. The machines don't cost him that much, though they cost more than the labor. So figure it out, nice and slow. He has three rum tanks going for him. Plus the lumber plus the rubber plus the cocoa plus the coffee plantations."

"Oh."

"Ooh. Something penetrated into your little head. Ooh. Now you see what's going on. Half a million doesn't mean much, but when you add half a million and half a million and half a million and"

"Yeah papa, I understand. So that's why Betty's hanging in there. She's not such a dope."

"Sure. Betty has her nose out for the money too. You know she already tried to leave Roger. She went home once for good, about a year ago. But she came back."

"I know all about Betty's leaving Roger. I think she really loves Roger. You know they're not even really married. Roger never registered the marriage with the Haitian government. So Betty has no possessions of her own, no money, she has no claim on Roger."

"Well, Roger's a nice boy. He's still a boy, understand. He can't get his head out of that black stuff."

"Roger just likes pussy. Black white red old young. He's rough."

"This damn bum leg. It's hurting me worse than ever."

Roger doesn't love me anymore. I know. He likes women too much. Even if he does love me, he's under daddy's control and daddy's stopping him from being with me. I know he is. She doesn't say anything out loud. "Why don't you have a doctor look at it, papa?"

"I have. I've had five doctors look at it. They all say something different. Why that Spanish doctor who lives over the hill there was giving me Vitamin B-12 shots every other day. Those things are dangerous. He had to stop them cause they were getting too dangerous."

"How'd you get the leg?"

"I was shipping fruits and vegetables out to the Caics. You know, you can't ship anything into Haiti. No one buys anything here. The only way you can make money is to ship things out of Haiti. Mangoes cost a penny, two pennies each when they're in season and in the Caics you can get fifteen cents apiece for them. All the fruits and vegetables here are that way. At that time I was shipping fruits and vegetables out to the Caics. There's nothing on the Caics you know. Just a lot of dunes and sand. Some natives. We were sitting off the Caics and we ate a bad fish and the lot of us got sick. Puking sick. I puked for three days straight and I wasn't the worst one. There was no doctor around and there was nothing we could do. Finally we got hold of this nurse. I mean got hold of her. She was something. Jiggling all over the place. I just love those things. Mmmm-mm. Well, she shot me up in the leg with that stuff, what do you call it? the stuff they use to make people sleep on airplanes."

"Dramamine?"

"That's it. Dramamine. She must have hit a nerve or something."

"Dramamine's not a medicine, I mean,"

"She must have hit a nerve or something, I'm sure it was a nerve cause immediately the leg swells up like a balloon. It won't come down for three months and it hurts like the dickens. The goddamn thing's still swollen." It is. "My heart isn't so good either."

"Why don't you get over to Florida and see a good doctor?"

"I've lived a good life. I've done everything I've wanted to and I can't say I've hurt anyone too much. I always try to avoid hurting anybody: I see no sense in doing otherwise. I always pay my girls as soon as I use them. That way there are no hard feelings. I sleep well at nights and you can't say that about anyone who lives in the States."

"I always sleep well at nights." She takes a sip of thick rich coffee.

"When you get back to the States, get a book called *Papa Doc*. That'll tell you everything you need to know about this country. Of course you can't get the book here. Papa Doc was a live wire. He had all the money and all the power in the country. He started out with nothing, and he got it that way. He was a rapacious son-of-a-bitch. When he died, you see, the family got together. They had to decide who would inherit what. Just a little family meeting like any family meeting after the funeral. They decided to split it. The mother and the sister got the money and Jean-Claude got the power."

"Jean-Claude's not poor."

"Of course he isn't, honey. But he's not bleeding the country for all he can get the way that mother and sister are still doing. Jesus Christ, women can never be satisfied. And his top ministers get all the graft they can get. They don't even think twice about it. Those blacks are still in power and, I say, they never completely came out of the trees."

"Everyone in this country's black."

"No they're not. There're the blacks and there're the mulattoes. Right now the blacks run the government, but the mulattoes have all the money. The blacks and the mulattoes: they've never liked each other. A mulatto man'll never go with a black woman. He doesn't even like American women. He'll go with another mulatto, or even better, with a French or French-Canadian woman cause that means he's overcome his African blood. Whereas a black prefers an American woman every time. The mulattoes are society: they do all the business and they have all the money. I'll tell you something: that's where your revolution's going to come from. Look at Henry. His father's English and his wife's father's French. Gerard is almost white. Those are the ones who have money in this town."

"But Roger's black?"

"Are you kidding? That father's almost as white as I am. And look at Nicolas, the second brother. He's barely tan. I'll tell you something. You look at Jean, Gerard's younger brother. His gums are black as anything. Now and then you get a throwback, and there's nothing you can do about it."

The boys and the white girl sit out on the stone wall. They don't do anything. They sit there for about an hour. Then they move back to the curb in the white dust. They sit down. They don't do anything else. A few more hours pass.

"Have you brought it for me?" Tony asks.

"Brought what, Tony?"

"You know."

"Don't give me any problems. I'm not in a good mood."

He raises his fists at her. "He wants to kill you," the nineteen-year-old boy says. "You want to kill me, Tony?" "Yes."

"Why do you want to kill me?" "You know."

"It's no good to want to kill someone. The bad energy you put out comes right back at you."

"No. It goes out to you."

"Tony only likes white girls. He refuses to go with Haitian girls. Last year he fought Ally over a French girl Ally was with."

"Was Tony fucking her?"

"No. Tony wanted to fuck her."

"When are you going to give me the something I want?"

"I don't know what you want."

"Yes you do. Don't lie to me."

The sun is white-hot the air and the cement and the cars are hot.

"Tony, I can't."

"Why not? You give it to the Mystere. I know you do cause I've seen you."

"It's different with Roger, Tony. He's the only one I fuck."

"Why's it different with the Mystere? You think he has money and he can take you places and I don't have any money."

All the boys cluster around them. "I've told you again and again. I can't go with you cause you're much younger than me."

"You think this 'younger' means something. I can do anything the Mystere does. I see him take you to the Poisson and buy you beers. You think I can't do that? I have plenty of money. I buy you one beer, two beers. I take you dancing and buy you things. You go with him just cause he's going to buy you lots of things."

"I love Roger. I don't care about his money. I've got my own money."

"Then why won't you give me a little kiss? I need comfort just like the Mystere needs comfort. You know what comfort is?"

"Yes." She pauses. "OK. I'll give you one kiss, if you promise not to bother me again. You have to promise not to bother me again. Just one kiss."

"I promise." With a huge smile on his face, he closes his eyes, purses his lips. All the other boys gather round, nudge each other, giggle, try to touch her. She bends down and kisses his forehead. He opens his eyes. "That isn't fair. That wasn't anything."

"I kissed you."

"That was for a baby. You have to kiss me like you kiss the Mystere." Alex giggles.

"He's right," Fritz tells her.

"OK. But this is the only time. I'm not going to kiss you again."

He lifts his arm and puts it around her shoulder. He places his thick soft lips on her mouth and gently inserts his tongue in her mouth. His arms press her into him. He moves his tongue slowly in her mouth. After a few minutes he lets her go.

"OK?" she asks, dazed.

"When are you going to give me eat?"

"Tony. You promised that was all. You're not supposed to bother me again."

"You don't have to kiss me again. Now you have to eat with me." All the other boys are giggling.

"Tony, I'm really getting angry. You're going too far."

"What do you mean I'm going too far? You're always making these rules. I don't make them. You won't even give me a chance."

"I understand what you're saying. I just can't. It's me. It's my fault. In my mind you're too young for me."

"You're crazy."

"That's true," Fritz agrees. "You know what the women over there say to you when you walk by them to go swimming?"

"I know."

" 'La folle Americaine.' Do you understand what that means?"

"I know I'm crazy. Everybody's a little crazy."

"I'm not crazy. Tony isn't crazy. You're the one who's crazy."

"Wait a minute. Just cause I do what I want and what I want

sometimes doesn't coincide with what women normally do in this town doesn't mean I'm crazy. I'm not insane."

"You do things you shouldn't do. You go bathing where no other white people go bathing, where only the poor black people go, and you make love with too many men."

"I don't make love with too many men. The only man I go with is Roger. I talk to a lot of men, sure, like I talk to you, I talk to you all the time but I don't go with you. You mean I'm not supposed to talk to you?"

"It's OK for you to talk to us little guys. But you shouldn't talk to anyone else except Roger. Otherwise people'll think you're crazy."

"I can't do that. If the people here think I'm crazy, I can't do anything about that."

"Do you know how to fight kung-fu?"

"No."

"You don't. We fight kung-fu all the time. Look, we'll show you." The khaki-shirted boy and another boy stand five feet apart, bodies turned sideways, forward legs face front, arms extend and bend, hands straight and stiff, forward hands point at each other. The khaki-shirted boy says "Kung-fu." They move toward each other as if they're kangaroos on downers. They're about two feet apart they kick at each other. "Don't they do this in America?"

"Sure they do. Everyone sees the kung-fu movies. Especially Bruce Lee."

"He's dead now. I'm going to be Bruce Lee when I get older."

"I guess he is dead. How do you know about kung-fu here?"

"We know everything. The movie house down the street, you know where it is, shows one kung-fu movie and one romance movie every week. You want to go see it?"

"Not right now."

"I can't see the movie cause I don't have any money."

"I see why you wanted me to see the movie. How much do you want?"

"I want to see it too. I want to see it too. I want to see it too."
Three other boys crowd around the white girl.

"I'm going to fight kung-fu," Alex says. "Look at me." He and
Tony take kung-fu positions. Alex lurches and when he tries to
kick his good leg in the air, falls flat on his face on his crippled
toothpick leg. "Alex, are you OK?" the white girl asks. The other
boys giggle. Alex gets up and waves his hands.

"How much do you want?"

"Fifty cents."

"OK. If you really want to go, I'll give whoever wants to fifty
cents."

"I want a coke," the red-head says.

"OK. I'll give each of you fifty cents and you can do what you
want with the money."

"You owe me a coke," Fritz reminds her. "Yesterday you said
you were going to buy me a coke and you never did."

"I'll give you a dollar."

"That's not fair. Why should he get a coke and get to go to
the movies? We all want to do that."

"Shut up. I should never have said anything in the first place.
I'll give you all fifty cents and that's that." She doles out the
money.

"You owe me two dollars when I got that cab for you that day.
The one you took to visit Mr. Mystere," the smallest of the lot
says.

"Are you bringing that up again you scoundrel? You know
damn well I paid you. Listen you kids, I do not have endless
money. Compared to you I'm rich, but back home in the States
I am poor."

"When are you going back to your home?" Fritz asks. "I think
you're going back very soon. I think your mother and father are
waiting for you."

"I don't have a mother and father. I have a brother who's
waiting for me. He's terrific: you'd like him. I'm trying to get
him to come down here. If he does, I'll stay here a lot longer."

"If your brother comes down here, he's going to be very angry with you."

"Why?"

"He'll see you doing your something with Mr. Mystere and he'll make you stop seeing Mr. Mystere."

"No he won't. My brother doesn't care what I do."

"I don't believe you. If you were my sister, I'd keep my eye on you all the time."

"My brother's terrific."

"I think you're going to leave us soon. I don't think you're ever coming back," Alex cries.

"Oh Alex. That's not true. I'm not going to leave soon and if I do, it'll only be for a few months. I love it here. I'm happier than I've ever been anywhere else. All I want is to sit and do nothing. I have to leave cause I have to get some money so I can come back here. I'm not rich."

"I think you're going to leave and you're going to forget all about us."

"I'll never forget about you. I couldn't. I'll send you stuff from the States and I'll be back here soon as I can. I don't like it there; I like it here."

"I want the address of your mother and father so I can write them," Fritz says.

"I'll give you my brother's address. He's much nicer. My parents are creeps." She gives him her brother's address. The white ball grows small enough that some blue appears and long thin clouds moving rapidly past the blue and the burning white. There are no more fishing boats on the ocean. Girls in blouses and tight skirts walk together, giggling, on the boulevard. Tall young studs race by on motor scooters. A gray car whirs past and honks.

"That's Mr. Mystere."

"Where's Mr. Mystere, where's Roger?" she screams.

"His car just drove by."

"That wasn't his car," Fritz tells the girl.

"Was that Roger? Please, tell me. Please."

"That wasn't Roger," Fritz says. "They're just teasing you. Don't you worry about nothing."

"I don't think there should be any white people here," the smallest boy says. "This place is going to be like Jamaica. In Jamaica the black people tell all the white people they have to get out."

"I agree with what you're saying, but, it makes me feel funny, that you don't like me, well, cause I'm white."

"We have to be by ourselves. We have to do everything by ourselves," Tony says.

"I understand what you're saying."

"Can you do the Kingston walk?"

"The Kingston walk?"

Fritz sticks out his pelvis, lifts his legs high in the air, doesn't move his hips, shuffles.

"I've got to go to the hospital," Tony says.

"Tony, what's the matter with you?"

"You know why I've got to go to the hospital."

"I don't know why you have to go the hospital. Are you sick?"

"You know why he has to go the hospital," Fritz says.

"People stop me and I tell them 'Don't talk to me you can't talk to me anymore I'm dying.' I'm going to take myself to the hospital they'll say 'Tony, you're never going to recover. We can't do anything more for you.' I'll tell them this evil woman caused my death she's going I'm going to die now."

"Oh Tony, you're not going to die." They all do the Kingston walk. "Oo be doo oo be da na-na na-na, na-na na-na, oo be do oo be oo be be da."

"Les poissons, ils nagent dans la mer, Les poissons, ils sont tres cher," Fritz sings.

> "I wanna go home,
> Where-ere I belong,
> Cau-ause now I'm just a
> Lonely teenager, lonely tee-eenager.
> Seventeen, I ran away,"

"Chk a buka buka dchuk shlik ya hung, hung,"

"What's that, Alex?"

"That's Chinese."

"Oh. I didn't know you could speak Chinese."

"I'll teach you how. Hung guk, good good, hu hu long ha."

"Foe wah, li con good good lung chk hak."

"La spaghettina esta bono."

"Hey, that's a good one." The ocean leaps up into spray and covers them.

"Guk li pong ya, ma tay fong tu li pik so shlik punk li poe nah nah foe tay hong."

"Do you know Gene Kelly? When you go back to New York, you have to see him. He can give you comfort."

"Everyone in New York goes to see him. They bring him their problems and he takes their problems away. You know, a doctor? He's a doctor. When you go to see him, you have to bring him your problems."

"I don't have any problems."

"You have lots of problems in your head. I see them. Gene Kelly can make you better. He cures many, many people."

"How can I find him?"

"Everyone in New York knows where he lives. He's as famous as Bruce Lee."

"I think I've heard of him."

"Gene Kelly's a good man. You have to see him when you get back to New York, and then you be OK."

"I'm making big trouble for you," says the red-head. "I make big trouble for you and you don't get out of it so easily."

"What'd he do?" she asks Fritz.

"Nothing. Nothing." He waves his hands at the red-head boy to go away.

"I talk to Mrs. Betty today and tell her what's going on. She says she's going to make trouble for you and Roger."

"What'd you do? What'd you say about me and Roger?" Her eyes blaze.

"Go away. Get out of here." Fritz raises his fists at the red-head then turns around to the girl. "Don't you listen to that little fellow. He wants to make trouble. He's telling lies."

"Fritz, this is my affair. I have to find out what he said to Betty." Her blazing eyes turn to the red-head. "What did you say to Betty?"

"I didn't say anything. I don't cause any trouble. Mrs. Betty's my friend. I just tell her what's going on."

"What's going on?"

"You know what goes on. I see you and Mr. Mystere kissing on the roof. I see Mr. Mystere go into your room night after night."

"I see that too," Fritz says.

"Mrs. Betty doesn't like this. I think she's going to make a lot of trouble for you."

"Betty can't make a lot of trouble for me. There's nothing she can do. Look. The only person you're hurting by sticking your nose into this business which you know nothing about is Betty. You don't have any idea what's going on and you don't know what you're doing. You're just causing a lot of unnecessary trouble."

"I cause trouble to you," he mocks.

"No. You're stupid. Betty and Roger have a lot of problems which have nothing to do with me. Their marriage has been on the rocks for awhile and I'm not going to save it or break it. I don't matter. Betty knows all about me and telling her is only going to hurt her feelings more. It doesn't hurt me. So just keep out of this."

"Mrs. Betty doesn't like it when her husband makes eyes at other women. She's going to get Mr. Mystere's father to hurt you."

"What're you talking about?"

"I think the police are coming after you."

"The police? You don't know what you're talking about." She's trembling.

"Don't you listen to that little fellow. Come away from here." Fritz pulls her left arm.

"I'm going to cause a lot of trouble for you," the white girl says. "I'm an American so I can do it. You'd better watch your fuckin' step." The red-head throws a rock at her head. She ducks. "You try that one more time and you're going to be in more trouble than you've ever been in your life." He throws another rock at her head. She starts crying. "I think the cops are coming after you. Whore. Miss Whore."

"I'm going to kill him." She can't talk directly to the red-head. Her fists are clenched.

"Are you going to kill him?" Fritz asks. "Are you going to fight kung-fu?"

"How much money do you take from men? I tell you what everyone says." None of the other boys say anything.

She turns around and starts to run. Only she can't figure out where to go.

"Gerard. Can I talk to you for a minute?"

He shrugs through his blue-green jeep window.

"Are you sure you've got five minutes?"

"I've got five minutes and only five minutes. Open the door and climb in. It's more private in here."

Through the dirty jeep window the beggar boys sit in the dust and watch, Ally comes out of the pension, gooses a maid, drives away on his red Honda, the white dust covers everything, Fritz and Tony fight kung-fu. "It's about Roger. I don't want to bother you or anything, I just have to know I don't want to dump my private life on you."

"Spill it. We're all friends here."

"It's about Roger." She takes a deep breath.

"Want a Marlboro?"

"Sure."

"Here's a light."

"That night I met you and Roger at L'Ouverture, Roger and I spent the night together."

"That's great. Roger's a wonderful person."

"I think so too. Uh . . ."

"Roger wanted me to drive him back to Le Roi. At six o'clock he came pounding on my door . . ."

"I know. He was pissed off you didn't drive him back. He says you're not his friend."

"Roger's a nice guy, but he's full of crap. I have to work on that mountain five days a week. I only come down here for the weekends. The morning he knocked on my door was the only morning I had to sleep till eight o'clock instead of getting up at five o'clock. I wasn't about to get up for no one. Roger has plenty of friends who can drive him back to Le Roi."

"I want to know about his and Betty's relationship," she blurts out. "I'm all mixed up. Roger says he and Betty aren't at all close, he can do whatever he wants, but he never spends a whole night with me and Betty talks as if she and Roger are the same person."

"Roger doesn't care about her at all. He wants to get rid of her and live alone so he can do exactly what he wants to do all the time."

"I know that. But the day after I met you and Roger, I went to Le Roi to visit Betty and Roger, Roger told me to come. Betty kept saying "we," she never said "I," she talked about her and Roger as if they're inseparable. Then she told me Roger's family is crazy. I liked Betty. I thought we were friends. But today I get up and go out on the terrace for breakfast, the first thing I see is Betty and I feel these totally weird vibes. She's talking to papa and I just know she's talking about me. Something tells me not to say hello to her. She wants to make trouble. I just ran. I couldn't handle the situation. And two days ago I had a date with Roger. He didn't show up. He's never done that before. He didn't call or nothing. I haven't seen him in two days. I don't think I'm going to see him again."

"Calm down and take it easy. The main thing is to enjoy your vacation. Roger likes to have his fun. He's probably been at Le Roi, working very hard. He'll be back."

"Does Roger have a lot of girlfriends? I just want to know."

"Roger has never had women problems. Don't worry about

Roger. Take a little sun, make love when you want to make love, go out drinking, see Roger, the main thing is when you get back to New York you'll remember you had a nice vacation."

"Roger tells me he loves me. I don't know whether to believe him or not."

"He does?"

"That's what he said to me."

"Roger has lots of girlfriends."

"He does?"

"Why don't you forget it."

"You've told me what I wanted to know. Thank you," she starts to climb out of the jeep.

"Wait a minute. If you want to stay down here, I can offer you a job."

"A job! In Haiti! What kind of job?"

"What can you do?"

"I can't do anything. I can write, but that's nothing. I used to be a professional dancer."

"You can write for me."

"Write for you? No one in Haiti does any reading."

"I want to start a magazine here. I haven't thought this through clearly yet. But I have a conscience, I see what goes on, and I have to do something."

"You could give me the information and I could write it up under a fake name. No one could know you're the source."

"I don't know. It's very dangerous here. I want to do something, but I don't know what I can do. The main thing that's needed in this country are Creole schools. All the people except for the government elite speak Creole, but the government won't recognize the language, they say it isn't a real language. They make all the schools use French and all the newspapers use French, so most of the people never learn to read. My people speak Creole; they're African, not American or European."

"If you could get me a job, Gerard, I'd stay here. I'm only going back cause I need money."

"We'll talk about this some more."

Kathy and Fritz sit huddled, hidden by the shadows, at Pension L'Ouverture.

"There are lots of evil people in this world."

"No there aren't. There aren't evil people. People do what they have to cause they're stuck, and poor and miserable and they've been hurt so much. The main thing is you have to realize why people act the way they do."

"There are evil people. They made you cry this afternoon and I couldn't do anything about it." He starts to cry.

"I was crying. That little red-head wouldn't leave me alone. Why does he hate me so much? That wasn't so bad, what really hurt me was that all of you didn't stick up for me and you're my friends. Don't you know what friends are for? How the hell could you believe I'm a prostitute? That little boy kept saying things and you just agreed with him."

"I kept out of it cause I couldn't do nothin' against all those big boys. I walked away. You saw me." They sit in the shadows of the steps, the corners, huge white blossoms in the air hanging over the front porch their odor everywhere mosquitoes slight breezes, the white girl covering him cause if the pension owners and servants see the beggar boy, they'll kick him out. He starts to cry again.

"I don't know what to do. Knowing why people hurt me doesn't help."

"Those little boys wanted to hurt you. They wanted to hurt you. I'm going to beat them and kill them."

"No you don't. That wouldn't do anything. Fritz, Fritz, don't cry. There's nothing to cry about. I love you." She puts her arms around him.

"You don't understand what happened. You're in a lot of trouble."

"What do you mean?"

"I don't mean nothing. There's nothing I can do."

"Fritz. You've got to tell me what kind of trouble."

His fist digs into his eye and wipes away the tears. He lights a cigarette. Raoul the head-servant walks by and she tells him it's OK Fritz is here. "That little boy, Tommy, says you're a prostitute."

"I'll tell you what happened between me and Tommy. One night one of the first nights I was here I heard a knocking at my window. I was asleep I didn't know what was happening I thought it was Roger cause that's where Roger knocks so I said, 'Who's there?' 'It's Alfred.' It sounded like Alfred: I don't know I was asleep. I don't know any Alfred. I said, 'I don't know you. Go away.' The doorknob started turning. The doorknob to the back door that's always locked. It wouldn't stop turning. I get really scared. I freaked. I thought someone was going to rape me. In New York City women get raped all the time and they don't like being raped. I ran to the front door, threw the door open, and there was that little kid. Tommy."

"Tommy told me about that. He said he knocked on your door cause he wanted to be with you and you slammed the door in his face. You hurt his feelings badly."

"I didn't know who he was. It was the middle of the night."

"You know what that little red-head told Mrs. Betty?"

"What?"

"You can't tell this to anyone. I don't want to get into trouble."

"What'd he tell her?"

"Today he told Mrs. Betty that you and Mr. Mystere are doing your something."

"I know that."

"He told Mrs. Betty you're trying to break apart her and Mr. Mystere cause you want Mr. Mystere for yourself cause you want his money. Mrs. Betty said she's going to get Mr. Mystere's father to make Mr. Mystere stop seeing you."

"Roger'll do whatever his father tells him to do. Well, that's that. Jesus Christ, why don't you kids get your nose out of other people's business? This didn't concern you. It didn't matter to you in any way whatsoever. But you had to butt in on something you didn't understand and now you've hurt a lot of people, for no reason at all. Just for no reason at all."

"I tried to stop that little boy, but there was nothing I could do. I told you he was going to cause trouble."

"Well, now he's caused trouble. I hope you're satisfied."

"I didn't know what to do."

"Don't cry, Fritz. Please Fritz, don't cry anymore. Everything's OK. Nobody's been really hurt. Fritz, I love you, please don't cry."

"I didn't know what to do when you started to cry this afternoon. You made me cry."

"Well it's all over now. That little red-head boy is my problem, not yours."

"Those little boys are making you bad. I don't know what to do about it."

"I don't know what to do when people hurt me. The best thing is to forget about it."

"That's no good." Crickets made a lot of noise and an occasional wave splashed against the wall.

TWO DAYS LATER

Roger: "Hello."
  Kathy: "Uh."
  "How are you doing?"
"Uh."
"I've been wanting to see you a lot, but I haven't been able to."
"Why not?"
"We can't talk here. Let's go into that little garden in back of your room."
"I don't want to."
"I want to talk to you."
"OK. What do you want?"
"You know why I haven't been here? My parents forbid me to come here."
"Why'd they do that?"
"I told you there's been a lot of drugs here. The last day I saw you, the Chief of Police told my mother there's going to be a bust here."
"In the pension?"
"The police say there's an American who's staying at the pension who's distributing a lot of drugs."
"But I'm the only American who's been staying here for any length of time, except for those damn missionaries, and I'm not dealing drugs. I don't even use drugs. Not that that matters. Do they think I'm the dealer?"
"The Police Chief told my mother they have a complete list

of everyone who's been dealing and everyone in the town who takes drugs. They know everything. My name's on it."

"What do you think I should do, Roger? Is my name on the list?"

"I don't know."

"You know when those tontons macoute came after me, maybe that's why they were after me. There are drugs coming out of L'Ouverture, but they're not coming from me. Ally directs all the drug traffic. He's getting strung out these days on pills: a few days ago when I said I was going down to Port-au-Prince for a few days, he went down on his hands and knees begging me to bring him back some grass. Imagine being desperate for grass. Then when I mentioned my brother might come to Haiti, he asked me to ask my brother to bring him some reds. My brother should risk getting caught at the border just for Ally. Ally must be out of his mind."

"Ally's gone crazy from too many pills. I've seen it happening for a long time. He goes crazy when he can't get drugs and he wants to kill the women who won't sleep with him. The police know all about him. We shouldn't talk about this so loud."

"When did your mother tell you the bust is going to happen?"

"The policeman didn't tell her. But she made me promise I'd stay away from here cause I'm in a precarious position. If the police could find any member of my family with even a joint on us, they'd be able to arrest all of us and take away all our money. Have you noticed I've been dressing like a businessman instead of a worker lately and eating at the expensive hotels? My parents told me I have to start acting like who I am because of my position."

"Do you think they're after you?"

"The cops wouldn't dare touch any of us. But just in case my parents want me to go down to Port-au-Prince for a few days until the heat cools down."

"Do you think I ought to leave too?"

"Maybe you ought to get out of Cap Haitian for a while. You could go back to your country."

"Why'd you say that?"

"I'm worried about you. You have to be very careful in this country."

"Maybe I should get out of here for a while. I could use a change of air. Once things die down, I'll come back here."

"I'm going to get out of here myself. When this is all over, we can see each other again."

"How are you going to get down to Port-au-Prince? Are you going with your family?"

"I'm going in a car with my sister, my parents, and Betty."

"I thought you weren't going to take Betty with you to Port-au-Prince. At least that's what you said a week ago."

"Betty doesn't want to come with me, but I'm taking her. I don't want her staying alone in the house while I'm gone."

"Oh."

"Have you missed me a lot?"

"I don't know."

"You must be going with a lot of other men and have forgotten me."

"I haven't been fucking anyone else."

"I thought about you all the time. I came to see you the first moment I could."

"You did."

"I kept seeing you making love with Duval. I know he wants you. If you're not going with him, you're going with some other man. I think I must care about you a lot."

"You do? Oh Roger, I've missed you so much. I thought you didn't want to see me again. Two days ago I saw Gerard I asked him what was going on with you cause I didn't understand why you didn't show up for that date you didn't call me nothing. I think I really bugged Gerard."

"What'd Gerard say to you?"

"Oh. Well . . . I asked him about your and Betty's relationship cause I didn't understand what it was."

"I told you. Betty doesn't mean anything to me."

"That's what Gerard said."

"Did he say anything else about me?"

"He didn't really say anything . . . He said you were probably working hard at the factory and too tired to come to town. You'd see me in a day or two. That's all he really said."

"Well here I am."

"I know. I'm glad you're here."

"I'm going to take a walk now."

"What d'you mean: going to take a walk now? You're gonna leave?"

"I'm going to take a walk now. I'll see you later."

"Roger. Wait a second. Don't you . . .?"

They kiss.

"I'll see you later."

"You can't see me later. I won't be here. You go to hell."

"I hate your guts. You think you can do whatever you want to and just walk off . . ."

They kiss for a long time.

"Goodbye."

"Roger, wait a second. Just talk to me for a second."

"What do you want to talk about?"

"I don't want to talk about anything. Goodbye."

"I'll see you later when I finish my walk."

She pulls him to the ground. "Fuck me. Fuck me right now Roger." They make out for awhile.

"Let's go in your room."

"Stick your cock in me as hard as you can and fuck me here. I don't care who sees us. I want you."

"You've gotten me all wet."

"I'm wetter. Please fuck me. Here."

They stand up. "What d'you do that for? My new pants are torn. There's mud all over me. You're crazy."

"I was right in the mud. That was terrific. Why didn't you fuck me?"

"I'm not going to have anything to do with you anymore."

"Are you really angry? It's only mud and water. Roger, I love you."

"You tore my pants. Why'd you jump on me?"

"You were walking away from me and I didn't want you to. I haven't seen you for days and suddenly you show up and then you say you're going to take a walk."

"I told you why I haven't been able to come here. I have to talk to you further. Let's go to your room."

"Are you still angry with me?"

"Pull this chair to here and sit down on it."

"Like this? I don't like it. I like sitting here by your knees. I always liked sitting on floors when I was a kid I used to sit on the floor in front of my mother's bed all the time and watch TV."

"If you're sitting on the floor, I have to sit on the floor."

"Roger."

They make out.

"Do you like this?"

"I'm so hot for you. The minute you touch me, I start to come."

"Let's go to the bed." They go to the bed. "I've got to go now. I have to see another girl."

"You have to see another girl?"

"I made a date with another girl. I'll come back later."

"OK. Get out of here."

"You don't like that, do you?"

"I said: GET OUT OF HERE."

"I'll make love to you once and then I'll leave."

"You're not touching me."

"I thought you said you liked making love with me. I have to hurry cause I have to meet this girl."

"Jesus Christ. You're out of your mind. What're you trying to do? Do you think I'm some ragdoll or something you can throw around?"

"You don't like it when I go out with other women, do you?"

"I don't give a shit."

"I've never seen you this upset. You're very jealous."

"It's not that you go out with other women. Look. The men in New York treat me like I'm something special. They buy me

presents, they take me out for meals, they treat me very gently.
I'm a special kind of woman. I have to be treated well. No man's
ever treated me like you're treating me."

"I'm not acting badly."

"You make a date with me and don't show up for days, when
you show up five minutes later you say you have to take a walk.
Now you tell me you've made a date with another girl while
you're supposed to be seeing me. If you don't give a shit about
me, why are you coming around and seeing me? I didn't call
you up. I didn't tell you to come here."

"You have to act the way I want you to act. I'm much nicer
to you than I am to most women."

"Most of the women you go with are dumb fluffy cunts who
don't know what the hell they're doing. That's why you can treat
them that way. I know a lot about how to treat men I'm good at
sex and I want respect for my knowledge. I'm a woman."

"That's why I go for older women. I like them my mother's
age."

"But I'm special. There's something special about me as far
as sex goes. There's always been. You have to treat me that way
or else get out."

"I've told you I love you more than any other woman."

"Then why do you treat me so badly? Have I hurt you in some
way? If I have, I did it by accident I didn't mean to. I'm very
egotistic."

"I already told you what it is."

"You did?"

"You're going back to New York and I won't see you again.
That's why out in the garden I told you I was going to take a
walk and that's why I made plans to meet another girl."

"But you're going to Port-au-Prince tomorrow. And you're
taking Betty with you; you told me a week ago you weren't going
to be taking her."

"Betty doesn't want to go with me, but I told her she has to
cause of what my mother told me."

"Oh. Look Roger, it doesn't matter about Betty, I can't stick around here waiting for you to come back and never knowing when you'll come back. How long are you going to stay in Port-au-Prince?"

"Only a week."

"That's that. If I stay here more than a week, I'll have to give the airline another hundred dollars and it's ridiculous to blow a hundred dollars just so I can sit around waiting for your return and I'm not even sure you're going to return. You know you have to go back and forth just as your father wants you to. Do you think I should wait for you?"

"No. You're going to go away."

"Well, what the hell can I do? We're going to see each other again."

"I'm a realist. I know that most affairs, no matter how good they are, go away like the wind. Maybe ours will remain, and maybe it'll go away like it never happened."

"If we want to, it'll remain. If we work at it."

"This is our last night together. You know what I'm going to do? I'm going to stay here all night with you until my brother returns to pick me up. We're going to spend the whole night together making love."

"Roger . . . ?"

"What?"

"Roger? Would you do something for me? It's not really anything . . ."

"Tell me what you want."

"Would, would you give me something before you go away. I don't care what it is, just something I can wear. It doesn't have to be expensive or anything. It can be a beer ring. I just want something so I can hold you while I'm away from you."

"I don't have anything. You can have this necklace I'm wearing."

"Oh no. It's much too expensive. I just want something little."

"You know what I want. I want to suck your cunt again. Do you like that?"

"You know I love it. I like it the best. Oh touch me. Not that hard. Yes. Oh, just like that."

"That girl who used to be my mistress: once I sucked her cunt for hours and I came in my pants twice. I never took my pants off."

"I wish you'd suck me for that long. Oh don't move your finger. There. Just like that."

"Take me in your mouth while I suck your cunt."

"No. I'll get confused. I'll just suck you if you want, but I don't like doing both things at once."

Suck.

"That feels good."

Suck.

"Don't stop. Just give me another few minutes."

Suck.

"Please. Don't stop. I'm just about to . . ."

Suck.

"Don't stop. Not now. Oh no . . ."

"I'm going to leave now so I can see that girl."

"Roger, you bastard. You can't leave me like this."

"I told you. I have to meet someone else."

"I can't believe this is happening. You lousy stinkin' bastard. You stink like nobody's ever stinked in their whole life. You're a bunch of crap you don't have anything in your head your asshole's full of shit. You lousy little prick."

"I never made a date with no girl. I just wanted to see how you acted."

"You mean this has all been a lie? I hate you. Get the fuck out of here."

"You really want me to get out of here?"

"Get out of here."

"Are you sure you want me to leave?"

"Jesus Christ that feels good. Oh. Ooh oh. Oooh."

"Ah."

"Oh yes. Not like that. Faster. Please do it hard. Make me come. Ah. Ahh. Ahh."

"Ah."

"Ooh. Ooh. Ah. Ah. I can't do it."

"What's going on?"

"I'm too tight. I'm scared of you. I get this way when I've been hurt too much."

"You're trembling."

"Hold me."

They kiss lightly.

"Hold me like you care about me. I freak out sometimes and I have to be treated gently."

"Kathy, are you OK?"

"Just hold me a few more minutes. I'm OK now."

"Do you want me to leave you for a few minutes?"

"No. I'm OK now. We can start fucking again."

"I act the way I do cause you're going away and I don't want you to. I love you more than I've ever loved any other woman."

"Roger, please fuck me. Fuck me as hard as you can. Just fuck me. Ah. Ah. Ah."

"Ooh."

"Harder."

"Ah."

"Ah. Ah. Ah. Ah."

"Ah."

"Ah. Ah."

"I'm going to come now."

"You came, didn't you?"

"Didn't you?"

"Touch me a little with your fingers. Ow. That's too hard. I'm really upset. I can't come. I don't know what to do."

"Do my fingers feel good?"

"That feels good. That feels terrific. Don't go any harder . . . Oh . . . Oh . . . I love this. Roger Roger. Please Roger. Roger please please say Roger oh Roger. Ooh ooh ahaah ooh ooooh. Oooh. Oh. Thank you."

"Look at me."

"Mm. You're always hard."

"I love fucking you. When you go away, every day I'm going to remember how you smile when I fuck you."

"That's cause I love this so much. I'm going to come again. Oh."

"When you come, your eyes roll to the top of your head and you scream."

"I do?"

"Don't you hear yourself?"

"Another boyfriend used to tell me I screamed. Every time I was about to come, he'd put his hand over my mouth. Ooh. I'm going to come again. Come with me this time. I feel good now."

"You know why I couldn't see you these last few days?"

"I don't care."

"I was scared of getting busted."

"You told me."

"You don't understand. I'm bad."

"I like bad men. I'm not a nice person."

"I'll tell you something, but you have to promise you won't tell anyone." "I promise. What're you going to tell me?"

"I deal drugs."

"So that's why you were so worried when your mother told you L'Ouverture might be busted. You better get down to Port-au-Prince and stay there for a while. I hear in this country if you're busted for even a joint, it's a really bad scene."

"That's why I have to take Betty with me."

"Dealing a little grass isn't such a big thing. It's just that everyone in this country's crazy."

"I grow all the grass that gets sold in Cap Haitian out in the factory. No one can see me there. I also deal pills."

"I see. You'd better be really careful."

"You could be a government spy and I could be throwing my family's lives away by telling you this."

"Jesus Christ Roger do you really think I'm a government spy? You've been fucking me for weeks now."

"I don't know anything."

"Get the fuck out of here. I'm getting sick of all this suspicion and accusations. It isn't worth it. How the hell can I be a government spy when I sit around with the beggar boys and have the opinions I have? I told you to get out of here."

"Anyone can be a spy. There's no way to tell who the spies are."

"Well, I'm not a spy. If you think I am, that's your problem."

"If I thought you were a spy, I wouldn't be telling you all this."

"That's true. How come you've never been caught dealing?"

"I was caught twice in the United States. I told you about the time I went to school in Florida, with the blonde schoolteacher, I got thrown out of school for dealing."

"Oh yeah, I remember. You were in high school."

"I also got thrown out of another school in Arizona for carrying coke. I tell you, I'm a tough guy."

"I don't know if dealing drugs makes you tough. Aren't you scared of getting busted here?"

"My mother's good friends with one of the cops. He tells her when a bust's coming and then I go down to Port-au-Prince for a while. Also I'm very careful. Nobody here knows exactly what I do."

"You're telling me about it."

"You're the only person I tell and you're going back to America soon. You see I'm very very careful. Remember I told you the first time I met you it's dangerous to talk about drugs?"

"If you get caught, you're going to be in a lot of trouble."

"I'm never going to get caught."

"They all say that."

"No they don't. I'm the one who can do it."

"What else do you do besides deal drugs?"

"If I really tell you about me, you'll never speak to me again. You'd hate me."

"Don't you ever talk to people? That's a stupid question. Haven't you ever been friends with a woman so you could tell her what you're really like?"

"Nobody knows what I really do and who I am. You should stay away from me cause I'm bad."

"Well, I'm not going to stay away from you. I don't care how bad you are."

"Why not?"

"When people act bastardly toward me, it just doesn't bother me. The only two things that bother me are when people lie to me and when I get bored. I can't stand being bored. As soon as I get bored, I split."

"You won't leave me if you know all the things I do?"

"It'd probably make me love you more. I always go for the ones who burn me."

"You asked Gerard before if I go with other women and he told you yes?"

"I only asked him because I was confused about your relationship with Betty. I don't want to pry into your personal life."

"What Gerard told you is true. I go with many other women. I've always had lots of women. Does that bother you?"

"Why should it?"

"Before I married Betty, I used to go with five, six women at a time. Often Ally, Duval and I would trade off our women. I'd go with a woman, then when I was finished, Ally would take her, and he'd hand her over to Duval, or else all three of us would go out together and we'd share the girls we were with that night. Of course these girls weren't worth anything."

"Do you think I'm like those girls?"

"If I thought you were like those girls, I would have slept with you once and then let Ally have you. I only sleep with women once cause after once they start wanting things. Remember how upset I got when you told me that something happened between you and Duval?"

"Nothing happened between me and Duval. You misunderstood what"

"I got upset because you're going with me and Duval should have kept his hands off you. He knows that too because he won't speak to me anymore."

"Didn't all the girls you, Ally and Duval fucked mind you were doing that?"

"Most Haitian girls, all they want to do is make love. They're whores. They especially want to make love with Ally, Duval and me cause they know we have money and they think we'll give them things. When I was ten years old, we used to go down to the beach and lie in a circle. One girl would stand in the middle of the circle and take off her clothes. You know, she'd do a striptease. Then she'd go around the circle and give it to every guy who wanted her. We'd all lie in a circle and watch each other doing it while we did it. The other girls, the ones who come from wealthy families, no one sees. Their parents keep them under lock and key until they're fifteen or sixteen, and then they can only go out, under chaperone, with the boys their parents chose for them. They're being groomed for wealthy husbands because marriage can mean a lot of money to these people and their parents want to keep the money in the family."

"Historically that's how marriage has always been."

"I could never date one of those girls. You know the two girls who hang around here? They're Henry's nieces. You never see any men around them."

"They're really beautiful too. I wonder what'll happen to them?"

"One of them's studying to be a doctor. They'll get married to rich men."

"Have you ever loved a woman?"

"I don't give women presents. I had a mistress once before I married Betty. I gave her lots of money because she had to do everything I told her to."

"What sort of things did you make her do? Sexually."

"I gave her all sorts of money and then later, after we had broken up, I found out she had been seeing other men while she was seeing me."

"You didn't know at the time she was fucking other men?"

"She told me I was the only one she was with. Then she took all my money. The worst thing was: I found out after we broke up she was pregnant and going to have an abortion."

"So what?"

"It was my kid and she was going to have an abortion without asking me. She really hurt me."

"I hope you never get burned worse."

"I've been hurt by lots of women when I was younger. But now, no more. I don't let women get to me anymore; I'm very careful. All the women around here want to fuck me, oh brother, cause of who I am, so I fuck them once or twice and that's it. I make it clear each time I'm with a woman. I'm not going to do anything for her."

"There's nothing wrong with that. It's the lies that really hurt people."

"You're right. I don't act like Duval or Ally. This movie star came down here last year and Ally took her out."

"A movie star? Was she old or something?"

"No. She was young and pretty, if you like that sort of woman. I only like older women. She really went for Ally. Oh brother. He made her buy the drinks and pay for all the food. He brought me along whenever they went out. He told her I didn't have any money. One night he made her rent two cars so he could have one and I could have one."

"But Ally has a car."

"He wanted to ride around in a limousine. And he made her pay for all the champagne. I got really sick and puked."

"And she did all this?"

"He wanted her to buy him a car and she walked out on him. I think she was really upset."

"I guess she was."

"I told you not to get mixed up with Ally cause he's crazy. He just wants to hurt the women he's with. I don't do that. Since I've been with Betty, I go mainly with the women I find in the hotels and bars. All these women buy presents for me, oh brother you wouldn't believe the expensive things they give me bracelets and"

"I believe it."

"They want to do all these things for me and they want me to write them when they leave. I never send them letters. Once or twice I'll make a call. You know what I was really doing when I'd pick you up here, and we'd go from hotel to hotel?"

"I thought we were getting drunk and fucking."

"I was checking out the other hotels and bars to see if any new women had come into town. That's what Ally, Gerard, and I do here almost every night."

"I saw you looking around, but I never saw you pick up any women. You must be really clever."

"Remember when I met you that first night in L'Ouverture? I was checking out the hotel to see if there were any new women around."

"You didn't seem to be checking me out, I could tell Ally was cruising me cause he asked me if I wanted a present, but you were a cold fish. You wouldn't even say hello to me when Gerard introduced us. I thought you were a creep. That's why I was attracted to you: every other guy I had met was drooling after me and you wouldn't notice me."

"That's the way I am: I never go after the woman, I let her come to me. I didn't like you when I first met you. You know when I first started noticing you? When we were at The Imperial and Gerard was telling us that story"

"About your getting married. Gerard kept talking and talking and I kept looking at you. I wanted you before: when we were in the truck and you told me not to look at you. Remember?"

"I wanted you then too."

"The first thing I noticed was your Donald Duck T-shirt. I liked you cause I thought you were a hippy. I never would have gone with you if I had known you were a businessman."

"You don't act like you dislike me."

"Did you have a lot of girlfriends after you married Betty?"

"I don't have girlfriends. The women I sleep with don't mean anything to me. I'll tell you what I'm really like. I go with five, six girls at a time."

"How the hell do you do that? You are married and, since I've been here, you've been spending at least every other night with me."

"Every day I'm with four or five different women. I spend my lunch break with one woman: maybe I take her to the beach. Then I bring her home in the afternoon. I make a dinner date with another woman and I take her around to the hotels so I can check out what other women are around. Meanwhile I've made a date to meet another woman around ten o'clock in a bar. I go to the bar and spend an hour there. Like tonight I had made a date to meet a girlfriend of mine at Le Poisson."

"Then you were speaking the truth earlier: you really were going to meet some girl at a bar. I thought you were saying it just to make me upset."

"I have dates with women all the time. Sometimes I bring one girl with me to meet another."

"Don't your girlfriends get upset?"

"I've had girls walk out on me. One girl three nights ago slapped my face and said she wanted to murder me."

"Did anything happen?"

"There's nothing she can do to me. I like to see women upset. Sometimes I like to really fuck over women and see them cry a lot. I pull every trick I can think of."

"You don't like women, do you?"

"I love to make love to women. If I could, I would make love to women every minute of the day. When I can't fuck anymore, I suck pussy and that makes me hard again. I can suck pussy for hours and I still want more. I love to make love to women in bars and places I've never done it before. Where have you never done it?"

"Huh. I can't think where. I've never fucked in a sewer. Or a police station."

"Women love to be loved in public places. I can do it to any woman in a bar. Often I can do it to two or three women together: they don't mind."

"So how do you fuck women over?"

"I go into a bar with one woman and make her wait while I make love to another woman. Then while the first woman's sucking me off, I tell her what just happened. Remember that night we walked into the Poisson and that girl in the brown dress kissed me. She was waiting for me."

"But you didn't fuck her in the bar, you fucked me."

"I wanted her to wait for me, and then when I finally showed up, nothing would happen. I saw her the next night and she wouldn't talk to me. One of these days I'm never going to fuck women again. I'm going to be all alone."

"Why do you keep on fucking women? You obviously hate them."

"Women are whores. That's my opinion. I'm a male whore."

"Someone must have frightened you badly."

"I know how the world is. We're all animals. Anyone who thinks otherwise is fooling himself."

"Roger, fuck me again."

"You like it when I fuck you?"

"Fuck me as hard as you can. Make me forget everything that's ever happened."

"You like me when I fuck you?"

"How come you married Betty? You're a sex maniac and she's so innocent it's unbelievable."

"I tell you something. I married Betty cause she's a donkey. She has no friends and she has no one she can run to for help. I wanted someone who was nothing. Who was like an animal to me. I don't want her anymore anyways. I've told her to leave me, she could find men who are much richer, more handsome, and smarter than me, but she says she won't leave me. Yesterday she told me if she ever has to separate from me, she's going to enter a nunnery."

"That's what you get for marrying a donkey."

"I've hired lawyers who've offered to give her money to leave me, but she won't go."

"Papa says the only time a man hires inexperienced help is when he gets married."

"I'm going to get rid of Betty this year."

"How are you going to get rid of her? You've been trying to for the last year and you still haven't succeeded."

"I'm going to get rid of her this year and live alone."

"Why do you hate women so much? You know you hate women?"

"It's the women here: they all lie and do everything behind your back. They're real sweet, you know what I mean? Women act like they want to give you everything and then when you think you have them, they disappear."

"That's the only way they can act. They don't have any power."

"I see women lie to me all the time and I act the same way. I've never let a woman get too close to me."

"I'm the same way."

"I went with this one French woman last year a couple of times, but it didn't mean anything to me. She approached me and made me come back to her room with her. Then when she was sick of me, she went on to Ally."

"I've heard that most of the women tourists who come alone are looking to get laid as much as possible."

"The women always leave me. They say all these sweet things they tell me they love me like they've never loved any man, then they go back to their country and I never see them again."

"Well, you're a bastard too."

"You know why? When I was staying in the United States, not only in New York City but in Arizona, all the people who lived around me wanted to beat me up cause they said I'm a black person. They didn't care whether I had money or not. I was really innocent then. In Arizona this one guy who was a cop taught me how to defend myself. I hung out with cops cause they knew how things were. They taught me the things I needed to know. I like cops; I own two guns already. They know how to treat women. I saw this one cop give it to a woman, he almost took her scalp off. Oh brother."

"Why don't you try being friends with women?"

"I make love with lots of women."

"If you tried talking with women, you might find out they're as mean and vicious as men."

"I never talk to any women. If I let some woman find out what I'm like, she won't go with me again."

"I'm still with you. I'm talking to you right now. I'm as bastardly to men as you are to women only I'm more indirect about it. I've lived with three men and walked out on every one of them."

"That's cause you like sex as much as I do. The next time I marry, I'm going to marry an older woman like you and not a dumbbell like Betty."

"Someone like me wouldn't marry you. You can talk to me: that's the point; you can say whatever you want to me. I don't give a shit. I just don't like when people lie to me."

"I'm always honest to women. I tell them what I'm like and if they don't like it, they can go away."

"As long as you're honest, you can do anything you want with me. You can fuck around, fuck me over, I don't give a shit. I just have to know what's going on."

"As much as I've ever loved any woman, I love you."

"You know what I'm going to do? I'm gonna write you everything that happens to me: all the details. Who I fuck, how I manage to get money, all the weirdest things I do. That way you'll find out what a woman's really like and you'll know I'm being honest with you."

"Do you promise you'll write me? Maybe you won't so I'll wait until you write me and then I'll call you. You know what? You call me when you get back to New York and charge it to me. I'm going to write down my phone number and address on this paper."

"I'd be embarrassed to call you collect."

"You're going to call me as soon as you get back to New York. You're my girlfriend A-number-1."

The gray car honks. "Honk. Honk."

"That's my brother's car. I have to go."

"No. I don't want you to go."

"My brother's waiting for me."

"Just give me a minute. Just wait a few minutes."

"I want to fuck you again quickly. In your asshole."

"Oh please, in my asshole. I've got to have you again."

"Does that hurt?"

"It feels wonderful. You've got to come with me, fast."

"I've got to go now."

"Honk. Honk."

"Roger . . . I . . ."

"We say 'Goodbye' like this. We have to smile."

"Goodbye."

A TRIP TO THE VOODOO DOCTOR

A FTER a week and a half of anxiously waiting, Kathy decides to go to Port-au-Prince to look for Roger. As soon as she reaches Port-au-Prince, she forgets about Roger. Completely dazed, with a huge smile, she wanders around the hot docks that are the pits of Haiti's main city.

The congested streets, rotting pastel-colored wood walls piled on top of each other, legless and armless beggars on wheels, male and female one-basket merchants, rows of food and leather and plastic shoes and notebooks and hair curlers, one or two scared white tourists, starved children looking for the rich white tourists, nonexistent sidewalks and cars, lots and lots of cars, Chevrolets and Pontiacs and Plymouths and Fords and VW's and jeeps and a few American sportscars and the trap-traps, cars of every color and year, cars that don't run and hopped-up cars, all going at the same speed: slowly, and lots and lots of garbage, and rooms without doors in the rotting pastel-colored wood walls, and rooms without walls, everything and everyone piled up on and squashed next to each other, a big pounding scaly pregnant fish: all give way to wide empty streets. Wide empty sidewalks. Low block-big rectangular buildings. Everything here is white. It's hotter than where the people and all the buildings are crushed together. There seem to be very few people here because sidewalks and the streets are so huge. The air seems to be the same color as the buildings and the streets.

Moving from the congested market-slum-city, through this whiteness, to the ocean, each block gets longer and wider. The third and final block is the longest and widest. It's huge. It's surrounded by emptiness. The few people walking up and down look like black marbles lost in the sand. A white person wouldn't be seen at all. Moving from the congested market-slum-city, through this whiteness, to the ocean, no one can breathe. The ocean is a green plate. There's no sound because the streets and buildings are big and empty and almost invisible. As if they're shadows.

What are they shadows of? One narrow wood pier extends into the water. The water makes no sound against the wood. A two-sail boat lies a quarter of a mile off of this pier.

It's this hot and white because dust and pollution sweep down from the mountains and the upper city into this pit. Then the air and pollution move from this pit across the ocean and leave a vacuum.

One wide black street lies parallel to the ocean front. Three huge empty squares, amputated fingers, lie off of this street. The cement squares don't contain anything.

A group of males are standing on the corner of the sidewalk of the middle square. They're talking to each other. Two cops in cop uniforms're yelling at a smaller group of men, a few whites in this group, who're trying to get past the closed wire gates and on to the far end of the pier. Kathy walks out of the middle of the smaller groups of men and off of the pier. She's leaning against a pole and watching what's going on. The world's hot.

"Hey, Kathy."

She looks around, but doesn't see anyone she knows. She doesn't know anyone in Port-au-Prince.

"Hey, Kathy."

She looks over the street at the large group of men on the sidewalk and sees an arm waving. She crosses the black street and walks over to the waving arm. "Don't you remember me, Kathy? I'm Sammy's brother. Don't you remember Sammy?"

"Jesus Christ. How are you? I've been away: I just got back to Port-au-Prince yesterday. How's Sammy?" She feels embarrassed.

"Sammy wants to see you."

"I don't know. Uh, I'm kind of busy right now. Actually I'm looking for Rue DeForestre. I've got to make an airplane reservation so I can get back to the Cap as soon as possible. Can you tell me where the Rue DeForestre is?"

"When should I tell Sammy to meet you?"

"I don't know. Sometime later today. I have to get to the Rue DeForestre and I got totally lost . . ."

"It's just a few blocks from here."

"Where?"

"You can't walk there by yourself. I'll get someone to help you."

"I don't need any help. I just want to know where it is."

"Patrick, this is Kathy. Kathy, Patrick." A short-haired good-looking twenty year old.

"How can I get to the Rue DeForestre?" she asks Patrick.

"I'll show you. It's not far from here."

"Just tell me how to get there."

"You can't walk there by yourself. It's too far."

"I like to walk."

"White women don't walk around this city by themselves. The men won't leave you alone and you'll get lost."

"I can take care of myself. I just want to know how to get there."

"Do you not want to talk with me because you think I'll do something bad to you?"

"Don't be ridiculous. I just don't see any reason you should go out of your way so I can get to where I'm going. I like you."

"I have nothing to do. I'll walk with you."

"I can't pay you or anything."

"Why do you mention money? I want to be your friend. Do you think I want your money?"

"I'm sorry." She tries to explain. "I get so used to people asking me for money. I . . ."

"You don't want to be friends with me?"

"I don't even know you. I think I want to be friends with you."

"What hotel're you staying at?" the brother asks her.

"The Plaza."

"Sammy'll pick you up there at five o'clock this afternoon. Don't forget."

"OK." She turns again to her new friend. "I have to go to ABC Tours. It's on the Rue DeForestre."

"I know where it is."

They start walking upward, through the city. "Is it far?"

"Why do you ask so many questions?"

"I just want to know where I'm going."

"Why do you want to get to ABC Tours so badly?"

"I want to get back to Cap Haitian as soon as possible." She tells him how much she loves Cap Haitian, all about Roger and the beggar boys. "Are we almost there?"

"What're you in such a hurry for? Americans're always in a hurry. I lived in America for a while, that's why I speak English so well, I didn't like it except when I lived in Atlanta, Georgia. The life in Atlanta, Georgia is like the life here. Nobody hurries there, no one works, and there's lots of dope. Do you smoke dope?"

"Yeah."

"Do you want some now? I have some really good smoke. I can stop by my house and get it."

"Not right now. Maybe later."

"Don't you trust me?"

"I trust you. I mean, you're a strange guy and I don't know you very well."

"I don't want to hurt you. Do you think I want you to be my girlfriend?"

"Well . . ."

"Look. Put your hand in mine." She stares at his outstretched hand. "Go on. Take my hand." She's holding his hand. "See. I don't want anything more. Do you know why you can trust me?"

"Why?" Her big brown eyes look up at him.

"You look and act exactly like my older sister. How old are you?"

"Twenty-nine."

"No you're not. She's twenty-three."

"I AM twenty-nine."

"You can't be more than twenty. That's how old you are. Call me your brother."

"OK, brother."

"Take my hand again." He takes her into the green rickety wood room that's the travel bureau and out of it. "Why do you want to take the plane to the Cap?"

"How else could I get there?" They continue walking up and down the sometimes nonexistent sidewalks past the fake store-fronts.

"Why don't you rent a motorcycle?"

"Gee, that's an idea. When I was a kid, I used to spend days hitchhiking on motorcycles. I've always had this thing about motorcycles and black leather. But if I drive a cycle up to the Cap, I won't have any way of getting it back. Maybe I can return it there? I could learn to ride a cycle in a day."

"I'll ride with you. Then I'll drive the bike back to Port-au-Prince."

"How much money would you want for that?"

"I don't want your money. I told you this already. I do it because you're my sister."

"No. I don't think I want to do it. How much would it cost me to rent a cycle?"

"Nine dollars a day."

"That's not much."

"Plus you give them a deposit. You get the deposit back."

"How can I get the deposit if I'm going to Cap Haitian and not coming back?"

"I can get it for you."

"No . . ."

"You still don't like me. You think I'm going to take all your money."

"I don't have enough money for you to take."

"If you rented a motorcycle, you could be in Cap Haitian tonight. You don't want to waste all your money on a plane. Why don't you take a look at the motorcycle store? It's just around the corner."

"Wait a second. If it costs me nine dollars a day I won't be able to get the cycle back till tomorrow, it'll cost me at least eighteen." She's adding everything up in her head. "Plus the deposit. That's more than a plane ticket."

"So you're not going to do it?"

"I have my plane ticket. I'm going to go back to the hotel now."

"Why don't you rent a bike just for the day? You can take the plane tomorrow or the next day. We'll go to the Barbancourt rum factory."

"I don't have nine dollars to blow on a cycle. I want to go home."

Patrick informs her there are other cheaper ways to go to Cap Haitian—the vomit bus and the government airplane, so she asks him about the government airplane. They decide he'll take her to the government airport so she can reserve a ticket.

They've been walking up and down the sidewalks for hours. Sometimes there's a huge bottomless hole in a sidewalk. Sometimes a sidewalk disappears. Sometimes the sidewalks and streets are clean the wood store walls are solid. As they descend through the city, the sidewalks getting narrower until they almost disappear, the streets disappearing, the stores are on top of each other. They're in the marketplace. The sidewalks lie under shoes, carved fake mahogany cause there's no real mahogany left in Haiti cause the woods that used to cover the island have been decimated, straw baskets full of plastic barrettes, Ivory soap, and underpants, mangoes, baskets full of all kinds of burnt sugar confections, dried fish. The long cigar-black street lies under brightly-colored private cars, private taxis, city-run taxis, tap-taps, bicycles, young boys with no legs, young boys with shriveled legs, and old big-belly women. One huge block contains one no-door building. Inside this building, space is immense. There are no walls except for the outer walls of the building and those walls are almost invisible due to the lack of light. Tables cover all of the sawdust floor, tables far as the eye can see, wood tables covered with baskets full of short and long rices, millet, wheat kernels, ground grains, dried corn and white and yellow corn flours, dried fishes, fish freshly caught from the ocean still unscaled and ungutted, different varieties of mangoes, canaps, figs, bananas, breadfruit, sour oranges, lemons, limes, onions and garlics, tomatoes, co-conuts, cashews, roasted cashews, sugar, brown sugar, almonds, peanuts, raisins, Camembert cheese, more. Scales hang over some of the tables. Narrow pathways in the darkness separate the tables. Women and men and children all dressed in brightly-colored cloth, almost hidden by the darkness, stand by the tables or shuffle by each other. Almost under the table, in the half-light, here and there, an old woman squats and separates kernels of corn in a huge straw basket and scales a fish with a big heavy steel knife in her hand. Outside the people are walking on top of each other, over each other; the sky's so bright its yellow is blue even though it isn't.

Kathy and Patrick stumble into a tap-tap. A tap-tap is a small public bus that's colored with green red pink yellow brown blue and black paint. The tap-tap's white. Virgin Mary's La Sirene's Jesus Christ's Duvalier's private girlfriends' names adorn every inch of the bus' walls. GRACE DE MARIE. PAIX POUR TOUJOURS. LE SAUVIER EST ICI. The tap-tap lets Patrick and Kathy off at the government airbase.

The government airbase is a huge almost empty field that's brown gray and, a little, olive green. A brown man stands in a gray metal booth in front of this field and controls who goes in and out of the field. There are a few other men inside the field. There are a few two-engine gray airplanes. There are a few huts on the ground. The airfield seems empty cause it's so big and cause it looks like death.

She walks out of the airfield and they climb back into a tap-tap. She thanks him and tells him she's going to go home now that she's done what she had to. He doesn't want her to go away from him. He tells her he wants to go to the beach. She doesn't want to go to the beach. He wants to rent a motorcycle and ride around Petionville. She doesn't want to rent a motorcycle. He wants to go dancing in Carrefour. She doesn't want to dance.

"I know this doctor I'd like you to meet."

"Do you mean a voodoo doctor?"

"He's a very important man. I want you to meet him because you mean a lot to me."

"I'd love to meet him."

"You have to realize this could be the most important thing that's ever happened to you. I want you to realize this. This man can change your life."

"I want to meet him."

"He's going to do a lot for you. I know he is. This man has helped a lot of people. He's a very good man."

"I don't want him to do anything for me. I just want to meet him."

"There's just one thing. You have to be willing to realize who he is."

"Do I have to pay him anything?"

"You'll have to buy him candles so he can do his work. That won't cost you much."

All the tap-taps in the city meet in the marketplace. They're back where they started from. Limbless beggars crouch under them. Skateboards attached to half-bodied people roll by.

They go off to see the voodoo doctor. The city cab soon leaves the straight black tar streets. It winds basically upward and to the left, sometimes round in circles, sometimes in huge snake-arcs, sometimes it goes opposite to where it wants to go, there's no time in Haiti. It goes everywhere. Through driveways and around falling-apart single building single-room stores. On gray broken cement roads that go under while the old mansions alongside the road go up so it seems to go under mansions. Ahead up a narrow street hedged in by two-story wood houses into a narrow gray wood garage then straight back down the street in reverse.

The neighborhood changes completely. The taxicab turns left on a corner, and stops.

A narrower pebbly unrideable road juts off of the dirt road the taxi's been riding on. The new road is covered with dust. Thick yellow dust. This dust hides women carrying huge parcels on their heads, walking in the ruts, and two-story stucco houses, painted all colors, yellow and black. They walk into the dust. The sun seems to get hotter and hotter. There's lots of noise and hot dust and heat. On one side the dust sharply descends through the air into a ditch crossed over by a modern trestle. They keep on trudging upward.

The pebbly road turns sharply to the right. About ten yards below this turn, there's a dark red stucco house. The red house has a porch.

The sun is very very hot. Kathy feels tired and excited. Kathy should wait on the porch while Patrick sees if the doctor's available.

Kathy's waiting. A huge man appears. Would Kathy like to go inside?

Kathy does what anyone tells her. She follows the man around the porch and the house past a tiny woman washing and hanging laundry to a tiny room in the back of the house which is only big enough for the narrow cot and cabinet-desk inside it. Photos and newspapers cover the walls and glass windows of the cabinet.

"Are you the doctor?" Kathy asks the man.

"The doctor?"

"Uh, I'm supposed to meet a doctor. A holy person. I thought that was you."

The huge man sits down on the bed next to Kathy and laughs. "Non. I am Kung-Fu."

Kathy looks at him in total fear.

"There are pictures of me at my kung-fu."

She sees pictures of him dressed up in his uniform. "Oh, you're a black belt."

"Do you know about kung-fu?"

"Not very much."

"I am very good, I like doing that: I don't like violence. I don't go with women because they're tricky. They don't do things honestly. I only go with men."

She relaxes and looks at the girly pictures. "Are those your relatives, that woman over there?"

"That's a picture of my aunt and her two children. They now live in Boston. Do you know Boston?"

"Very well. I used to live there."

"I'd like to go there." There's a huge market for the private yacht owners in smuggling Haitians to anywhere in the US. They talk about their relatives and kung-fu for a long long time. Kathy and the huge gentle man like each other very much.

When Patrick returns for Kathy, she doesn't want to leave.

"You said you wanted to see the doctor."

She tells the kung-fu man she'll return as soon as she's finished with the voodoo doctor.

Patrick and Kathy're walking upward in the thick dust. When they reach a black Pontiac parked by the corner, he tells her to wait there until someone comes for her.

How will she know who that someone is? She'll know.

Fifteen minutes pass by. She sees a girl in a bright bright green skirt walking toward her. She sees, in the distance, Patrick's hand waving at her. The girl smiles at her so she follows her.

The girl walks part ways up the same road, then turns to her left. There are no more roads. The girl walks into a mass of dust, on a mass of dust, down ten feet of only slightly horizontal rocks, into a section that's unlike anything Kathy's seen in Port-au-Prince.

There's a mass of dust-ground and approximately ten feet by

eight feet and six feet high thatched huts. People are everywhere. Small black goats and roosters and black-and-white hens and lots and lots of children. Everyone squawking and cackling crying gossiping. Hotter than ever. Women sitting in the dust and women sitting by round straw baskets full of one kind of food and one woman sitting under an improvised cloth canopy by a table holding a tray of some homemade confection and women walking around and women washing clothes in some bowls of water and women holding babies maybe suckling them. The girl walks past these people without stopping, she walks around a hut, down, turns a sharp corner around another hut, straight onward, past almost a row of huts. Kathy follows her.

The girl stops by the door of one of the brown ten feet by eight feet huts and enters. Actually there's no door, only a red curtain. The roof is corroded metal. A narrow cot lies against the back wall of the hut. A rough table lies against the left wall. Two wood chairs. To the right, a middle-aged man so wrinkled and thin he looks old sits in a chair facing a smaller wood table.

Patrick's sitting on a chair between the old man and the back wall. "You have to buy some candles."

"How much money?"

"Three dollars."

Kathy gives Patrick this money. He gives the money to a woman who's sitting in the hut. There are three women sitting in the hut: two on the bed and one (the girl who led Kathy to the hut) on the floor.

The père lights a white candle. Then he lights a cigarette with the candle flame and gives it to Patrick. He lights another cigarette and gives it to Kathy. He lights another cigarette for himself. Everyone smokes. The père sings a song something about Jesus. He speaks only Creole. Patrick translates for Kathy but Kathy suspects that Patrick isn't saying to her what the père says to him.

The père opens a small Bible and begins to recite a passage rapidly in a monotone.

Then his head sinks and he makes loud hiccups. "He's receiving the spirit." Patrick tells Kathy.

The père shakes Patrick's hand, then Kathy's hand. His grip is unusually strong and sharp.

The père rubs some liquid from a bottle covered with red cloth over his face and hands. He puts a match to the top of this bottle; the bottle lights up; immediately he puts his hand over the bottle top. The bottle sticks to his hand. He passes the hand-and-bottle round his head. When he pulls the bottle off of his hand, there's a loud pop and it looks like the skin of his hand is going to come away with the bottle.

The ceremony's begun.

It's very hot inside the unlighted hut, much hotter than it was outside the hut in the dust under the direct burning sun. Everyone inside the hut's sweating.

Kathy doesn't remember exactly what and when happens from now on because she's so hot and because she's getting dizzier and dizzier. Certain incidents stick out in her mind.

The père takes a drink from the red-cloth-covered bottle. He hands the bottle to Patrick to take a drink. Patrick drinks. He hands the bottle to Kathy to drink. Kathy drinks. It's cheap rum.

The père pours rum into an approximately foot diameter tin bowl. Many objects are in the bowl: a Virgin Mary, some rocks, some sticks, a small skull, some beads, the white candle. He puts a match to the rum, poof! Everything's alight.

The père asks Kathy to write in a small green notebook. She writes down her name. "Anything else?" Kathy asks Patrick. She writes down her age.

The père says he needs something so he can begin his work for Kathy. He writes about fifteen words down on a small piece of white paper. "Give him some money" Patrick tells Kathy. "How much?" "It'll only be about three dollars." "Is this going to cost me any more money?" "This is important. You have to realize that you're doing something that could be the most important thing for you. He wants to work for you and he needs certain things to work with." "I only have a twenty." Kathy gives one of the women the twenty. She goes out of the hut to purchase the somethings.

The père gives Kathy a small dusty bottle with some clear liquid in it. She swallows. He smiles and takes back the bottle. "That'll be better for you," says Patrick. "You'll see what'll happen."

It's incredibly hot in the hut. Sweat runs down everyone's face. Kathy doesn't think she feels anything.

Everything takes incredibly long.

The père's singing again. The women on the bed join in singing. Kathy sings along. How the hell am I able to sing in a language I don't know, Kathy says to herself. The père and the women're happy Kathy's singing with them.

The père lights a cigar with the white candle's flame. He gives it to Patrick. He lights another cigar with the white candle's flame. He gives it to Kathy. He lights another cigar with the white candle's flame for himself. Everyone smokes his cigars.

The père talks to Patrick. Patrick tells Kathy she'll have to give the père some money because he's working for her. She understands. He's a worker. "How much?" "Ten dollar." Kathy gives the père a ten-dollar bill. He carelessly throws the bill on the wood table next to a huge beaten-up skull. "I don't have any more money," Kathy says, "I can't give you any more money." She's worried.

"How much money do you make in the United States?" Patrick asks Kathy. "Seven dollars a day when I work." "Wooo. You know why all the people up there," Patrick points to the invisible hills where all the rich people in Port-au-Prince live, "are rich? The doctor works for them. The doctor is going to work for you. This is very very important. The doctor is going to work for you for six . . . seven hundred a week." Kathy looks into the witch doctor's eyes. "I don't want money," she says. "I want you to understand. More, I want to do good for others."

The père smiles and says, "You have a great force in you. You

must go upwards." His hands motion strongly upwards. "I can
help you to go upwards." Kathy smiles. She feels she and the
père understand each other. She thinks Patrick's becoming a
nuisance. "I would like that." The père shakes each of Kathy's
hands quickly and firmly.

The père begins singing. Everyone starts singing.

The woman returns with about ten small envelopes, a bottle
of cheap perfume, a bottle of rum. She gives fifteen dollars to
Patrick. Patrick gives the fifteen dollars to Kathy.

The père takes the envelopes, perfume, and rum. He opens
the rum, pours it into the dusty bottle, and drinks. He gives the
bottle to Patrick. Patrick drinks. Patrick gives the bottle to Kathy.
Kathy drinks. Everyone drinks a few more rounds. "I work with
rum this first time," the père says.

The père lights up a cigarette with the white candle's flame.
Gives it to Kathy. Lights another cigarette with the white candle's
flame. Gives it to Patrick. Lights a cigarette with the white candle's flame for himself. Everyone smokes.

"Give me twenty cents for more cigarettes," Patrick tells Kathy.
Kathy gives Patrick the money. "Also three dollars for another
bottle of perfume. The father wants to do something special for
you." Kathy thinks the père hasn't said anything to Patrick, but
she gives the money anyways.

The père pours the perfume into an old thin bottle, about five
inches high. Then he opens one of the small envelopes. He
carefully shovels some of the lavender powder from this envelope
into the bottle. Each of the envelopes contains a different color
powder. The envelopes say things such as AMOUR, REINE DE
GRACE. After he's opened and closed all the envelopes, he pours
some of the rum from the dusty bottle, raw white rum, into the
five inch high bottle. Everyone drinks some more rum. He shakes
the five inch high bottle. He puts some brown dried leaves and
branches into the five inch high bottle. He takes the rattle that's
lying on the floor to the left of the wood table, shakes the rattle
over everything. He puffs on his cigarette, blows smoke over

everything, blows smoke into the five inch high bottle, and seals the bottle with an improvised paper cork.

The père rubs his face and hands with some liquid. He pours the same liquid on Kathy's hands and motions for her to rub her face. She does.

The père takes some salve and rubs it on her lips. He motions her to do she doesn't understand what. She kisses her arms and breasts. He smiles.

The woman returns with the cigarettes.

"He's given me a secret for you," Patrick tells Kathy. "What is it?" "I'll tell you later. I have something to tell you later." "Why can't you tell me now?" "He said I should tell you after we leave. He said you have to sit by the sea after we leave here. It's necessary you sit by the sea. I'll tell you then."

The père holds a pack of filthy cards in his hands. He puts three cards down on the table. Jack of Diamonds, dark queen, Ace of clubs. He reshuffles the cards and cuts. He puts some more cards down on the table. He reshuffles the cards and cuts. He asks Kathy to cut the cards. She cuts toward him. He smiles. He puts ten cards down on the table. He quickly puts them back in the deck.

The père speaks to Patrick in a quick monotone. "Recently someone's been speaking to you badly," Patrick translates for Kathy. Pause. "Is this true?" "Uh yeah . . . yeah maybe. I had a fight with a boyfriend in Cap Haitian right before I left. But it's OK now. We made up. That's not really speaking badly." The père speaks again in his rapid monotone. Patrick translates. "You've missed a very good chance in the US." "I dunno," Kathy says. The old man's not really hitting the mark, Kathy thinks to herself. "The father says he's going to work for you for six to seven hundred dollars a week. This is very important. He says you have bonne chance." Kathy talks directly to the père. "Je ne veux pas d'argent assez que je veux travailler pour des autres." The father smiles.

The father starts singing. Everyone sings along. One of the

middle-aged women who's sitting on the bed leads the singing.

Patrick talks to a woman next to him, who suckles a baby.

"He wants to give you something else," Patrick says to Kathy. The père's carefully spooning some powder from each of the small white envelopes on to a crumpled piece of paper. When he finishes with the last envelope, he seals the paper and says something in his quick monotone to Patrick. "When you're alone, you have to rub this all over your body. If you don't do this, nothing he's doing for you will work." The père nods. Kathy nods.

The père takes the red-cloth-covered bottle. He lights its top with the white candle's flame. Poof. Quickly he places the palm of his hand over the top. The bottle sticks to his palm. He passes this hand-and-bottle three times around his head.

The leading woman, a middle-aged woman, starts drawing a vever on the stone floor. Everyone else sings lackadaisically while she sprinkles the white corn flour from a china dish on to the floor. The sign's a long backbone line with curlicues coming out of its sides. One heart in the middle. At the bottom of this vever she draws a funny hideous head. Then she draws a second vever which Kathy's too out of it to see. When the woman's finished using the flour, he nods his approval.

The père places the human skull that's on the wood table on the funny hideous head. He places two rocks near the skull. He shakes the rattle all over the skull. He's not satisfied. He takes the light blue nailpolish bottle that's on the wood table and pours some small gray beads from the nailpolish bottle on to the center of the first vever. He holds the lighted white candle next to these beads. The beads light up, explode. He places the human skull on top of the exploded beads. He puts two rocks near the skull. He's very careful to put everything in exactly the right place. He sticks the lighted white candle into a depression in the center of the skull. He sprinkles rum around the lighted white candle without extinguishing the light. He takes a small red-plastic-frame mirror and passes the mirror three times around the center of

Kathy's body. He sticks the mirror in front of her face so she has to look at herself. Kathy's almost unconscious. He passes the mirror around her head three times. He places the mirror on the vever near the skull but not touching the skull. He places the five inch high corked bottle next to, leaning against the side of the skull. He picks a string of many-colored beads up from the junk of the floor to his left and throws the beads around the lighted white candle. He says something to Patrick. Patrick says, "She can't give you fifty dollars." The père and Patrick argue about how much money Kathy must give. Patrick says to Kathy, "Wait a second. Listen closely to me. You have to give something more. Otherwise all that he's doing won't work for you. What he's doing is very important. This is very important. You must realize that what he's doing could be the most important thing in your life." "How much?" Kathy asks Patrick. This is an art piece, Kathy thinks to herself. "Ten dollar. And when you get back to the United States, you buy him a watch. Not a good watch, you understand." Kathy gives a ten-dollar bill to the père. She has no more money left. He throws the ten-dollar bill on the skull. It falls in back of the skull. He pours rum around the lighted white candle without extinguishing its flame. He shakes the rattle over the skull and the vever.

The père draws a cross on Kathy's forehead.

The père motions Kathy to get up. He turns her around three times. He pushes her around the vevers three times clockwise. He pushes her around the vevers three times counterclockwise. He picks up the small plastic red-frame mirror and passes the mirror around her body. He shows Kathy to herself. He pushes her around the vevers three times clockwise. He pushes her around the vevers three times counterclockwise.

Kathy's facing the red curtain. The père tells Kathy she has to return here. She can bring a friend with her. He gives her the filled five inch high bottle and a green plastic soap case containing the powders. He tells her she can't look back.

Chickens and goats run around. The ground's so dry, it's almost sand. This sand flies everywhere. Children squall and yell. Women sit on the sand-covered almost nonexistent doorsteps of huts and low wood chairs outside the huts. Women talk to each other. Women with baskets on their heads walk in the fine dust. Women carry huge amounts of wet clothes in their arms. There are a few men.

"Goodbye," says the girl in the bright green skirt.

Kathy turns around and walks outside into the sun. She's more dazed than before.

MY DEATH MY LIFE
BY PIER PAOLO PASOLINI

My Death

D ID I ask to die? Was my murder a suicide by proxy?
In 1973 I wrote: "Up until the 1970s the ancient world, the world which is daily life and thinking and loving, existed—but it was swept away. From the age of innocence we've passed to the age of corruption."

The scene: Increasingly overt control of dynamic materialism by Multinationals in Italy expresses itself particularly in rise of terrorism (right-wing media strategy and expression of the populace's inability to act functionally and politically) and in Americanism, that homogenization of daily lives and identities.

I left my home after lunch on 1 November 1975. As usual I took the Guilia GT. I was planning to eat with Ninetto later that evening. We ate in the Pommidoro restaurant in the Tiburtino quarter. I left Ninetto who of course was uninterested in fucking me and drove to my favorite quarter near the Piazza dei Cinquecento. A young boy seemingly on the down-and-out practically stood in front of my car. I stopped, got out, approached the kid. He looked OK. He was interested. He got into the car. I drove him to a deserted soccer field outside and near Idroscalo. One house only and still undergoing construction. The poor don't live in houses. We'd have sex here.

Did I leave my car as I was trying to sexually coerce the boy?

Witnesses: Various thugs had attacked Pier during the past few years. Pier had become very cautious. He wouldn't now step out of his car in front of strange young thugs. We saw him stay in his car. He told some young hustlers he was waiting for a friend.

They tried to touch him. Suspiciously he rolled up his window. He quickly locked his door. No, Pier was very careful.

A boy, Seminara, went into the bar and told Pelosi to try Pier. Pasolini went for Pelosi without showing any suspicion. Why?

We stopped at the Biondo Tevere trattoria on the Via Ostiense where the kid bolted down spaghetti al'olio. Then I again stopped at an automatic to refill the tank.

A car with a Catania license plate was following us. The kid knew the four men who were in this car made their livings from mugging young hustlers after the hustlers got their takes.

We reached the soccer field. I stopped the car. I unzipped the kid's pants and stuck my face into his young crotch.

The Kid: He took my dick into his mouth, but it was just for a moment and he didn't do it to me. He dragged me out of the car. He threw my body against the car so my ass was sticking out. Then he tore my pants halfway down I didn't want him to do that. Pissed cause he couldn't get into me, he tried to stick a goddamn wood stake into my asshole. He wanted to murder me. I said, "You're crazy, you son-of-a-bitch. I'm getting out of here." He had left his glasses in the car. His naked face looking mad really frightened me. I ran. He ran after me; he wasn't going to let me go. You're crazy. He fell on top of me. Hit him with a stick. A hand grabbed the stick and threw it away. Violence takes the place of sex. I half-ran, crawled, started to run through the night, he grabbed my shirttail. Down on me. Hitting me. I struck his head with something. I kicked him in the balls. They felt soft. He didn't scream. He didn't react. He kept on hitting me. I just beat him up as hard as I could as much as I could. I was good and scared.

I leapt into his car, the keys were still in the lock, and drove off. Really the whole time is a blank. (I can't remember whether I drove over Pasolini's body or not.) The next thing I know I'm standing in the water fountain and washing blood off my hands and pants. There was no other person involved in the night.

The next day, when they arrested me, I asked them for my Marlboro's and lighter but they were no longer in the car. Instead there was a shabby green sweater that didn't belong either to the old fag or me.

The kid was more than willing to do whatever I wanted sexually. I took his shirt off cause I didn't want to touch that. He had a gorgeous back. The way the muscles stick out when there's been too much starvation and there isn't enough flesh. Just as I was about to touch my cock tip to what was inside those tight little spheres, as tight and hard as his eyes cause poverty had made them so, something bashed my head.

At first I didn't realize what was happening cause I was so intent on my desire. The blood dropped over my eyebrow. What? I realized something's happening. I fought back.

They hit my head as hard as they could with a stick and some unknown weapon. Blood fell all over the face. This blood was spurting. They held me still. One person kicked out my balls. The kick broke a hole in my lower abdomen. The hand holding my hair tore out the hair it was holding.

Witnesses: Pier passed out. His body slumps to the ground. One of them driving the Giulia 2000 runs over his body and actually kills it.

The evidence shows one or more men either using Pelosi or in cahoots with Pelosi offed me. Why did they off me? If I can

find out why they offed me, I could or might be able to learn
the identity or identities of these creeps.

First question: Was it a political assassination or just a cheap
street murder? It could just be a street murder, something that
stupid and thoughtless, that takes away my life: despite what your
parents taught you when you were a kid, there's no reason anything should be a certain way in our lives; as far as you're concerned there's no reason why you should get anything good.
Justice is our leaders' hype. No reason for you or anyone else to
have any preconception whatsoever.

I'm talking to you who are moralists, too.

Another piece of evidence. Ferdinando Zucconi Galli Fonseca
the judge of the Appeals Court on 12/4/76 stated officially that
only Pelosi murdered me. His verdict further said that Pelosi was
lying when he had sworn in court I had tried to rape him, that
actually Pelosi had been willing to get fucked, and that there's
no way of knowing why Pelosi killed me.

Why did the Appeals Court ignore the obvious evidence that
more than one person had slaughtered me?

I had just finished making *Salo*. In *Salo* human male sexual
desires especially homosexual and sadistic are raised both within
the movie and in the movie's audience at the same time that
I'm showing the close connections between these desires and
fascism. Because the state's now fascistic, sexual desire is totally
reasonable that is separate from caring. This is great for a pornog-
rapher to say.

Ernie and Cindy Gernhart had a daughter Sally. Ernie said Cindy
just like my mother never wanted a kid but the society said she
should and most people are too weak to buck society, and she
got pregnant just to hold on to her husband—the only way you
can still hold on to a man is by having his kid, look at all my
friends—but he split on her just like my father walked away from
my mother. Of course she hated her baby. Cindy hated Ernie

or at least is scared of him because Ernie walked out on her like
my (first) father walked out on my mother.

Ernie Gernhart remarried and Cindy remarried Ross Hart.
Their second marriage lasted just as my parents' did. Cindy said
Sally hated Ernie. Ross stated Sally hated him and adored Ernie.
Ross loved Sally because he explained she's the closest thing I
have to a daughter.

Sally since she understood everything that had happened tried
to run to her real father, but the law forced her to remain with
her mother.

SUICIDE CONSIDERED AS A MODUS OPERANDI.

Ross Hart had been shtupping Sally since she was fourteen
years old. That's when I lost my virginity. The guy who took it
didn't believe me that I was cherry so I didn't get any reward,
but two years later when I was fucking another guy for the first
time (in a cemetery) and simultaneously got my period, the guy
cause he thought he had just fucked a virgin fell for me. When
I was seventeen, my father tried to fuck me. Hart loved fucking
his daughter so much he wanted to run away with her. She could
try to get away from him only by keeping everything a black secret
and acting in blackness. Cindy, your second husband these past
four years has been fucking your daughter. He loved her, not
you, because she's young and you're old.

Cindy wanted Ross to fuck Sally so he wouldn't fuck her. This
is too grotty to believe. Do people really act like this?

As soon as Sally turned puberty, she was a problem. Though
she was a top-A student, she stopped studying so her grades fell.
She robbed stores all the time especially big department stores.
She hitchhiked especially on motorcycles. Then she began taking
whatever drugs anyone gave her. She got busted a few times, but
this didn't put any fear in her cause she was already so scared.

By this time she was in (protected by) a motorcycle gang. When
they arrested the gang, they sent her to probation school. If it
hadn't been for our money, she'd be spending her whole life like
a dumb animal in juvenile. Probation school at least taught

excuse me trained her to act normal. She didn't have any boyfriends because she didn't feel anything about boys.

Susan Sabin who used to be Sally's best friend said Sally is
very sensitive and doesn't trust anyone.

The whole problem revolves around who Sally Gernhart really
is.

Sally thought everyone in the world hated her, just like I do;
no one cares for her. She acts indifferent. She doesn't act insecure.

What about her father (I don't have a father)?

She loved her first father and wants to abandon the parents
she was living with. So she was lost. Then she started hanging
out with motorcycle hoods. She had her first boyfriend. Sally
said Ross Hart and her mother owe her money. She's very angry.
His name was Gype. The motorcyclists are heroes because they're
against society even though they rape and murder.

Jack Lewis Habermas, known as Gype, 29 years old, 5 feet 11
inches, 185 pounds. Long brown hair, moustache. Either ex- or
H-addict. Born in Valparaiso, Indiana. Divorced lower-middle-
class parents. Mom now third-time married Bob Smith. Smith,
a child abuser. Habermas always in trouble. Uses drugs but no
addictions. Consistently insubordinate. Habermas' domicile: The
houses in LA don't look like houses. Habermas' gang The Skulls
say they'd never kill a brother money isn't important enough.
Morality.

Sally looked around for help. She confided to the head of the
Jesus Freaks and to the guy who was trying to deprogram her
from the Jesus Freaks that her second father has been fucking
her. The deprogrammer blackmailed her second father.

Andrew Noble is the head of the Jesus Freak group. When he
was a kid he made money by trading God. Then he stopped cause
he saw he was doing wrong. Then he got a call and started doing
what he used to do. Now in these times of depression he nets
$15,000 a month and owns prime California land. His cohort's
a Vietnam vet who's organized his group militarily just like

Naropa when I was there four years ago. Every group in this country's an enemy.

Noble says Sally (this is still all about Sally) never took God into her heart, had committed the foulest of acts he doesn't say what, and constantly thought sinfully.

While Sally was in Jesus Freak camp, Gype was sprung. He has and only loves one girl: Sally.

On 4 September Ross Hart gave Furston a thousand dollars to deprogram his daughter. Ernie wouldn't have hired Furston to kidnap her because Furston is morally worse than the Jesus Freaks. Who's worse in a bad world? Eric Furston, who makes his living this way, programmed or deprogrammed depending on how you look at it, and sent her back to her hateful parents. A couple of days later which is six days ago Sally again ran away from her parents.

Ross and Cindy Hart hire me to locate their daughter Sally. Ross Hart gives Furston $500 to find Sally cause he's trying to protect Sally. He admits to me he gave Furston $500.

I ask Ernie Gernhart where's Sally. He says she's old enough to be where she wants. I ask Andrew Noble where's Sally. Noble says he hasn't seen her since Furston kidnapped her from his people. I ask Gype's landlady where's Gype. The landlady in a draggling bathrobe says, "He left five days ago. He came here with Sally for five minutes and left. That's true love."

Bob Smith a fleshy slob whose belly hangs out over his trousers drooling after every possible penny hating children even though or because he has two boys of his own rats on his stepson by giving me his address and if that doesn't work the gang's hangout's address.

At their hangout, The Skulls are lounging. Unlike this father, they protect their own. When they challenge my guts, I beat one of them up.

They plan to avenge themselves.

Furston phones Ernie Gernhart and says he has something important to tell Gernhart but he doesn't tell what it is. Ross

Hart kills Furston before Furston can tell Sally's real father and
Sally her second father are fucking. In this world of death. Is he
my real father? I investigate.

Gype and Sally send Ernie a letter in which Sally announces
she's back with the Jesus Freaks and she believes in God. I meditate.

According to these two youngsters' plan, in a bar Gype tells
me Sally split on him two days ago but he doesn't give a shit and
she's probably offering herself up to Jesus. I'm getting this information because outside the bar The Skulls are waiting for me.

Gype and Sally send Ross a $25,000 kidnapping note. If he
wants his daughter back.

He would sit for hours, a finger in his mouth, looking almost
stupid. The calm child who reacts poorly when spoken to. He
has no social graces. He doesn't want to speak to other people.
He makes himself speak to other people because he thinks he
socially has to but the words mean nothing, the images he uses
mean nothing. Affection remains inarticulable and ineffectual.
A secret preference for the inarticulable and inarticulate. I figure
out Gype and Sally are still living together and trying to con
Sally's parents out of $25,000. These parents, making the worst
decision they can as they always do, will give the kidnappers the
money without involving the cops or anyone else. Money's always
the easy solution. Gype phones Ross Hart to drive to the drive-
in restaurant phone in Trancas canyon. As if words themselves
instead of merging with possible meanings retain for the child's
consciousness their resonant materiality. That is, comprehension
has been arrested before its completion.

Ross Hart obediently leaves the $25,000 at the crossroads of
Canyon Road and Mulholland. Gype on motorcycle picks up
the money. Drives back to a small wood house. There's Sally. I
knock but Ross:

When I try to walk out on all this, Ross kills his daughter.
Gype's gone. Besides, lacking the reciprocity—however ephem-
eral—that establishes complete comprehension with all its forms,

the speech of another person seems to him a word that has been GIVEN, in every sense of the term, like a commandment, and I experience the world (word) as fear. Ross carves up Gype especially his face and cock.

One could say that he seeks to merge with unnameable nature, fleeing the weight of nomination in the unnameable texture of things, I want people to treat me as an animal, in the irregular indefinable movements of the foliage, of the waves. To be matter. To be matter to matter. The cops find Gype dead badly buried. I don't produce meaning. Truth is alien to him. That's why he's the most credulous child: since he doesn't possess the truth, since only other people do it is their language, he can only recognize truth because it always causes him pain; when he has to deal socially or in the world he relies on the principle of authority because socially nothing matters.

When we arrest Hart, he looks like he's mad. You killed your daughter. Every human being has intentions. Every human being is connected to every other human being and the intentionality of these connections is language. What happens when there's no language or when language doesn't mean? It's too soon to answer these questions. His first stories deal continually with his childhood. He hasn't stopped nor will he ever stop being that murdered child.

I, Pier Paolo Pasolini, will solve my murder by denying the principle of causation and by proposing nominalism:

NOMINALISM

1 SEX

1. *Sexual desire*

1. Claudius', King of Denmark's, corruption infects his family and all society:

Ophelia (*to her father Polonius*): Daddy, can't I go out? I'm bored. You're keeping me locked up here like I'm a piece of dry goods.

Polonius: No, honey, I'd rather you were wet. Do you think I want to see you blackface up your pretty white party dress?

Ophelia: I'll dirty up more, pops, if you don't let me out of here. I'm no nun.

Polonius: Shut up. I'm bigger than you. (*Changing his tone.*) How dare you talk to me like that: I'm your father. If you set one foot outside this house, Pheelie, I'm telling you right now: there are rapists in this world. Little girls like you can get in serious trouble. Take that boy Hamlet. My baby isn't safe with a criminal like him.

Ophelia: Not even if she's supporting her father?

Polonius: What're you saying? Pheelie, all men except for me are evil. When you go outside, they're going to rape and murder you. Do you know what'll happen to me, darling, when you're raped and murdered? I'll have horns on the top of my head. I'll be horny. I'm going to tell you something, Pheelie. It's all right for a woman, but it's not good for a man to be horny. A man who doesn't achieve full sexual satiation becomes ill. If you walk out of this house, young lady, you're going to give your father a heart attack.

Ophelia: My mother's already given you two heart attacks. She's better at it than I am. Besides, the only people you can perceive are murderers and rapists and you're always miserable and you sit in bed and do dope and don't do anything else cause your mind's a stinkin' mess.

(*All these characters stink and have lousy motivations.*)

Polonius (*swigging out of his Scotch bottle*): You're running out to see that Hamlet, aren't you? You two have something going on with you. I'm not going to let you go! I'm going to protect you! He doesn't respect you, Pheelie: no man respects you except for me; I give you a home and everything you want. He's going to leave you.

Ophelia: Why don't you fuck your wife, Polly, instead of me?

Polonius: We're too old to do that sort of thing.

Ophelia: Mother wants it. She sends you all those birthday cards asking you why you can't get your cock up and shows them to her friends.

Polonius: Phelia! Where d'you ever learn such foul language! I'm going to wash your mouth out with soap, young lady.

Ophelia: You ate up all the soap yesterday when you ran out of your liquor. (*Tries another tack.*) Why don't I go around the corner to get you another bottle of Jack Daniels, daddy?

Polonius: That would be very nice of you. (*Catching himself, but he wants it too much.*) You come back here immediately, Ophelia! Don't say a word to a man.

Ophelia: How would I know what a man looks like the way you keep me locked up, daddy?

Ophelia's First Nurse (*entering room*): "Man"? I don't know where she picked up such language, Mr. Polonius. She was brought up to be a nice girl and she talks like a two-bit . . . I can't even get the word out of my mouth.

Ophelia: Slut. Whore. Hooker. Prostitute. Pretty girl. Cunt. Tramp. Floozy. Flounder. Dead fish. Wet fish. Teeth. Trollop. Cock-twister. Slut scumbag scallops. Box. Bitch. (*To her nurse.*) I know this is what you are because I've seen you and this feeble-brain (*pointing to her father*) who's holding me prisoner in this house doing it together and he can't even get it up.

Nurse: You ungrateful child! I ought to slap your face. Your father has given you everything a child could possibly want and brought you up in this hard world like no child's ever been brought up and this is the gratitude you give him.

Polonius: Shut up, Grace. Ophelia, your nurse loves you. Is this how you treat her? I don't care how you're acting towards me, but your nurse is a wonderful person. Everyone loves her. I'm not going to let you hurt her as you're doing.

First Nurse (*in a little voice*): It doesn't matter. Parrot.

Polonius: It matters to me, Grace. I'm not going to let her keep on taking advantage of your sweetness. I'm going to take her trust fund away from her; well, I legally can't; but I can do my best to see she is never happy.

Ophelia: How're you going to do that, Impotency?

Polonius: You're not twenty-one yet, young lady. I still own you. You cannot leave this house, Ophelia. From now on, these doors are locked. Moreover, no man's going to enter this house.

Ophelia: There's sure no man in here now.

(*Polonius' walking off high-and-mightily arm-in-arm with the Nurse. Polonius is off the stage.*)

Ophelia: I don't care about love.

In Honor Of Brendan Behan And The Irish Society Who Revolted: The prisoners sing: they are in one of the punishment cells.

Claudius (*to his Queen*): I bought you a Christmas present.

Queen: Oh, Claudius. How sweet of you. Tell me. What is it?

Claudius: A maid. Would you like to see her?

Queen: A ready-made?

Claudius: Ready and willing. (*Tries to rub his cock and misses.*)

Should I call her? (*Rings the buzzer "Emergency" for the guard. A moment later the cell door opens and a tiny, pretty girl is shoved through the door.*) These are your new employers, Mrs. Claudius and Mrs. Polonius. You shall help them out, Al'Amat, in whatever ways they require you to do so.

Al'Amat: Yes, sir.

Queen: What's your name, child?

Al'Amat: Rebecca.

Queen: What a horrible name!

Claudius: I changed her name to Al'Amat.

Queen: Why don't you go outside and bring us some Turkish coffee, Al'Amat? They serve the worst dishwater in here.

Mrs. Polonius (*looking at a wall, as if through a window*): Nice day for murder.

Al'Amat (*looking confused*): Yes, Ma'am. (*She rings the "Emergency" bell*).

(*A guard appears and lets Al'Amat out.*)

Queen: Claudius, would you like a piece of bread and cheese?

Claudius: Yes, please.

Queen: We haven't got any.

(*Again, the cell door opens. Al'Amat, overloaded by a tray full of Turkish coffee cups, stumbles through and falls down.*)

Queen: Don't you feel awful working for strangers, Al'Amat?

(*All these distinctly different verbal elements go together because nothing makes sense anymore and this putting together of various cultures is an act of hatred.*)

Al'Amat: I don't give a damn about anyone anymore, Mrs. Claudius. I'm Irish.

Queen: Oh. Why don't you just call me Gertrude?

Al'Amat: Yes, Mrs. . . . Gertrude.

Queen: If I was working for the first time for strange people, I'd be so shy I wouldn't know what to do with myself.

Al'Amat: I hate the English. They infiltrated and made me with their culture. I don't know how to speak English very well, Mrs. Claudius.

Queen: Gertrude. I'm afraid you're going to have to get used to our life in jail here just as we have had to, Al'Amat. Humans, you will learn, can adapt to anything, even to society. Inside jail we use neither sexist nor classist nor racist, such as "I hate the English," language. Although words don't mean anything anymore.

Al'Amat: What do you mean "Words don't mean anything"?

Mrs. Polonius: Polly told me he likes to fuck black sailors because he's making up for the way his parents, when he was a kid, mistreated their black maids.

Al'Amat: I'm not black; I'm Irish.

Queen: You are now that we've changed your name. I hope you don't mind.

Al'Amat: Of course not, Mrs. Gertrude (*Now the audience sees that a knife is sticking out from under her arm.*) The culture I grew up in and by is the culture the English imposed on my country to make us learn that is stop perceiving the absolute lack of pride or abject poverty, they are the same thing, in which we were living. Culture is that which falsifies.

Queen: We are all sisters.

Mrs. Polonius: There's a man down there.

Claudius: Is he wearing a trench coat and beret?

Mrs. Polonius: How d'you know?

Claudius: He's a fortuneteller.

Al'Amat: He's going to tell all of your fortunes. You're all going to die.

(*Two men, one thin-faced in a trench coat and black beret, the second in a black leather overcoat and pimp hat, enter the cell and begin searching it. They test the plaster, stamp on the wood boards that are beds.)*

Al'Amat: I've been waiting for you.
Thin-Faced Man: Who's in charge here?
Claudius: I am.
Thin-Faced Man: This cell is full of rubbish. (*Kicking the Turkish coffee cups.*)
Leather-Coat: You'll have to clear this cell totally. It's an escape route.
Mrs. Polonius: Are these the sanitary inspectors?
Thin-Faced Man: Where are the toilet arrangements?

(Al'Amat walks him around a thin three-foot high partition in back of which a cracked urinal sits on a concrete square.)

Al'Amat: When may we expect the prisoner?
Thin-Faced Man: Tonight.
Al'Amat: What time?
Thin-Faced Man: Between nine and twelve.
Al'Amat: They had not, under the heavens and on earth, one single weapon. They don't control the land they live on, the schools which train them, the heat and food their bodies need to live through the winter's cold, the media which gives them language, the military weapons for which they give most of their money. There is no more time in this city. Reasonable people don't let themselves dream because no dream can be true. They have a cry that brought them back to first causes: But we who have no mothers, no fathers, no homes or love: Where are we going to run?

Hamlet is the only member of this society who perceives this disease. Because he's perceiving the disease, he's being ostracized by the society:

1. *The art world of New York City.*

Hamlet's Maid: Then an artist can't live these days by his art?
Hamlet: That's a very important point. I'm going to conquer the world. Whatever I have to do to myself to achieve this.

Hamlet's Maid: But, sir, you don't have any money.

Hamlet: So what. Are you a materialist? Am I a materialist? . . .

Hamlet's Maid: Yes.

Hamlet: . . . If it's not money that matters, it's the idea. Oh, the world! Anyway, money is the main thing those who are really in power are using—they actually *make* it—to control us. Rich men don't have money, they have power. I hate the rich.

Hamlet's Maid: But not their money.

Hamlet: The mental world is the cause of the physical one. Two knobs, so to speak. Two nips tits bazooms. Since I can't have one, money, I'm going to clamp my teeth and chomp on the other.

Hamlet's Maid: Mother Earth's going to love that one.

Hamlet: Shut up. Don't I pay your wages?

Hamlet's Maid: Just like Reagan pays out Social Security, Welfare, and the NEA.

Hamlet: No more dumb jokes. No one reads me now so I'd better write for posterity though the world's ending. Like a good artist, I'm going to marry Ophelia for her money!

Hamlet's Maid: That's real love.

Hamlet: And so by chomping on the sacred tit of money, art will spurt out her milk for me!

Hamlet's Maid: You don't have to be weaned, baby, because you don't have a head. Why is Ophelia who's beautiful rich and so shy she can't even talk to a normal person going to let you near her secret underpants?

Hamlet: This desperate poverty commingled with the purity of my artistic action will, by rendering her ashamed of her richness, annihilate both her pride and fear. I, the person who considers himself, will be much more desirable than any rich man!

Hamlet's Maid: You've certainly got the brains of a rich man.

Hamlet (*aside*): This absence of love, noticed only as a hole, a gnawing which never goes away. You rats at the edge of my mind! Get out! Get out, I say to all you characteristics.

While the sinuses around my brain are pounding. This hurt.
I'm not going to bother again with psychologies, relation-
ships, those sorts of damned human contacts. I've been too
hurt. I now know now nothing lasts. More precisely there
is no true belief, is any belief true?, in any security between
human and human. I have experienced this. I have been
taught my blows that split apart the world. Crack. Why
should I give in to any relationship, love or hatred?

Hamlet's Maid: Your plan to marry Ophelia for her money is
as intelligent as the American Cancer Association's decision
to research synthetic rather than natural cancer cures. Synthetic cancer cures maintain the pharmaceutical industry
and the cancer plague. Meanwhile, the men who eat the
most food in this country, the doctors, are the ones who
have the highest incidence of cancer.

Hamlet: I'll take away some of their trade.

Hamlet's Maid: What? Are you going to open a mortuary?

Hamlet: I'm going to make dead people. I'm going to write a
play.

Hamlet's Maid: The last time you wrote a play, the printer stole
all the money you gave him to print the play, the lawyer
you hired turned around and sued you for three thousand
dollar court fees though no one ever went to court, three
famous people sued you for libel, and now all the women
refuse to fuck with you cause you might write about them.
You don't have any friends left. And your parents hate your
guts.

Hamlet: There's you.

Hamlet's Maid: There was me. Poverty, living without heat or
hot water, catcalls as we walk down the street just because
of what we look like, envy, loneliness: every part of your
life I can stand. The only thing that turns my stomach is
poetry.

Hamlet: I'll be a representational painter. What's in a name these
days? I will represent the poverty of spirit that the powers

behind Reagan endorse. Economic poverty. Social poverty. Political poverty. Emotional poverty. Ideational poverty.

Hamlet's Maid: How much you want money. I wouldn't mind a little bit either.

(*Hamlet exits.*)

Hamlet's Maid (*alone*): Choosing to be an artist means living against this world. Why would anyone choose to be an artist? Cripples didn't choose to be crippled.

The spirit of famine is appearing to me: Now he's fucking rich women to stay alive. Now he's pulling white scraps out of his holey pockets and saying "These are my poems" in a deserted airport. Now he's standing in the doorway of a rich woman's dining-room during a crowded party, one eye on the moldy pink ham and stale white bread on the dining-room table and the other on his death.

(*Exits as Hamlet re-enters room.*)

Hamlet's Maid (*re-entering, followed by men*): Hamlet. They're here to arrest you because you haven't paid your bills.

(*Hamlet flees.*)

1. *The cure for disease.*

Romeo: I look up to you so much, my just being around you must hurt you so let me increase this disease.

Juliet: I don't mind you being around me because I'm made to have human contact. I'm not made for separation which is the sickness of this society.

Romeo: Which means I can make you more diseased.

Juliet: You're going to hurt me?

Romeo: There's always danger when we aim for everything.

Juliet: I don't think it's possible for humans to do anything. They can listen.

Romeo: Until there is no thing.

(*He kisses her. They shiver.*)

Juliet: And back and forth so that we are both nothing.
Romeo: We're descending into blackness.

(*They kiss again more hotly. Their tongues are slapping against each other.*)

Juliet: You kiss like your mother taught you to.

2. (*There is no light on stage because Juliet is the only thing who exists.*)

Romeo: I would do anything for you. I would do anything so you would let me near you but I know if I say this to you, it'll scare you so much you'll freeze up to me.
Juliet: Oh me!
Romeo: Just, please, listen to me a second and give me one chance. I'm living in the pain of absolute longing like leaning over a chair that is a sharp razor blade.
Juliet: Give up your life in New York and come to me. Or I, I'll give myself, I will, because being loved is the only thing that matters. I'll accept death and be cured.
Romeo (*aside*): Can I tell her I want her? The life I'm living is like being dead. The hell with this fame. Her speech is the first living I've heard. (*To Juliet.*) You, mistress, name me.
Juliet: Who are you? Now I know who you are. You're my enemy.
Romeo: If you want me to, I'll kill you.
Juliet: You've hurt me before but that doesn't matter. How do I know anything? What does this language mean? I'll have to trust nothing. I know I trust nothing too much, I will do anything for nothing. Tell me what's true now. Tell me what's true now.
Romeo: The truth?
Juliet: Don't leave me hanging.
Romeo: The only thing I believe in is nothingness.

(A *gleam of light grey appears in the lower sky.*)

Juliet: Go to hell. I don't like you anyway. I don't live anywhere. My life is shit. I need someone to love me.

Romeo: I want your body.

Juliet: I wish I knew what I want.

Romeo: To hell with these politenesses! Tomorrow I'll marry you.

Juliet: For ever?

Romeo: For ever.

Juliet: That's what I want to do.

Nurse (*from within Juliet's parents' house*): Juliet, are you talking to yourself again?

Juliet: I have to go.

Romeo: I'll give you all my money if you just let my tongue lick your cunt juice.

Juliet: Tomorrow, for the rest of our lives for ever we'll be able to lie to each other and we'll be able to lie on each other. What time tomorrow will we be able to fuck?

Romeo: As soon as the morning sun has shot its sperm over all blackness and the Wall Street lawyer is masturbating in his office.

Juliet: From now on let every second be a year until this ache this smell of dead fish takes over the world. I am being driven crazy. When I will lie with you I can no longer think. When I will lie with you I am no longer happy.

Romeo: Then I'll make sure you'll never fuck me.

Juliet: I'd rather have you next to me so I could increase your absence by a thousandfold. Absence upon absence until . . .

Romeo: I will eat you out.

Juliet: I'd rather be manipulated.

(*The nurse drags away this brat.*)

Romeo: This isn't real.

3. *Society: The doldrums of this season, winter, wet like drabs the maids made of these waters, ugly, along the streets they gleam*

black no matter what the hour, late at night small black human figures, caps over the tops of their heads, toss crates of sticks, fishheads and parts of fish bodies the scales now dulled into the huge dark green bins, and no one says hello to anyone, in the narrow alleyways, these few cobblestones left, surrounded by the long grey smooth streets which during the day the businessmen with their briefcases cover. (Tybalt and Mercutio, two business-men, walk on to the street and kill each other.)

4. *Romeo at home.*

Romeo: The war's my real father.

Mrs. Montague: It doesn't matter who your real father is. You just have to have some father cause every child has a father or else you're not a real child.

Romeo: I don't have a mother either.

Mrs. Montague (*showing emotion*): What do you mean "You don't have a mother"?

Romeo: Since you open your body to my unreal father, you're not real and I'm an abortion.

Mrs. Montague: I gave birth to you only cause I was too scared to get an abortion. You need sex too much.

5. *Romeo is in the Priest's cell.*

Romeo: I'm going to get married.

Priest: You're crazy. What're you going to get married for?

Romeo: This time I really want to get married. When are you going to marry me?

Priest: One of us is the wrong sex, honey. It isn't legal yet.

Romeo: The person I want to marry is more wrong than you. (*Juliet enters the cell.*) I will do whatever I have to to get her.

This scene break, though not a logical one, has become conventional; we have retained it merely because it is generally accepted and to depart from this convention might affect the scene numbering of the rest of the act in a way that would cause referential confusion.

6. *SITTING* here I see, through the glass restaurant door, a three-foot wide rivulet of black water, flowing, now stagnant, against cobblestones each one slightly apart from the ones surrounding it. Towards the back of the street near an uneven light grey sidewalk, smaller black pools obscure the stones. The more rapidly the water moves, the lighter it seems. Out of the sidewalk which is nearer to the eye a thick aluminum cylinder whose function is unknown and the same sized fire hydrant rise up. Inside the restaurant several small hideous woodcuts and drawings of a classical representational style hang over the walls' sanded red bricks. Varnished unstained wood slabs six inches wide and two inches long frame the glass windows and doors. There is a lot of natural and electric light. On one rectangular wood table a cigarette burns on a shell. Near the cigarette a small glass contains half a cup of sugar. An aluminum spoon sticks upward. From the sugar cup, about the same distance as is between the burning cigarette and the sugar, a white china dish holds salt and a dark green-brown spice. A girl sits at this table. The pen in her right hand moves rapidly over a blue-lined page of a spiral notebook. Sitting on the seat of a dark wood chair which is next and similar to the one she's sitting on, whose back holds a copy of *American Heritage*, the open section of a worn-out leather handbag reveals a crumbled piece of white paper. Easy-listening Greek music is playing. The girl is thinking that most people are saying the human world is ending. This landscape is without propaganda or obsession. This landscape without any given meaning is as present as any statement such as the world is about to end.

Memory and association
Back to the same restaurant. In Zurich, after I crossed the large river, the streets moved as if streets can move by themselves while away from me upward and slightly winding. The most interesting streets, I remember, were the narrowest ones. Small bars with bad food, not catering just to rich people, clean sidewalks and buildings, light browns light-light not light. Of course there was

nowhere to go on top. Better than Berne: there, there was no
hiddenness: Levels on levels of buildings and their streets, the
archways are archways, the shops under the archways sell gold
coins and antiques which are more economically stable than
money, there are levels of roofs, steppingstones of roofs, staircases
outside. All which is understandable. On one middle level at the
end of the archways cobblestones and small squares of greenery,
a large park lifted up to another level. At the bottom of this park
a round circle of masonry sunk in the ground contained two bears
and some rocks. The American and one Italian-Swiss and two
German-Swiss for breakfast ate one poached egg and a slice of
Swiss cheese over a piece of white bread. The bread tasted winey.
Some say he is not in that grave at all. That the coffin was filled
with stones. That one day he will come again.

Hynes shook his head.

—Parnell'll never come again, he said. He's there, all that was
mortal of him. TO SEARCH IN ALL THESE THINGS (OF
COURSE MENTAL) WHICH SIMPLY PRESENT THEM-
SELVES FOR THE ROAD OR MEANING:

When I lived in San Diego, I had three cats. The cats used
to jump out of the kitchen window of my apartment which was
on the second floor, over to a black flat roof. Once they had
jumped off this roof, I couldn't see them anymore. When they
became hungry and when they wanted to, they reappeared in my
kitchen. At times another cat, a huge black stud searching for
my oldest female, appeared on the black flat roof. To me these
appearances were magic or causeless because I couldn't follow
my cats because I can't leap across roofs.

I thought I knew every section of this small beach town. My
male cat adored my body so much whenever he was around me
he pressed rubbed his back into my belly. One day while I was
walking on a sidewalk I met my male cat strutting along the edge
of the green. I said "Hello." He refused to recognize me. I decided
to follow him. He met twelve other cats behind an old car in
long grass a block away from the beach. As soon as the cats heard

me, they ran where I couldn't follow. I began to trace dogs. The dogs had a different town. Definitive meeting points and certain streets or paths that linked the points defined each town. I almost but couldn't know these towns that were my towns.

How available are the (meanings of the) specifics of all that is given? Language is a giveness like all other givenesses. Let the meanings not overpowering (rigid) but rather within the contexts, like Hamlet's father's ghost who tells the first meaning, interpretation of nothing, be here:

On this table which is in front of me which is just a fancy wood crate: on the first half, a chessboard on whose black-and-gold plastic top dust cookie crumbs some chess pieces, behind the chessboard a white plastic coffee cup over, to the left of the board and cover (my eye doesn't want to see too much). What is given: one almost empty jar of dried soy granules, one tin of cinnamon, one book entitled *The Book of Ebenezer le Page* on top of the light-blue-covered book *The Complete Plays of William Wycherly*, two filthy chopsticks, one empty white china cup with an aluminum spoon sticking out of its middle; on the other half of this crate, a stack of nine books two of whose titles *The Art of Positional Play* and *The Marble Faun* right against a bottle of Lancôme red nail polish and right in front of a small white candy box and a box of herbal cigarettes, a small black-and-white TV which isn't on, a small computer chess set a quarter way through a game.

What's the meaning here? Compare this list of just what is given to another structurally similar list to find the key:

Gross-booted draymen rolled barrels dull-thudding out of Prince's stores and bumped them up on the brewery float. On the brewery float bumped dull-thudding barrels rolled by gross-booted draymen out of Prince's stores. —There it is Red Murray said. Alexander Keyes. —Just cut it out, will you? Mr. Bloom said, and I'll take it round to the TELEGRAPH office. HOUSE OF KEY(E)S —Like that, see. Two crossed keys here. A circle. Then here the name Alexander Keyes, tea, wine and spirit merchant. So on.

Better not teach him his own business. —You know yourself, councilor, just what he wants. Then round the top in leaded: The house of keys. You see. Do you think that's a good idea? The foreman moved his scratching hand to his lower ribs and scratched there quietly. —The idea, Mr. Bloom said, is the house of keys. You know, councilor, the Man parliament. Innuendo of home rule. Tourists, you know, from the Isle of Man. Catches the eye. (I), you see. Can you do that?

Compare these two lists:

Comparison: Paris rawly waking, crude sunlight over her lemon streets. Moist piths of farls of bread, the froggreen wormwood, her morning perfume, coffee coffee court the air. The milk of architectural tits. *Têtes.* Frenchmen can only think. We invited two hookers to sit with us cause Frenchmen are only polite to language and food before you've fucked them. There Belluomo rises from his wife's lover's wife's bed, the kerchiefed housewife stirs, a saucer of sunk gone oh below the cement. I say, pick up skirts. Show cunt. Smelly fish all over the sides of flesh going slowly arising

I can no longer speak English:

7. La Chambre du lit

Juliet: Si je ne suis pas fouquée à damain, je vais mourir par une malâdie. Il est necessaire que je fouque ou je meurs. Je pense que je suis souffrante parce que le seul chose que je demande—fouquer un homme—est l'unique acte que je ne peux pas faire. Je suis pourtant plus écoeurée parce que tu ne me désires pas subitement tu me désires maintenant tu ne me désires pas. Dieu je te tuerai. Je suis à bout de mes forces. Les hommes sont des bébés. Ils doivent pronouncer la réalité, déclarer à moi qu'il est necessaire pour moi faire d'accord avec leurs grandes modèles de la réalité, et à la même temps mentir. Leurs mesonges ne sont pas intelligents. Par conséquent leurs mesonges nous insultent et nous rennent incapables de la langage parler.

La Bonne D'Enfant: Les hommes sont des merdres. Regarde-toi le morceau gros de la saucisse entre ces reins.

Juliet: Je l'aime. Si j'ai besoin de choisir entre ma famille et fouquer, je chois fouquer. N'est pas problème. Je chois fouquer si fouquer existe joint au pouvoir, la renommée et tous les phenomena qui existent. Par conséquent je préfére fouquer les hommes qui sont les plus puissants les plus fameux. Comme moi décadents avec la plus complexe perception obsessifs droits comme moi et ne me désirent jamais. Est-ce que peut-être il est bon pour moi me suicider?

La Bonne D'Enfant: Pourquoi? Comment peux-tu aimer un homme que tu possedes? Comment peux-tu aimer ce qui est présent?

Juliet: Par conséquent je ne pourrai jamais fouquer un homme. Commence-toi avec le renversement des humains qui est la fierté humaine. Laisse-toi l'imagination dégager. Je signifie surtout les types de l'imagination les plus débiles. Supposant l'expression de ton visage sur ce moment tu me fouques.

Cette écriture est réelle. Cette réalité est mon message á vous.

8. *Dans le cachot du prêtre*

Juliet: Est-ce que possible que quand nous nous fouquons je touche l'amour pour toi et tu ne le touches pas pour moi?

Romeo: Mon corps a voulu rester pour un moment.

Juliet: Aprés deux jours je m'allierai à Paris.

Romeo: Par conséquent j'ai besoin de toi. Pour un homme l'amour n'advient pas et ensuite sans cause il advient. Je ne t'as jamais vu avant ce moment. Qui êtes-vous? Je sortirai en trombe tes cheveux.

Juliet: Les cheveux de mon poisson s'etoufferont tes narines.

(*Elle met un doigt couvert par un gant du cuir noir sur sa joue.*)

Juliet: Au revoir; je vais partir.

(*Ses dingdongs s'écrasent follement contre l'un l'autre.*)

(*Cette chose n'est pas supposée être obsessife.*)

Le Prêtre: Juliet!

(*Les prêtres ne sont pas obsessifs.*)

Juliet: Huh? (*Elle est une gosse seulement. Romeo disparaît. Juliet ne peut pas tolérer cet acte. Il ne peut pas me laisser.*) Romeo! (*Seulement un peu de lui apparaît.*) Pense-toi que nous nous rencontrerons de nouveau toujours?
Romeo: Je t'aime. Au revoir.

(*Il me baisse tendrement.*)

9. *Le seul moyen que j'ai pour guérir la maladie sociale est pour moi devenir plus malade. Plus de gens ne veulent pas nuire aux autres gens et nuisent aux autres. Plus d'hommes de l'authorité social et politique ne veulent pas endommagent les autres humains et les endommagent. Au contraire de ces hommes malades je consciencieusement désire faire ma maladie consciencieusement a l'extrême. Je me réglerai plus jusqu'à ce qui est mes besoins deviendra insensé;*

Juliet: J'aime votre sexe. Vous n'aimer pas mon sexe.

(*J'aime votre sexe. Vous n'aimez pas mon sexe et ne voulez pas voir mon sexe.*)

Le dixiéme vue

Paris: Veux-toi m'épouser?
Juliet: Vous? L'oubliez. Je seulement désire me marier Romeo.
Paris: Romeo ne te désirera jamais. Il devient fameux de sorte qu'il a trop d'intérêt personnel qu'il ne peut pas prêter attention à une autre personne.

Juliet: D'accord. Je ne suis pas assez riche de sorte qu'il m'aimera. Je ne vais pas me marier même si, si je ne me marierai pas, je mourirai. Je ne parle pas du sexe.

(*Elle est physiquement malade et se tord avec une inflammation de la syphilis.*)

L'onziéme vue:

Juliet (*seule*): Si tu plais, cesse mon coeur et les lèvres de mon sexe et ces qui sont mes pensées d'incendier de me réduire en cendres. Je ne peut pas supporter désirer tout ce rien reins.

Dear Monet, Would you like to go away with me? A bribe. For a week. We will go anywhere in the world you want.

How can I get him to talk to me? He isn't going to fall in love with me because he's becoming too famous.

12. **Juliet** (*déguisée comme un jeune garçon parce qu'elle est un jeune garçon quand personne ne s'aime pas*): Merde, est-ce que je suis un garçon beau jeune?

Orlando (*brusquement*): Que voulez-vous?
Juliet: Quelle heure est-il?
Orlando: L'heure? Que pensez-vous? Que je porte une montre?
Juliet: Alors vous n'êtes pas amoureux avec personne, monsieur, parce que si vous êtes amoureux avec quelqu'un vous savez ce que le temps est.
Orlando: Maintenant je n'ai pas de temps pour l'amour.
Juliet: Votre déclaration est exactement ce que je signifie. Si vous soyez une jeune fille venante revenir á la cité á l'homme qu'elle désire fouquer et avec lequel elle pense être inanimée va arriver et qu'elle n'a pas eue dans un an; vous sachez ce qui est la nature du temps. Le temps est couché entre les reins.
Orlando: Pas le temps, mais des piéces de dix cents. Il est

necessaire que cette affaire est vraie parce que le temps, qui
est changement, ment.

Juliet: La monnaie dans mon porte-monnaie! La monnaie dans
mon porte-monnaie! (*Frictionnante les lévres de son sexe
avec ses doigts.*) Tandis qu'un homme qui ne fouque pas ou
un prêtre, qui existe joyeusement sur la fertilité de la nation
et sur son propre embonpoint, ne peut pas mentir. Par example notre prêtre President Reagan.

Orlando: Tandis que les voleurs et les meurtriers se taisent à plat
dans leurs tombes. Alors avez-vous de temps, garcon?

Juliet: Je suis trop jeune pouvoir parler de sorte que je mens.
Seulement, merci à Dieu que je ne suis pas une femelle.

Orlando: Pourquoi?

Juliet: Je ne veuille pas être une femelle dans le monde de beaux-
arts à cet instant comme si le monde de beaux-arts ait changé.
Les femmes: les hommes courent après lesquelles et leur
disent "Je te veux" sans d'intention ou de signification; les
femmes, pas comprenantes ce qui se passe, sont quittées
dans une condition du désir échauffé à côté de l'incapacité
de compréhension de quelque chose.

13. *Heathcliffe et Catherine sur les terrains incultes*

Catherine: H et moi, nous nous vont rebeller. Ce soir nous avons
pris nos premiers pas rebeller.

Mardi 5 mars. J'instruis mes leçons de l'école à H de sorte
que ils ne peuvent pas nous désunir. En dépit de et joint à
tous ces choses que j'apprends, je ne vais pas devenir adulte.
Je ne vais pas changer la férocité. Cette férocité est: je ne
fais pas l'attention à quelqu'un mais H parce que H n'est
pas quelqu'un je ne fais pas attention à quelqu'un H est cet
univers. Moi et H cet univers: une sphere. Ce vent qui se
tourne sans gêne est moi. J'aime les cheveux de la fille dans
la peinture de Monet.

Aujourd'hui ils ont fouettés H et ont pris mon animal
empaillé. Quand je les atteigne, je vais les atteindre sang-

lantement. Mais H, il est necessaire que je regarde à la
hauteur de H que je me donne à H parce qu'il n'a pas eu
un merde pour quelqu'un. Ils sont les monstres sur moi si
je les permette je ne peux pas le permettre je dois maintenir
le contrôle sévère sur moi-même. Il y a toujours le besoin
absolu que je fais exactement ce que je désire et veux et H
H il naturellement, sans se faisant consciencieusement, fait
fait tous ces qu'il souhaite.

   Les vents, faites vos existences damnées! Soufflez à fond
à ces bâtiments bétons jusqu'a ce que vous désintegrerez
proprement puis démolirez leurs quartiers de tête! Soufflez
fouquer! Soufflez mon désir pour! Parce que H et moi nous
sommes étés si brûlés les brèches que nous sommes outre
sentissants des émotions. Chaque carré de cette peau rouge
violacée combat. Ces lacérations, les lacérations que ma
mère-mère et mon père-père me donnent chaque jour: ap-
prenants par coeur la Bible, l'abus physique, la nourriture
mal, la peur de rien de la nourriture et du refuge: Contre
vous, nous dessinons nos revanches. Nous vous vengerons—
pour nôtre perception est rêvant—seulement afin de faire
nous éclater de rire. Nous n'avons pas d'amis.

H: Il me dégradera Heathcliffe épouser pour cette raison il ne
   saura pas combien je l'adore. Heathcliffe n'est pas moi.
   Heathcliffe est plus moi-même que je suis. Quoi que ce
   soit qui fait forme cette matière humaine l'âme, le sien et
   le mien sont semblables; je hais définitement mon mari
   futur, il est aussi différent de nous que la glace de la glace
   sec ou la drogue la mort. Aujourd'hui je pense que je désire
   mortir.

La Bonne D'Enfant: Si tu épouseras un homme que tu n'aimes
   pas, tu ne pourras jamais fouquer et devenir cet homme, si
   il possiblement existe, que tu adores.

Heathcliffe: Jamais le fouquer! Jamais l'être! Unimaginable. Nous
   ne pouvons pas êtres separés, il s'est exclamé avec l'indig-
   nation. "Qui par enfer puisse nous separer? Pas aussi long

que je vis parce que mon être est le sien. Chaque Linton
(chaque étranger) se dissout en rien avant que je m'incline
avant que je puisse partir de Heathcliffe! Oh cette chose
n'est pas ce que je signifie par mon mariage—je ne voudrai
pas être la femme de Linton si faire cette fonction de la
femme de Linton touchera mon être réel. Heathcliffe est
pauvre. Si j'épouse Heathcliffe, il n'ait pas d'argent; mais si
j'épouserai Linton, je pourraie élever Heathcliffe au pouvoir
extrême qu'il est de sorte que mon frére ne puisse jamais le
nuire.

The cure for desire.

1. *In bed.*

Juliet: Get away from me, you fat old creep! I want to be alone.
Nurse: Why?

(Exi((s))ts.)

Juliet (*alone*): Because I am alone.

(She's not alone: she's a brat.)

I'm getting to be so incredibly famous when I walk down
the city street, people have to stop and ask me for my au-
tograph. As I walk into my gym, a man who has no hair
asks me if I'm really Juliet. All this attention only foils this
space I have lived and am living in which is solitude. I'm
not going to get weak-minded and babyish. (*Desperate.*) Nurse!
Nurse! (*Her nurse doesn't answer.*) Good. She didn't answer
me. I'm alone do you hear me God therefore I'm going to
poison myself.

(She drinks down a gram of poison not opium.)

What if I'm doing the wrong thing?
Nurse (*entering the bedroom as the sun rises up, full gorgeous*

colors, therefore as joyous a day as has ever existed): My God. My baby, oh my little lamb.

(*One of Juliet's stuffed animals is a lamb.*)

(*Feeling her pulse.*) There's no pulse. She was an angel because she never wanted to hurt another living being even a human though she was too innocent to live. (*Picking a piece of scrap paper off the floor.*) She left this note to her poodle and no other suicide note. Everyone loved her so much there's no reason for her to suicide.

(*Maniacally screaming so loudly at the top of her lungs, Juliet's mother hears her and enters.*)

Mrs. Capulet: Wha . . . why Juliet's dead. Well, that's no reason to wake me up in the middle of the night. She deserved to die since she wasn't worth anything, especially economically, and she was too crazy for this family.

2. *In the grave.*

Romeo: Fuck this social political and economic sickness. I am sick. I am diseased. I am in love.

Juliet: I can cure you, honey.

Romeo: How can you cure disease? You're dead.

Juliet: You'll become well if every day you come to me, kneel down beside my body, and kiss me and adore me and want me want me want me.

Romeo: That's sick. You're a dead person so I'd be wanting to death precisely what I can't have, and the sickest thing in the world is to want who you can't have.

Juliet: Do you want to get well?

Romeo: Yes.

(*The next day.*)

Romeo (*looking at a filthy decaying corpse one of whose feet is clubfoot*): Here I am, blue lips, but how the hell are you

going to notice? I might as well be making love to a dead
woman. All my other love affairs have been like this: for
me the language of love, the only language I've ever used,
is talking to myself.

Juliet: You're full of bullshit, hole not even good enough for an
ass. You've never actually loved a single person.

Romeo: I deserve this.

Juliet: Furthermore, you don't even want to fuck me.

Romeo (*aside*): You're a corpse. (*To Juliet.*) Since I'm feeling
love rather than lust for you, you've got to give me some
time.

Juliet: Time? Can the sun ask for more time when he has to
begin each morning by orgasming into light and shooting
whiteness over the tops of this universe? Do irrationality and
nonsense know anything of time?

Romeo: It's not that I don't love you, Juliet . . . Corpse, but if
I want to marry a girl, I need the time to consider how I
can support her in the style in which no one lives and to
which everyone should become accustomed: endless richness, and how we can live in the same ten rooms without
tearing out each other's hairs and mangling like mindless
mental beasts.

Juliet: I'd rather you'd fuck me like a bitch-in-heat right this
second.

Romeo: But as an upper-middle-class Jewish boy, I'm trained to
do what's right by my wife.

Juliet: Fuck me! Fuck me! What do I care whose wife you are?
If you care about me, you should be saving my life. When
I'm this horny, I get bad sexual disease.

Romeo: If you were the woman I worship, my lips would be
pressed on the dripping red-violet of your cunt lips.

Juliet: So you don't love me. (*Takes in this fact.*) You're supposed
to be pretending you love me and the more you don't,
because love is confusion, the more love you're feeling for
me. In this way pretense becomes reality.

Romeo: Run that by me again.

Juliet: Get rid of your reasons. I'm out of my clothes. And either take off those clothes or don't have anything to do with me and get out of here. (*To you two men who don't love me.*)

Romeo: I'm not going to take my clothes off in front of a woman I don't love. I'm no hippy.

Juliet: Then you're sick.

Romeo: This is the way of desire: Either I'm sick and don't fuck, or I fuck a corpse.

Juliet: No one ever said the world is perfect. Human beings have been mean to themselves and each other in various un-countable ways ever since they were orangutans, yet all the time, as far as I know, no one's ever died from fucking a corpse. Men fuck corpses all the time. Most men would rather fuck corpses than other women. How do I know this? Because men pay prostitutes but they don't pay other women to fuck. Yet the prostitutes don't give a damn about the men who are humping on top of them, and if they feel anything, they like the money they're earning. Now have you ever heard of a John dying, or even being put in jail?

Romeo: Rockefeller died.

Juliet: He was a politician.

Romeo: I'm glad you're not the woman I love because you're a corpse so you can't love in return.

Juliet: Most men would find that an inducement.

3. *I must make writing the real thing.*

I am almost sick for a cock, though I would not have it grow upon my chin:

(*Viola, a young boy, following around everywhere the man she loves even though he will have nothing to do with her.*)

Duke: Boy, I will no longer love.

Viola: I love you more than I love these eyes of mine, therefore more than I love what I see, more than I love the causes of my eyes: my life. I would follow you to the ends of the earth, but I'm scared you don't want me. I don't want to do anything you don't want.

Duke: For a month now you've been telling me you'll do whatever I want and you don't care for a woman.

Viola: Everything I say is always absolutely true and absolutely false because I'd give my will and judgement to you if only you'd have me.

Duke: Let me see what you look like when your legs are spread as wide as they can spread.

Viola: (*with her hand in her cunt*): I'm giving myself up.

(*She joyfully runs away. Joe enters, with letter.*)

Olivia (*to Joe*): What's that, fool?

(*Joe ignores her because she's over eighteen.*)

Read your letter.

Joe: This is the same as children learning in our schools: idiots telling crazies what reality's like: (reads the paper sententiously:)

YOU ASKED ME TO COME OUT HERE AND NOW YOU WON'T HAVE ANYTHING TO DO WITH ME. YOU WON'T TELL ME WHY. THIS IS THE SECOND TIME YOU'VE BURNT ME. I'M NOT A CHILD ANYMORE SO I DON'T CARE SO I'M NOT GOING TO MAIM MYSELF LIKE I DID THE FIRST TIME YOU HURT ME. I DON'T KNOW IF I SHOULD WRITE TO YOU.

Olivia: I'd better talk to Howard in person. Shit. (*To Joe.*) Tell Howard to come here.

(*Joe exits as Viola enters, naked and fantastically muscularly beautiful.*)

Duke (*to Viola*): As soon as I find myself in a room with you, I have to fuck you.

(*Joe and Howard enter.*)

Olivia: What's going on, Howard?

Howard: I don't know. You hurt me.

Olivia: Explain to me how I've hurt you.

Howard: You called me up over the phone I didn't call you. Over the phone you told me to go out on the streets, not wearing any skirts, with my cunt hairs and string black bikini showing through my half-white half-black tights, so everybody could see everything I own.

   still saying you want me, when then are you keeping me locked up in a dark house, visited by no one else but a priest, so I have no more friends? I'm screaming against unjust loneliness. Do humans treat each other in this way?

Olivia: I don't know if I ever wanted you or not, but I don't want you now. Learn to hear changes which are human or else die.

Howard: I hate you!

Duke: All of our desires are always changing.

2. *The world resembles sexual desire*

I Remember seeing my mother's dead body: It was Christmas Day so the morgue-men or the policemen or whatever-you-call-them wanted to get out of the morgue by four so they were kind of pissed-off I wanted to see my mother or had to see her. At that moment we (my sister and I) weren't sure it was my mother. She had been missing five days and the cops had found this dead female, etc. body in a room of the Hilton Hotel. We (my sister and I) walked down these plastic-like, they were probably metal, hospital-like steps. I can't remember the color of the steps. The door was the same material and (I slightly remember) pale green. I was frightened to look inside. There was nothing in the room. He wheeled one of those slabs hospital patients lie on when they're about to be cut into about a foot from the door. A dark green garbage bag lay over something on the slab. The morgue-man, I think he was black, pulled the garbage bag down from the top about one-third its length. The man standing behind us said, "You're going to have to identify her for us." The face was pale white until its lower third. The lower third was horizontal stripes. There was a bright bright red stripe. Below that was a white stripe. Then there was a swollen blue-purple brighter than any color. Actual seeing didn't give me the information this was my mother. All of me knew I was seeing my mother so I screamed. I said, "Yes, that's my mother." I didn't know. I said, "I don't recognize her." The morgue-man answered. "That's because she's been dead five days. Decayed bodies look like that." I replied, "I didn't know."

Upstairs they told me they didn't know how she had died. From the evidence they were sure, though it wasn't clear why they were sure, she hadn't suicided. We (my sister, I, and the family lawyer) thought she had suicided. Then it was either an accidental overdose of pills or murder. The police were not going to investigate it if it was murder because there wasn't enough evidence it was murder, an autopsy would take two months and by then all the evidence would have dissipated, and they had enough to do with important cases. Since I didn't have enough money to hire a private investigator until the money from the will came through, which my family lawyer informed me would take at least two years, I would have to probe myself or else walk away from this mess.

The uses of reductionism: the same desire to go over any edge or passion I had when I started to write; only now, having become frigid, I am choosing to want to go over the edges. Now uncontrollable violence or expressionism occurs within a chosen framework or will.

My father was a fascist. My mother, Susan, intensely repeated the matriarchal pattern of her side of the family. She never considered fucking a man other than my father once they were married, though he probably fucked whores to keep up his (male) business relations; but her fantasizing betrayed her daily with me. I willingly served her as much as I could until I began to revolt.

(I remember the taxi. Inside of a Checker cab I squeeze my mother's arm tightly I dare to touch the black baby seal of her coat. If I stroke it upwards, it's dark black. Downwards, it's light brown. I smell her armpits, a mixture of cold and warmth, of mud and those flowers that are absolutely tight unbloomed there is no fragrance. I'm allowed to touch. This desperation is)

When my mother was on the point of giving birth, I started to suffer from burning eyes. My father made me hold still on the kitchen table, opened the eye with his finger, and put something black in it.

My father is the power. He is a fascist. To be against my father is to be anti-authoritarian sexually perverse unstable insane. My father was tyrannical at home and extremely kind to and loved by the people who worked for him because he was alcoholic and paranoid. He was madly in love with my mother in a mistaken passionate possessive way. He drank more and more because the woman he loved didn't love him. He died when he was fifty-one. When he died he abandoned me. He took away my father. He believed in certain moral and social truths or ways to act just because that's what everyone believes and that's what he was taught to do. This is what liberalism is. Hypocrisy. He never really dared to question. He never had the courage to think. This is what centralized power is. I won't accept this.

To think for myself is what I want. My language is my irrationality. Watch desire carefully. Desire burns up all the old dead language morality. I'm not interested in truth. My father willed to rape me because in that he didn't want me to think for myself because he didn't think for himself. My father isn't my real father. This is a fact. I want a man. I don't want this man this stepfather who has killed off the man I love. I have no way of getting the man I love who is my real father. My stepfather, society, is anything but the city of art.

I will resurrect the city of art, I mean this, because it is there I and you this is the real desire.

For *City Limits:* I have nothing to do with the future: I don't envisage it. Writing, along with everything else, if they are any-thing, is right now. Writing is the making of pleasure as are everything else including death. Some nut a so-called publisher he looked like a hippy and was a multimillionaire which probably means he's a hippy just told me he intends to rewrite *Blood and Guts in High School* by taking out the violence. Why am I violent? Because I like violence. When something means something, that event (the first something) can't be just what it is present in itself. The abolition of all meaning is also the abolition of temporality.

In the City of Pleasure, and I mean we can are live there,

((the body, the body, that which is present, is the source of everything, and it has been made to disappear))

The Art-World Or The World Of Non-Materialism Is Becoming Materialistic Therefore The Society's Dead:

Pasolini's City: What I like sexually is that which outside the realm of sex disgusts me. So of course I am alone. Most people think I fuck around. I don't fuck around because in the words of Cavafy one of those voices to whom I listen I won't go after what I don't want. In the presence of want, there's no decision. I relish this loneliness and call it pleasure. I shut myself up in the Chia tower, purchased in 1970, sometimes with Ninetto sometimes alone. On top of a buttress placed over two gullies surrounding two conversant streams an outer castle wall protects a high tower. The tower is shut. A few rooms lie in the outer wall. I can never be adult. I absolutely don't understand how adult people act. I have been this way since childhood. Nothing changes none of the psychological characteristics which are presented like a terrain, but I am what I choose. I won't deal with the adult world and I refuse to make more than a surface pretense. Therefore one of my more stable desires is a man who'll take care of me in the world. Outside desire, I'm scared of men and despise the men who tell me what to do. My next-to-hugest disgust is people who want to own other people like certain poets who write to teach people. Therefore I like to fuck men I don't care for: I can't resolve this contradiction in myself: I don't fuck: this loneliness is masturbation. I could pay people money to fuck me or bribe with expectations of increasing fame and other worldly opportunities. Gay guys easily find young poor hustlers who'll spread their cheeks for a few tens. Older men offer young women a secure home, learning a career, etc. I likewise could offer something besides myself to get what I want, but I don't. I don't want what I want. This division in myself is infinite. I don't want what I want because if I got what I wanted I would have to give up because I don't know: the swarming and shouting of the architecture of the city I live in, junkies shoot up on the roofs two feet from one of the windows of the room I live in, a Mafia palace has hidden itself within the most poverty-stricken buildings streets. The rules by which we live: Sex and friendship don't have much to do with each other. To take desire cast it away and at the same time exaggerate the desire or ugliness in us so we can express it. To be honest with a person that I want to lick the feet, but to not care. Exaggerate pain because the government wants me to ignore what I feel. Never break up a friendship when a friend knifes you in the back. New York has made me open enough to disbelieve the validity of principles. Friendship, not love, is sacred and so must encompass violence. Work is everything.

(break into the above) His gallery dealer sold a double painting of his to a rich man. A portrait of two people. Three days later the gallery dealer phoned the artist said he had to paint another portrait because one of the portraits reminded the rich man of a friend he didn't like the rich man wanted another half though he had bought the double portrait. The artist agreed to paint what the rich man wanted because he justified to himself he thought it a commission. He finished the painting in a week then gave it to his dealer. The dealer said, "The rich man wanted a woman, not a man. You have three days in which to make a proper painting," and the artist agreed.

The two most powerful Roman galleries for relatively experimental art when they collaboratively present an artist's work make that artist's career (insofar as any one event can make an artist's career). One rich woman tells these gallery dealers who to show. Recently, the two galleries presented the work of a young painter who had had an affair with the woman and whom she fell in love with. The show sold out before it opened. The paintings are good. (Bitchy gossip. No art magazines or biographies mention these nexuses.) The wealthy woman still says this painter is the finest of the younger painters.

For art, as you will see, there has never been a favorable time; it has always been said that it must go a-begging; but now it will die of hunger. Whence might come that unaffectedness of spirit that is so necessary for its enjoyment and making, in times like these when sorrow is dealing everyone blows?

The most interesting: Everyone talks about these two young painters. Their paintings make a lot of money. In the past five years, when most people are becoming poorer and poorer, the selling prices of their paintings rose spectacularly. Today these paintings, despite the fact these painters are about thirty years old, dominate the market. What matters to me? Art. Art equal to sex. As soon as he got to Rome, he met artists. He hung around with them, alternately being a hermit and in the wildest most poverty-stricken areas of the city. I will give anything to do art. I think this is the only way to do art. But I must be more specific:

What is language? The discovery of the urban peripheries has so far has been essentially visual—I'm thinking of Marcel Duchamp's rationality or autism and Sheeler's social-realism that is discontinuity that is seeing without psychology. Wittgenstein seems to understand language as function, therefore, without psychology (by psychology, I mean the Freudian model of mentality); but by depending on a model of intentionality, he incorporates dualism. If I understand language in this manner: by saying something I intend something, then whatever I say means some other things because one event can be equivalent only to itself, (the Law of Identity). What is real is what is both real and unreal. The main controversy in the art world these days is money. You can call this controversy artistic and social. Are the paintings of the two young painters who are earning scads of money any good? The question is: Can paintings which aren't by dead or dying people and sell for fifty thousand each, I sell myself for fifty dollars, be any good? The question is: Are art and monetary profit compatible? The question is: Does capitalism which must be based on materialism or the absence of values stink? The question is: What is art? Is art worth anything in the practice of art making (of values) or is it craft? Can the making of values and nonvalue (money) occur simultaneously? In the Renaissance, the artist did what his patron told him to do:

I guess what's happened now is that everyone has died. If writing is the making (of values), I don't know where I'm supposed to find any values.

3. *The denial of sexuality*

Abolished. And her wing atrocious in the tears. Of the pool. Abolished whoever mirrors fears. Of naked gold whipping the bloody space a dawn has, heraldic feathers, chosen my tower of ashes, all the sacrifices which have happened. Fucking grave from which a beautiful bird flew away; whimsy alone black feathers dawn in vain. Again and again. The manor of decayed and sad countries. Pools of stagnant water, if these pools exist anywhere. The water our mirror reflects the relinquishment of the language here goes, drawn out autumn extinguishing in its own self its brand: Of the cunt hair when in the pallid mausoleum museum or when the plumage dipped its head, abandoned and made mad by the pure diamond of some—made desolate, but all this long ago. I can't remember. I'm whatever has been. There's no memory. Who will never shine. This is crime. This is butchery. Old dead dawn. Masochism. The blood of my cut-up eyes. Pool of blood (by mirroring) accomplice (to this death). There must be something else. And over the flesh-colors (that lie over the blood), open to its fullest the stained glass window.

Through the stained glass window: A peculiar room in a frame. Apparatus from when they used to wage war all the time. Extinct gold jewelry. In this room everything that seems to be alive is just memory. The upholstery, seeming to be mother-of-pearl, is useless; the in-tombs' eyes of sibyls present their old claws to men who've suffered. One of them, withered by history on top of history, on my dress bleached in whiteness and shut off from a sky of birds strewn among black-silver, (beginnings/flights/robberies perfumed and phantomed), a perfume which carries of cunt hairs a perfume far from the empty bed which a huge candle blown-out hid, a gold cold stink slipping beyond its holder, luxuriant and branched. The branches have been abandoned.

For two years every morning I woke up I thought about suiciding. I thought I was going to act like my mother who wildly spent two million dollars then suicided. I don't care about anything now.

Me—The World (this is what expressionism is):

I: Don't anyone come near me. I don't want anyone touching me. I'm an old woman. The shit-colored torrent of my immaculate cunt hair in the toilet when it's bathing my solitary body this fear of eternal solitude is making me ice. These tiny hairs which the light nets don't know death. I

am a picture. A kiss a real kiss not a one-night-stand would
kill me but beauty is frigidity . . .

Nurse: Masturbate yourself.

I: What can possibly attract me now? Do I even know these
mornings like every other mornings, no gods to believe in
therefore nothing, only the materialism of the government
of society all is the same therefore no more space no more
time: a constant melancholy. I'm not anymore relative to
this.

The Past Of Memory: You've seen me, nurse of the winter, under
the heavy prison of stones and iron where my old lions used to
drag along the lying ages enter.

The Entrance Into The Past: and I, fatal, walked, my hands bestial
claws, into the waste stink of ancient Egypt where they used to
fuck so much brothers would fuck their sisters.

I'm an object. Do you, reader, know anything about human
objects, what caused them: you with your clawings, your gripes,
your grippes, your petty boyfriend complaints? This, all this, is
object. Scream. I dream of being punished. Scream. I dream of
torment that will carry me over the edge and make me act without
considering the action. I dream of having a body and it and
thinking being one monster.

At The Same Time These Unless Thoughts're Occupying My Mind:
Obsessed from staring at the listless wreckage descending, I could
tell you about all the men I've loved who haven't loved me. I
think this is only I don't want to be loved. Cold mirror. Without
decreasing desire if you want to stay alive turn my desire into art.
My cunt hair imitating these too savage manners any return to
the bestial, help me, because all of you are no longer able to I
don't know if that's true because all of you're no longer simply
seeing me; just help me masturbate myself in front of this mirror.
I'm scared I'm going crazy.

Nurse: Rejecting myrrh bright in its closed bottle and the essence ripped out of the most faded roses, are you actually choosing only the faculty of death?

I: I keep trying to kill myself to be like my mother who killed herself. I kept working on the "Large Glass" for eight years, but despite that, I didn't want it to be the expression of an inner life.

Nurse: I'll always help you in crime.

I: You're still romantic. Stick this mirror like a stiff cock in front of my puss. Last night all I directly dreamt about was sex. I fucked men and women alternately. Why isn't there any sex in my waking life? Mirror: the above: water made into ice by boredom in your frozen frame, how many times for how many hours each time, cut off from dreams cut off from desire itself examining each memory which is everyone a leaf under your ice in an endless hole; no, the memory's not worth anything it's a false indication therefore of nothing; therefore I don't exist because there's nothing to see me with I live on the edge of existence; horror: nights, in your severe fountain, total nonconnectedness is my dream like being as naked as possible for everyone to see me stare up and down me pry into me. Why do Hydrox cookies taste like cunt juice?

Nurse: You're celibate so you're the object everyone wants to stare at.

I: Stop this romantic crime which's chilling my blood.

Nurse: Why stop it?

I: Stop your gesture. Against life.

Nurse: Why?

I: Why do you have so many feelings? Why be for or against anything? I'm against myself only because I hate any feeling and a human has feelings. How dare you, nurse, want to touch me and I can't be touched? I so desperately need to be touched. I can't be touched.

Nurse: This sick society that worships money or the lack of values has petrified and immortalized all our monstrosities. Your

mother's dead. Your father's dead. Your husband walked
away from you. You have no one in the world. You have
some money. You can do anything. New fury, mad and
scared of your madness which is just loneliness because,
being alone, you can only act and not react, . . .

I: Not even you're going to touch me?

Nurse: Will he come sometime?

I: What man would want to touch me? I'm savage. I don't want
a boyfriend now. I want no sense.

Nurse: You mustn't use violence except purposefully.

I: Woman born into this malignant society—according to all the
histories I've read humans are always malicious—you who
like all liberals work to hurt other humans; you can have
your humanness and your good intentions. According to
you, from out of my tits, smelling like delightful wild animals, leaps out the frigidity of my nakedness. Wild frigidity.
Take over everything! If just once the tepid blue of summer for whom every woman sheds herself would see me
in my shame/just as I am/unsocialized/celibate/dead. I am
pure.
     I die.

Nurse: So you're going to die, dope?

I: I am dead. I'm confused now because I'm being awakened.
     Now: waves rock each other and, there, do you know a
land where a dismal sky contains the sex which is always
hatred: this is where I am.
     Expressionism: So after six years of meditation, I'm back
to where I was: a life based on instant desire. Childish you
say in the same desperation, not to want to change.

Nurse: Goodbye.

I: My lips and I love you lies. I love you I lie. This is where I'm
at. I'm waiting for something I don't know. That's the truth.
Or maybe, not knowing that the unknown or screams exist
and are the only things that matter, keep expressing in writing and action your fascination with suicide which is just

childhood searching in its dreams to break down its precious frigid images. I want passion.

4. *War*

Beginning:

Already I can tell everything's closing in on me.

I want to list the possibilities or the lack of possibilities: I can no longer ask real questions. There's no way I can stop this from happening or even pretend it isn't happening. I can't control my looks. I have no power over what I do. I don't even understand what's happening. I don't understand what any event means. All I have is to hold on to each thing as it appears as it happens. The public CIA disclosure that they've discovered the Egyptian tomb changes everything and absolutely ensures he's going to die. But the details are the same. The details of death are always the same.

The apartment's house's entrance looks like every other entrance. A red or black door (of the usual size) and a few moldings in the frame top. The only thing that's unusual though it's not noticeable is that there's no door handle. There's a hole instead of a lock, latch, knocker, doorbell, etc. So the door might open to the right or it might open to the left. It's also possible the door's a fake. Don't consider any possibility which leaves you bound.

A classic triangular pediment is sitting over the stone frame whose columns are flat and flutings, vertical. The triangle holds in its lowest point a second triangle whose three points touch the first triangle's sides. The center of the second triangle is a bas-relief eye. But whereas most eyes in nature and in pictures are horizontal, this one's vertical. Its pupil is deep or a hole. The pupil is so high above the door it's impossible to tell what it is.

An electric device obviously works this door. A portable

machine small enough to be set up in one of the inner panels must be—now don't assume anything—I am always assuming everything—what can I say to you if I don't make assumptions?—how can I say anything about what's going on with me if I don't make assumptions?—the only thing I have are the words in this text I'm now looking at which I can give you only as I see them: these words are the details, whatever they mean. The detail of the stone eye sitting above the door frame doesn't mean anything. That's why it's forcing a new world.

My statement to you begins after a probable interruption all this giving the feeling that everything is uncertain and there are decreasing possibilities unlike an opera overture in which everything is false. I am catatonic.

Catatonic, yes, to be sure, but still there's something provisional, fragile, something tenuous a seashell enclosing a skinless creature. A cunt. In this world where the law of probability governs reality a quiet invisible threat hangs over everything. Fear now dictates all of our actions. Let me tell you I'm a what-you-may-call-it I can't move out of this room. Right before or rather at the moment of my father's death, I was at my father's death, I noticed a similar stopping; but that stopping (I think) was a stopping due to complete knowledge; whereas this stopping is only half-way. Maybe the whole thing is slowly dying, always this silent, at the edge of nothing; an imperceptible breath or whistling

The beginning of my report of what I saw:
as if a wind coming from nowhere is displacing every grain of sand of the beach. Without any apparent movement of its own it carries each grain to an abandoned terrace. A mass of tiny snakelike ripples, each ripple being parallel to every other, accumulates on top of the gray wood planks. The gray wood planks though they don't touch each other are one object. A blaze of sunlight powders paint which the footsteps of those who can't

sleep have already broken up. The ocean is pounding itself (into) a wave. Again and again the ocean is pounding itself (into) a wave. The wave is always tiny, long. So there seems to be no linear time. Owl hoots sound regularly. The dawn that makes the world rigid conceals every other sound. Ten feet above the ocean a huge pelican stands in the air. When he flies towards the right picture edge, the solid land or river-line or foam ripple being skirted, his wings' thundering noises mask the other beginning sounds. One foam wave disappears so rapidly and another foam wave appears so rapidly that there are no visible changes. I stand too far away in too low and secluded a spot to be able to tell what's going on.

On the opposite side of the picture than the one the pelican has now disappeared into, facing me, a colorless silhouette, a writhing spiral complexity, a thin boy who climbs on a horse. The horse's hairs move all over the place. The people in California insofar as I remember ride this way: trackless and pathless; now this side of him is in my face; now that side; so I see every aspect of his appearing and love. Coming closer and closer to me (as with love my objectivity disappears) the lengthy blue-black hairs twisting in the flakes of air he paws the ground and is circling almost around himself. A girl who's riding with neither spurs nor stirrups is trying to make her white mare go into the ocean; the mare is shying water is spurting out from all sides under its shaking hoofs among the clear laughs of the Amazon whose body is as sharp and bright as metal, suddenly, what I see, in this shifting light this.

Having almost reached the front of the picture, the male rider disappears behind me.

I see that I'm standing in the middle of jumbled chairs. These are piles of folding metal chairs on the terrace. Three men who're wearing leather jackets and weapons are coming towards me. They walk faster. They walk parallel and next to the ocean. Each one points the gun in his left hand down towards the sand. They are tracking something. They cock their guns. Having walked from the left to the right side of the picture, they walk even faster in the same step behind my back.

(A sound like a gunshot.) An even shorter silence. (A cry like a human who's being knifed.) Dead silence. A neigh. Silence. (A second identical sound like a shot from a Mauser which is the gun the National Guard uses.) The scream that's been going on this whole time stops. (*In the forest a gorgeous animal whose feathers're made out of flesh's name is female.*) The splashings from a body falling into the water at the same time as heavy steps at the same time as water throwing itself against the jetty, water throwing itself against an unexpected rock at the same time as the convergences of the unseeable minglings of its back-turnings and waves with the frightened-now-wild horse's clops. All these animal noises stop.

The world's gone dead.

With the return of calmness of the dead breath, there's unity that is I now have the possibility of naming and knowing what I see. *This is "partial death." Here is my punk expectation of the New Order.* (I mean the music group.)

A seagull who's holding a fish in its mouth flies over the almost dead ocean in a straight line across the picture. It's flight is such an exact reproduction of the pelican's flight that I'm not sure what my perception is. There's a shorter interval than the one between the first and second bird. A third bird flies over the almost dead ocean in a straight line across the picture. Its flight is such an exact reproduction of the pelican's flight, its wings batting sluggishly against the thick air bits of cardboard boxes condoms soda pop tops pieces of a stocking top a bullet; either it's one bird or it's all three birds disappearing into the horizon at the left side of the picture. I understand that "naturalness" depends on my perception or on who I am. The grayish vomit sands like the men with guns are closing in on me, little tongues are alive, snails move, without any hope of stopping. A fragile call girl is walking along the beach. She wears a dress I can see through.

*   *   *

*I'm telling you what I see with my own eyes. I'm reporting to you
who are my judges the only things I have: Robbe-Grillet's words.
. . . the cloth is floating and torn . . . the edges of the waves
. . . drags behind her . . .* The sands contained all kinds of crap:
bits of cardboard boxes condoms soda pop tops pieces of a stocking
top a bullet. The girl has stopped walking. Her whole back is
sticking into my face. The left foot which is resting on its toe
lifts upwards almost vertically. The shape of her breasts doesn't
change. The pale flesh gains a pink tinge. (What is perception?)

Her huge gray-green eyes' lost disconsolation staring at me a
few feet away from me what is it? I'm forced to turn my face
disguised by a false beard. Here a wood fence encloses an abandoned café. A partially mutilated advertisement still visibly presents the picture of a famous circus rider's blood-filled battle
against a mad bull. The circus rider's dress is red. I will do
anything for love.

What was really puzzling and at the same time totally fascinating
the cops who were investigating the murder was the fact, at least
they surmised that though the victim had been strangled, stran-
gling hadn't been the cause of his death. The murder must have
been more complicated than it appeared. For instance, despite
the skin's ghastly whiteness and the long marks ground into the
flesh under the cord that was lying around his neck, none of the
vertebrae had been broken. And the whole corpse was still luke-
warm, flexible, and intact. Also there were a number of miniscule
red points. These, unnoticeable and unevenly distributed over
the body, seemed to be needle marks.

The rest of the murder scene surprised me; I felt I was walking
into some kind of ceremony. Could it be the still-as-yet-unknown
Criminal Of The Second Hand had entered the room to finish
off his punishing?

Naturally I kept my ideas to myself. In as casual a tone as I could manage I asked the cops if they had gotten back the blood analysis. As yet no one had said anythng at all about the red stains under his fingernails and on the insides of the lips and knees, much less about a less apparent wound. But I hesitated, out of fear, asking them another question.

For instance: do these stains have anything to do with the mass of bloodstains could he have died as it seems by reacting to his massive blood transfusion or a heart attack from the amount he obviously had to fight the marks on his nails and teeth against something-or-other were they about to torch him or some other such horror as described in the UN account of torture in South America?

Actually I've become more interested in the mystery of the fur mantle. Had it disappeared just before the cops entered the room? They say they didn't see it then. I saw it when I came into the room. So who put it back into the room and why? Such an oversight or confusion isn't typical of that organization who again and again give us evidence of their meticulousness. Their execution is precise and to the second. I didn't have the time, unfortunately, before I had to get out of there, to look more carefully at that mantle made from a huge cat's skin or the luxurious curls of some other animal's back. They had rolled this object which I find the most significant of all into a ball and shoved it into a dark corner of the room. Unfortunately, I say again unfortunately, it had caught my attention at the very moment I realized I had to get the hell out of there.

Once I was away from their evil faces I must have been able to think because now I realized this was the cloth that was being dragged along the beach right in front of my eyes. Again I saw that mysterious girl, now even more clearly, the bloody animal skin she's trailing along the sand: This picture is reddish-gold, despite the dust from the shellfish who're sticking together between the black hairs and winding into a unity of corkscrews, so the dust is exactly the same color as her wild hairs. The only thing I can see is her back. Her right arm holds an old violin tightly against her hip. The violin's caseless. Now I know why her neck's bent the way it is.

Since she was walking too fast for me to follow her for very long, for the cane on which I was leaning was quickly sinking into that spongy ground, I swiveled my head towards the abandoned café. Two trench-coated men, hats over one of each of their eyes, were in the act of sitting down at one of the tables. They must have assumed there were waiters. He's holding a platter and has a napkin draped over his arm. (I perceive what I've been told to perceive.)

Just as I'm gazing fixedly, two hands clamp down on my arms. They hold me in a double stranglehold. They are looking at me. They are telling me what to do. The world is my desire. It's so simple. I don't need eyes to know that several men are surrounding me. I have dreamt this many times. I cannot escape. There's something genetically wrong with my hormones. If I perceive it, I've been told it. If I dream it, is it true? They haven't made a mistake. I no longer need to be told or given art in order to perceive what they want me to perceive.

This is my last thought before I disappear: I'm living without emotions because desire's the only thing that can save me.

That's it. I can no longer speak. I've been trained to be catatonic or a dog. I might as well tell you the same story again and again. *This is the season of my torment.*

It began at the same time as or just as the *Daily News* article said just like a fairy tale. A police chief named Frank V. Francis on his holiday and wandering around for the first time in his memory is walking down a certain street. On this street, stuck into one of the gutter-grills whose purpose is to get rid of possible rain overflows but is rather an inefficient garbage disposal he finds a woman's tiny shoe. At first he doesn't notice this object though it hardly goes with the usual jumble of cardboard boxes condoms

soda pop tops pieces of a stocking top and bullet shells that have
fallen out or that the rats and bums have taken away from the
garbage cans and only half-eaten or hidden. The shoe is almost
new. The only thing that seems to be the matter with it is that
its red stiletto heel has been almost totally torn away from the
sole—but it's easy enough to fix this with a hammer and three
nails—there's no need to go to a shoemaker. (The objective conditions of what is.)

Immediately after that they started their questions. As a rule
there were two of them. It was impossible to recognize any of
them cause you could never tell one from the other. They are
all the same height. They never move from the positions in which
they're standing. Their coats which look dark are always totally
buttoned over their bodies and their hats, slouched over one of
each of their eyes, put the rest of their faces into shadow. I can't
tell forms anymore because the camera lights are directly in my
eyes. (If sight's no longer a tool, are any of the perceptions?)
Although they ask me questions, there's no way I can rely on
my ears to understand what's happening because the rotation of
these questions is robot-like and they say nothing out loud to
each other. When they communicate to each other, they use
tiny, almost imperceptible gestures. One hand or a head nod.
One of these hands must be holding an umbrella handle because
every time they interrupt my speech, there's a violent knocking
on the metal floor.

The unknowns (you the readers) are questioning me the writer so
you can judge me. This writing is the way it is so I can escape
you:
—"Because such a situation might occur, the student, let us call
him a student, had taped a syringe to his lower thigh. Over the
syringe he placed the soft calf of his boot. Was she wearing the
same kind of shoe for this very reason? Your defense system, as
we've recently learned, doesn't call for white boots. And in the

second version of your story, you said she was wearing a shoe with a red stiletto heel. Do you remember this writing?"—"I don't remember any writing cause I don't know what I write so you can't pin me down. I might haphazardly take away parts of the writing. Even if I don't these are just the words I copied from a book by Robbe-Grillet. I don't even know French and I don't care. I don't want to control you by telling you what reality is just as you try to control me." This answer is easy for me cause I'm bored with this writing: that is, I'm not into it because it isn't obsessive what isn't obsessive I call torment. (Directly about perception.)

—"I want to find out just why you're telling us this story. Take those tables you told us about . . . an empty room . . . the hotel in ruins . . . the waiter who's really a waiter . . . You told us the tables in *Maximilien's* stood in straight lines around the fountain. You've certainly been precise about all the details in the story that are absolutely irrelevant. Again: you're just trying to escape us. You'll have to tell us about the parts of the story that matter if you want us to believe you. For instance, remember we're talking about murder, did that waiter who you made such a point of saying was acting properly, put your food on your table or on the student's?"—"On neither. He placed coffee and a basket filled with brioches on the third table. This table which stood a bit in back of ours formed a sort of isosceles triangle . . ." (Again the sound of the umbrella handle hitting the floor violently)—"Was this the reason you forgot to bring your black notebook?"—"What black notebook? I don't know what you're talking about."—"We're talking about the black notebook in which the so-called student was in the habit of putting down what was happening and what he thought was happening during his work. You know this notebook and you know what's in it: the way you described those tables is exactly how they're described in the notebook. That's why we were asking you about the tables. We want to know about the notebook.

"There are some further points to consider: Now, there was a bottle on the student's table. There's no way the waiter could have brought this bottle. Remember your saying the waiter didn't put anything on the student's table? You say this bottle was still full at the moment you intervened. You also say this bottle contained an antidote to the intravenous injection, an antidote which a little later all of you tried out on her. Now how was this antidote supposed to work on the student if he hadn't drunk it?

"We're going to start again with you. We want to find out why you've been telling us what you're telling us. We want meaning that is we want control."

The only thing I want is all-out war.

2 LANGUAGE

1. Narrative breakdown for Carla Harriman
In the year 1413 I went in search of my true love. There was a
camp full of milling people. A beautiful young boxer who's the
son of a rich man is buying horses. I called him to me. I told
him he's my brother by our father. I put him up for the night
in my house. In the toilet he fell into the shit. I stole his money
while he escaped from my house. He knocked at the door of my
house and my servants: "You're crazy; we don't know who you
are." A bum told him to stop disturbing his sister. They found
him out by the smell of his shit. An old woman told the following
tale: It is a place of sacred practice. Art isn't about the sacred. A
beautiful young man sneaks up to the garden. The beautiful
young man pretends to be mute. He is the new gardener and the
nuns treat him as a pet. The nuns want his cock. Cock is the
action that makes you go mad. The nuns hit him with a stick.
Then they drag him into a hut. His cock's small. Oh ooooh ooh.
Heaven, for all we know, has arisen. Both the nuns are smiling.
All the other nuns want to. All the women are after cock. Will
the man die? Old ugly hag Mother Superior gets hold of this
boy's cock. Ten men (much less this boy) can't even satisfy one
female and a cock is a miracle. "You're a robber you're a forger
you've raped women, etc; maybe you should get out of town a
bit until things cool down. You're so evil, you're the person to
collect my debts." So I went to a town out in the grass. Men
pushed along a cart of skulls. The queen wore a basket over her
head and extended a shovel with a skull sitting on top of it.

Giotto's best pupil has come to paint Naples. The painter who is one of the finest painters around wears rags. Are all our friends poor? The painter looks like an imp. This imp is maddened. Mauled. Big plump Casaba melons lie on the road. Don't make me die of love. If you fuck me, I won't die. When the painter eats with the monks, his table manners are atrocious.

I am a slave because they're auctioning me. I'm a young boy. I pick a young boy to buy me. I give him my money. I tell him where to get us shelter. We fuck there. He's so very young, he doesn't know how to fuck. Soon he figures it out. No: I show him. I'm a great artist. I tell my new boyfriend to sell my art but not to a white man because a white man'll separate us. When I sell it to a white man, he follows me. My girlfriend tells me a story. Can the poets speak about what they haven't experienced? Slowly I penetrated her. My cock wouldn't go in easily cause she was tight along the upper part of her mucus tunnel. The muscles felt good around the end of my cock. I had to come. As soon as it sprang out of me I passed out. When I, the girl says, woke up I saw him lying in the bed next to mine, looking like the rose fallen out of the midnight. I had to have his cock, she said. I had to have his tongue. I had to piss over his flesh. I rubbed my clit and the upper cunt corners against his pelvis bones sharp I came five times. I fell asleep. When I woke up, he was gone.

In the Fifth Precinct which is where I used to live the cop who's the head likes to arrest anyone he sees fucking or making Voodoun or hustling and libeling or robbing the local churches or forging checks or issuing false contracts or priests who use their parishes to get rich or lending money or simony whatever that is. Most of all he hates sex. He takes all these offenders' money. When they can't pay him what he wants, he makes sure they're locked up longer than they should be. This is the way he remains the head cop (rich man). Also he eats at any restaurant in the neighborhood he wants to free of charge and gets any store object he desires. If a local store owner doesn't pay the police chief the monthly garbage bill, the owner has to close his store because he's been violating sanitary laws. The East Village, part of which is this Fifth Precinct, is the filthiest space in the world.

The police chief has a Special Assistant. This Assistant is thin sly greasy locks dribble down his forehead and he collects five to eight-year-old boys who're greasier and fart more than he does. They must have been spit out of their mothers' assholes between fits of constipation because they're so much smoother and more poisonous and gaseous than turds these little sausages can slip around everywhere and see everything. The children know every-thing. They know where the Families in the neighborhood (I'm talking about the Mafia) keep their money in secret mansions way inside surrounded by rows of the poorest apartment buildings around Tenth Street. The Special Assistant uses these children for information and also to capture the few people who still dare to fuck. These people fuck because they need to fuck so badly and it's now so hard to get laid they need to fuck so badly, by the time they announce to themselves they have to fuck they'll do anything to fuck, they'll fuck anyone one of these slimy kids. The kid tells the cop. The Special Assistant has his junky des-perate for his junk so he makes whatever terms he wants. The Special Assistant is a sexual pervert but mad because he never fucks but gets exactly what he wants without ever compromising himself. I'm telling you all this because I'm a monk.

The Special Assistant also has a squad of pimps. You under-stand that he's not a hypocrite. By no means. He'd use any means if he was smart enough. He tolerates pimps whom otherwise he would be joyously grinding into the nonexistent dirt and the existent shit on the street because they tell him dirt the children can't tell him. Their girls or trash learn where the businessmen (dealers, gunmen, etc.) hide their monies and tell the pimps and the pimps tell. This way also the Special Assistant is constantly checking the children's information against the pimps' infor-mation and vice-versa and no one's ever let off the hook. This is democracy: no overt governmental control. The Special As-sistant isn't as moral as his boss which is why he's lower down the business hierarchy so he pimps on the side. He pimps so he can run his own blackmail sideline. Unlike his boss he loves sex because he's making a fortune from it.

One day since the sun was shining the Special Assistant decided to go after new ducks: old women because old women walk around mumbling to themselves drop their purses and are helpless. While the Special Assistant stood on the corner of Fifth Street and First Avenue and looked for an old woman, a tall Puerto Rican walked by him. The Puerto Rican wore a large black hat and a black jacket. The Puerto Rican looked at the Special Assistant. "What d'ya want, white boy? Do ya want anything with me?" "I don't want anything. Yet. Right now," the white boy replied. "I need a real criminal." "So you can't go after anyone you want. You white boys don't have any power no matter how many badges you wear. You just do what the big tops tell you to do." The Special Assistant couldn't admit he was powerless. "Me, I'm after someone myself," the Puerto Rican flips some kind of card into his face. "I also belong to an Agency. If you're looking for some-one, why don't you hook up with me? I own the territory over there," pointing south towards the Lower East Side, "and there're lots of junkies over there. It's easy to make money." The Special Assistant knew a good money deal. They walked down the street.

"How're we going to make money? And, especially, how do you make money, you who live on the other side of the law?"

"Since my life's always in jeopardy because of the color of my skin, I blackmail, extort and simply take as much as I can from those who are more helpless than me."

"I have a job and I do the same thing," said the cop. "I have one moral: If it's too hot for a fence, give it to a cop. You have to be tough to live in New York. I'm so tough, there's no tragedy that could make me even blink. I'm beyond those intellectual liberals because I don't depend on anybody's opinion. Are you as tough as I am?"

For the first time the Puerto Rican realized he could have this white cop, so he began to smile. "I'm a dead man," he replied.

"I live in hell. Just like you I spend all my time looking for humans I can get something from and just like you I don't care how I get it."

"I see. You're Vice Squad."

"No. I'm not human. I'm using a human form because I'm trying to fool you."

"If you're not human, who are you?"

"I'm nonhuman. We nonhumans unlike you humans who are stuck only use forms to get what we want."

"If you're so powerful, why do you even bother with human beings?"

"You're so much more powerful than old women and junkies and young girls and yet you prey off of them. This is the way the world is. I'll give you an answer: When you're murdering someone, you think you're murdering because you're getting something out of it. But like me you vulturize because you get nothing. You and I are made. We are part of this almost un-bearable worldly pain which isn't disappearing."

"Do you always lie?"

"If I always lied, a lie wouldn't be a lie. Sometimes Puerto Ricans tell the truth. Sometimes we Puerto Ricans are so ro-mantic we tell some woman we totally love her she believes we adore her we can fuck over her whole life we do she learns that another human being is capable of absolutely conscious decep-tion. You don't have to learn anything from me. From this moment onwards you're going to see so much pain because you're going to cause so much pain that no artist will be able to tell you nothing. No human being can remain naive. If you hurt somebody, nobody can hurt you. There's no natural laws. There's no natural justice or morality. Politicians or rather those in power have made up that liberal jive so they can keep their slaves or excuse me cuntstichyouwents in check. I'll just trot along by your side, bro', until you do so much evil, you're ready to stick a knife in my back. This is the way people in New York City live."

"I won't become so evil," the Special Assistant swears with his hand over his heart, "because I'm a New York City cop. I've sworn to protect human life. I'm going to take a second oath. I swear that I love you and regard you as absolute evil and that I'll do so until the end of time. I'm white and you're black and you're my brother."

"And you are mine," the fiend replies. This is the neighborhood he was speaking about. Half of the buildings have broken glass for windows. Behind each broken glass is an unseeable space. The doors and some of the windows are wood boards. Men waiting for their junk sit on what there is for floors inside these buildings. Children and fat women whose tits are hanging out of their bras crowd the doorways and doorsteps of the occupied brownstones. Seven men are sitting on chairs outside the corner bodega. On the sidewalk two children fight each other with sticks. "Give me that junk," the child says as he raises his stick. "I hate you," says the other child, "because last night you had my sister." "I hope you die. Jesus Christ should come down and forsake you and the Evil One should hold you in his arms." They fight again.

"Those kids need to be taught what's right and what's wrong," the Special Assistant thought to himself, "and I can make a little money on the side." He whispered to his friend, "Don't you want to take him?"

"They don't mean what they're saying," his friend replied. "They're only imitating what their parents say." The children are kneeling on the edge of the sidewalk. There's a huge spider trapped between a glass jar and the cement. They let the spider free. The moment the spider moves, they trap it again.

"Human beings say one thing and mean another. That's what they mean by language. Let's get further into this neighborhood where there's more desperation. It's only when humans are totally desperate that they speak the truth."

The white man speaks. "I know where I am. There's a Jew in this Puerto Rican and black hovel who doesn't give up a penny even when a mugger's holding a knife to her eye. Either she's going to give me a hundred and twenty dollars for a payoff or

I'm going to jail her. I'm a cop, aren't I? I have to make my living. The taxpayers won't give me enough money."

"You're still using liberal excuses," the fiend instructs him.

To show how evil he is, the cop kicks in the old blind dumb and almost deaf cunt's stomach. "What do you want?" in a little old woman voice. "Excuse me, ma'am." Kick again. "I've got orders here to arrest you." She doesn't bother asking what for. "Now?" "Open up this door. I have to take you to jail." "I don't want to go to jail. I just had an operation yesterday. My doctor said if I don't stay still, I'm going to die. No one takes care of me cause my daughter's husband just left her so she killed herself so there's no one to help me go to jail." "The law doesn't take account of disease, ma'am." "How can I stay alive?" "Pay me a hundred and twenty dollars." "I don't have a hundred and twenty dollars. Do you think an old woman who lives with junkies and alcoholics and sub-welfare families has a hundred and twenty dollars lying around the house?" "If I don't either arrest you or get a hundred and twenty dollars, may I go to hell."

"OK. What did I do wrong?" "When your husband was alive, you fucked another man." "I never got married. So whenever I fucked, I fucked out of love. Madly for love. Desire has nothing to do with justice anyway. Go to hell." Quickly the fiend asked, "My dear, do you really mean what you're saying?" The foul old bitch who was foul only because she was old and not because she wanted to cause anyone pain answered, "I hope you die or go to hell if you keep trying to rob me."

"Rather than rob you, I'm going to take everything you've got."

"Don't be angry, bro', cause now you're getting everything you wanted. I'm going to take you to hell where the only thing you can do is evil."

If God has made all of us in His image, part of this image is pain and hell.

They go down to hell. On the way the cop sees a painted forest. There, the trees are knotted, stubby, and leafless.

The pickpocket. Bloodless Fear. This smiling man carries a

knife under his coat. Black smoke lies around the fire of the burning block. Humans murder other humans asleep in their beds. The body opens wounds blood all over all the flesh. There're all sorts of sounds in this place. I see the man who commits suicide. I see the mother who commits suicide. The blood in her heart, slipping out of, soaks her cunt. At night the hammer pounds a nail through the forehead. The dead people's mouths are open wide.

Bad Luck's sitting in the middle of the floor. His face is all weazled and squinched up. Madness in the center of Madness laughs which is total pain. Complaining bickering hating all feeling jealous keeping all this hate and anger bottled under the skin; all the isms are the psychology here. Every group of skinny trees has under them dogshit and a body whose throat is cut open. The tyrant takes whatever he wants. Simply. As a result a country is destroyed. Haiti. Vietnam. There's nothing left to the country. There's no time here. Ships are burning up. Wild bears sink their teeth into the man who hunted them. The pig struts into the bedroom and eats the child in the cradle. Madness goes everywhere. The cook scalds his arms by his long ladle. Above the poverty-stricken peasant lying under his cart's wheel Conquest or Fame, which is the only One people honor, rises; criminals are the politicians; conquest 1 gives way only to conquest 2; humans are killing themselves because they're choosing to love humans who don't love them.

From this time onward, war came to Ectabane. Lots of slaves escaped, went to those conquering, but when the conquerors tried to make them give specific details about the resistance of the occupied, the slaves refused to tell their former owners' names. And their situations became worse; the slavery was more intense. Ectabane is the largest Western capital. Every day the beaches below the boulevard which line the sea wear as clothes corpses. At the ocean-front guards shoot all the resisters who land during the nighttime. The conquerors took over painlessly: the city wanted to get rid of gods and masters. The shoed helmeted armored

conquerors halted the sexuality and the perception of the con-
quered. For a hundred years they had halted everything. Then
the Ectabane wise men in secret made a weapon capable of
resuscitating their land. The conquerors stole the weapon. They
constructed an airplane into which they could put the weapon.
They flew the wise men and the weapon to their city Septentrion.
The remaining dissidents the adventurers con men mercenaries
fighters they pursued even beyond Ectabane's boundaries. They
had to use both informers and cruelty to control some of the
families who lived in the city's center: at night their children
ran to other parts of the world; other children started out for
those underground rivers in the Southern coast which the
Buxtehude Archipelago joins. As of yet the Archipelago is
still free, but blackened every moment by the enemy bombers'
shadows.

On the day his country capitulated a young Ectabanese officer
whom the General Staff despised because he had been trying to
modernize their army fled to this Archipelago under the aegis of
diplomatic immunity—as the ambassador extraordinaire of his
country. They had instructed him to convince the as-yet free
Archipelago to fight the enemy as much as possible. Buxtehude
gave him a hotel room in a spa. He put photos of his wife and
children who were still in Ectabane on a shelf. Then he set up
a small radio with which he could send information back to
Ectabane. He told the Archipelago to resist the enemy as strongly
as they could. Get rid of all political apathy. Use all the arms
and weapons you've left to rot in your forgotten barracks. Soon
all of Septentrion, the whole Western continent which is only
part of the East, will be flaming! The conquerors will never have
enough fires to burn away the secret ashes and wastes and garbage
of their souls or of their blood so that tears can start flowing! In
downtrodden defeated Ectabane, dawn the day the city was over-
taken, I sat on top of a balcony of the triumphal arch and watched
the whole city which was still asleep: A boot hit the sidewalk. A
rat scurried across the balcony. A security guard sticking his head

under a bunch of flowers banged it on the table outside. The wind which was alive dried up his blood. One of the enemy security bending down wiped up the dried blood with his handkerchief. He tapped the knee of the Ectabanese guard who slowly managed to get vertical, "The old dolts, the priests and everyone who loves this our country have freely elected a president who pleases the enemy."

The people in the world blow up the world. After the end of the world.

One. One and one. One and one. One and one. One and one. One and one. One and own. One and one. One and one. One and one.

One and one and one. One and one and one. One and one and one. One and one and one. One and one and one. One and one and

One and two. One and two and no more. One and two. One and two no more. One and two. One and two no more. One and two.

One two and. One two and. One two and. One two and. One two and. One two and. One two and. One two and. One two and. One two.

On. On. On. On. On. On. On. On. On. On. On. On. On. On. On. On. On. On. On. On. On. On. On. On. On. On. On. On. On.

On and. On and. On and. On and. On and. On and. On and. On and. On and. On and. On and. On and. On and. On and. On and.

Candor honor. Candor honor. Candor honor. Candor honor. Candor honor. Candor honor. Candor honor. Candor honor. Candor honor.

Can do one more. Can do one more. Can do one more. Can do one more. Can do one more. Can do one more. Can do one more. Can do one more. Can do one more. Can do one more. Can do one more. Can do one

Can murmur murder mirth. Can murmur murder mirth. Can

murmur murder mirth. Can murmur murder mirth. Can murmur murder mirth.

This is. This is a saying. One. Can murder mention one. This is a saying.

Stop. Not it. Can it is. Can it is. Can it is. The hat on the steps of. The windowpane is by now.

The sea flows scaffold for the sheep. I came come of the being. Androgynous draggles.

Two and three and five. Two and three and five. Two and three and five. Two and three and five. Two and three and five.

Accent her. Hand armors on wonder. Orphan forces war or instance of ovary. The manor of stove.

An instance of romance. Or form. Or form. Or form. Or form. Or form. Or form. Or form. Or form. Or form. Or form. Or form.

An land. An land. An land. An land. An land. An land. An land. An land. An land. An land. An land. An land. An land. An

And scape escape romance. And scape escape romance. And scape escape romance. And scape escape romance. And scape escape romance. And . . .

2. *Language breakdown*

Bats of boxes in the houses. Delight layering the accesses. Exquisite and excess urinals devour. So we. Glowerings glowerings sail.

Reins breasts and the polar rains turmeric. Along of in the polar down and police no dark no ark sightings away sight. To the lines long eerie aeries are we we we. The owes. He whispers whimpers whimpers.

Come out to the light: of squares of sturgeon of sturgeon and on on an under the dark and dark. Dark. On. On. On. On. On and under one. On and under two. On and under three. The sticks hunt vertical. Three sticks hunt vertical. Murderers remain demands. Murderers remain subversion. Houses veer bicy-cles. I.

Daylight. Obstetrician. Axe. Demanding. Who they are. Swing. A restaurant.

Do you disturb eyes? Do you disturb tampax? Eyes foment off. Of reminiscing. Waste rebellion fast you lose.

In the square. What did she do? Hands flouresce. The tip of the clit suggest augmentation. Of treacherous. Lights murmurs. Hair egomaniac.

Was there danger? There usury. There objects of. There ec-centricity. There notorious. There you. There accumulation. There simultaneous. There acquiescence. There dumb. There upset.

While walking, she was dreaming. Policeman wings boards off how. And under thatches of under of this. The lights blank how whispers a lot. To two lips.

Of these projects backs on bouquets. Wastebaskets glowing stabs knickers.

She moves. Therefore ways of moving. One sound done. Two the reduction to what is essential.

Two the reduction to what is essential. We don't reduce: we start nothing or bottom up. Hands hang rape. Hands flatter bad. Hands wing flutter. Hands lost record. Hands record corduroy. Hands grip colds angry black knife. Hands weaving blasts wonders often frozen. Hunger aggression.

The late skies of listening recalls claims two. Toward. The blisters baskets squires rues under hay and wise men anger. Her-ald blisters hunger is plausible lubberings crows an. Language thinking.

3. *Nominalism*

I want to talk about the quality of my perception. I want the quality or kind called childhood cause children see the sadness which sees this city's glory. What does this sentence mean? I can wander wherever I want. I simply see. Each detail is a mystery a wonder. I wander wonder. The loneliness feeling is very quickly lost. So I can see any and everything. I can talk about everything as a child would. The interior or my mind versus the exterior. Art proposes an interiority which no longer exists for all of us are molded. The nightmare that I fear most is true. This writing's outdated. Yet you walk around the city. Is this realization the source of your melancholy? I love you. You're my friend. I'm masturbating now. I have someone to talk to like I talk to my stuffed animals. Of course this life's desolate, it's lonely when there's no mentality. This sentence means nothing. More and more submerged the mind, you trace its submergence through Baudelaire; now it's gone. Fashion is the illusion there's a mind.

Walking through the cities, being partly lost, the image (in the mind) change fast enough that the perception which watches and judges perception is gone, is the same as the living in the place where I can do anything in which every happening is that which just happens. Saint-Pol Roux, going to bed about daybreak, fixes a notice on his door: "Poet at work." The day is breaking.

Language is more important than meaning. Don't make anything out of broken-up syntax cause you're looking to make meaning where nonsense will. Of course nonsense isn't only nonsense. I'll say again that writing isn't just writing, it's a meeting of writing and living the way existence is the meeting of mental and material or language of idea and sign. It is how we live. We must take how we live.

To substitute space for time. What's this mean? I'm not talking about death. Death isn't my province. When that happens that's that; it's the only thing or event god or shit knows what it is that isn't life. To forget. To get rid of history. I'm telling you right now burn the schools. They teach you about good writing. That's a way of keeping you from writing what you want to, says Enzensberger, from revolutionary that is present. I just see. Each of you must use writing to do exactly what you want. Myself or any occurrence is a city through which I can wander if I stop judging.

It could happen to someone looking back over his life that he realized that almost all the deeper obligations he had endured in its course originated in people on whose destructive character everyone was agreed. He would stumble on this fact one day, perhaps by chance, and the heavier the blow it deals him, the better are his chances of picturing the destructive character.

Wandering through the streets and creating a city: Berlin's a deserted city. Its streets're very clean. Princely solitude princely desolation hang over its streets. How deserted and empty is Berlin!

The first street no longer has anything habitable or hospitable on it. The few shops look as if they're shut. The crossings on the streetcorners are actually dangerous. Puerto Ricans whiz by in cars.

At the end of the next event is the Herkules Bridge. There's a block-long park that runs along the river. Here when I was a child as soon as I could walk I spent most of my days. I had a nurse. At first I didn't have as many toys as the other children. Then I had a tricycle. Later I had a cap gun. We would try to shoot pigeons with our cap guns. If your cap gun shot a pigeon in the eye, pigeons are the only living animals around, you blinded the pigeon and then could capture it bring it home to make pigeon soup the most wonderful delicacy in the world. Neither I nor anyone else ever captured a pigeon. The river which was pure garbage brown was crossed by a bridge on my right as I looked from the park out over the river. This bridge was the Herkules Bridge.

I used to have a strong dream about the garbage river. It was the most magical place. If only I could cross it, on the other side. Desire is the other side. During the day I can't cross it. Suddenly, in my dream, I can. Go over the low cement wall black iron bars curving out of upwards towards me, down a three- or five-foot hill that's mainly dirt and some bushes, my feet kick small rocks rolling, downwards. Here's the water at my feet. Here's flat sands forming a triangle narrowing towards the north I can walk on it. I'm walking on top of a narrow evenly wide sand ribbon across the river which isn't deep. I reach the other side. The other side is a carnival. The beach is still here. Here's a merry-go-round. All around the beach's white and onwards. I walk onwards on the magic ground. There are many adventures as I walk straight northwards.

The other park I used to go to, the park that contained New Lake on Rousseau Island, was much further from my house. I'd go only with my grandmother who lived a few blocks away in a large hotel, I'll talk about her later, or with mommy although mommy almost never spent her time with me. In fact, I now remember, I never went to the park with mommy unless other friends accompanied us. The park or rather this part of the park which was its southernmost tip, in my mind the boot of Italy, bordered on a line of almost white expensive residences and hotels. Differently colored cars whirring back and forth separate the residential buildings from the park. There was a lake and ducks. On the far side of the lake, luxuriant dark greens brown. I can't get over to the luxury. I sit on a large rock. The rock's not large enough to be a hill. It's large enough to have two holes to crawl within, not really into, and to climb for five minutes. Three roads, one dirt and two asphalt-and-stepped, swerve through the short dog-shit-covered grass, down to it. I'm sitting on top of the rock and looking across the lake, to my right so far in the distance I don't know if it really exists there's a carnival. During one winter, when it's very cold, I can skate on this lake which has grown very small which snow surrounds. A small brown terrier has placed his butt on the northeast end of the lake. Two and three foot high ridges of snow surround the lake. There aren't any children here as there are in the other park. At this time, I liked this park better than the other park. Then my grandmother would take me back to her hotel room.

Everything's alive.

When I was older, a boyfriend would walk with me through other parts of this park. No, first I went to school. When they couldn't drag us for exercise on the chilliest coldest fall days out to the level short green hockey fields way uptown, they took us for a treat to the part of the park nearest the school. Several asphalt and dirt paths of varying widths having absolutely no order crossed here and quickly changing growths of trees still thickly-green-leafed high among densely green valleys not big enough to be valleys and curving like eye contact lenses; I remember metal statues of Alice-in-Wonderland and the Caterpillar-on-the-Mushroom my boyfriend who was bearded and I would crawl under, ladies in precisely tailored suits walked their dogs, near one of the long rough stone walls that separated this park from the very wealthy residential and religious buildings was a park only children under a certain age played.

Only spaces in which I can lose myself whether I'm now sensibly perceiving or remembering interest me. It's because I live to fill a certain dream. I have penetrated to the innermost center of this dream. The center has three parts.

1. My most constant childhood experience is pain.

No, no knowing, just the present. A wholly unfruitful solution to the problem but all fruit these days is death, no as I grow older I don't think it's any worse or better now than before historically for humans I don't know I know less and less as I get older, the flight into sabotage and anarchism. The same sabotage of social existence is my constantly walking the city my refusal to be together normal a real person: because I won't be together with my mother. I like this sentence cause it's stupid.

2. Who do I know? I go over this question again and again because the people I know in this world are my reality stones. I know Peter and David and Jeffrey, and secondarily Betsy, and lots of other people whom I only half know. Peter and David who live together half of each of them is my grandmother. They have a small three-room apartment. They have certain nice belongings. They're proud of their living. They live more quietly than the people in the neighborhood they live in do and the people they know who are mainly rock-n-roll stars. I often debate with myself whether they're kind or not.

They're my closest friends. Sometimes I start to cry cause I feel so glad and lucky I know them and have been admitted into their hearts this feeling is almost too much so I say to myself you're just transferring your need for the affection you're not getting from a boyfriend. Lacking a boyfriend's one of the many thoughts society's taught me. All the thoughts society's taught me're judgemental, usually involving or causing self-dislike, imprisoning, and stopping me. When I just let what is be what is and stop judging, I'm always happy. Peter and David are two of the most happy people I know.

I got a cat this week, but the minute the cat kitten long light dark gray black white hairs hints of brown pale blue gray green eyes jumps into my house I can't give this much affection the kitten torn away from its mother demands something mental in me rends, I don't want to love inappropriately, I'm too something to be touched. I invent an allergy and run the cat back to its mother.

3. I didn't know anything about death (the first time I experienced death and saw a dead person it was my suicided mother when I was an adult) nor about poverty. The first time the word "poverty" meant anything to me (to understand this word I had to wait until I was judging my experience and not just experiencing), I thought I was poor because I had less than the girls in my grade who were of my class and because my boyfriend in the fancy nightclub to which he had taken me said, "Tell your mother to get you a nice dress," and I knew she would never. In college I learned for the first time that my family was rich. (How does the word "poverty" differ from the word "death"?) Does this kind of knowledge which is really only belief change my actual experiences? Of course:

I'm making my dream. The mappings, the intertwinings, so hopefully there'll be losing, loosings, my mother said I hate you.

Let the rocks come tumbling out. Move crack open the ice blocks. You hurt me twice. No one hurts me twice, bastard. You said "Don't talk to me again" and "I'm saying this for no reason at all." First off (in time), after six years of living with me one night you said. "This is it." I said that I didn't know it had been getting so bad and could I have one more chance and you said no. My whole life busted itself. I recovered almost I almost didn't I do everything you want I always have, to, of, from, for I love you, you don't love me. One month ago you said, "I don't want to be friends with you any longer." This time I was innocent. You've hurt me again, I want you to know this time really badly. I don't understand how someone can be such a shit as you are. I think you are really evil. No one hurts another person for no reason at all. No one believes in him- or herself so totally, the other person has absolutely no say no language. This' how this country's run.

The media's just one-way language so the media-makers control.

I'm diseased. I hate you. There's this anger hot nauseating in me that has to seep out then destroy.

I hate the world. I hate everyone. Every moment I have to fight to exert my will to want to live. When I lived with a man, I was happy. I always was miserable. I like banging my head into a wall. I'm banging my head my head into a wall.

One might generalize by saying: the technique of reproduction detaches the reproduced object from the domain of tradition. Meaning, for example: a book no longer has anything to do with literary history so the history of literarture you're taught in school is for shit. The art work's no longer the one object that's true; sellability and control, rather than truth, are the considerations that give the art object its value. Art's substructure has moved from ritual and truth to politics.

Meanwhile this society has the hype: the artist's powerless. Hype. Schools teach good writing in order to stop people writing whatever they want the ways they want. Why do I like banging my head into, against the wall? I always have. I could go stand by your door and ring the doorbell. This is what I think every day: I'm going to phone him. No; he told me he didn't want to speak to me again. I shouldn't want someone who needlessly hurts me because such a situation hurts me. You haven't liked me for a year. You only talked to me when you wanted my money so I hate you. But that's the way you are with everybody because you're crazy because you're so scared. You think when you're hurting someone more than anyone would normally (maybe my idea of "normal" is incorrect) the person is irredeemably hurting you, because you're so coked up. As I walk along each street I think: I can do whatever I want so I'll walk to your apartment and ring the doorbell. My attention's distracted from this by wanting a mystery book. I walk out of the bookstore. I don't care enough about you now to experience your hatred of me again and I'm proud of me for sidestepping my masochism my masochism.

By not getting in touch with you I'm keeping this situation alive. I'm keeping this situation alive because there's no one alive who physically loves me. This' false. When I was in high school, unlike the other kids (I went to an all-girls' school), I was never in love. I didn't feel I-didn't-know-what-it-was for boys; I just liked sex. I crave sex.

Presumably, without intending it, he issued an invitation to a far-reaching liquidation. Now I want to give you an analogy. A painter represents or makes (whichever verb at this moment you prefer) reality by keeping distant from it and picturing it totally. A cameraman, on the other hand, permeates with mechanical equipment what he's going to represent, thus for the sake of representation changes breaks up. Reproducible art breaks up and ruins.

I must give people art that demands very little attention and takes almost nothing for me to do.

3 VIOLENCE

Purpose: To Get Rid of Meaning
for the German Expressionists
who believed nothing
and the primacy of language over form
cause society suicide
In total blackness
dedicated to The Fall:
I want to fuck one of The Gang of Four or The Fall:

She was always losing her stockings. (Shot of leg whose toe is high in the air, black sheer stocking slipping off, finger in cunt)

All females are dykes

She wanted to get a man, and she didn't know how to get one.

1. *The women*

Lesbian Guerrilla Army all gunned up enters stage:

Dyke Leader: OK girls. Here we are. (*They look around the factory.*) Not much here to put up our cunts.
Sparrow Cunt: Not even a cock to chop off.
Blonde Beauty: There's no cocks left in New York.

Adele-Just-Out-Of-Reform-School: You're getting too old. I make my own. (*She takes out a bunch of black dildoes.*)

Girls: Yay! (*They fuck up and down on the dildoes.*)

The Madonna (*to her girlfriend who's a whore*): I've been telling you I'm not racist.

Whore: Well you wouldn't take that lousy trick I handed you last night over by Forsyth.

Madonna: I don't have to fuck every black cock on the street to show I like blacks.

Alice: But if you don't fuck a guy, you can't possibly like him.

Dyke Leader: We're here to kill men.

Whore: Maybe you, honey. I've gotta make a living. You want me to be a secretary? Anyway, if there were no men, there'd be no secretaries, no file clerks, no lickers. We'd all starve.

Madonna: I believe in God.

Blonde Beauty: You mean *cock*. We don't need men like God, dumb shit, because we don't need money. We need cocks.

Whore: Well, I don't know about you, but I need lots of money. Some people need places to live, not me. I need Krizia dresses, sheer black stockings, Valentino shoes, Yamamoto sweaters, and above all Issey Miyake when he's not designing for the masses. What else is a revolution for?

Madonna: What revolution? This isn't Europe.

Dyke Leader (*inspecting factory*): I don't know what the hell this is. I don't know why anyone goes out of their apartment anymore.

2. *The men*

All the lights go out in such a way that even the people in the audience get spooked. Shadows, here, and there, what's going on?, loneliness, from romanticism to fear.

(*The factory remains black. Areas and lines of dim grey light. Two black shadows ((humans)) crouch in this light against bare walls.*)

Second Shadow: Where's the bomb?

First Shadow: Don't use that word. Reagan might hear.

Second Shadow (*SS man*): So what's he going to do to us? I'm going to die anyway.

First Shadow: Fear isn't so reasonable.

Second Shadow: He isn't a guy; he's a woman.

First Shadow: Who? Reagan?

Second Shadow: No, the transsexual.

Transsexual: Are you talking about me? (*Now we can see the three male faces. One of them is a woman.*)

Second Shadow: I have no wish to hurt you.

Transsexual: You do so. You know you hurt me? You know why all of you hurt me? I'm gonna protest against all of you men. All I want is someone to love me. (*Still very calm and soft.*) Is that so much to ask for one lifetime? (*Tears out cunt hairs; lies back down on floor; kicks legs straight in air. Out of her mind.*)

Second Shadow (*coldly*): Not again. (*Slaps her. To the other terrorist.*) OK the bomb's set. We have to get out of here soon as possible.

Transsexual (*screaming at the same time*): I'll do whatever I want because I need.

Second Shadow: I'm leaving.

Transsexual (*now very quiet*): Please don't leave me. I'll do anything you want.

Second Shadow: Either you're going to do what I want or you're going to do what you want. Make your decision, Elvira.

Elvira: You know I'm a woman and I'm weak.

Second Shadow: You're not a real woman.

Elvira: No one's a real enough woman for the likes of you. All you men, the big conceptualists the revolutionaries. You tell me you love me only when you want to stick your thing in me.

Second Shadow: You're a piece of trash who can't think, all you know is how to be lonely. You pretend you have all these

brains when actually everyone is laughing at you, and as
you're growing older your body is so ugly how could any
man desire your puckered asshole? You? Love? You don't
even know enough to keep your mouth shut.

Elvira: You used to like my mouth well enough even if it is flabby
and ugly.

Second Shadow: I like every hole when I'm drunk. A man doesn't
mean anything he does when he's drunk. And you're not
even a man or a woman.

Elvira: Whatever I am, I've been something to you for three
years' deeps of nights.

Second Shadow: The deep of night, yes. We live there. I'm
leaving.

(*The First Shadow is at the doorway, now a shadow.*)

Elivra: If anybody leaves me again, I'll suicide. I'll ask you one
thing. (*Looking straight up at the ceiling like Frankenstein,
as Second Shadow also exits.*) If any of you have any dot of
human pity at all in you, please give me some help and stay
with me until I can get on my feet.

3. *My childhood*

A *dyke walks over to Elvira and kicks her.*

Adele: What're you doing here?

Elvira: I'm lonely.

Adele: What does that have to do with sex?

Elvira: As long as I can remember I've been lonely. My parents
had this apartment on Sutton Place. The corner of the sixth
floor of the building was their living room. I'd sit on one of
the window seats, looking down over the people and tiny
cars, and sing, "Somewhere Over the Rainbow." Even when
I was married. I was lonely because I was always in love

with an artist who wasn't in love with me. When I turned thirty years old, I was desperate. When you're young, you find pleasure by sticking razor blades into your wrist. The desperation of old age, being over thirty, is frightening because you don't know if you'll be strong, or lobotomized, enough to bear it. I met Christoph in the bar I hang out. For two years I supported him by doing sex show shit. I'm not a hooker. I can't touch strange men's flesh. Touching their flesh freaks me out. That's the way I am. I can do anything in front of men as long as I don't have to touch them. Chris wanted to be a mercenary, but he couldn't get it together for a long time. He kept getting his gun barrels clogged. Even back then everyone I knew back then says he was the most ambitious person around, but I never knew it: I thought Chris was the kindest and most gentle man I had ever known. I couldn't believe there was a man such as him. We never fought once or raised our voices to each other. He must have loved me. I used to tell him, "In this brutal world you can't let people walk over you and use you. You have to grow up." He was my world. He became a man by taking more coke, acting like more of a shit to women, and closing off his feelings. Now he's able to take care of me. I'm not going to be a whore anymore. I know he loves me.

4. I lose my home forever

Elvira in her home. Shot of a dark green wall.

Elvira: Chris? Chris, where are you? (*She's intuitive enough to be worried. Sees a note pinned to a bedframe, hanging as if it's all bloody. Reads it to herself. Can't believe it so reads it out loud.*) "Elvira, I'm leaving you as you know I have to because you're a mess and nothing can be made up between us. Christoph."

5. *Looking for friends*

Sparrow Cunt: What're you doing back here?
Blonde Beauty: Huh?
Elvira: I want to join you.
Madonna: Oh, you do believe in God.
Elvira: I want to help you get rid of men.
Dyke Leader: We're not getting rid of men; we're getting rid of our controllers.
Whore: We're artists.
Elvira: Who's controlling me? (*The Whore points to Elvira's cunt and the Dyke Leader to Elvira's brains.*)
Blonde Beauty: Hermann Kahn's controlling you.
Elvira: Hermann Kahn? I used to fuck him. He must be Jewish.
Whore: Oh gee. Was he any good?
Dyke Leader (*slapping her*): Shut up, whore.
Elvira: I'm sorry. He used to fuck me.
Whore: Was he any good?
Elvira: Gee. I never know if a guy's any good cause I'm always desperate.
Whore: That's what makes a woman a great fuck.
Dyke Leader: That's what makes a woman hate men. You cunts're scared.
Elvira (*looking at her cunt*): You should see inside my asshole. (*Proudly.*) I've been to the hospital twice. One time the doctor said I might not recover.
Madonna: She is religious.
Beautiful Blonde: Feeling sexual love is like being in prison:

Prison scene:

Prisoner 1 (*sitting up on her wood board*): Goddamn I have to shit.

(*In a nearby corner, night, three prisoners throw dice on a board. They're the matron's baby dykes.*)

First Dice-thrower (*looking at Prisoner 1*): She never shits.

(*Prisoner 1 falls flat on her face and goes back to never-never land.*)

Prisoner 1 (*sitting up on her wood board*): I really have to shit. (*She's sound asleep. As she climbs out of her bunk, she steps on her bedmate's face.*)

Bedmate (*instantly awake*): Cindy, you can't have to shit. You never eat.

Cindy: I have to shit. (*She goes over to the box of yellow paper, lays two papers on the floor, squats over the two pieces of paper. Nothing comes out. She waddles back to the wood bunk.*)

Bedmate: You're dreaming.

Cindy: I can't help wanting to shit. I still have normal body reactions.

Bedmate: You'll soon get over that.

Cindy: What'll be left?

Bedmate: Nothing's left to us or anyone else. Soon enough we die.

Cindy: I do have to shit. I've got these terrible stomach contractions. (*Pause*) Maybe I'm sick?

Bedmate: At least you're not pregnant. How many abortions have you had?

Cindy (*now totally doubled over*): I am sick. God . . . (*Runs over to the pot.*)

Bedmate: Is it coming out?

Cindy: All I can do is urinate.

Bedmate: Dig your fingers in and pull it out.

Cindy: I can't shit, I'm asleep, and I have lumps in my breast.

Bedmate: At least you're not pregnant.

Cindy: Doctors tear apart bodies and make me sick. Most of all they increase my fear with their talk of death death death. I'm scared out of my mind.

Bedmate: Of what? Of death?

Cindy: They've scared us out of our minds. Deeply threaded by my prick, he'll become something other than himself, something other than my lover.

Dyke Leader: Humans have to die, but they don't have to feel pain.

Elvira: But he made love to me.

Whore: Tom made love to me last night four times in a row. But that doesn't mean he knows who I am.

Elvira: Maybe I'd better see Hermann Kahn again and find out whether he still loves me.

Madonna: What happened to Christoph?

Elvira: Hermann Kahn came before Christoph. He was my first.

6. Back to the nunnery

Elvira leans against one of the white columns that holds up the stone porch roof. In back of her are green gardens and penguins.

Elvira (*running over to a penguin*): Mommy!
Penguin 1: I'm not your mommy.

(*Elvira goes back to her friend, the Beautiful Blonde.*)

Beautiful Blonde: Don't you know who your mommy is? I thought you were looking for Hermann Kahn.

Elvira: All these penguins look the same to me. (*A penguin passes close to her. She runs over to it.*) Mommy! (I dreamed one night that one of the angels of the Lord came down to me. Blue lights were rising up from the city below me. The blue lights were pale yellow, pale pink, violet, and blue. I know now that the angels are coming. The angel of the Lord said to me, "The murderers are after you." I ran through the city. I have been to this city before. The streets are narrow and wind past the small stores set in the bottoms of two- and three-story townhouses. There're no large businesses. Each geographical section of townhouses has the shape of a human liver or something similar. In the left part of the landscape, to the left of the liver through which now I'm running, there's a green park. Throughout the city there are small parks. Of course the heavyset brutal killers are going to catch me. You who I love are heavyset.) Do you remember who I am?

Penguin 2: Who are you?

Elvira: You're my mother.

Penguin 2: I'm the mother to all children.

Elvira: If you can cut through your shit, Holy Mother, remember you once spread your legs screamed in agony and I came out. (*Yanks the pinned arm upward.*) Now do you remember?

Penguin 2: I've changed, my daughter.

Elvira: Cut the daughter shit too. I used to be your son. (*Yanks the arm higher.*) I want you to tell me about the first man I fell in love with.

Penguin 2 (*as hard as she really is*): Why bother? (*Recovering her surface.*) Why disturb the good life you've managed to make for yourself by remembering anything?

Elvira: That's shit too. (*Yanks the arm up as hard as she can and breaks it.*)

Penguin 2: For a Catholic pain is ecstasy. (*Raising her eyes towards heaven.*) I'll tell you what you want to know so you too can be in pain. Maybe you'll be in so much pain you'll kill yourself.

7. *Mexican lust*

Penguin 2: It's the Mexican-American border below San Diego. The American government's maneuvering a war between the Mexicans who have snuck across the border to the American side and the local Blacks cause the American government wants to off both groups.

A highfalutin' Mexican Vice cop lands on the American

side of the border for the first time with his newly-married wife. Three feet away from where the honeymoon couple stands, a car blows up. The head of the Mexican Family this Vice cop recently busted threatens the Vice cop's wife if her husband doesn't lay off the scum, while the Vice cop watches the big fat cop who runs this border town hates Mexes and whose name is Hermann Kahn arrest a Mexican greaser for the car bombing. In return the kid is screaming, "You fascist pig! You're only arresting me cause I just married the rich white girl of the town. You don't get off on black dick plus white-and-red puss." The Mexican Vice cop watches this, but has to keep his mouth clamped because he's Mexican. Today being Mexican black female gay and everything else is being dead because this is Mexico.

To protect his wife from further harrassments, the Vice cop puts her in a nearby motel. She's safer in America than in Mexico because the Americans live by rules. The Head of the Family owns this dump. Family punks proceed to rape, dope up, and set up the wife as a junky on the Mexican side of the border so the cops'll think the Vice cop's a junky. Hermann Kahn and the Head of the Family collude in this strategy. When the wife rolls around in junk delight, three inches from her eyes Hermann Kahn strangles the Family Head just so he, Kahn, is sure her husband'll be framed and get out of his, Kahn's, affairs. Meanwhile the Vice cop has found incontrovertible evidence that Kahn is really crooked, shown this evidence to the other cops, and one of the cops is helping the Vice frame Kahn. During the frame Kahn kills this lower cop and at the same time it becomes public that the Mexican greaser was the car bomber just as Kahn said he was.

Elvira: Did they kill Kahn?

Penguin 2: No. They incorporated him as head of the American think tank scheme.

8. *Suicide*

In Hermann Kahn's building (the factory), which is now totally deserted:

Man in empty room: I'm going to commit suicide. (*To Elvira entering.*)

Elvira: Good for you.

Man: Don't you want to know how stinko the world is and how it hurts to be alive?

Elvira: Not really.

Man: I'm going to kill myself in the most disgusting way possible. I'm going to drown in my very own vomit which will be as red as nipples of cancer. As it gleams the bed at night, through which love is passing.

Elvira: Go ahead. (*Pulls out her purse and lights a cigarette.*) I'll watch you. (*Looks at her watch.*) Do you think you're going to take a long time?

Man: First let's fuck. Oh my darling, I've waited for you for so long.

Elvira: I don't know. (*Rolling her head.*) I can't believe.

Man: (*two hands on her cheeks so the eyes in her face have to look into his eyes. Stares intently at her*): I want you. Say "I want you."

Elvira: I want you.

(*He puts his small stubby cock in her cunt. They haven't quite gotten undressed.*)

Man: Say, "I love you."

Elvira (*still looking at him so she'll be possessed*): I love you.

(*He releases her. She goes back to normal or feelinglessness, then realizes she has to change: of her own will her righthand's fingers are lightly tapping up down his left cheek, the softness of her eyes as she gasps her cunt opens. Her cunt is opening and his cock is opening and*)

Elvira: Oh. Oh Jesus Christ I don't believe.

Man (*at the same time, loudly*): Oohhh, ooohhoohh, hOOhoohoohh.

Elvira: Can we maybe be friends after this?

Man (*turning Elvira's face into his*): Neither of us expected this would happen, did we?

9. *Elvira*

Elvira (*as she's committing suicide*): Merry Christmas, Elvira. (*Takes a pill.*) Your mother won't give you money. You don't have any money left. You're going to starve to death. (*Takes another pill.*) You pretend to everyone you have a boyfriend so your friends won't think you're a freak though you know goddamn well there's no boyfriend you liar. (*Takes another pill.*) All your life is an illusion you crummy liar you lie to everyone you are a liar everything is a fake because you pretend you have money and you're happy you have to pretend these things, and you're none of these things. (*Takes another pill.*) There is no one you can turn to. (*She is teaching herself.*) There is no way because there is no one to whom you can yell "Help." There is no human shoulder. There is no one. (*Takes another pill.*) Scream. No possibility of screaming. Scream. No possibility of screaming. (*Takes the rest of the pills.*) Why the fuck should I commit suicide? I'd rather kill. (*She goes into bathroom. Sticks her fingers down throat and vomits up pills.*)

10. *Rebirth or human suffering is stupid*

Elvira (*lying in her apartment on her couch. Smoking some opium*): Now what'm I going to do with myself?

(*Chrysis, entering. Takes my cunt in his palm. Starts rousing me. In one minute there are chills up and down my spine.*)

Elvira: This stuff always ends up hurting me.
Chrysis: Don't you see I've started a hunt and now you need a
   hare?

*(I threw myself into his arms, not only my body, and I started to go out
of whack. I could no longer keep control of myself by pretending I was
a zombie. I threw myself into his arms.*
   Lots of kisses.
   *I got him to fuck me by refusing to leave his side and looking into his
eyes. Lips mesh. Hands go all over the place. Bodies go crazy bodies
really want cause souls)*
*Getting up right after the fuck, Chrysis: I hate your cunt, you dog, why
do you think you amuse me? You don't mean anything to me, spindle-
cunt, spoiled fish-teeth, trench-mouth, herpes. (He beats me up.)*

Elvira: The witch can cure me.
Man: I'm the witch.
Elvira: Suppose there's a person who by birth naturally is off.
   Weird. Sick. Unbalanced. Just not like other people. Do
   the Leftists and the Marxists and the Socialists care about
   this person?
Witch (Man): What do these people mean now?
Elvira I mean: Why help a bum? I see bums every day. Why do
   they keep living their hard lives? Why help anyone continue
   what is useless: living? I get wiser as I get older and then
   when I'm wise I die, so what's the use of all the wisdom?
   There's another thing I think. Say I fall wildly in love with
   a man. Why do I feel all these powerful things? Does my
   feeling them mean he has to feel something? What's reality?
   I mean I'm not under physical torture all of the time, but
   there's always all this mental pain, but suicide . . . ? Let's
   take an example of this situation: What do I do without love?
   Is sex necessary?
Witch (Man): Even rats live better than us.
Elvira: We'd better say this life is almost intolerable. So, witch,
   what am I going to do?

First Jew: It's the old story. They beat us up. They beat up our children. In the middle of the midnight they appear in our houses, drag us out of our beds, take us into their hellholes.

Second Jew: Suffering! We are the chosen people! Aren't we the chosen people? Chosen for suffering therefore we make good art!

Witch (Man): I don't give a shit as long as I can fuck.

11. *Implosion*

I. THE BACKGROUND OF THE FRENCH REVOLUTION. THREE SCENES.

1. *Europe. The people mutter political discontent.*

Kathy (*an American visitor*): How do you make love?

Father (*a Frenchman*): I make love with my fingers. My fingers are magic. Are you feeling them now?

Kathy: Oh yes! (*He beats her ass while he fingerfucks her.*) Oh. OH! (*Comes twice.*)

Father: I have other kinds of tastes. I'm a feminist: I like to watch two women fuck. Sometimes I beat them with my belt while they fuck each other. (*Frank and Patricia enter.*) Frank! What is the matter with you? Are the Dutch people calling you a fascist again?

Frank (*a Dutchman sitting on the bed between Father's and Kathy's bodies*): I'm no goddamn fascist. I don't have any politics. I'm like an American.

Patricia (*also Dutch*): I'm thirsty.

Frank: I'm sick of moralists. For the first time their economy's going under and the Dutch are beginning to realize their posh ways of life might no longer be available to them. At this moment they're acting scared cause they'll do anything to avoid rocking the boat.

Father: Of course. I'm a good Frenchman.

Frank: . . . They've always worshipped anything that's safe. That's why they're Liberals. The Dutch Marxists in announcing themselves as the only opposition to this reaction have grouped and defined themselves so rigidly that they've got no political power. They're as bureaucratic academic and rigid as the Right Wing.

Patricia: How long will we be as bloody and dirty as children?

Kathy (*masturbating*): Oh oh oh.

Patricia: For how much longer are our toys—the coffins of friends out on heroin—going to be the only things we can love? For how much longer will severed heads be the only people I place my lips upon? I love death. The Committee of Happiness better begin its work.

Father: Your statements are reactionary cause you can't so simply put ideals on top of what's actually happening to you. If this society in which you're living shits, you have to shit. (*He's such a big guy, he farts.*)

Patricia: But ideals can pick holes in the social fabric. "True" and "false" are beside the point. Even if they did nothing, they're the only tools we've got.

Father: Look, I'm a musician: I know language like music isn't stating big things, but breathing. Otherwise, poetry opera art painting aren't only dead they also cause death. That's why Rockefeller sponsors them. Throw everything that's dead up the assholes of those who're too tight to fuck in the ass.

Kathy (*stopping masturbating for a moment*): I'm too crazy. The only thing I want is feeling. Talking to friends.

Frank (*feeling up her cunt*): How're you going to do that? They either worship you or they despise you, but you'll never be human because you feel.

Kathy: This talk shits. Go crazy. We're going to cause a revolution. I tell you. I'm going to cause a burning revolution. (*Disappears.*)

Father: The hell with her.

2. *What my grandmother saw in London.*

In America:

Tom (*barely audible and fucking*): Love.

My Grandmother (*can't stop herself from saying it*): I love you I love you. (*She starts coming and can't stop coming. Gradually they calm down physically.*) I have to go to Europe now. (*They kiss a lot.*)

In England:

My Grandmother (*phoning Tom*): This is Florence.

Tom: Who?

My Grandmother: Florrie.

Tom: Who?

My Grandmother: Florrie . . .

Tom: Oh. Florrie. Where are you?

My Grandmother: I'm drunk.

Tom: That's nice.

My Grandmother: I'm in London. (*Pause.*) Am I disturbing you?

Tom: There's someone here with me.

My Grandmother: I'm sorry; I didn't mean to disturb you. (*She hangs up the phone.*) Oh, thank you. (*She looks through the window and sees the following scene*):

(*An outside street. The bright sunlight is evident mainly in all the colors which are so bright they're almost white. There are working- and lower-middle-class three- and four-story tenements in back of and around the streets. There are groups of typical that is small and eccentric English people on the streets.*)

A Middle-aged Housewife: You know those fuckin' upper-middle-class women. They say a woman who's a whore is the pitfall and living cancer of human existence. I'll tell you something. No woman wants to be a whore. Oh maybe some bitch who went to Oxford and has to have daddy needs to be a whore or gets her thrills whoring. I have nothing to

do with the rich. Most women who whore whore because
you need to be supported. You, daddy. You hire fuck and
arrest the whores.

A whore needs a pimp. A whore doesn't need a pimp
because she's weak. A whore needs a pimp because a pimp
controls the territory. To control this whore the pimp, just
like a record company with its rock-n-roll stars, gets her
hooked. Your daughter is now supporting two daddies and
a habit. Who did this to her? I ask you, who did this to her?
Is she doing it to herself? (*She turns to a Frenchman who's
standing on the street.*) You think whoring is fashionable?
You think women who're too young to come whore because
it's "heep"? Being a whore beats being a secretary (*back to
her husband, who we now see's a drunken tailor*) or a wife
cause, for the same work, work cause there's no love, only
a whore not a wife or a secretary gets paid enough she might
be able to escape men.

Tailor: Our daughter doesn't love me.
A Middle-aged Housewife: I used to have a fantasy you loved
me. Then I had a fantasy some man could love me. Now
I can't find any fantasy inside my head. I can't find anything.
My Grandmother (*to herself*): What do I want? I'm a woman
too.
Tailor: It's natural it's a Law of Human Nature: My daughter
has to whore to support me. Give me a knife so I can increase
the pain.
My Grandmother: Give his daughter the knife cause it's the hurt,
not the hurters, who feel pain.
Tailor (*to his wife*): I will increase the pain. I will go crazy. I
hurt; let all of us hurt more.
A Middle-aged Housewife: To you everything's your cock. You
worship your pain.

3. *Art-criticism and art.*

The office of ARTFORUM, *Mulberry Street, New York City.*

Situationalist With Italian Accent: I just saw an American film. The title of the film is *Bladder Run.*

His Girlfriend: *Blade Runner.*

Situationalist With Italian Accent: I think it is a real American film. In this film which is a film and not a real event . . .

Girlfriend: . . . but it's a real film . . .

Situationalist With Italian Accent: . . . the filmmaker proves to us the audience that robots are as human as we are. Since simulation can take the place of reality . . .

Girlfriend: . . . non-simulation . . .

Situationalist With Italian Accent: . . . we no longer need money to make germ warfare, lobotomy, and other weapons as does Mr. Reagan, Inc.

Girlfriend: We don't want germ warfare, lobotomies, and Tylenol.

Situationalist With Italian Accent: We make fake germ warfare, fake lobotomy, and good medicine which doesn't hurt anybody and yet works very well destruction of governmental control.

Girlfriend: Destruction of corporations.

Situationalist With Italian Accent: Yes. Corporality.

Marxist Feminist: But how can I tell the difference between the real and what isn't real that is, for our purposes, between their disgusting weapons and our good weapons?

Situationalist With Italian Accent: You can't.

Marxist Feminist: I might end up a Right-Winger.

Girlfriend: For you that's better than ending up in someone's bed.

Tom (*who's an Irish artist turned American*): No, this woman's correct. There's definitely a problem with Situationalism as it now stands. I therefore propose we get rid of all judge-

ments. No more you v. me v. Reagan or rich v. poor. We
don't mean anymore. We Americans and our allies the British (*in thick Irish accent*) will give the world a fine example!

Marxist Feminist (*not understanding anything*): Of what?

Tom: Of the new politics: no politics. Everything. We can and
do everything. We are theater.

Murderers (*all dark, black. The skin. Murderer*): Why do you
keep murdering?

My Grandmother: I have to, my dear.

Murderer: You're a shadow that murders the body that casts it.

My Grandmother: So then I'll be left with shadows . . .

Murderer: . . . different textures of blackness . . .

My Grandmother: . . . my skin. Where's Danton? Fiction. I tell
you truly: right now fiction's the method of revolution.

Murderer: All this is talk. (*Sharpening his knife.*)

My Grandmother: To dream's more violent than to act.

(*End of my version of art-criticism.*)

II. ACTION. TEN SCENES.

1. *On heroism: Robespierre decides to kill Danton.*

Robespierre: Danton's getting too famous. Let's kill him. (*Rubs
his hands.*) Hee hee hee. (*Robespierre's Polish. All Polish
people are gnomes who run around in tiny circles and act in
malicious ways.*) You think murder's wrong. I'm going to
prove to you there's no morality (*a Polish proof*): My mind
is capable of and thinks every possible thought. Therefore
there's no morality in the mental world. A thought turns
into an action by chance. Therefore there's no morality in
the real world, only chance. (*A picture of Ronald Reagan's
asshole with shit coming out.*)

*Robespierre and St. Just (St. because today it's Christmas), being both
Polish jump up and down rubbing their hands together clap monkey feet*

together: Kill Danton the Powerful! Kill Lacroix the Foolish! Kill Hér-
ault-Séchelles Philippeau and Camille!

St. Just (*reading a long piece of paper which he rolls up and unrolls
    while everyone chants or chatters "Good" "Bad" "Good" "Bad"*):
    "Robespierre kills." That's a disgusting slander. The media
    lies.

Robespierre: I'll kill you for lying.

St. Just: I'm not lying. The paper's lying.

Robespierre: You die anyway. My friends only love me when
    they're dead.

St. Just: Or when you're dead. This is true in London not only
    in New York City.

Robespierre (*changing his mind*): You don't have to die yet,
    Justice. I just wanted to frighten you.

St. Just: You're frightening everybody to death. (*Walks off.*)

Robespierre: Who needs friends? I do everything I do only in
    accordance with myself: I act. I am the hero.

2. *Danton learns Robespierre's going to kill him and agrees to it.*

Danton (*sitting in his own room*): I don't care about anything
    except when I'm obsessed.

Lacroix: You think so much you're not going to be able to murder
    Robespierre. You're not only committing suicide; you're
    killing all of us. Stop thinking; slaughter the creep. I just
    heard he's planning to kill you. Worry about why you're
    murdering later.

Danton: I'd rather die than murder. I'd rather be fucked than
    fuck.

Lacroix: You're right: It's better to die than to die. (*All the Poles,
    bent over, shuffling around in circles, follow each other.*)

Danton: I don't care anymore if I die. The only thing I have is
    sex and I'm not so hooked on sex though the physical ecstasy
    keeps getting stronger. Maybe Robespierre'll kill me soon.
    (In London people can't afford to travel around the city.

Kids place wires on the soft spots of their brains so hopefully they're lobotomizing themselves. The beards of old men sitting in the pubs sit in their beers. The buildings of the rich overtower all.) We have to find our own pleasure.

(Pasolini died
by suicide.)

3. *Back to school.*

Kantor: I want you to tell me about the War of Roses.

Danton (*preschool age*): The War of Roses occurred in 1481. The House of Lancaster who were known as the red roses fought against the House of York who are the white roses. The red roses won because they were bloodier.

Kantor: Correct. Now tell me whether or not you are going to die. You don't know, do you? You're going to have to go to school. Let's go to school.

Danton: I don't want to go to school.

Kantor: All little boys go to school. Little girls don't do anything. Besides this school doesn't have any pupils and needs pupils cause a school needs pupils to be a success.

Danton: I won't be a pupil because I have pupils. I must be a school.

Kantor: If you're not at school in an hour, you won't have any more pupils. (*Picture of Polish people putting little Polish girl into the earth.*)

Danton: OK. So I'll go to school.

Kantor: Let's go to school right now.

(*The Spirit of Death takes my hand and wafts me to school.*)

4. *In school.*

All the teachers are female and all the boys are male.

Teacher (*gazing at little boys*): Boys! Boys! Boys! I need more.

Two other teachers talk to each other. (This is a pastoral scene: people occur in clumps.)

Teacher 1: I've already got herpes.

(I'm standing hand in hand with the guy who's brought me to school. I'm abnormal and abnormally shy. My toes quake inwards. I turn my face away. I don't want to go into this nasty place because I don't know nothing. In there. The Spirit of Death who's now a patriarch my uncle who's keeping me these days away from my own money, shoves me forward into the Schoolmistress' face. The Schoolmistress is part ogre and part pig. She has a fake English accent even though she's English.)

Me: My name's Johnny.

Schoolmistress: Well, here's little Johnny. (*Feeling my cock between my legs.*) You certainly are a little Johnny. I wish I was teaching future criminal offenders in the South Bronx. I always knew it was better to live in America.

My Uncle: Leave the goods alone, Mrs. Selby.

Headmistress (*correcting him*): They're virgins. (*Moving away to a beautiful grove of trees.*) Look how well all the students are coming back. They know how to walk. They all know how to walk. We have a very fine establishment here.

Beautiful Blonde: They ain't innocent enough. I always said, we don't get enough virgins and so the others ain't worth anything to us, they's just used rags cause they parents gets 'em first, an' they ain't worth anything to the people we's sell them to. Now, you's a father. Do you know how hard it is for a teacher to make a boy fresh and innocent again? You can't do it with young girls which's why young girls don't go to school. There ain't no use for them to go to school. We men have to be really highly trained and it takes a lot of the taxpayers' money to make an already rotting vegetable into a strong carrot. You wouldn't believe how much work cause you's a father.

My Uncle (*to himself*): Let 'em rot. At least these rotters are willing to stand up. (*To Beautiful Blonde.*) Madam, it is your job to train these young pliable minds to want goodness. These pliable minds will be the owners of the world and the world will rest on their shoulders. Goodness or godliness, you know, is a taught desire: the social caviar. You must persuade their frail wills to want goodness rather than coca-cola.

Boy: The only thing we want for our coca-cola is hard drugs. (*Shoves his ass in the Beautiful Blonde's face then runs away.*)

For the Punk World

5. *Love scene.*

My Grandmother: I miss you so much.

Danton: I'm not near you. I'm in England.

My Grandmother: I wish you were next to me so I could lick your ears. The tips of your ears tip tip. Then into two eyes. My love. We've never said anything affectionate to each other. We don't really know each other.

Danton: We don't know each other.

My Grandmother: Shit. You're less capable than I am. I should forget about you.

Danton: A person should be as self-sufficient as possible, but I don't know what the hell for. Robespierre's coming to arrest me.

6. *Robespierre and his gang plan.*

St. Just: In two hours Danton's going to announce his son's engagement cause he knows people love a wedding so that way he can keep them under his thumb.

My Grandmother: But George, the son, is a Siamese twin. Half a Siamese twin.

St. Just: They just need this wedding to keep the people happy. That way they don't have to have sex.

My Grandmother: An advertisement wedding is as good as a real wedding and better than the sex I'm getting these days.

Robespierre (*looking her body up and down*): I hope you're speaking about yourself.

My Grandmother: You don't have anything worth speaking of.

Robespierre: The semi-Siamese son is a human booby and basket phenomenon; the non-married semi-twin, Arthur . . .

My Grandmother: —he's the one who ruled Britain—

Robespierre: . . . is the one I want to use.

My Grandmother: What do you do in bed?

Robespierre (*annoyed*): Arthur's going to help us kill Danton.

My Grandmother: He won't commit patricide. He's too intent on fratricide.

Robespierre: If Arthur kills his father, the people'll decide Danton has to be a shit.

My Grandmother: I'll go back home and tell Arthur his other half's getting married. He's so dumb he doesn't even know it yet. He must have been born on the other side of the brains. When he learns Danton's marrying off George, he'll be pissed off enough to slaughter George but he can't because then he'd die too. So he'll murder his father.

Robespierre: A family scandal'll really kill off the Danton family. Murder advertisements always top wedding advertisements. The people'll know we're just as pure as driven-over snow. We can even kill a few more people.

My Grandmother: Due to that Watergate scandal—when even dummies as dumb as the Americans had to know their leaders, Nixon and everybody else, lie steal murder cheat and take hard drugs—these same leaders simply gained more power. Don't throw your money into advertising. What matters is that you get all the political power.

7. *Danton*.

Danton: I want to be less nothing. There are some thoughts that shouldn't ever be heard. It's not good if they cry out the

second they're born a baby out of the womb, it is good: they
can blow up the world.

8. *Robespierre's coming for Danton.*

*Lots of battle scenes, small battles, all around. Only street fighting
no more major characters.*

9. *Robespierre's coming For Danton 2.*

Make more and more like a painting.

My Grandmother: Do you know who I am?

Danton: How can I know who you are? I only fucked you twice.
(*Lots of sunlight and little battles.*) What I believe is what
I see. It's harder to live than die for what you see.

My Grandmother: What do you see? (*Lots of sunlight and little
battles.*)

Danton: Last night I had this dream: I was fishing. I caught an
eel. As the fish I had caught flapped on the wood dock, my
hook slipped out of its mouth. This made me very upset.
Surprisingly, when I put my hook back into its seemingly
smiling therefore sly mouth, the fish readily accepted it.

(*The audience beginning to see Robespierre and his men advancing on
Danton realizes Danton's faster and faster closer to his death, at the
point of punk ecstasy, in the daylight.*)

My Grandmother: You have to say what you are. Tell me what
you see.

Danton (*even faster no fighting against the speed at the same
pace*): We are particulars. We are this world. (*Now, the
people are on him. A housewife digs her fingernails into his
thigh.*) There's more and more world a proliferation of phenomena. How, you religious people and more important
you politicos who believe in your wilfully therefore violently
changing this world who believe in your wills, how can you
be apart from the world? Who is doing the changing? All

phenomena which include me being phenomena are alive.

My Grandmother: And it's OK that the rich maul the poor?

Danton: Hello, Robespierre. You're slaughtering me for being a revolutionary and I don't believe in anything I didn't choose to be the freak I was born to be. (*As Robespierre's arresting him, in a weak uncertain voice.*) I would like to love Florrie.

Robespierre: I'm taking over this world because I'm strong and you're weak.

My Grandmother: The moments are gone: Tell me what you see.

Danton: Your eyes work the same ways mine do, you cunt. I see a three-story brick building whose bricks the sun is wrapping, a bloodstain on a white collar, a black window frame. I'm hoping, my love, that you love me cause I'd like to live in love. Since I'm given I don't give, I can't create love I can only hope it's here. (*Robespierre leads away Danton.*)

10. *My Grandmother.*

My Grandmother (*alone on the sunlit street*): Today I've been deeply wounded in my sex: I've had two viral warts scraped off my clit. My cunt cut open at my clit.

III. THE AFTERMATH OF WAR. TWO SCENES.

1. *My Grandmother talks to Danton.*

My Grandmother writes a telegram. The telegram says:
I'M CRAZY I MISS YOU ARE YOU MARRIED I CAN'T WAIT SIX WEEKS FOR YOUR RETURN. *She waits for the phone to ring. She waits for a return letter in the mail.*

My Grandmother: He hasn't phoned me. There's no telegram coming back. There won't be any letters because letters from England take too long, a week, and by that time my memory's over and, besides, there are no letters in a revolution.

I'll forget him. It's better to forget the people you care about. Being free: that's what I know. I hate this fake freedom. This fake freedom's being in prison. It's social; all psychological is political. I hate.

I'm strong. I need to be part of a family and this world; and when I have to feel needs that are unsatisfiable, needs are only anguish.

(*Her phone rings. To phone.*) Let's go see 'Line.

Phone: 'Lina? Lisa Lyons? What's she doing?

My Grandmother: 'Line. She's fucking some white guy on stage in the middle of the poorest Puerto Rican section. Maybe there'll be a riot.

Phone: Sounds like a riot. There're riots all over the place. Let's go.

My Grandmother: Pick me up at eight-thirty. If you don't get killed on the way. There're already two corpses on my doorstep.

Phone: They're dead. Dead junkies can't hurt me. How long will she be?

My Grandmother: How long does a fuck take? Ten minutes?

Phone: Five minutes?

My Grandmother: How the fuck should I know?

Phone: It takes longer than a death.

My Grandmother (*immediately hanging up phone retaking it off hook and dialing*): Melvyn. I'm desperate. Just listen to my story. It's about this guy I saw in England. Now I'm going to tell you exactly what happened so you can give me advice. I met him by accident in England. The next day we fucked. I wasn't expecting anything to happen. I was too busy. I could barely sandwich him into my life. We didn't talk about anything. All we did was fuck. The minute we saw each other we fucked. It wasn't that we didn't have anything in common. We really like each other's work. We just fucked fucked. I'm a real dope I didn't ask him if he had a girlfriend. We didn't say anything to each other. The next day we saw each other in the afternoon, but I had to see the TV people that night. And the next day I had a dinner date and couldn't take him along. You know how it is. But we see each other all the next day. It was really great. We really got along. That night I was upset I couldn't say anything well what do you expect? I had to leave England. At the end I asked him, "Am I going to see you again?" "I'm coming to New York in February." When I got back to New York a few days later, there was stuff about the magazine he works for, I phoned him. It was all right to phone him. We said we'd work together on an art piece. I said I couldn't keep phoning him cause it cost too much so I'd blow all my money. He said he'd phone me. Robert, the woman who actually runs the magazine, was supposed to be here last week but she won't be here till next week. I haven't heard from him since I phoned. I sent him a telegram. He didn't reply to my telegram. Now, I want to know if this means he doesn't like me.

Melvyn: There's obviously something between you. When did you send the telegram?

My Grandmother: Fifteen minutes ago. Five minutes ago.

Melvyn: Maybe he's not in town.

My Grandmother: That could be.

Melvyn: Look: You're very far apart. Let him know you keep caring and at the same minute, protect yourself: don't obsess. (*They both laugh.*) Fuck someone else.

My Grandmother: It doesn't work like that. (*She hangs up phone.*) You're not around me and even if you were around me, I'm just dealing with my own desires. It doesn't matter if I name these desires because every desire acts the same: Either, if I let myself be overcome in desire I'm being sentimental so not letting the mind have a resting place I should take every desire which rises up in me and shove it; or, I should be dumb passion! Let desires and revolutions act! The last choice makes my happy because it's true there's no will.

    Where are you? Please call me.

2. Everything is gone.

Paul Rockoffer (*in mourning*): Shut up, bitches! I'm returning
to Art I'll be an artist and now I'll be happy. I'm an artist
I'm an artist! I don't believe in breaking traditional form.

Ella (*a pretty eighteen-year-old girl*): You're 46 years old.

My Grandmother: I'm 22.

Ella: Well, you're fat enough to be 46.

My Grandmother: My body doesn't matter. It's always trying to
die anyway. The hell with it. My mind matters less. It's a
conditioned piece of shit. Keep your mind on what matters,
girl.

Ella: What matters?

Paul Rockoffer: Tell me please, what is life really?

Ella: Now I don't know anymore so I feel dull.

Paul Rockoffer: Don't force me to make speeches. I could tell
you things, beautiful and horrible deep and drastic, but it'd
be just more lies.

Ella: Now the artist's talking sincerely.

My Grandmother's Memory:

(**Old Man-Teacher:** Now, Cleopatra's nose . . . Cleopatra. Cle-
o-pa-tra.

My Grandmother-In-Old-Age: What about Cleopatra's nose?
C'mon, fellers, what about it?

The Other Pupils: The nose, the no-o-se, her no-o-o-se. Cleopatra's nose!!

My Grandmother-In-Old-Age-As-The-Good-Student: It's the nose
of Cleopatra, her no-o-se. (*She sits quickly down.*)

Old Man-Teacher: And the foot of a mountain . . . ? (*He's clearly
at the point of losing his self-control.*) Well, the foot of a
mountain?

My Grandmother-In-Old-Age-As-The-Good-Student: Foot. Foot
foot foot foot. (*Epileptic fit.*) Footfootfootfootfootfoot-
footfootfootfootfoot (*drooling*).

Old Man-Teacher-More-Anxious-Cause-He's-Realizing-The-

Dumbness-Of-The-Kids: And what about Achilles' heel? Quickly. Achilles' heel, Achilles' spiel, heel and toe around is woe, don't show your cunt bare, bear. (*The Man-Teacher's penis now becomes real for the Man-Teacher a thing of flesh and blood it grows and grows.*) Heel! Heel!!

My Grandmother-As-A-Young-Child: Out of love.

Convict: Get me vittles. Pork pie and steak 'n' kidney pie 'n' tomatoes 'n' cabbage. I got a young man with me and this young boy eats up children like you for supper. If you don't get me those vittles, this young man will eat up your nose, then part of your cheeks, your eyes. He likes big chunks of young girls' thighs. (*Grabbing her nose.*)

My Grandmother-As-A-Young-Child: I'll get you your vittles! I'll get you those vittles you want!

Convict: I'll tell you something. You might run away, but you can't run away. A child might be warm in bed, he might pull all the covers over his head, but my young man gets into the house, he gets under your covers, he gets at your toes, your legs. There's nowhere you'll be able to escape him! You can never run away.

My Grandmother-As-A-Young-Child: I'll get you the vittles! (*Running away.*)

Convict: Remember, child, remember.)

My Life

1 CHILDHOOD: CATHOLIC BLATHERINGS

1. *The Son*

(to Charlotte Brontë in
Brussels)

Dear Charlotte,

I don't know how to write with you, but I can for you.

I'm holing up like a bear now. I'm cuddled up in my sofa and
here, under the endlessly heavy ocean, I peek eyes, two eyes
round peer beep beep, our mother she was warm she was a warm
person. Her big breasts sagged low and the flesh on her skin was
thick. She wasn't warm to us because we were children and she
was a child and wanted to be *the* child: she was warm to her
mother. Childhood was green. The house's hall's walls were green
and our bedroom's walls were green. Green was the color I hated.

Father (*my* father, not the man who adopted me and had you)
was really a murderer. I haven't found out who he is. He left
mommy when she was three months pregnant with me because
she was pregnant with me. Mommy adored him so since then
she's shut herself off. I've shut off myself. He's our family ghost:
Among all the things we and especially I can't touch, he's the
most untouchable. When ten years old I asked Nana about him.
(This was the first time I had ever asked anything.) Nana answered, "He's sick. You can't see him." "What's he sick with?"
"He's dead, Emily . . ." "Oh." "He's a murderer, Emily. You
can't have anything to do with him." This sentence made me

know she was lying. Three years ago I traced his family. His first cousin, meeting me, propositioned me then told me his daughter fucks Soho bums and my father's mad. A year ago he murdered someone who was trespassing on his yacht. It might be dangerous to meet him since I'm his daughter.

It was the end of winter. It was one of those London days when the rare snow's melted and grey wetness is overlaying our eyeballs. The air stinks that the end is almost over. And the wind blows, wind so strong it was more powerful than a human being, it was the dog in our building who knocked us off our rollerskates every time he said hello to us.

In those hours the hours of not knowing just before we went out on the streets to play with other children, just feeling. Air pink satin hot air lots of time anxiety about the gigantic mother being left alone is peace glory from words in books. All the emotions are violent. I say to you, "If you enter my life and who am I kidding you're already in my life which is the heart, I'll care about you there and want you there. I don't let people go easily. The more they're wedged in my flesh, the more I get sick screech when this skin's torn apart." Everything is the body. Disease is just apparent pain. I can cry with all this life. I used to run around and fly, it was like running down mountains, the stars made my ecstasy the other side of anguish. I ran into the school library and dumped all the books on the floor. That didn't take much time. I told the girl they had ordered to room with me if she roomed with me I would knife her. From then on I lived alone. What are colors? They taught us names, but there are no names but impressions and connections. Our drawings were full of cruelty, pitfalls and aggression.

(*next day*)
Mother ordered us, "You can't stay home all the time. You have to go down to the street to play with the other children." We were kicked out of nothingness. There was no more nothingness. There were no ways we could fight her orders. She was absolute.

We went downstairs, though we didn't want to. Outside (the sixth floor) was alien that is known. A thing is alien because I don't want it. We walked outside into this cold gray-brown. I held your hand. In front of the apartment buildings equally-sized squares divided the sidewalk. A bunch of girls played handball against the building walls which lined the street. Each girl owned a line of squares from the street to the wall. Whenever a pink rubber ball was in her territory, her open palm had to hit it once down on the sidewalk then into the building wall. If she didn't, she lost her territory. The girl who usually had the first territory or the head of the line was the most powerful girl.

Maggie, the most powerful girl, is my friend. We don't talk to each other. I don't know whether other people talk to each other because I only know how people act when they act around me. I'm not comfortable with language. I have nothing to say to anyone. Now I'm second-in-command to Maggie even though I don't have anything to do with language and other people. Language for me is private. If someone gives me the allowance to play then I can use language. My best game is when Maggie and I walk up to the whitest oldest most distinguished-looking guy we can find walking down our block:

: Excuse me, Sir.

The gentleman barely notices us. Then, bending down his crane's head: Yes?

: We want to know Sir, . . . (breaking into giggles)

The Gentleman, very kindly: What can I do for you?

: We want to know what (can barely get word out) a pee-nus is.

The Gentleman: Do you really want to know?

Bobbing our heads: We really want to know. (Giggle. Giggle.)

The Gentleman: A penis is a part of the body every man has. It is long and straight and . . . (We run away giggling.)

Now our world where language isn't communication our world now, there is sex and masturbation but have nothing to do with communicating anymore,

I can talk by plagiarizing other people's words that is real

language, and then . . . then I make something. Tonight I don't
fuck someone who has a girlfriend anyway cause I want to be in
this nothingness.

Dear Charlotte,

For those who live in silence: to sing.

Dear Charlotte,

1968 is over. 1981 is over. Future is between my legs ha ha.

Dear Charlotte,

So people do come here in order to live. I thought everyone
just died. Today I went out on the street. I'm just a mouse.
R___ because he poisoned me tells me I'm crazy. If I'm crazy,
what's sane? That is it's impossible for any person who likes herself
to believe she's crazy. Today R___ told me I'm crazy so did the
Dyna-Vent man because the Dyna-Vent isn't working because I
make it not work, but when the Dyna-Vent man is here the
Dyna-Vent works. Today I walked outside this room. When I'm
outside this room, I become well. I think writers make themselves
sick to write. I spent today crying. In a movie on TV an-English-
earl-giving-a-little-boy-everything-he-wanted was my mother, but
I wasn't included in this circle of giving because my mother gave
me nothing. Whenever I don't do anything, I cry. I have to work
as much as possible. I was crying because I was feeling the pain
my mother felt right before she suicided. Or am I making this
up? Is my picture of her pain actually a picture of my own
loneliness? I want to talk about loneliness. Lonely people stink.
I constantly think: I'm not talking to anyone these days. I've cut
out all my friends. The less I talk to people the less I want to,
so this wanting solitude or being solitudinous is a sickness. The
next thing I say to myself is: I've lots of friends. The next thing
I say to myself is: the reason all the parts of me don't fit together

is that I'm not fucking enough. Whenever I talk to one of my friends I perceive my friend is even lonelier than I am because he's less willing than I am himself to see the loneliness horror and awkwardness: solitude: nothing: what I call "the actual state of existence." These people have to act normal to avoid seeing what really is, because if they did see like my father the day he was dying they wouldn't be able to bear it because it's not bearable.

Dear Charlotte,

I'm thinking about loneliness again. All you think about is sex. You say it's love but it's not: it's cunt. I think: I have to meet my loneliness face-on right now. Love I mean sex doesn't matter. I am alone. Melville says love does matter: we can be kind to each other: sweet your flesh why are you staying away from me?

You describe your acute physical horniness for me yet you're staying away from me but I'm not staying away from you. I become physically sick when I sexually want somene and I don't get that for an extended length of time. You write that also in you sex is almost death because when someone whom you sexually want rejects you you come close to physically dying. So I want, instead of death, flesh in the nose, waking up, sniffing, smelling, surcease ease. Now there are two times: no time and slow time. No time isn't the capitalists' substitution of commodities for values, as you say it is; no time is loneliness and the absence of love. The other time, slow time, is touching someone.

Love, Emily

Dear Charlotte,

Black hole black magic. All so tragic . . . Sus (I can't read this word) fantastic. An anti-hell.

Dear Charlotte,

Today three English spies violently died. The first died in New York City; the second died in the Caribbean; the third died in New Orleans. Who killed these spies and are their deaths connected? The Circus tells James to find out.

A fortuneteller predicted James' arrival. "He's coming here to ruin us! The devil. The world's going to end!" In New York City there are many cars and most of the cars, driven fairly equally by whites blacks and Puerto Ricans, are following each other. This is one of the reasons we can't live together. When James' in his taxi driving from the airport, a sniper shoots but doesn't kill him.

James walks into one of the voodoo shops. In a corner of his eye an amazingly fat black guy is disappearing behind a curtain. James follows this edge of vision to where the car in which the sniper was sitting stands. Two black men're driving this car and James', as they've planned because they're now controlling James, following them. In this way the blacks lure James into Harlem where every black's one of them. James' new taxi driver's one of them. The newspaper vendor is one of them. This is one of the reasons we can't live together. Because he's white, James is a dope and dopiness is his intelligence. He walks into a black bar in Harlem which every white man knows is a dumb thing to do. Of course the wall against which he's sitting flips around so he's down in black bestial animal hell voodoo in where black man says "Mr. Big gonna take care of you woo." James cause he's stupid tries an identity bluff. The fortuneteller whose territory is identity answers James, "No cause and effect, baby. Voodoo. Nominalism. The blacks cause they know reality'll take over this world." Mr. Big: "Hey, baby James. I is big so I take over you and this world only cause." Mr. Big wears white which is the color of Jesus Christ the conqueror as every good voodoo person knows. His steel arm shows the union of human and nonhuman and of life and death within this living world. In a typical abandoned lot on to whose rubbish floor and graffitied rat and roach walls the sun daren't penetrate, this is one of the reasons we can't live together, a black CIA man cause there're only blacks in this land stops James from being murdered. That is: the whites are trying to set blacks against blacks.

My only question, darling, about reality is: Why does Mr. Big want to knock off English spies?

Knanga is an important black diplomat but I don't know from where cause I never read newspapers. He is heading for San Monique. Innocent now-plucky-instead-of-dumb James is taking a bath in his luxurious San Monique hotel when a black-and-white snake jumps for his jugular. Wham! James since he's white has super-technology to burn up this snake energy. A black hat sparkling a bloody white feather.

Where in San Monique was the English spy offed? James' CIA (that is good) cohort is a black (that is evil) female (that is suspect). Having smartened up in matters of the world James tells her, "You're evil. I'll fuck you anyway cause I have to fuck." Fucking dissolves all evil. So in this voodoo land as she fucks she becomes white. Now vulnerable to voodoo, she sees big one-eyed voodoo mask in which life and death are inseparable. White people say: "Too dangerous to be between good and evil. Got to be all good or all evil cause we want war."

White people got love and black people got sex. (Except if you're like me you fuck everyone but your friends, but I'm koo-koo.) Not like the dead black slut the beautiful female fortune-teller is white (that is good). James understands even though she seems to work for Mr. Big she's good cause he knows understands that this world is only appearances and that these appearances are real only symbolically. Since the only reality of phenomena is symbolic, the world's most controllable by those who can best manipulate these symbolic relations. Semiotics is a useful model to the post-capitalists. White man say: Voodoo is power. For-tuneteller is pure white virgin. If you make her red, she die. James makes her red so she's no longer black (that is she can no longer tell truth, fortunes). Mr. Big is going to kill her.

"Everyone on this black island is black therefore after me. Everyone I see. Motorcyclists policemen washingwomen actors. I've got to run away. No matter how fast I'm moving, I can't move fast. I've got to get away from dying. Voodooland is dreamland. White people, if you can cut out your dreams you'll never lose your power." James can run fast. James can get away: "Voodoo doesn't exist. It's just a cover-up of the real stuff, the heroin trade which is the only liquid-money business left in this world." Evil versus good has become unreal versus real. "I can protect you," James tells his red and dead girlfriend, "cause I'm all-powerful."

The next world is New Orleans. In this total dream or belief the same taxi driver who drove James to Harlem is now carrying him to Mr. Big. Cause everything now means something James' black funereal mourners though James hasn't died yet are whooping it up. Our deaths are their lives. James walks into the same bar. The same wall, rotating, seats James in front of Mr. Big who's wearing one white mask one black mask and whose real face is our death. "James, did you make this girl red?" "Yes Sir Mr. Big I rape all girls." "Ha ha. Eyes' no voodoo man. You know reality. I'm just a little ol' drug man. I use white and black masks only to make money. My plan to make money is to give away the two tons of heroin I'm growing in San Monique through my American soul food restaurant chain. The Mafia won't have any business left, then I'll take over the stock during the lowest point of its depression. I learned my lessons from the American stockbrokers and CIA." All blacks are whites. There's nothing unknown. "You die, girl," so the girl dies. They send James to the farm to rehabilitate him. This world isn't dream, but death. Alligators eat you up. Crocodiles even eat each other. Africa's the land of predatory animals. Dank jungles the tops of trees and bottom foliage so high and thick through which no sunlight can penetrate. Black people are black cause they live in perpetual night. During night there's no possibility of rationality.

James burns up Africa. He rationally knows why the English spies were murdered.

Dear Charlotte,

I know what evil is. I've known what evil is ever since I was three days old though it took self-consciousness to realize evil happens in this world. Evil is human and not natural cataclysm; I see a huge fire for hours murder people; well human mind refuses to accept (understand) both of these. Childhood is dumb senseless world there aren't distinctions so open to everything. But at the edge: outside. When does this outside begin to happen? The strange world like sex surrounds the child. Or everything is strange: banks tall buildings too many turds all around the head and there is no friend anywhere. The child can't know how to make friends. Nothing nothing. The horror. No way given to make one's way. No way given in this society in which to live. Nothing taught. Rules that is lobotomies taught. And if you don't totally succeed where there's no possibility of succeeding, you die.

In a high and lofty loft, formed from iron pillars, whose walls are great black holes through which the thin gasps available air are blowing back and forth: the echoes of the city, the sound bounces up down especially in the top next to the sky; the hammers' pounding up and down mingle with the hissings of subways creeping over dead rats through the below unused city. The fire rages. At its edges: gloom, through which, lost, moving like the living dead among flames and smoke, one of their faces peeps, dimly and fitfully seen flushed and reddened by the near leaping flames. And nearer the fire men wielding great towers work like ants. Others the bums who get their daily salaries by dancing filthy wipecloths in front of car windows then spraying those windows with a liquid which renders them opaque, others, thin girls who by the time they're sixteen have only half their flesh left out of this gloom draw forth, as mosquitoes throw themselves on light bulbs rather than on sources of blood, to the great sheet of glowering existence which is emitting an unsupportable heat and whose light is either beyond white or the deep dull red Jesus Christ dropped on the cross.

Through bewildering lights and deepening sounds, with thoughts such as this and other thoughts of Utopia and hope and peace and human love and human calmness and personal happiness, the child, absolutely knowing nothing (and not even knowing this) and thus having only belief (Utopia and hope and peace and despair and horror) walked farther forward into this awful place: the green plastic garbage bags appearing again again never disappearing caused the form of unbearable because unending repetition. The same dream appears in every possible form. You are trying everywhere and every way to escape and can't the poverty that's no longer only or mainly material that is no possibility of friendships no love between man and the genital he pays for the end of marriages not even cried over she has to get out. To make escape possible. The whore and the old dodderer had abandoned themselves to the mercies of a strange world, and left all the dumb and senseless things they had known behind. What do I actually remember was childhood?

It's not so much a process of remembering as of now being a child. Now I say to myself. Mommy. I don't like you because I recognize you're going to hurt me. You're outside me. I don't say to you because I say the truth. Right now I like Jeffrey because he is my friend because he isn't hurting me. I am all alone so I have all my time with very few intrusions from the outside world to mull over my thoughts, for they are my dolls, though sometimes they torment me or rather the thought that I might be mulling too much torments me. R___ can hurt and can not hurt. These people have nothing to do with me. Due to my fearing, my world is apart. How can another person penetrate this childish world?:

2. *The penetration in the school in Poland*

1956. The Cegielski metal factory was the largest factory in Poland. As a result of the city communications and Cegielski factory workers' unfulfilled demands, the Poznan riots broke out.

The first thing we see is men, standing under doorways, shooting guns. There're no other people on the streets. We therefore have no way of knowing at whom they're shooting. During a workers' march to Kochanowski Street to free some political prisoners from the secret police, a cop killed a worker. The rest of the workers dipped the Polish flag into his blood and rioted. In this perpetual war there aren't any functional nations: the functional political distinctions are military versus civilians. The Polish police fled the city. The army entered.

Now we see one man. He's shooting, like all the other men. We and he have no way of knowing at whom he's shooting. All the newspapers therefore everybody blame the lumpenproletariat because the lumpenproletariat as stupid immoral drools in their inabilities to know and act define civilian life's actual conditions. The newspapers deny the lumpenproletariat's therefore ordinary people's existences: "All Americans are Reagan." "All Americans are impoverishing all other people because all Americans own toilets." The man who's been shooting comes home. He has to flee Poland; we don't know why; it's not because he's evil because he's a good man because he's responsible to his wife and children. His wife and children won't flee with him; we don't know why; so love is broken up.

Since the new reformist officials supported the Poznan riots, the civilians thought they had won. But the officials quickly centralized the workers' councils and reduced them to decorations. Military versus civilian seemed to equal centralized power versus non-centralized power. The military either corrupted or removed the popular worker leaders.

I am in school because I haven't learned anything. Maybe, a little, the cause of my suffering. Nothing matters unless it is right now. I see you so my heart is stopping still.

What is writing about; what is writing? If it is anything: (Adorno) "Art expresses the individual, the unique, the utopian, the critical, the new, the innovative vision" and is the opposite of, opposes media advertising commerciality or the market. If writing's nothing: it isn't presenting a story, it isn't presenting an expression of what's real, since it's present it isn't even this (time past); it is, going back to beginnings. Childhood beginnings.

Begin childhood from the very beginning. I have a great deal of difficulty beginning to write my portion of these pages, for I know I am not clever. Whether I shall turn out to be the hero of my own life, or whether that station will be held by anybody else, these pages must show. Among other public buildings in a certain town, which for many reasons it will be prudent to refrain from mentioning, and to which I assign no fictitious name for there's no need for fiction anymore, there is one for many many many years common to most towns, great or small: to wit no wit, a workhouse; and in this workhouse was born—on a day or date which I need not trouble myself to repeat because it isn't known and of course doesn't matter to you, the reader, at this point, at least at this point—the item of mortality whose name is prefixed to the head of this chapter. My father's family name being Pirrip, and my Christian name Philip, my infant tongue could make of both names nothing. In these times of ours, though concerning the exact year there's no need to be precise because it isn't known because everyone's a heroin addict, a boat of dirty and disreputable appearance, with two figures in it, floated on the Thames River, between Southwark Bridge, which is iron, and London Bridge, which is stone, as the wetness of life is closing in.

All Polish students think about is sex. I know my parents were some kind of revolutionaries right-wing or left-wing I don't know which back in 1958. The only thing I care about is how to get the boy at whom I'm staring to fuck me. Adam Mickiewicz in his play DZIADY shows that the kids who plotted against the Russian Tzar were heroes. The Russian ambassador closes down Kazimerz Dejmek's production of DZIADY. The boy doesn't want to fuck me because he wants nothing to do with sex. When the students protested the Russian-Polish censorship by occupying the university, students in Warsaw Poznan Krakow Wroclaw and Lodz supported them. For any revolution to succeed nowadays, the media liberals and those in power have to experience the revolt as childish irresponsible alienated and defeatist; it must remain marginal and, as for meaning, ambiguous. The Polish workers didn't understand why the students revolted, but gave them food. *His* older brother is the hunk of the school and the main revolter. The cops, acting normally, beat us all up. Some of us get physically jailed. None of us no matter how well-educated or whether our families are rich or poor are going to get jobs. In San Diego: Marcuse lived in fear of his life. Whenever we were in a car, the cops stopped the car because, they said, we were bank robbers. Now the cops no longer bother us because we don't exist. My life doesn't exist. What did I learn in school? This music isn't non-music; it's violence. *This text is violence.* The ruling elite stuck its own people into the now vacant university positions. Boy, you're not only going to fuck me, you're going to make love The whole Department to me of Philosophy and that of Sociology You has disappeared. do. There's no hope; there's only romanticism.

Well the main thing is to fuck only people you dislike, says the older brother,—that is if you want to save your friendships and ability to love—cause sex is the rampant disease. In my family, my mother never talked to me cause mothers are above their children: they don't have to love their children and their children have to worship them. In this way my parents taught me love is an expression of power. Sometimes mom blabbed to, not with, me cause none of her friends were around at the moment with whom she could talk. Mom was the first person to teach me the world is other than me and that I live in silence. I don't talk to anyone: I talk to myself; I either play images with other people or do whatever they tell me to do. Grown-ups and kids are my enemies. "Mom," at the dinner table, "I'm getting married."

"Kathy . . . don't tell me."

"Tell you what? I told you I'm getting married."

"You are."

"Are what, mom?" I know.

"We can get you a cheap operation."

"I don't want a cheap operation." My parents were always as cheap as possible with me; my mother spends every cent she can get her tootsies on even my allowance on gawky Gucci jewelry; "I'm not getting married because of that."

My mother has the usual look on her face of "this stubborn girl."

My father helps out my mother whenever she's too angry to lecture me: "You're not going to have the baby?"

"What baby? . . . There are other reasons to get married!"

"You might as well tell us if you're in trouble."

"Yeah, I'm in trouble." I shoved my right inside wrist covered with razor scars over the dining-room table. "Now don't ask me any more questions. I'm not going to tell you anymore."

My mother turns her face to the left. "Oh, Kathy," my father as my mother instructs me, "don't do disgusting things at the dining-room table." Each time I slice the blade through my wrist I'm finally able to act out war. You call it my masochism because you're trying to keep your power over me, but you're not going to anymore. This is the beginning of childhood.

Now there is no possibility of revolting successfully on a technological or social level. The successful revolt is us; mind and body:

Theory: The separations between signifiers and their signifieds are widening. According to Baudrillard, the powers of post-capitalism are determining the increasing of these separations. Post-capitalists' general strategy right now is to render language (all that which signifies) abstract therefore easily manipulable. For example: money. Another example is commodity value. Here Baudrillard differs from Marx: according to Baudrillard, political power is determining economy. In the case of language and of economy the signified and the actual objects have no value don't exist or else have only whatever values those who control the signifiers assign to them. Language is making me sick. Unless I

destroy the relations between language and their signifieds that
is, their control.

Christ is rising on the cross. In the nineteenth century truth
and beauty were. In the twentieth century use determined. Bohr,
Werner, etc. Now destroy the twentieth century. Is use value a
post-capitalistic construction? The value of this life is what I make
or do. I live in absolute loneliness. What's the value of this life
which is painful if it's not what I make or do in the world?
Assumption of this question: I am the subject of the making and
doing. I make (my) values or meanings. *I do* means *I mean*.

Given this syntax and grammar, functionality is the only possible value: I'm a Puritan; I write; I don't love; I.

But what if *I* isn't the subject, but the object? If the subject-
object dichotomy is here an inappropriate model?

(Note: the war is now, further than the body or sensible fact,
on the language level.)

I don't mean. I am meant. That's ridiculous. There's no meaning. Is meaning a post-capitalist invention?

The shits have made me. The shits have determined the sick
bad relations of these parts sexually to each other. What I'm
trying to say is that I can't just say, well human lives have always
been miserable pain is just another event like shitting. Be above
it (no meaning).

I buy lots of dresses. I don't need lots of dresses because I own
lots of dresses. I have to buy a dress like I did today because
buying it makes me into, one, a person who can buy and, two,
a person who's buying a frivolous thing. By buying (eating) I'm
bought (eaten). *I* am the commodity. The commodity buys me.

Take this formula farther. According to Marx: when I work,
there's the actual value of my work and the market value of my
work; the problem is that the market value is increasingly, now
fully, the determinant of the work's total value. When a file clerk
for Texaco, I spent all my working time in alphabetizing varying
pieces of paper. Texacco could have had this work done more
cheaply and quickly by computer. Why do they still hire file

clerks? So we'll have the money to buy their products. So we'll
have the money to be bought up. Marx's definitions of work value
don't apply to my situation: I don't work. I am worked. On the
one hand I'm in prison.

On the other hand everything's possible and is cause there's
no more eye there's only romanticism. Romanticism isn't fucky
fuck because at the end of the movie the older brother who's
totally political runs away from Poland which I know's useless
where's he going to run to, the USA? Even though your brother
ran away, you're coming back here to me in Poland because you
love me and you know your action is meaningless and useless
too this is what I call romanticism not love never just love.

Descent into not talking to anybody, only romanticism.

Dear Charlotte,

The first time I met you, the next night we spent fucking, after
two nights fucking, we couldn't see each other again. I want to
I want to be loved so desperately I've made myself invulnerable
to love though not to fucking fucking has nothing to do with
love. My mentality is a horror of burns and scars. By saying this
I'm making you guilty for not loving me. You have a number
of girlfriends. Your father has sent spies to separate us. Given all
of the above, and the following consideration, that the pain when
two people who have pledged their souls to each other and are
brother and sister separate is disgusting: I can't even mention sex
because it's too explosive. This scared running away from you is
my running away from my memories: I'm being sexually hurt.
I won't have anything to do with myself. I can't exist in such
violence and also work. I want us to love calmly (the only possibility). Now we're separate. If it happens you'll have nothing
to do with me for the next two weeks or forever, which I know
might well happen cause human desires stop and no will can
dictate desire, even though any contact with you is pain I won't
stop writing you. I write you who I really fuck and when I'm

celibate, though I know when we're physically fucking we're not
so honest with each other. What is writing? This is writing. When
I write you I just blab at the pen so I tell you all my grotty faults
the awful despair: the French men I know acting as if they want
to fuck or are fucking me whenever they're alone with me no
matter how they feel about me, my hatred of the intellectuals
who live on the Upper West Side of New York City, walking
down black Orchard Street, Vivian Westwood's dress, President
Reagan's using AIDS to control the American populace. These
writings are the fuels of love. Each statement is the absolute
truth—and an absolute lie—because I'm always changing. So,
despite all changes, despite and due to all our emotional fluc-
tuations and all the times you and I have to be in different parts
of the world, these writings, this work will fuel our love. Only
actors and actresses stably love.

    That passionless Finlandia who's sticking her cunt in your face
is a lesbian but keep on fucking her in London cause it's good
in London—lots of energy in the clubs and on the streets cause
the media doesn't control the streets there, yet, as they do here.
Dream in your deepest bed about me but don't tell anybody you
really know me, cause it's dangerous. Your father if he finds out
is going to murder you. And don't wake up in your own bed,
groin, and yell out to your nanny, "She's got cancer again. She
died. She jumped right off the Alps. A man ran a sword through
her body. I saw blood come out of her falling body."

    Wish me better luck. It was enough for me once to have had
your lips and arms on me.—

Dear Charlotte,

    What is this thing: human? What is the measure of human?
    In his early twenties John Donne was a fashionable brilliant
law student, avid for every kind of pleasure and worldly advance-
ment, not a debilitant, tidy, a ladies' man, a playgoer a theater

afficionado, and a great poet. Though he struggled and slaved, he wasn't a worldly success.

When he was thirty years old he had his first chance. Sir Thomas Egerton, Lord Keeper of the Great Seal, made him his private secretary. Donne was happy for the first time. His poems aren't sentimental—he doesn't care about beauty or love—and sex fascinates him: he can use sexual arousing as a tool by which to rebel against everything that's given. At the same time he secretly married his employer's second wife's niece. When her father found out, he got Donne imprisoned. On Donne's release, he made Egerton fire Donne. Because of his romantic passion Donne had to return to his former life of starving and groveling in front of the knees of rich moneybags only now he had a wife and kid.

Dear Charlotte,

I want to tell you how miserable I am cause you're not here. The only thing that interests me about this situation is that you're able to make me miserable even though I don't know you and 3,000 miles separate us. When I or anyone writes paints (makes) . . . that person is controlling. I make your body on top of mine. This isn't enough for me. The pain you write you feel and the pain I feel cause of this separation are just the unfeeling tools by which we're both making our new world. Like America. I bet the first Spaniards who sailed to America were scared. The first time a boy touched my naked flesh I was scared out of my mind. I thought I'm entering a new world unknown territory. Scared out of my mind, literally: this' what I like. What is this thing: human?

One day I want you so badly I'm going to die if I don't get you. The next day I'm absolutely uncaring about your existence. The weathers rage over the ocean; natural catastrophes happen. So known territory is the same as unknown territory. The world when I alone write (imagine) is the same as the world that we're writing and that's publicly happening.

This writing we're doing is the fuel of love and of indifference and of hatred and of the wish to destroy and of greed and of admiration.

Love, Emily

Dear Charlotte,

The more violent these weathers, this fearsome ocean hovering above my head (when I was a kid, once I had crawled into the triangle between the pink satin folds around the sides of my father's and mother's matching twin beds, two curled-at-their-tops bodies of ocean hovered above me. In that trough I was safe.): actual impersonal love. I'm safe in violence. To live in the realms of emotions. Though this might be too dangerous.

Taking this idea further: The main saying of the young boys I met in Haiti who knew that a third of them were going to die that fall cause the drought was ruining the avocado crop was "Pas de problêmes." The only words out of the only-rich-guy-I-know's mouth are "The world's about to end" (just like the *Village Voice*) and "All my friends do junk." He hates himself more than anyone else I know, not that I know any other rich people (the only people in the world). Why are poor Haitian boys happier than rich American men? Obviously love matters, not wealth. Fuck parental stability. Fuck parental security.

Take this theory of emotions further: When I was a child everything that happened (to me) was either totally good or totally evil. Now I'm adult, events are partly good partly evil even institutions. The United States of American government can't be all bad. Its organizing and administering are defective and so am I. Only unlike me it hides everything. Now I've been saying a lot of bad stuff about this government so please, understand, I'm just exaggerating certain imperfections. These imperfections in terms of the overall historical imperative don't matter; they just affect, here and there, now and then, a human life. True example of this: Once the CIA heard a gang they were after would be in a certain Baltimore bar on a certain day. At the correct time the agents bust into the bar shot everyone in the place. Two old hookers, one junky, one fat bartender, etc. The gang was in another bar. Logical example of this: A perfect 18-carat gold watch. Each tiny exquisite watch part has cost a fortune and is perfect. Two tiny parts don't properly fit together. It's a tiny unimportant flaw that makes this watch dysfunctional. When something matters to me, I return to my feelings. You and me.

Love, Emily

No Babylon love affairs no more.

3. *Christ fucked the world*

Dear Charlotte,

These last few days this MAN's been staring at me. He's ugly and he has only one eye. His eye is this hole which white drool comes out of. His mouth his very lips are thin thin-lipped people have no emotions these lips are wrapped into a snarl. The beard is gray. His color doesn't matter cause all beards stink cause they're snot. I remember when that Frenchman french-kissed me in France, his smell made me want to vomit though I was coming. Today, the house doorbell rang, though we can no longer afford a real house cause we're so poor; I opened the door cause I wasn't thinking I was daydreaming as usual about this romantic theater guy who absolutely doesn't want to fuck me. It's The Drool. I was so scared, I was surprised. Uncle's footsteps were coming all over through the floor, as usual wandering around, looking for his glasses. The Drool says: "Don't you know me?" I recognize you. Uncle's voice yelled, "Emily, I can't find my glasses." All rapists who come to my door are lovers. I passed out of this world. When I came to, my love, I was lying on auntie's satin, the maid

(I'm sounding like my mother who always said "The girl" or "She") *the slut* was in the room, so I said through my weakness to her, "Slut. Please find this drool who has one eye and looks like a mass murderer. Beg him not to love me, leave me alone," because you don't really love me and I've been physically sick cause I've wanted love so much, but now I'm recovering, a samurai. I serve only I don't know who I serve.

Love, Emily

(no heading)

The last letter I was talking about my health. I haven't told you the whole truth. I'm weak. It's hard for me to say this. Big farts are always coming out of my ass. My other disease is that I need love so badly—this is proof that either physical and mental are the same or that they're inextricably joined—when I fuck the wrong person I get sick and if someone I love leaves me I die. This situation's result is that I'm going to be an old maid. How can anyone be an old maid? I know the most horrible thing in this world is to be sexless. At the same time I know society's taught me to believe this cause men who don't marry aren't sexless, useless, and old maids: Men don't need sex to be real. It's better to be an old maid than to die. I'm being very serious now. Though I know I don't sound like it. I think I'm becoming an adult. But the thing that happened next amazed me. I was all set out to be an old maid. The Slut told me you had told her you're not a starving actor. Who the hell are you? I know we've never fucked. Worse: I don't know if you want to fuck me. Is my nighttime ending? She also, excuse me, the Slut said you have lots of money. I don't care about money; I do. So now we can marry each other. Do you want to fuck me? I think so. But I'm stupid. Slut has forgotten all the details of everything you've said so I have no way of knowing what's real and what isn't real. I haven't seen you since all of this happened. I know you're just lying, you're being romantic cause the English are romantic and they don't mean anything by their romanticism.

What is the truth? Everyone's totally apart in this city. Everyone is madly cause unsuccessfully trying through success to stave off fear. Is this true? How can I know what's true? I don't even know if I eat cause I'm hungry or lonely or nervous. Now: I know you don't want me because I'm not wantable. That's a belief. Another belief which I think at least once a day is that without a man's love I have to shit. If some man would love me, a miracle would be happening. I'm really good to a man I love; no, I'm a real shit: everything I say is false and yet, I love this life very much; I know it isn't mine.

Yours: I love you!
sklare wer wird dich befreien?

Dear Charlotte,

I don't understand what you mean by what you say cause you're English. I don't have a girlfriend. As for Miss Blacker (you keep mentioning her) (I should say Ms. cause I wouldn't want to offend you), I see Ms. Blacker now and then you see a number of women too. No one talks about you as if you're married—the women you've been with say quite the opposite. To go by what they say between the sheets, you have a lousy reputation. So either we're husbands or we're fuckfaces. Or are you agreeing with their dumb ways of seeing things?

This Blacker, though she's trying to blacken and end our friendship by drooling with lips meant for better past-times, is a friend. You say she's pregnant *enceinte* with child, etc. If this' true, it probably is my kid. I'm enormously fertile. Fertilities-in-action, that is pregnancies, are like cats: cats jump on to and paw the laps of people who're allergic to them. She's one girl who should be pregnant: her reputation stinks so badly anything could clean it up.

I'm thinking about this matter further: I'm probably not the father. I always get my sexual genders confused. The snake publisher made her pregnant just so he could get back at me. He knew my reputation's so poor, I'd get blamed. Men act like this (women are more dishonest than men because women know how dishonest men are and can't fight back any other way). In other words these people with whom we're living are degenerate—"degenerate" isn't a word I usually use and, when I do, I don't usually do it pejoratively—but in this case "degenerate" means "lives wasted in psychological dramas." Let them all get each other pregnant and gossip nastily about who the father is: If she says the baby's mine, she can have it and throw it into the garbage of the East River. I will not take part in wastefulness. If I have to, I'll send her fifty dollars. Why, I don't know. I'm not a total pig. Give her the enclosed fifty and keep my name out of it; otherwise the bitch'll think I'm guilty therefore responsible for her idiocy or idiot or shit that's why I'm giving her the money. Women don't understand they have to be responsible for their own actions.

The only person who visits us is M. the Abbé, the sole true grand family friend.

Dear Charlotte,

My uncle's best friend, the publisher (whom I mentioned in the last letter) Quinn, today semi-pissed in the steam-room though how anyone can be pissed enough to piss in a steam, told my uncle, "Living would stink in his nostrils if he didn't steep it in Scotch." My uncle and this man have been friends for years cause they never listen to what each other is saying only to themselves. His limbs were loosened; for love and longing and passion and pine were sore upon him; desire and transport got their hold on him and he turned pale. Such a political philosophy would avoid all war.

Love, Emily

Dear Charlotte,

Last night at my aunt's hotel, the Hotel Dorset, my aunt asked
Gus the waiter for fresh cream she could take up to her room
and then for a sixty-quid meal tipped sixty pence. "I saw you in
Hamlet," she says to Quinn.
"I'm not a ham, ma'am," replies the jokester.
"Of course not, I'm paying for your ham. It's much too ex-
pensive. You were a perfect ghost you look like a ghost now, and
your cock was huge."
"That was a play cock, ma'am."
"Whether real or not, his size's just what I need. If I could get
hold of him after the play ends, he'd be able to fertilize my roses."
"He tastes pretty good too, ma'am." The cocky word-slinger
is always thinking of himself.
"Sister," my uncle, waking up from his alcoholic stupor, "this
man was never a ham. You're confusing him with Nell Gwynn."
"I'm not a sexist," my aunt in her confusions gulps down her
seventh glass of wine. "Whenever a man tells me he's a feminist,
I tell him I'm a faggot." Being drunk she turns the conversation
to a less *entertaining* channel. "Are you a richie, Mr. Quinn?"
"I'm a sink of profligacy and extortion, ma'am."
These are the men I keep meeting.
When mom was three months big with me, auntie was fond
of soldiers. She even bought a few. She didn't care about money
like nasty Americans. 1947, then right after the war, so a lot of
soldiers didn't know what to do with themselves and how to earn
money now that they weren't killing. (Of course by now they've
learned how to kill in all sorts of ways.) As soon as she ran out
of money, cause even then the military was economically the
largest and most costly profession in the world, she went on to
the priesthood. They're the oldest militia and they know how,
the Jesuits have taught them, to wait for their money. Within
the confines of the confessional netting, the priest asked my aunt
her sins. Gradually, within her recital, she let in sexual sins.

Then a few descriptions. "He put his cock into my ass." The descriptions had more details. "His cock was almost too thick for my asshole," to personal details, "and I felt, I . . . I . . . ." "Priest, I'm masturbating." "Priest, do you want to know how I'm masturbating?" "The third finger of my right hand which is covered with red nail polish is touching a tuft of my wet cunt's hairs, oh, above above, as I'm . . . talking to you, I . . ." The priest is in the booth with her "Like this, baby?" "Do you want to hear more?" Priests and bums probably because both are Irish (I love the IRA) being the most moral people in the world, quickly bore nymphomaniacs like my aunt. A nymphomaniac is someone who wants constant attention. To get help my aunt ran to her doctor. The sicker she could get, the more he'd treat her like a baby. She was so love-starved—cause in any of its serious that is violent stages even physical sex is always really love—she went so far out as I am, she lay on her deathbed and almost moved from the doctor back to the priest. Now she wants to get married. I want to get married too, but only for love.

Love, Emily

Only in nighttime I see you. In darkness, I feel you. A bride by my side. I'm inside many brides. Fuck the mothers, kill the others. Night Shift sisters, await your nightly visitor.

Dear Charlotte,

Language begins in joy. Today I saw my publisher. He said to me, "All the phenomena in the world are just signs for other truths. Our job as humans is to find out what each thing represents." I think he was talking about my writing. "One of the truths," he continued, "of human existence is a malignancy. Malignant because it's real and we can't understand it. I hate this truth which manifests itself as the fact that human life is suffering. People have and do live in pain." He pounded his fist against the table until he bled in order to prove this point. "I won't accept this!" Pound. "That this is true!" Pound. "I will fight against what really is!"

"How will you do that?"

"In the same way you females are fighting against male hegemony."

"In the same way? Right now either a female dies of exhaustion cause she can't be a male and a female and live without love or else she's still in prison only now she knows she's in prison. Fighting against what's not changing—"

"Are you with me, boys? Are you going to fight with me, down to the death, the dungeons of existence, to fight for our own impossible possibilities more and more?" breaking into joy

"Yeah! Yay!" Our blood was boiling with his blood. My scarf fell over my bad eye.

"Drink." He raised the bottle. "Drink the wine that is the only blood we can drink until we halt this flow of cannibalism this greed and diarrhea that's now coursing through our world. Help! Help!" he cried.

"Captain," the second mate dared to interpose, intervene out of his strong beliefs about human identity and will that are common to New Englanders. "Don't you think you're willing too radically, and by doing so, by ignoring or going against all that is given the world, you're endangering not so importantly yourself as all of us your men?"

"Your blood must be my blood and your eyes must be my eyes."

The stubborn second mate continued, "You have given yourself over to your work. This' what's generally happening all over the American eastern seaboard, for there's no other pleasure anyone can find. Your goal or job has transformed you. You're now a monster: all your energies're against what's given; you're Walking Death; you're going to destroy us men."

"I will kill what is evil," the publisher who chooses isolation screamed. "If I destroy part of them, it's for freedom."

"The main characteristic of my American life is fame. Everyone wants media fame that is total isolation. For Americans, human identity has to be being against the world. What are the ramifications of this situation?"

Dear Charlotte,

I live alone. Anything else I write is nonsense. There's no other sentence except about knowing. I must tell you—I'm frightened. I must tell you—it makes me shiver.

What are the relations between pain and knowledge? Sometimes I'm lonely and I feel that that loneliness' painful. How can I deal with this pain? When I feel pain, I say to myself, since the pain I'm feeling is the same as any other occurrence I'm distant from it. Through analyzing and understanding I persuade myself I'm not in pain. But I know I'm in pain cause I feel it. Knowing (the cry, pain) isn't describing or analyzing or understanding.

How do I know I'm in pain? This isn't understandable.

Pain, or a cry, is primitive.

Any statement beginning "I know that . . ." characterizes a certain game. Once I understand the game, I also understand what's being said. The statement "I know that . . ." doesn't have to do with knowing. Compare "I know I'm scared" to "Help!"

What's this language which knows? "Help!" Language describes reality. Do I mean to describe when I cry out? A cry is language turning in on its own identity, its signifier-signified relation.

"To of for by" isn't a cry or language-destroying-itself. The language has to be recognizably destroying itself.

All of the above's description.

Cry: the incurable illness is the rule not the exception. Hiroshima is our rule, not the exception. Hiroshima was a historical instance of a meeting between two cultures, pre-industrial and post-industrial; my reality, between post-industrial and computerization. Today, the most interesting art is coming out of those countries in which political and cultural violence is its heaviest.

Cry: I want, above all, to avoid "doing something about" my life, and when, from time to time, the obligation is put to me to make some sort of career for myself, and to prepare for my future, I try to meet these demands and always fail.

Don't, don't go. You must stay with me now. It is the last time. Be with me always—take any form—drive me mad! Only DO not leave me in this abyss, where I cannot find you! Oh Jesus! it is unutterable! I CANNOT live without my life! I CAN-NOT live without my soul!

Emily

Dear Charlotte,

There was an air-raid warning.

A ball of blindingly intense light shone in the sky. Then all of Hiroshima became dark.

A light brown haze took over the sky. Finely ground-up chalk seemed to be falling from the sky. Most of the houses were flattened to the ground.

There were some upright building foundations. The finely ground-up white chalk lay over the surfaces. All of the skins of all of the people bled. They felt pain. Layers of human skin peeled off from layers of human skin. People felt thirsty. Some of the peoples' faces were swollen to double the size. Fires starting in a dozen places moved from left to right. The railway ties blazed. The railway poles smoked either at their tops or halfway down.

In the sky there was a great an enormous column of cloud. This cloud trailed a single thick leg below. Its top flattened as its body below the top swelled opening like a flower. The cloud seemed motionless. Its head blew first to the east then to the west then to the east. Each time it changed its direction, part of it shot out an illumination that was reddening purpling lapis lazuli-ing greening. Its inside boiled. Its stalk twisted and grew. It was bigger than Hiroshima.

The sky was an almost oblique mass of tiny particles. The cloud grew towards the southeast. On the Yokogawa railway bridge track a long freight train lay on its side. On one side of the Yokogawa railway bridge thousands of people squatted.

A loud noise happened. It shook the ground. Immediately a column of black smoke rose to the sky in the northwest. Another loud noise happened. This happened again and again and the columns of black smoke. Fires in the forest above Futaba-no-Sato roared downward and threw red-hot stones.

Many of the inhabitants were jammed around the train station although the trains didn't work.

A man's back flesh hung limply down from the lower part of his back and the flesh on the back of his hands was loose like pieces of wet newspaper. Broken tiles covered the road.

Out of the city's center a tremendous funnel of flame shot into the sky. The column of fire, growing, sucked in all the other fires burnt up the Fukuya Department Store, the Chūgoku Power Supply Corporation, the Chūgoku Newspaper Office, and the City Hall. Several human bodies floated in the water below the Miyuki Bridge.

Outside Hiroshima, the country floor was black. The thousand-year-old camphor trees burned and carbonized in the shapes of trees lay horizontal on the country floor. Silver drops of melted power cable lead dotted the sides of the roads. Live wires dangled from their iron poles. Most of the dead bodies lay on their stomachs and were naked scorched black and in a pool of shit. The corpses were many. Round black balls lay in the sand. Bodies floated down the river. A child tried to get milk out of her dead mother's breasts. The smell was nitrogen. A woman was carrying her dead baby. Many living people were diarrhoetic and vomited.

Dear Charlotte,

The main thought in the morning is that I need to shit. Only as soon as I shit do I feel good. If people telephone me before I

shit, I grudge at them on the phone. Today I grudged at my
English boyfriend he's not my boyfriend he is English cause he
hasn't fucked me. I don't know whether he wants to fuck me. I
don't fall in love with those males I haven't fucked in order to
protect myself only now I haven't fucked him and I have a crush
on him. After I shit, I keep thinking about the size of the shit.
Shit and rings are my main things. When I was a child, I was
safe (happy) if I had a ring. Every week with my friends I stole
a new wedding ring out of Woolworth's. If I let out a turd that
isn't a bunch of hard little pellets (the worst) or watery disintegrating (I can live with this) and I have a ring, I can talk crap
on the phone which I love to do.

I just found out my English boyfriend's very rich. Is this a
problem? I don't think so. I think I can love him even though
he's rich. My uncle, who used to hate his guts (I shouldn't use
such a word) when he was a penniless actor, is now in love with
him and will do anything to get us married. It's nice to get along
with uncle; I don't care about the fact that I despise his feelinglessness and materialism, for I'd rather get along than not get
along with the people who're in my daily life even if I hate them.

I've decided to not think about my shit due to my overwhelming
interest in love. The guy on whom I've got a crush might really
be interested in me cause he's been following me for the last
three months. So I think we're going to get married. Today I'm
going to my friend Rhys' wedding party. I'm going to drink a lot
of champagne and never lie again, especially to him, or to any
boy; I'm not going to pretend I'm not in love with him. It's a lie:
pretending to be feelingless. All these emotions and interest un-
clog my blood valves, unknot my muscles, let the shit move
through my guts. I've been shitting a lot more since I started this
regime (no regime).

Last night Brandon died.

This is a turkey, *this* is a wild duck, *this* is a pigeon. They put
pigeon's feathers in the pillows. In my sleep I don't die because
my pillow has pigeon feathers in it. Tonight, when I go to bed,

I'll throw it on the floor. Here is a moorcock's; and this—I can recognize it in a big pile of feathers—a lapwing's. Birdbird, whirring whirling over our heads in the middle of the moor. It wanted to get to its nest, for the clouds had touched the swells, and it felt rain coming. It dropped this feather on the heath; we didn't shoot it. That winter we saw its nest and its nest was full of little skeletons. H___ set his trap over it: the mother was too frightened of the trap to get to her dead children. I yelled at H___. I made him promise to never again be cruel to a nonhuman. Here are many lapwings! Did he kill those lapwing children? Are their bodies red? I will look at every bruise myself.

Love, Emily

Dear Charlotte,

Everything in the novel exists for the sake of meaning. Like hippy acid rock. All this meaning is the evil, so I want to go back to those first English novels: Smollett, Fielding, Sterne: novels based on jokes or just that are. Masculinity.

Love, Emily

Dear Charlotte,

When a young man was a child, his parents starved to death. A Buddhist priest found the abandoned child. He brought up the child.

Japan:

The child, now a young man, meets a famous wise old man who says he knows something. The young man tells him he himself hasn't learned anything. The old man tells the young man to go to Buddhist school.

As the wise man and the young man are conversing, policemen and the prisoners cufflinked to them, walking by, chant that

President Reagan is the best ruler even though Reagan'll be ending some of the prisoners' lives.

Two years later the wise man knows that the Reagan government's out to get him because he's wise and the Reagan government's ignorant. He's wise because, unlike most of us nowadays, he can touch what's really daily happening. The police arrest him.

While the cops drag the sage ignobly through the streets, a group of young novice priests stick a sacred chalice over the head of the young man who's now a priest. They can't get the chalice off his head. They ask the chained wise man to help them. The wise man can't help the young man who's lost his head because the young man, though he's in Buddhist school, doesn't know anything about himself. The young man can't change himself or anything else. The wise man tells the other dumb Buddhists that the young man will find his head only when he dies.

An unknown man tries to kill Reagan but instead drops William Casey. Reagan becomes more paranoid about his power. He and the sage plan to kidnap, bring up in secret, and if necessary murder the remaining Kennedy children. They have to act, as the wise man says, in accordance with the overall historical imperative.

Right now our main historical imperative is to preserve our imaginings, dreams, and own actings which Reagan is trying to decimate. The wise man says, if you government officials surrounding Reagan assassinate him, you'll save human civilization. We can't successfully revolt against our government because they control technological, military, and psychological information and power. But: there's one human power who's more ruthless, greedier, and stupider than Reagan. This power lives in the Far East.

An essay on the relations between government and morality: A presupposition of any government is that humans need social rules to curb their innate greed, angers, lusts, etc. Rousseau said that, to the contrary, social rules make us act in the ways we have to in order to destroy these rules. If this is true, why do we need to be governed? This solution is idealistic therefore useless. How can a government whose nature is power be good? Only if the governor knows what's good for his people. Human beings don't know in this way. A governor has to be in a morally impossible position. He has to become who his position says he is, just as an artist is exactly what is given.

This powerful stupid yellow ruler who lives in the Far East can only speak broken English. Missionaries who dared stormy seas to enter this foreign land converted his first wife to Christianity. At the present time the United States needs missionaries more than the foreign land does. Since she's only yellow and slant-eyed, George Bush tries to fuck her while the sage and the yellow monster are planning to overthrow the government of the United States of America.

Yellow people are taking over the United States of America. They own the vegetable groceries, golf courses, fashions, technological designs, and car-manufacturing plants. Unlike us, they believe in wisdom. They're going to make the sage the American Vice President and instil desperately needed anti-materialism.

For the last six months the American people have been reacting to the constant political nausea, fluctuating economy, and social breakdown by returning to their only memories of social and political stability: the McCarthy era. They are worshipping various post-capitalist phenomena such as the nuclear family. Such contents are now hollow or formal; only the forms are sacred, thus the hypocrisy of the middle class; no American believes in anything. If nothing's real, how can anything be real and is this hell? Yellow gooks are infiltrating our civilization and now they're destroying it. They wear two-feet-high purple hats trimmed in fur. Their eyes are the eyes of insects. Their men have tongues which move up and down a hundred miles an hour. Their men like whips better than cunt hair. They are, one, stopping the freedom of our civilization; for instance, artists in their country have to do exactly what the government officials tell them to do.

They are, two, eradicating all Western anti-social heroism in-
dividuality and weirdness, all blackness, all our civilization is
really depending on. The yellow gooks are taking away our selves.
"Without white minds, white people be much happier." Wise
men says, "If white people can be lobotomized white people want
lobotomy: white people have no dreams."

Actually beyond our cliches which are beliefs, actually outside
our cliches which are beliefs:

President Reagan.

What is Japan?

Wittgenstein: Can I describe (know) anything truthfully? No.
I: For me when I love I don't know and this is Japan.
My love, the quality of love.
My love, pain's within rather than is love.
Solitariness.

As for solitariness, the great forests of the north, the expanses
of unnavigated waters, the Greenland icefields: still the magic of
their changeable tides and seasons mitigates their terror. But the
special curse of the Encantadas is that to them change never
comes; neither the change of seasons nor of sorrows. Finally ruin
itself can work little more in this place. They were cracked by
an everlasting drought beneath a torrid sky. Man and wolf alike
disown this land. Little but reptile life is here found: tortoises,
lizards, immense spiders, and that strangest anomaly of outland-
ish nature, the iguana.

The yellow men have captured Reagan. They bow to him and
say, "We are not original. We take what is given such as American
know-how, do it better, then send the products—such as clothes,
machines—back to America. We adopt everything. We adapt to
everything. We adapted to Hiroshima. (Bowing.) Hiroshima was

the way we adapted to your non-adaptable civilization. Now we give Hiroshima as a reality back to you. (Bowing.)" Reagan's head appears stuck on a white pole yellow with dog piss. Blood drips down the pole's sides. Reagan's head appears stuck on a white pole yellow with dog piss. (Bowing.) "The self is the object, not the subject. We don't adopt; we are adopted. We don't know who our father is and our mother hates us because our father abandoned her because she was three months pregnant with us. Language knows only when it cries. (Bowing.) A child who's been hurt is the devil and must cause social pain. (Bowing.) How is it possible to govern? (Bowing.) During Pearl Harbor, not as in *The Winds of War*, the white people screamed the yellow devils were going to decimate them and the yellow people, who like my mother were very sensitive, killed themselves. (Bowing.) Somewhere there has been a breach of honor."

Love, Emily

Dear Charlotte,

As far as I can tell, both Nietzche and Wittgenstein thought their lives were painful.

Ludwig Wittgenstein was born into the midst of all possibilities including great art and wealth. When he was a young man he gave all his family wealth to his siblings even though they despised him. He wanted nothing or he had turned against himself. He turned to studying mathematics then philosophy with Gottlob Frege then Bertrand Russell. He left his graduate studies to live in Norway as alone as possible. He wanted nothing or he had turned against himself. In the end of World War I he wrote his doctoral thesis in an Italian fascist prison. He had given away so much money, he couldn't afford the travel fare to return to Russell. When he asked Russell, Russell sent him the money.

I think he hated his body rather its demands, for he was celibate except now and then there would be two or three weeks of violent nights, fuck every young boy by the river, the body pleasures until the desire for love and friendship turns around and vomits. As in me the fierce longing to unite affection and sexual desire or the mind and body is the basis of living pain.

He loved his job teaching just-adolescent boys in southern Austria. The hicks took away the job from him cause they thought he was corrupting his students though he probably wasn't.

I say I'm in pain. Is my pain hidden from you? Can you see my pain? Say, there's a group of people who don't know what pretended pain is. If one of them says "I'm in pain," the others cry. Someone teaches these people the phrase "to simulate pain." A beggar says, "I'm in pain so please give me money." Now: Is simulated pain a kind of pain? (By analogy, if I accept the model of analogy, I'm asking about the relation of falsehood to reality.)

I can only be in pain if I know what pain is. I'm in pain so I know what pain is. If I know what's pain; when I'm pretending pain, this false pain can't be pain.

Now take the example of "hidden pain." Example: when I feel pain as I am now with this ulcer, I pretend I'm not feeling it so you'll keep believing me and so you might still love me. Hidden pain is the same as simulated non-pain. Therefore simulated pain is overt pain. This kind of logic's useless cause it has nothing to do with human intentionality.

"Your inner self is hidden from me." This means: I'm unsure how to describe your words and acts. I can only guess at your feelings. I am burnt and cry out. I wouldn't call this "pretending." We teach each other language. We don't teach each other to cry out. What, then, is "pretended pain?" Am I pretending to cry out to you?

Nothing is hidden from you; if I were to assume something's hidden, I would be assuming a psychology or description less interesting than your intention, the cry. I affirm life and life doesn't need affirmation. I am lying down for you, Charlotte, and spreading my legs.

                                                            Emily

2 TEENAGE MACBETH

The English are the good guys and the Irish are the bad guys.

Note: All the characters can, obviously, be played however the actors and actresses want. Total schizophrenia or freedom, including any distance between player and character, reigns.

All the English characters are either upper- or upper-middle-class or identify themselves as such.

Macbeth as a chess game: repetition one

ACT I

1. The two sides.

As yet there's no language. These words, therefore, must just be shown: what is war? War happens when one side fights another side.

Side One (*still no speaking*): Nothing given to or understandable by humans. The appearances of nothing in the world: In geographical terms, the desert. In psychological terms, those who aren't rational logical or understandable to humans: the witches. In epistemological terms: not-knowing. In verbal terms: prophecy. In temporal terms: only the future is reality.

(*There are huts made of earthen sods, or of mud strengthened with straw; the rank reek of the wet turf on the heath; the smoke that blinds the eyes as one creeps into the interior: (Rain brown-dripping through the thatch; in this webbed murkiness men and women and children and animals huddle. Human beings live like this. Description of nothingness.)*)

Side Two: Something: We English who are honorable and just. In geographical terms: our stronghold in our empire: Ireland. In psychological terms: reality is only and exactly that which appears. We aren't liars. In epistemological terms: we understand reality, therefore define good and evil. In verbal terms: simple declarative statements. In temporal terms: the past which we're naming or history is the present.

2. The two sides have identified themselves. Now war can begin. Each side starts fighting by trying to lay out its territory.

Let's say that the English or Side Two is White and The Irish or Side One is Black:

England: The past is the present. Ireland challenged our natural hegemony. We own all that's natural or the world because we're upright and honest. (They do stand very straight.) The rebel Macdonwald, though he was a Protestant being a Mac-, fought us and we, because we're in the right, have defeated him. The Irish who identify with us are English. The Porter who though Irish is English killed the traitor Macdonwald. Therefore, The Porter will be allowed to be Protestant, English, and noble.

The Irish Bitches. *(They don't wear anything. Neither shoes nor stockings, nor any covering whatever on the head and have no churches but unnatural ones. Some shreds of flannel which might have once been a slut's underpants. One tattered shirt of unbleached linen ties around one old crone's waist. Another sports a rotted blanket over her bone-thrusting-through-flesh shoulder. The final bitch has made herself out to be, at least in her opinion, feminine. Her hands have shoved her hairs so filled with filth they can be moulded like clay into the shapes of birds.*

    (Pride, passion, and disdain dilate their eyes' pupils.

    (Human beings are these Bitches' drudges, slaves, horrors, and conveniences. The ruling idea or the only perspective

*they want to communicate is that no event fits into its context
and, at the same time, necessity compels every event.*

*(The Second Bitch's a child. Passions predominantly avar-
ice're owning her mind and therefore actions)*: We're malicious and cause causeless revenge. In this world Nothingness' chaos. We'll make The Porter and his friend Banquo,
who're coming here, our territory by convincing them our
Irish future's more real than their English past. *(The Porter
and Banquo arrive in front of The Bitches.)* Porter, you will
be our leader therefore you're our leader.

The Porter: I believe you not cause I've any reason to believe
you, only cause I want to believe you. This world's desire.

Banquo: I never believe in cunts or holes. Females always lie
cause all they do is talk from feelings. All of my friends,
cause all are English, are male. *(The Porter and Banquo,
once friends, glare at each other. Civil war begins.)*

3. *Nothingness or the Irish uses the Porter to advance its territory.*

The Porter *(thinking alone in the maze of the forest)*: I believe
the Bitches: I'm going to rule Ireland. But how can I rule
a country that belongs to another country? England owns
Ireland. England'd rather start World War III than give up
her favorite colony, the economic portal to Western Europe.
England's more powerful than me. I can't fight such power.
I can only fight by being devious. Deviation is my war
strategy.

Now: Our Irish Prime Minister—ours?—is relying on
trusting me. I'll murder him. The Irish character isn't
straightforward.

4. *Nothingness extends its territory not only through the Porter
but also through his wife.*

Mrs. Porter: I'm confused. On the one hand, I'm human just
like my husband; on the other hand, I'm unnatural because
I'm female. Females are those beings who only want re-

venge. My humanity has tempered infinite revenge into caused revenge or ambition. Irrationality, Animalism, and Night: own me. Since I can't know, I don't want clinging to my thoughts fucking up my mind.

5. *The other side, something, defines its territory.*

In the Porter's castle.

Duncan (*the Irish Prime Minister. Very properly*): We English are good, honest, and kind. Natural owners.

Mrs. Porter: We hope our hospitality'll reflect at least half Your Kindness.

Duncan: I'm sure you're as good as us.

6. *Nothingness repulses something by rejecting something's goodness.*

The Porters talking to each other in their castle.

The Porter (*pondering*): Either events are caused or rational, or else there's no causes no morality no justice. If the first is real, I should keep being a fake or English. If the second's real, the Irish must control Ireland. Since I'm ambitious, babe, I'll opt for the second. This reasoning's circular. So I've no reasons for choosing nothing.

Mrs. Porter: You're back in the nineteenth century! How can your reasons or so-called rationality be separate from you? And if your reasons're you, there's only desire and will. Therefore there's no morality in the twentieth century: there's only ambition.

So either play at being a good boy like the English and as the English want you to do, or by recognizing who you are and being responsible for it, be adult.

The Porter: You mean: "Kill the Prime Minister"?

Mrs. Porter: In this century what we know as "natural" our conquerors have invented as their identities and use as tools to control us.

The Porter: I'll destroy this human malignancy to our land by acting hypocritically and spying.

Mrs. Porter: You'll take over the rule of Ireland then?

The Porter: It's evil to want political power.

Mrs. Porter: In this century the only way a human can't be a slave is by being evil.

The Porter: You're arguing rationally for irrationality.

Mrs. Porter: I guess I'm nuts.

The Porter: I guess we've chosen to be mad rather than good and knowledgeable . . . (*It's nothingness' advantage.*) . . . OK, Voodoo, since I can't know anything: I don't know this body therefore this body's dead; I don't know anything therefore language is all lies. (*In uppity English accent.*) Welcome, Your Highness. (*Bowing.*) We're so proud to have you here. May we eat the scraps of filet mignon off your plate? That's better food than we usually see. Your spit is our blood. Are your mummy's polo ponies teething properly? Perhaps they would like to teeth on our corpses? Here a corpse's bones're supposed to be full of calcium. (*Pauses. Now in a very lowly peasant's tone as if his mouth's full of shit.*) I'm not sticking this knife in your back, Sir, cause I'm ambitious. You've already made me a Caw-tholic or Protestant or whatever the Hell religion is. I'm killing you. Shit, in order to kill you. I choose to be the head of the IRA.

ACT II

1.   *Having repulsed the first English attack, the Irish, getting courage out of nothing, try to extend their territory to the Porter's friend Banquo and to everywhere or nature.*

In the same castle.

The Porter (*blurting it out*): Banquo, what d'you think's more important? Friendship or political morality?

Banquo (*standing up very straight*): Political morality. (*Not taking The Porter seriously.*) Am I correct?

The Porter: You *are* English (*Aside*). So I'll murder you and
your children. I choose political morality too. But I'm not
pretending I'm not contradicting myself. (*Looks at Banquo
to see if he notices anything.*) Jesus Christ! The sky's so fuckin'
beautiful: Masses of clouds on clouds bluer than the sky.
This' the first time in months I've felt happy: the sky's making
me feel space. I'll never sleep again. Every human must
become space all the time! I will space! So I don't have the
time to relax. If I had the time to relax, I'd fuck men by the
score cause having a man love me's the only event that
relaxes me. My life's without rest; my life's now made; my
life's now hollow. Goodbye, life! Goodbye, ambition! I had
to die anyway because all humans die. I'm dead: I'm unnatural: I'm alive only because I make. The hell with wanting to fuck. Let Banquo be his natural naive self. The English might rule the world, but they're more innocent than
us.

(*Outside the castle.*)

A Tree: They're against us because we're natural.
A Baby Bird: I'm not natural. I'm full of cancer cause they stuck
hypos full of carcinogens into mommy's eggs before I was
even able to fight.
A Tree: You have to be natural: you're Nature . . .
The Water: I'm polluting my brothers and sisters.
Reality: The Irish don't have to destroy us because they're so full
of self-hatred and hypocrisy we, being out-of-balance, are
reacting. The pendulum'll swing more and more violently
cause there's no way out of Nature.

(*In the castle.*)

The Porter (*all alone*): Morality makes a-morality and a-morality
makes morality. Human will makes causality; causality de-
stroys my ability to perceive. (*Screams. His wife runs in.*) I
want a lobotomy. (My main nightmare: that of getting one.)
Mrs. Porter: To Hell with you. To Hell with you.

The Porter: I'm already in Hell.

Mrs. Porter: They've been lobotomizing me for years. I'm more of a man than you are.

The Porter: You could win out over anybody. You're like Mike Arguello.

Mrs. Porter: Who's he?

The Porter: A fighter.

Mrs. Porter: I don't approve of macho shit sport. (*Her egoism wins over her good judgement.*) How's he like me?

The Porter: He's the greatest bantamweight cause, not only has he fought at every different weight, but he gives and takes an unbelievable amount of punishment.

Mrs. Porter (*spreading her legs and throwing them over The Porter's blood-smeared mouth*): Is that why you won't fuck me now?

The Porter: I'm about to murder. Go away.

Mrs. Porter: You know you're a sadist only your sadism isn't confined to your bed. All I want to know is how conscious are you of your obsessions?

The Porter: If I'm going to be a good artist, I have to judge myself as little as possible. (*So The Porter must even get rid of human knowledge.*)

Mrs. Porter: I think I'm falling in love with you cause you won't fuck me anymore.

The Porter: Unnatural has become natural: You love me only cause you're repeating your father's unwanted rape. Cause you said "No" to him, you can only say "Yes" to a man who doesn't want you who's rejecting you. Victims like you, not the victimizers, suffer. If not, the victimizers would be victims.

2. *The IRA kills off the Irish Prime Minister.*

Macduff (*an Irishman who loves the English cause the English have enrolled him as Chief of Police*): Knock. Knock. (*Knocking.*)

The Porter: Who's there?

Macduff: Ida.

The Porter: Ida who?

Macduff: I don' do anything

The Porter (*still not opening the door*): What *do* you want?

Macduff: I wanna fuck you.

The Porter: Oh then, come in. (*Opening the door, sees Macduff.*)
Shit, you're going to hurt me.

Macduff: Our English Lord is dead! Our English Lord is dead!

The Porter: Cut out the capitals: you're not Caw-tholic.

The RUC (*entering and shouting*): Treason's somewhere in this
castle!

Mrs. Porter: Alas.

The Porter: I don't want to be fucked anymore.

Macduff (*to The Porter*): Give a damn.

(*The Irish Prime Minister's sons, Malcolm and Donalbain, one who's
ten and the other who's twelve years old, enter.*)

The Porter (*to these two boys*): Give a damn. This' Hell. Your
father's been murdered. Don't make a sound.

Donalbain (*the elder*): Is it suicide?

The Porter: Absolutely not. The evidence points to unknown
causes.

Macduff: Let's go to war! The Falklands! Who killed him?

The Porter: The butler, of course. (*Mrs. Porter, who's been fucking the butler, faints. The Porter kicks her.*) Ignore her. All
she wants is attention because she's a failed actress. Women
can't go to war to get what they want.

3. *The English fight back by arranging their defense.*

Same room.

Donalbain (*to his brother in secret*): Keep your trap shut. It's
better to have neither your own language nor identity these
days. Just like Arguello, be reservedly polite continuously
until it's time to come out: Then, kill.

Malcolm: I'll retreat to England. England's peaceful cause she's
    making her colonies, especially Ireland and Scotland, fight
    civil wars.
Donalbain: I'll retreat to America who learned imperialism from
    England.
Banquo: I don't know.

4. *Because the Irish are beginning to control their territory, they're
wrecking their territory. 1845.*

*Outside The Porter's castle, the tips of the potato stalks wither.
The decayed tubers' stench flies into the hovels and turns the air
into gas. Thousands of people are starving, but the Irish don't
care about their own people.*

Young Irish Lad (*tousled-haired and freckled*): This fall I'm prob-
    ably going to starve to death. So what. My mother's starving
    to death now.
Daniel O'Connell (*the famous Irish leader who uses language to
    lie to the Irish*): We've conquered England, babes. Robert
    Peel our main English enemy, has just slit his own throat
    cause he won't back down from opposing the repeal of the
    Corn Laws.
Robert Peel (*in haughty British accent*): You're right. I'm re-
    signing from the English Cabinet. The Cabinet's all yours,
    Lord John Russell.
Lord John Russell (*even more haughtily*): Excuse me. I can't form
    a Cabinet because I'm an aristocrat.
Robert Peel: OK I'll take back the political responsibility. The
    English people'll have cheap corn. The Irish colony'll have
    no corn. And there'll be an Irish Coercion bill.
O'Connell: Death by fighting for our country's better than this
    slow mass murder of the Irish. (*O'Connell, because he chose
    to deal effectively politically lost his human judgement of
    human beings. The non-IRA Irish, who think the English
    bring order to Ireland, have to retreat from this human wreck.*)

Macduff: I'm going to hole up in the Belfast.
Ross: I'll go with you. We'll fight from there.

ACT III.   IRELAND IN ITS YEARS OF SELF-INDEPENDENCE

1. *Political power as a living existence to stay alive must expand. Nothingness keeps trying to extend its control to Banquo.*

Outside the IRA stronghold.

Banquo: I know who killed our English master. The Porter who's now the Thane of Cawdor Glamis and the head of the IRA offed him. (*Now Banquo considers.*) Since The Porter acted against the English, he became politically successful. Should I do the same?

(*At the same time, inside the IRA stronghold.*)

The Porter (*to Mrs. Porter*): We have to make Banquo one of us.

(*Outside.*)

Banquo: In a corrupt political society if you fight that society by the opposites of corruption, you don't get anything accomplished. In a corrupt society to fight society you have to be corrupt. I'll stick with The Porter and be Irish. It takes an Irishman to hate an Irishman. I'll be corrupt.

(*At the same time, inside the IRA stronghold.*)

The Porter: I'll murder Banquo. It's the easiest.
Mrs. Porter: What about his children?
The Porter: I'll murder them too.
Mrs. Porter: How many terrorists do you think we need?
The Porter: Two.
Mrs. Porter (*going for the phone*): I'll get two. I'll get two who are so autistic, they don't care what's going on.
The Porter: They'll be easy to find. Murder solves my fear.

Mrs. Porter: Murder some more. You're a whole country and if the English don't care about the Irish, why should you?

2. *The Irish territory.*

Same scene continuing.

Mrs. Porter: I'm unhappy.

The Porter: Don't lay it on me. I can't handle my own problems.

Mrs. Porter: You don't understand. I don't know what to do. Even thought hurts me. It hurts me to think.

The Porter: You'd be better off dead.

Mrs. Porter (*considering*): If I was dead, I'd be really asleep. I'm dying to sleep.

The Porter (*whose egoism has to override her*): Everything I do's out of fear. I hate this kind of existing. How did I start living this way? (*She tries to answer.*) You, shut up. We're all going to die anyway. Why's my whole life governed by fear of the one event that has to happen to me? Then if I'm not scared of death, what's there to be scared of? Why am I still always scared? The life which I know which is anxiety and fear is a prison. I want to be out of prison: I want to be dead. Why should the one thing we want most scare us the most?

Mrs. Porter: You're not going to kill yourself so you might as well consider your ambition. The IRA isn't, to say the least, in the solidest of positions. Let's grant what you're saying's true: this living isn't worth considering cause it's just a prison whose director is fear. Therefore: There's no morality here. No causation for us. We can do whatever we want. Anything including hypocrisies and lies are just tools. Every event's unreal and separate from meaning. If this' all true, why am I feeling so much pain?

The Porter: My mother trained me to always kiss my elders "Hello" even if I hated their guts. So I hate hypocrites. I will say "I hate." I will go for ambition. All that's so-called "natural" is neurotic. I'll tell you what's really natural: sex

. . . (*He doesn't fuck anymore cause he has so many political responsibilities.*) . . . holocausts, murders, any extraordinary events, peoples'-fingers-getting-cut-off, sexualities that make people crazy always: these're natural.

3. *The IRA lose a battle.*

The two Terrorists Mrs. Porter phoned plus one other who isn't recognizable it might be The Porter, in black masks, stand inside an office building. The flourescent light is even.

A Terrorist: Are they coming?

(*Banquo and his children enter the building. He wears a businessman's hat. They're regular little boys. The Terrorists jump them. Just as Terrorist 1 has his left hand holding one of the son's hands at the back of the son's neck and, in his right hand, a knife two inches in front of this same neck, the lights go out. In the black.*)

Terrorist 2: What happened to the light?
Banquo (*gurgling in blood*): Murder . . .
Terrorist 1 (*as Banquo's son gets away*): Where'd he go? (*Scuffing as he looks for the child.*) The lights went out so the kid's escaped me.
Terrorist 2: Who turned out the lights?
Unknown Terrorist: This' the first time our side's failed.

4. *The Irish territory's insecurity.*

A grand IRA feast's taking place in The Porter's castle which, of course, is a hut. The food is potatoes and nettles. Irish people eat all the time. They eat only with their hands. Their noses're red. Terrorist 1 and Terrorist 2 barge their ways into the unruly drunken mob.

Terrorist 1 (*to The Porter*): We got the father.
Terrorist 2: But not his son.
The Porter: The son's more important than the father.
Terrorist 2: How come?

The Porter (*hitting him*): How dare you question your leader? This' military rule. (*Aside.*) The son's the first human I haven't been able to murder.

Terrorist 1 (*being Irish; quickly*): We'll do whatever you want, sir. For money.

The Porter: Do you think the IRA has money? That's why we use terrorism. (*Looks behind him, starts back in terror.*) Blimey. What the hell's going on here?

Banquo's dead body: Hell. You know that, dummy.

The Porter: I know that. I killed you. (*Looks around to see if anyone can hear him. The Porter's scared of his own mother.*)

Banquo's dead body: Death isn't your business.

The Porter: What *is* my business?

Banquo's dead body: The Irish don't have any business. Give up, Porter.

The Porter: I can't give up nothing. I won't give up nothing.

Banquo's dead body: Shh. Someone might hear you. Don't you have any social sense? Look: (*A scene of The Porter getting married. He's very happy.*) Is a man who fucks English or Irish? Look, Porter. (*Shows him two long very thin snakes like paper strips who, as they rise out of the African river, grow. The snakes rise to The Porter who, then climbing upward, they begin to reach because each time they rise they grow. The Porter's about to scream in the land of Apartheid.*) Is a man who lives according to fear Irish or English?

The Porter: I don't know what to think. I'm the IRA leader and I'm as confused as Hell.

Banquo's dead body: Englishmen're never confused cause they don't concern themselves with death and they know to not think. Stop murdering, Porter.

The Porter: I'm not murdering: I give the past present and future Irish their self-control.

Banquo's dead body: No person can give another person power.

The Porter: I should give up. (*Banquo, having won, disappears.*

The Porter turns to his IRA men.) Stop eating as if you've the ability to be hungry and go on home.

Tousled-hair and freckled lad (*who's now anorexic*): We don't have homes.

(*Outside the IRA stronghold, before the humans begin to dribble back somewhere like tiny black figures.*)

Morning: I'm the secret man of blood. I have to fight. Let all the mourning in this universe come out.

(*Back in the IRA stronghold.*)

The Porter (*to Terrorist 1*): Now. Where's Macduff?

Terrorist 1: You won't be able to get at him. He's holed up in his home in Belfast.

The Porter: I didn't get Banquo's son and I can't reach Macduff. (*Decides.*) I don't care if it's useless, I'll fight for the Irish. Now that I've made my decision, I won't think: I'll plan. (*Calls all his men to him.*) This' guerrilla fighting. Don't think. Follow orders.

5. *Sex lies under power.*

Eleanor Courtenay's public memory.

Eleanor Courtenay (*to O'Connell in his Merrior Square home*): Sir. I hate to bother a busy person like you. Everyone says you're more than kind and I don't know where else to turn. My father, he just died, left me a small estate in County Cork.

O'Connell: You were here before, weren't you?

Eleanor Courtenay: You asked me to return.

O'Connell: I did? Oh yes. What can I do for you?

(*End of Eleanor Courtenay's public memory.*)

Eleanor Courtenay: Vain were all my struggles, all my prayers, all my cries for sustenance: the man O'Connell descended into the brutality of the monster and wouldn't leave me to

sink into apathy until he had finished and finished and
finished the most amoral remorseless and revengeless atroc-
ity which humans have ever perpetrated on each other.

Priest (*masturbating behind the confessional's bars*): What happened next, child?

Eleanor Courtenay: I had a bloody kid.

Priest: Why was it bloody? (*Suspiciously.*) Was it conceived un-
naturally?

Eleanor Courtenay (*properly*): Of course not, father. Rape's very
natural these days.

Priest: I simply meant that you had no money.

Eleanor Courtenay: A woman who doesn't have any money has
to get money out of a man. After O'Connell raped me, he
put his right hand on The Book and swore by the Virgin
Mary he'd support me.

Priest: Does he know you had his child?

Eleanor Courtenay: You bet your ass. Sorry: fathers aren't asses.
I gave that bloody nuisance up to Major Macnamara . . .

Priest: . . . O'Connell's political agent . . .

Eleanor Courtenay: . . . who put the son who had been torn
out my soft feminine arms into one of those charitable institutions in Dublin that are favored with many of Mr.
O'Connell's illegitimate offspring.

Priest: Are we going to share the booty?

Eleanor Courtenay: We're going to destroy O'Connell.

*6. The English're strong because they don't engage in double-
dealing. From this strength they start their second attack against
the Irish.*

England, the land of perfect goodness.

Malcolm: We know the head of the IRA offed your Irish Prime
Minister.

King Edward of England: A land that needs to murder isn't a
good land. Ireland needs Our help.

Malcolm: You'll help us to attack the IRA?

(*North London.*)

Macduff: Uncle, we need assistance against the creep Porter.
Siward (*an English general who's Macduff's uncle*): I could use a little war.
Northumberland: The Empire could use a little war. There's a bit of poverty going around these days.
Macduff: In this place of safety, let's start cautiously slowly planning our attack now so we don't take no chances in keeping England safe.

ACT IV. *While the Irish army violently rages, the English're building up their attack: active versus potential power. Which is the stronger?*

1.

The Irish: We are nothing. We talk nonsense. We hate human beings. We write poetry.

(*The Porter again comes into this area of nothingness. The world is horror and screaming if you see it that way. There are huts made of earthen sods, or of mud strengthened with straw; the rank reek of the wet turf on the heath; the smoke that blinds the eyes as one creeps into the interior: ((Rain brown-dripping through the thatch; in this webbed murkiness men and women and children and animals huddle. Human beings live like this. Otherwise there're just soap operas and there's also pain.))*)

The Porter (*in pain*): Bitches! I know I can't know the future. You have to tell me the future. I'd give myself to pure evil in order to enable the Irish to realize their own self-control. I know as an Irishman I don't have the power to order around anyone. I'm ordering you to obey my wishes.
The Bitches: We love you and'll give everything you want.
The Porter: I am the *violent one* who sets forth into the un-said, who breaks into un-thought, compels the unhappened to happen, and makes the unseen appear . . .

Bitch 1: . . . another ego artist . . .

The Porter: The *violent one*'s the adventurer. Ireland risks dispersion . . .

Bitch 2: . . . is dispersed . . .

The Porter: . . . instability disorder mischief.

Bitch 2: . . . etc.

The Bitches: If you want to know the future, boy, we'll show it to you: (V*isual: A big brain and war weapons.*) You're going to die, boy.

The Porter: My personal fate doesn't concern me. Tell me what I'm dying to know.

Bitch 1: You're dying to know: (V*isual: Blood covers children.*) The Irish children're covered by blood . . .

The Porter (*getting fed up*): That's not what I need to know: that's what I see every goddamn day. Instead of children we Irish have abortions. I want to know how to make Ireland self-independent!

The Bitches: You still think you can know abstractly? An unnatural child'll kill you, boy: (V*isual: A blood-covered child is wearing a crown and holding a tree.*)

The Porter: Is that me? That's not me. Who's that?

The Bitches: Who isn't you? We love you.

The Porter: My wife's had five abortions. Is that one of her abortions? Abortions're alive. What's this have to do with Ireland? Oh Ireland, where the hell are you? You're cut up and bloody. You don't exist. There's an open stomach, cut, the blood gushes out. Is the bloody child coming out of this? Can something be born out of nothing? If I don't make something out of nothing, if I don't make a self-sufficiency where there's now, if anything, chaos and blood: there's no possible Ireland. Is this what you're telling me, bitch-holes? We can make something out of nothing?

The Bitches (*masturbating*): Still too abstract, boy. When Birnam Wood comes to Dunsinane Hill, you're gonna die.

The Porter: Why're you always harping on my personal death?

Is that all there is? (*Understands.*) I'm going to die, bitches, aren't I? (*Visual: Banquo's dead body's the Prime Minister of Ireland. The English're still controlling.*) Something can't come out of nothing. Who the hell're you to tell me what's true?

(*The Bitches laugh. As he rushes at them, they burst into nothing.*)

In wartime the only possible females're whores. (*Changes his mind.*) OK. The English're so powerful, they'll always control Ireland and eliminate the Irish. I don't care. I'm still going to fight.

Lennox (*an Irish pro-English lieutenant, entering*): Porter. Macduff's now in England. He's working with the English against you.

The Porter: Is Macduff a bloody child? He can't hurt us. Nobody can do anything relevant in this world of Hell.

(*The Irish, cause they're stupid, are disintegrating their own territory.*)

2. The Irish fight back against Macduff and win.

No visuals.

The Porter (*reconsidering*): Macduff's working against us in England. I'll stop him . . . the only way I can . . . indirectly. I'll go after his territory here.

(*Now visuals.*)

Mrs. Macduff: Macduff lied to me. He told me he loved me, he was going to take me to England where it's safe, as soon as we were safe he'd be able to fuck me again: they are all lies because he was all the time planning to go to England by himself. By abandoning me and our son here, he made every part of our former life together a lie. Memories're hurting me.

Ross: How can a man love in a world that's humans knifing humans?

Mrs. Macduff: I think you have to love.

Ross: You can't love by yourself. You can't trust anyone anymore you can't believe another person. It has to be every man for himself . . .

Mrs. Macduff: . . . "Man." It's worse: it's the abandonment of love . . .

Ross: . . . so, what is there?

Mrs. Macduff: We don't use each other, but we're scared. (*With understanding.*) Macduff ran away from us out of fear. The only thing I know is how to be scared and that stinks.

Macduff's Child (*picking up her fear therefore screaming*): Mommy!

Mrs. Macduff (*looking at her child*): I don't want to live always by fear.

Macduff's Child: We can be animals.

Mrs. Macduff: They say the poor're eating dogs. There can be nothing as natural as a human or an animal anymore.

Macduff's Child: Why do you call "human" such a small thing? When an animal's hungry, it does everything it can to eat. I've seen Flopsy do this. Animals've always been eating each other. Isn't this how the world is?

Mrs. Macduff: Oh my baby. Should I eat you? If it's natural to eat you, human motherhood must be unnatural. Humans've always been unnatural.

Macduff's Child: You taught me, mommy, to lie, not to care if I lied believably, and to use other humans. Do you love me, mommy? Is it natural for a mother to love her child? If it's natural, why do you lie to me and really not give a damn about me too. Humans're all things.

Mrs. Macduff (*obsessed by the memory that a man's lied to and abandoned her*): Humans are criminals. (*The Terrorists enter and start murdering Macduff's Child.*) There's only my will. (*They murder Macduff's Child.*) Since there're no more people, I don't have a life. Since there're no more people in my life, it doesn't matter what I do. (*She runs away, but the Terrorists murder her.*)

3. The English keep building up potential force. Does the Irish active side attack on the Macduff territory succeed in weakening the English Macduff-Malcolm build-up?

Malcolm and Macduff in a pub in England.

Malcolm: The Porter's after you. You might have to play ball with him by giving me up to him.

Macduff: Forget it, kid. I don't act like The Porter.

Malcolm: You live in this Porter's world. Are you the only man who's honest?

Macduff: Then what's the use of fighting? We can just stay here and drink.

Malcolm: Because when reality's horrible, there's no way you can get out of horror. Are you honest? You just abandoned your young wife and child to our enemy. In order to sit on your ass and swill Scotch? That makes you less human than a pig. Oh shit. Who'm I to judge? I'm horror too in this horrible world because I'm not trusting anyone so I don't know what people mean by what they say. Are we totally conditioned by this world we live in? Are we zombies? Yes: You betrayed your love. I rely totally on my brains and I know my brains're deficient. We'll assassinate The Porter. We'll get rid of thinking: You a traitor and I an idiot'll run Ireland for England.

Macduff: How can a traitor and an idiot govern a people who don't yet exist?

(The English have the possibility of trying to figure out why they fight cause their backs aren't every moment against the wall. On the other hand, The Porter can only think actively cause he has to act every moment.)

Malcolm: I can damage anyone. I'm more of a fighter than The Porter. I wouldn't get near me to fuck me or even with any intention of being nice.

Macduff: You're just self-centered. You're not anywhere near as evil as the Irishman what he's now doing to Ireland.

Malcolm: I'm more vicious than The Porter: I've endless bottom-less hunger. When there's just a hint an inch a speck of hunger in me, that hunger's the only thing in me. I or my will is hunger; else, I'm empty. I'd do anything to fuck you. It's only cause a certain level of me is scared that I seem one level below my surface honest and trustworthy.

Macduff: Every human's hungry in this same way. Why do you think you're different? You have to learn to control these hungers which're energy, like you work your muscles.

Malcolm: Repressive and hypocritical.

Macduff: Hypocritical only if you call these attributes "you."

Malcolm: What else are there? I love being evil.

Macduff: On one side of the coin you're good; on the other side, evil. On one side of the coin this world's good; on the other side, evil. You don't know anything cause all you see are your attributes, so you say there's nothing and no one else.

Malcolm: If I'm not English and I'm not Irish, what am I? I see: I'm twenty-two. I'm an Irishman who's pro-English. I'm going to assassinate The Porter so I can run Ireland for the English.

Macduff: You're OK. At least you've stopped being an intellec-tual. Use Siward and the ten thousand men under him.

(*Outside.*)

King Edward of England (*walking over to a crowd of Pakistanis, rats, sailors who lost their legs in the Falklands, and self-lobotomized kids*): No more poverty.

(*Inside the pub.*)

Malcolm (*through the window, watching King Edward*): The English King is good.

Ross (*entering the pub, to Macduff*): The IRA burnt down your house and slaughtered your child and wife.

Macduff: No. I've no life left. Not the IRA, *I* killed my wife by running away.

Malcolm: You told me I wasn't my attributes. Are you your attributes? Does IRA terrorism control you?

Macduff: No. There's no causation. I'm giving my life away to defeat the IRA.

(Irish active force doesn't defeat English potential force. English potential force's secure.)

ACT V. DIRECT BATTLE

1. *The Irish defense's weak.*

Mrs. Porter (*holding her hands in front of her, a bloody white cloth hanging off of these hands, and stumbling over everything*): I've got to get to sleep. When it becomes late at night, I feel sleepy. I go to bed. When I'm in bed, I relax. All these thoughts I've been keeping out of my head now my defenses're down infiltrate my head. All the thoughts're alive. Where's sleep? The more I can't sleep, the more painful I become.

Doctor (*overlooking, to The Porter*): She can't get to sleep.

Mrs. Porter: Every thought, no matter what its content, 's pain. The only way to run away from thinking is by sleeping. And I can't sleep.

Doctor: Her disease's mental. We can't cure schizophrenia.

The Porter: We can by killing.

Mrs. Porter: If I can't will sleep, at least I can will death.

2. *The English extend their territory into Irish territory.*

The English army march through the Irish countryside (no seeable countryside). Malcolm, Macduff, and Siward are in front. When they reach Birnam Wood they meet the RUC, UDR, UDA, and the UVF.

Siward (*saluting a young man*): Son.

Siward's Son: Our ex-Irish Prime Minister's younger son, Don-albain, is missing.

Siward: Bad manners. Nowhere to be seen.

(*All the English and the Irish soldiers shake each other's hands.*)

3. *The Irish territory that's left is Dunsinane.*

Dunsinane.

The Porter (*to the IRA soldiers in the room*): Don't think the English can hurt your leader cause our witches and mad-women and prophetesses say no living man can touch me.

Young Soldier 1 (*to Young Soldier 2*): He must be closet.

Young Soldier 3: The Irish language and madness're holy.

The Porter: The English can't hurt you because they're pansies and've been lobotomized by their culture.

Young Soldier 4: Our culture is madness and drunkenness.

The Porter (*aside*): This life's hollow. Is this really a life? Every-thing's now war and I'm a soldier. What's ambition? What's success? There's certainly no fucking. Am I descending into sentimentality? Adult living is making decisions. I've made my decision. You don't go running to a doctor to cure your decision. You don't judge a decision. This violence's life.

4. *The English further extend their territory to IRA defectors and by decimating the Irish land.*

Malcolm (*to four mixed English and Irish-Protestant Soldiers*): Cut down this wood to use as camouflage. In that way approach the Irish stronghold. I know you think the Irish don't fight according to agreed terms.

The IRA're turning against their head cause he's a drunk.

5. *The Irish territory or the Irish language further disintegrates into meaninglessness.*

The Porter (*talking to himself*): The good-for-nothing Irish're revolting against me. We're slaves.

I'm all alone in the room. My wife she killed herself out of loneliness. Why can't women go beyond their personalities? Is it cause they're dependent on men? Slaves. I won't be a slave to the English. I'm all alone in this room and everywhere else. I'm beyond thoughts, needs, and emotions.

I'm no exceptional person to follow. I'm the same as any other human: phenomena come and go, become and die. Phenomena: you see outward; you don't see inward.

If every phenomenon no matter what it is comes and goes, how can there be any value? Fuckin' human life's worth nothing. This world should be war cause all human living is useless.

IRA Soldier (*shivering against the wall*): Trees're coming at us, sir.

The Porter: So what. Nothing's real and nothing matters. There're just different events. That's all there are. That's what I see: phenomena; that's the only thing I can see. My business is with becoming or phenomena, not with Platonic ideals. We soldiers're realists.

We soldiers're brutal realists. My business' this country's actual conditions. First and foremost I'm not a social revolutionary: I'm a political revolutionary. Political change or war first: social change later. (*Yelling.*) Men! Men! Let's arm against the English! (*The Porter alone arms himself.*)

6. *The English begin to fight to control the last Irish territory . . .*

Dunsinane.

Outside Dunsinane.

Malcolm: Siward and young Siward. You lead the first attack. Macduff and I'll clean up behind you. We should kill The Porter.

7. . . . *which's now only The Porter.*

The Porter.

The Porter versus Siward's Son.

The Porter: Since you're normal, you can't kill me.
Siward's Son: I'll kill you.
The Porter (*after knifing him*): I killed you.

(*Outside The Porter.*)

Macduff: I'll kill him off and then we'll control everything.
Siward (*to Malcolm*): We own everything else: The Porter's lost
    the IRA. He's all alone and soon won't even be a man.

8. *The Irish territory.*

The Porter: I believe in witches. Nothing's real and nothing
    matters. The witches base their reality on the lack of caus-
    ation. How does one phenomenon relate to another phe-
    nomenon? The Irish language and madness're holy. I have
    to die. Should I commit suicide or kill? I have to give
    meaning. Since there can be no safety for Ireland without
    a repeal of the Union, I'll kill.
Macduff: Turn around. I'll kill you first.
The Porter: It's not worth it. Neither life nor death matters. It's
    not worth killing. Why'm I always concerned with absolutes?
    I don't want to be a slave while I'm alive. I don't care,
    Macduff, whether you're alive or dead.
Malcolm: I'm gonna kill you whether or not you fight back cause
    the only thing I want in the world's to kill you.
The Porter: No normal man can kill me. I can't die. The Irish
    prophetesses predicted this.
Macduff: I'm not normal.
The Porter: You're English.
Macduff: They ripped me in gushing blood out of my mother's

womb cause she not wanting a kid but for medical reasons got pregnant aborted herself.

The Porter (*realizing absolutely*): I'm gonna die. I don't want to die.

Macduff: Fight, goddamn you, fight. You're still looking for reality which doesn't exist.

The Porter (*fighting*): Since there can be no safety for Ireland without a repeal of the Union, I'll kill. (*Keeps on fighting.*)

9. *The World.*

The English Soldiers're all talking to each other.

RUC Lieutenant: Which leaders do we have who're still alive?

English Soldier (*saluting*): Sir. Siward and Malcolm.

Siward: My son died like an English gentleman.

(*Macduff enters, holding The Porter's head on the tip of his sword.*)

Macduff (*giving this head to Malcolm*): You're our head and the new Prime Minister of Ireland.

Malcolm: Our only purpose'll be to negate. (*Hail falls.*)

Macbeth as voodoo: repetition two

ACT I
1.

The Witches: Now we'll start the world. Bang. (*Nothing happens but this noise and a string of blue glass beads.*) The first phenomenon's power or territory. (*A frightful human skull on stage. A heart like a jewelry heart not a human heart hangs out of its mouth.*)

Witch 1 (*walking to the right side of the skull and writing a black dot where the skull's right ear should be*): This is good or being born or the world. (*Walking over to the left side of the skull and painting a black snake where the skull's left ear should be.*) This' evil or lack of humanity or nothing.

Witch 3 (*walking over to Witch 1 and holding a mirror so the skull can see itself in the mirror*): Reality or the relations between something and nothing are: Something comes out of nothing and nothing disappears.

(*The world fully appears: air as a nail-polish bottle full of Orlane Vermillion 18; fire as a black burning candle dripping red; water, a red plastic Casio watch; earth, a string of brown similar-to-shit beads.*)

Witch 2 (*a child*): Humans, appear!

(*Two Ulster Defence Association officers who're friends, The Porter and Banquo enter.*)

Banquo: Now we own the world, old chap (*in thick Irish brogue*) . . .

The Porter: (Everyone always disappears.)

Banquo: . . . we English. The head just raised our ranks for killing that lousy IRA rebel.

The Porter: That's not enough. I want what doesn't disappear. I want to know what's real.

Witch 1 (*to Witch 2*): This' the nature of these humans.

Witch 3 (*answering The Porter*): You're the ruler who does a lot of damage to a lot of people. (*Rubbing her clit.*) You like that one, boy. (*To Banquo.*) You're not the ruler; you're the father.

Banquo: You're not telling me anything! But how can he be ruler when we already have an English leader?

The Witches: We're starting Ireland as best we know how.

2. Reflection of Scene 1: The skull looks on.

In The Porter's castle in Ireland.

The Porter (*repeating*): The only way I an Irishman can rule Ireland is by terroristically assassinating the English Prime Minister. I have to cause terrorism.

(Two of The Porter's henchmen, now IRA Terrorists, dressed in black trench coats, black hats slung over their eyes, assassinate the Prime Minister of Ireland. There's lots of blood.)

The Porter (*in shock*): What'm I doing?

Mrs. Porter (*who looks like The Porter*): You've caused destruction so now you're destruction. I'm tied to you by the heart. Lemme give you a heart. We have to cause the death of the world so there's only passion. May blood be matter. Blood's matter.

The Porter: I'm responsible. I have to cause the death of the English world.

ACT II. IRELAND: THE BALANCING OF BLACK AND WHITE

Inside The Porter's castle, all in black and white stylized shadows.

The Irish Prime Minister's sons, Donalbain and Malcolm, who're very tall teenagers, running around; their arms flap the air: Our father's dead! Our father's dead! What're we going to do now?

Donalbain: Since he was good, whoever murdered him's bad.

Malcolm: There's evil in this fair land. We must find out where it is . . .

(Outside the castle, The Irish're drunkenly rolling around. They look like swine.)

The Porter (*to Donalbain and Malcolm*): I can tell you how your father died. All the gays're dying from AIDS.

Donalbain and Malcolm (*murmuring to themselves*): Oh dear. We have to defend ourselves.

The Porter: Man's main psychological defense or immunity system is identity and his principal political defense, centralization. Any breakdown is madness and death.

Donalbain: We have to restore society.

Malcolm: Who's causing this breakdown?

The Porter: If there's no identity, how can anyone be guilty?

Donalbain (*turning back to The Porter and whispering to Malcolm*): I don't know what's going on in these portals of Hell. I can't tell anything here.

Malcolm: We have to get out of here. I'll go to England where it's safe.

Donalbain: And I to suburban America. There we'll be able to be good.

The Porter (*aside*): I can't get out of my bed in the mornings. My only real life is that hour I'm not supposed to have—between waking and getting up—when I can be obsessed by a private figure, when I've a private life. Otherwise I want to die. That's a cliché. Now I've died. What's possibly natural about this life? My life's only what I make. So any event other than my will is murder: sleep, falling in love, being drugged. If I'm going to be happy, I can only be my will. Donalbain and Malcolm made up their *good versus evil*; I make up *natural versus unnatural*.

I rule Ireland because I decided to rule Ireland. But the witches said I'd rule Ireland. So maybe I'm not making, but seeing. I've got to find out what being human is.

Donalbain and Malcolm (*whispering to each other*): Let's escape from this evil.

Macduff (*whoever he is*): I don't know anything and I don't have any power. Ross, disappear with me. I don't want to be real anymore.

Ross: Yes, sir.

ACT III. RED AND WHITE

A portrait of Ogu the God of War.

The IRA stronghold.

Banquo (*The Porter's childhood friend*): Harsh homeland, the falsest, the most miserable imaginable. I'll never return to you hatred. With these eyes closed: enveloped in the blurry ubiquity of sleep, thus invisible, but nevertheless cleverly and subtly suggested, foreshortened and far in the distance; with even the tiniest details recognizable with such scrupulous activity as to border on the maniacal: an insolent light, a perfect sun: your loved memory and memory of love bring pain and sorrow to anyone who holds you; your name is forever cursed by those who mention it.

The Porter: Don't be ridiculous.

Banquo: You assassinated him.

The Porter: Ireland?

Banquo: Our Prime Minister.

The Porter: Yours? If Ireland's going to become its own country, it needs men such as you to find your own power.

Banquo: By following you?

The Porter: No. By following Ireland. By doing what Ireland needs.

Banquo: I presume you're Ireland.

The Porter: If someone doesn't do provisionally what's necessary, how else's Ireland going to exist?

Banquo: You're presuming you know the future.

The Porter (*aside*): Ride me, horseman. "I rule, then his child rules." The Witches said so. We, we Irish, mightn't be real, but we've real ways of knowing and being: bitches wild behavior winds. So Banquo'll never believe the Witches. I'll have to off him and his son.

(*Pacing.*) That's going against the Witches' prophecy.

(*Still pacing.*) Those Witches're more powerful than me cause women don't make sense. Ireland doesn't make sense. Ireland's a hypocritical cunt bitch. (*Holds himself in.*) Since I'm responsible for our lives, I don't have the luxury of considering. I've taken my course, so now the curse runs itself.

(*The Porter and his Terrorists in the stronghold.*)

The Porter: I've a job for you, boys.
Terrorist 1 (*counting money between his fingers*): What d'you want?
The Porter: Murder and a half.
Terrorist 1: Who?
The Porter: Banquo and his kid.
Terrorist 1: OK.
Terrorist 2: Banquo's your friend.
The Porter: I don't have to explain anything to you.
Terrorist 1: We have to eat.

(*Terrorist 1, Terrorist 2, and a third Unknown Terrorist who is The Porter getting his kicks at the crossroads. Baron La Croix watches.*)

Terrorist 1: He'll be crossing soon.
Terrorist 2: Jesus Christ.

(*As Banquo crosses, they kill Banquo, lots of blood, but're unable to kill his son.*)

(*The Porter's holding a dinner party Irish-style that is lots of potatoes for his friends. Everyone's drunk therefore swine. Terrorist 1 knocks on the portal. The Porter opens the door.*)

The Porter: Come in. Over here. (*His eyes're rolling red from drink.*)
Terrorist 1: It's been done. There was lots of blood.
The Porter: Enough.
Terrorist 1: Not enough: We didn't get the kid.
The Porter (*eyes wide open*): The kid was the main one. You didn't obey my orders. (*Terrorist 1 looks at him as if he's disobeyable and mad.*)
Banquo's dead body (*as Irish Prime Minister, sitting in The Porter's rickety wood chair*): Hey, boy.
The Porter: You calling me, sir? (*Catches himself. Looks around. Sees no one has noticed him cause they're all drunk. The Porter's not drunk, now he's crazy.*)
Banquo's dead body: Shine these shoes, boy.

The Porter (*walks over to Banquo's feet, kneels down, and sticks his tongue out. Looking up*): Sorry, sir I's can't do this for free, sir. No, sir. I's a free man now.

Banquo's dead body: I'll free you. (*Kicks him hard in the belly.*) Here's your quarter. (*Tosses a quarter into a piss pool.*) Go lick that up.

The Porter: Better than licking whites. I want to lick your blood. (*For a second catches himself. But he's beyond caring about people.*) In anticipation of the great and not too distant day when a world will dawn in which a slave will be the equal of a king, in which the lambs of God who've been last'll be first: the niggertrash—dogs, that bite, leash them tight!— have accepted whatever comes their way. In anticipation of the great and not too distant day on which you say you'll give me your love, man, I now eat all the shit you give me and say, "This violence's my sexuality." No longer, king, does your future murder my present. (*His sword slashes through Banquo's dead body.*)

Drunk RUC 1: He's murdering Our Holy Mother Mary.

Drunk RUC 2: Your mother's not supposed to be holy, only a hole.

The Porter (*screaming*): Having depopulated whole regions, you swept away your now unprofitable slave trade like water in hungry sand. Since we wouldn't work for you, zombie-like, your taxes simply bled out our money. Our nobility, our foremost warriors have become trivial art-world power-mongers. I'll sing the history of all slaves.

Filthy Prostitute: I think he's trying to kill himself.

The Porter: Not far from the bodies of the countless children of ours you've aborted, the gaping entrails of women gasping in the agonies of death shot forth seventeen fetuses. The raped females hated themselves so much, they suicided themselves. One of the women's brothers was watching. The scene of his sister killing herself erased some of his fear. Does human exist? (*Turning to the Orderly.*) Where's Macduff?

Orderly: He went back to Belfast.

The Porter: I have to kill him and I can't kill him. I can't kill Banquo's child and I can't kill him right now. My power's gone. My power to know's gone.

(*White:*)

(*The English court in London. A bunch of poor people sit on the streets. Across, inside a rich room.*)

Malcolm: You are good. You have to help us save our country.
The good King Edward: We'll help you.

(*The English countryside. A small pub in the country.*)

Macduff (*to Siward*): I'm glad you're going to come to Ireland with your army and destroy The Porter.

ACT IV. MY PSYCHOLOGY

(*Dream 1: Visual of me fucking. The man with whom I'm fucking's a friend of mine. Though it's real hard, I come and'm happy I do. As soon as I come my phone rings.*)

The Porter: This means "I want to fuck."
The Witches (*preening themselves and showing spread shots*): I'm beautiful.

(*Dream 2*)

The State: I need terrorism to keep a good front. I either use my own agents, or better, cause I'm cheap, infiltrate and use my enemy's organizations' members. Your hierarchical organizational form, Left, makes this easy: your autonomous clandestine militant cells, being separate from and ignorant of each other, don't communicate with each other. Since you function from blind discipline, not out of knowledge and questioning, you can be infiltrated. If you ever suspect one of our infiltrators, which you're usually too stupid to do, we have him arrested, get the media to play up the arrest, then let him "heroically" escape so he can re-infiltrate. In this way, we destroy your ability to distinguish between good and evil.

The Porter: This means "Blood's gushing out of my body."

(*Dream 3: A visual of Banquo's child with a crown on his head and a huge tree trunk, ten times his size, in his right hand.*)

The Porter: That's the child I couldn't kill. His mother wanted to have an abortion but was too scared so had him instead so he's a living abortion. Now all children who're freaks rule.

The Witches: This means "When unnatural's the only nature we've got, you're going to die."

The Porter: Since unnatural's the only nature I've got, I'm going to die now.

(*Scene change.*)

I (*in Ireland*): Fear motivates all my actions. I act only with regard to my memories so I won't be hurt again or so I can avoid the horror which's outside my home (my physical extension). I've three memories: 1. My mother hated me. 2. My husband left me. 3. My mother suicided. These memories're history or myself. If I don't act in accordance with them. I don't have any identity and certainly no nationality. No wonder Ireland's either a horror populated by ghosts or a nonexistent country.

(*To my child, a girl.*) Macduff's left us. I'd kill myself because I can't live without him, but I'm not going to.

My Child: How're we going to live, mommy?

(*The Terrorists're lurking in the trees.*)

I: However I have to live. There's no such thing as "natural" anymore. (I mean "love.")

My Child: Animals who live as they have to live're natural.

(The Terrorists kill me and my child. There's lots of blood. Unlike classical Greek drama, this play displays more blood and violence than's necessary.)

(Macduff, in England.)

Macduff *(to Malcolm)*: I guess I killed my wife by abandoning her.

Malcolm: You can't be responsible, man, for another person's life.

Macduff: I did evil by abandoning my wife. She didn't do anything but good. She's the one who died. What can justice be?

Malcolm: You killed your wife in order to fight the IRA. Your methods're as inhuman as the IRA's. You're a pig.

Macduff: I'm Irish.

(The skull's looking at the skull.)

Malcolm: Who'm I to judge? I'm horror, too, in this horrible world cause I'm not trusting anyone so I don't know what people mean by what they say. Are we totally conditioned by this world we live in? Are we zombies? Yes: You betrayed your love. I rely totally on my brain and I know my brain's deficient. We'll assassinate The Porter. We'll get rid of thinking: You a traitor and I an idiot'll run Ireland for England.

(The skull's looking at the skull.)

Macduff: If we're all fascists, why should I do anything but drink? Did I kill my wife and kid for fascism?

Malcolm: How can I act? All this' idealism. How can I act?

Macduff: What's an appropriate action now?

Malcolm: To kill our controllers.

Macduff: Kill the controller.

Malcolm *(walking over to the skull and splitting it)*: Ogu. I'm a warrior.

Macduff: It's hard for me to say "I love you."

ACT V. THE IRA'S DEATH

1. *Death.*

In bed.

Mrs. Porter: I'm a horrible person: I want power so much I've
    disregarded every friendship and love in me and I can only
    see my point-of-view. I confess to myself, like Catholics have
    the health of confessing to someone else, so there's no world
    but me. Since there's nowhere for this energy to go, I have
    to live with too much energy. I no longer want to be alive.

2. *Animal life.*

Marching to Birnam Wood.

Malcolm: The time's ripe to smash the Provisional IRA.

(*Malcolm, Macduff and Siward with five other soldiers meet the Irish
Protestants, parts of the RUC, UDA, UDR, and UVF. They shake
hands.*)

Protestant Private: Kill 'em. (*Shows his teeth.*)
Protestant Lieutenant (*to the English imports*): Our army and
    the local security forces've been released from their years of
    low-profile and're going on the offensive.

3. *Humanness.*

The Porter (*very big-eyed*): I'm going to die.
His Butler: Sir, your wife just killed herself.
The Porter: Tell her not to bother me. (*Back to himself.*) The
    news' Birnam Wood is moving here, to Dunsinane. I know
    I'm going to die.
       Not only the Protestants, now even my Catholics're sup-
    porting an anti-terrorist campaign. I've no support. I'm up
    against the wall. (*These cries come from unseen: "Mrs. Porter's*

dead!" "*Mrs. Porter's dead!*") Another person has died because people die. I'll fight.

4. Death.

Inside the closed IRA territory.

Siward's Son (*very young so cocksure. To himself*): Me. I'm gonna
    kill that son-of-a-bitch Porter. (*When he sees The Porter,
    runs at him.*)
The Porter (*turning around*): What a child! (*Easily kills him and
    wipes the blood on his sword off on his pants.*)

5. Animal life.

Goat: I'm gonna tear The Porter's brains out of his head.
Jaguar: His men've abandoned him so it'll be easy to kill him.
    Just kill him.

6. Life and death're fucking each other.

The Porter (*all abandoned*): I'm going to die. I'll kill myself. I'll
    kill other people.
Macduff: Either you're going to die or you're going to kill me.
The Porter: You can't kill me.
Macduff: Then kill me.
The Porter: No.
Macduff: That's not possible. You either have to kill me or I'm
    going to kill you.
The Porter: I'm not going to die. (*He fights Macduff.*)
Macduff: Either you're going to die or I'm going to die.
The Porter: No, neither of us're going to die.
Macduff: Either you're going to die or I'm going to die.
The Porter: Do I have to be human? Do I have to be in this
    world?
Macduff: You who're a slave: aren't you every slave who's ever
    existed? What do you call "human"?
The Porter: May the spirits of the living and the dead help us to

laugh at our slave human beliefs. I'm going to either die or kill you, cause I'm the hero. (*They fight.*)

7. *Ireland.*

Macduff, walking out of The Porter's castle, carrying The Porter's cut-off head, gives it to Malcolm.

Malcolm: I'll tell you how to stop the slavery. Kill all the slaves.

Macbeth as Daniel O'Connell: repetition three

The English are the good guys and the Irish are the bad guys.

ACT I

The Irish world begins in and as nothing. The Irish fortunetellers who're nothing foretell the beginning of the world. In this beginning which is the hope for power and about power because the Irish don't have any power or the establishings of territory because the Irish don't have any territory, the nothing of the Irish equals evil, and anything cause the Irish're so desperate equals good. Everything because it must come out of nothing will die, the Irish will always lose the war, or, as Ireland really is nothing, so evil or Ireland has to win.

The English overrun the stage.

The King of England: Who's that bloody man over there? The English are taking over the world for once and for all. A bloody man can tell us what the real state of the world is.
Man Dripping in Blood: Thanks to The Porter and Banquo we cut off many Irish heads.
The King of England: Oh valiant cousins! Worthy gentlemen!
Man Dripping In Blood: Now we own all of Ireland.
The King of England: Porter and Banquo, I dub thee Knights.

(The world's nothing again. Dust and smoke and penicillin swirling around the stage. Don't bother with stage props because it's too difficult. Kind of blabbing noises.)

(The Porter and Banquo enter the scene.)

The Porter: Here we are in nothing to learn about nothing.

Banquo *(to nobody)*: Who're you? You should be women because the only people I talk to're women only I don't feel any desire to fuck you.

Females *(to The Porter)*: You'll become evil and by becoming evil powerful.

Banquo: But what about me though I don't give a shit about you, females?

Females: You won't become evil that is Irish. Your child'll be powerful.

Banquo: Does that mean my child'll be good or evil?

(The Plan)

(In The Porter's southern Irish castle.)

The Porter: I hate the English! I'm going to assassinate the King in order to save our homeland. *(It is night. He kills the English King.)*

The Porter's Irish Wife *(to the Porter who comes bloodily out of the English King's bed not cause he actually murdered the King but cause his hands touched the arms of the young punks he had paid to murder the English King)*: I'm glad you murdered that upper-class snob. I'm part of your blood, my husband my love, because genitals when they touch make the blood flow together so my blood's your blood. Like you I'm Irish. Like you I'm nothing and want nothing: not Knighthood nor any other baubles the socialized English uphold. We're prophets and evil. We don't want to own our own country.

The Porter: We don't want to own our own country. That's not enough. We want to destroy the world.

ACT II. THE PORTER HAS A CONVERSATION

The Play's Writer: A definition of this world's a portal.

A definition, my first, of this world's AIDS. AIDS' the breakdown of the body's immunity system: the body becomes allergic to itself. At this moment in New York City fags Haitians and hemophiliacs're all getting AIDS. I just heard this heterosexual garbage collector got AIDS.

What's AIDS? A virus. A virus' seemingly unknowable who gets identity by preying on an entity, a cell. Writers whose identities depend on written language're viruses. I'm trying to break down the social immune system. Even this sentence's false.

If there're no identities, there're hallucinations. The first portal of this world's hallucination.

The Portal: Knock. Knock.

The Porter's Voice (*still in sleep*): There's no reality. Go away.

The Portal: Knock. Knock.

Morning.

The Porter (*in his bed, sheets knotted around his body with the sweat that indicates he fell asleep drunk but couldn't sleep*): You hate my guts. You hate me, so I'm nothing. Your lips are the most wonderful things. I don't care if this fantasizing is you rejecting me, I still want to stay here.

The Portal: Knock. Knock.

The Porter: I don't want to get up in the morning because I want to die.

The Portal: Knock. Knock.

The Porter: I don't want your fraternity pin. Is he talking about us, Tad? Oh, Alfred, you're breaking my heart.

The Portal: Knock. Knock.

The Porter: Amanda, come on in. Oh, you brought that book

of essays they assigned you in English class. The teacher's
cunt's a set of falsies. Oh no, you're at the portals of Hell
only I'm drunk. But I'm out of booze. Hell, this place's too
boring for Hell. Try another city. (*He knocks himself.*) Knock.
Knock. Well, I'm going to make a new resolution. I just
murdered the King of England. I've got blood on my hands.
I'm gonna wash it off. Out, out, bad blood. Life's just a
walking shadow allowing everything. I'd pee on life only
coke's made my cock too small. Oh horror horror horror.
Who's going to alter my bloodstained hands? I'm more cou-
rageous than you, big boy. Who thought that a human
contains so much blood?

(*The English princes, Malcolm and Donalbain, they're about eight and
ten years old, run in and start screaming: Daddy's murdered.*)

Malcolm: I'm going back to England where I'll be safe cause the
only dirty Irish there the English kill or starve.
Donalbain: I'll go Brazil. Let's not tell anyone where we're going
cause now the forces of nothingness Ireland're ruling the
world.
The Porter (*in his bedclothes*): I smell sex. (*Smelling old blood.*)
Macduff (*to Ross*): Even though we're really Irish we can still act
English by retreating.
The Porter: Here are the manipulators who manipulate everyone
but God.

ACT III. THE PORTER TALKS TO THE GHOST

Banquo's dead body: Porter, this's your cock.
The Porter: I don't feel sexual desire.
Banquo's dead body: I'm Banquo.
The Porter: Fuck you. I killed you. Where's your cock?
Banquo's dead body: I'm not a cock; I'm a ghost. You know
why you can't get it up, don't you? You're guilty as hell.
The Porter: If I were guilty as hell. I'd be the Devil.

Banquo's dead body: You killed our King. That's the same as killing God.

The Porter: Your *King* said she was female.

Banquo's dead body: That's why you can't fuck.

The Porter: Then no Englishman can fuck.

Banquo's dead body: It's called "The English Disease."

The Porter: As long as I can't fuck, I might as well be social. (*Throwing open his arms in a royal gesture and indicating his dining-room guests.*) Everyone gets ahead in their top-level jobs the most possible by being social.

Banquo's dead body: Well, be social with me, honey. (*Patting the chair.*) A ghost like me needs company. (*Crossing his legs.*) Now, tell me something. I've got this thing for Mrs. Porter. Does she . . . put out?

The Porter: She's Catholic! Listen, Ghostie, I've done so much fuckin' shit to this land by fighting the English, if I make the slightest mistake now that is if there's the slightest flaw in my territory, I'm a dead duck.

Banquo's dead body: You're worse than that, honey. (*Again patting the chair.*) You might as well admit what you really are. You've lost everything anyway.

The Porter (*sadly looking down*): I know. (*Changing.*) I will not lose! My will will keep going! Now I'll kill Macduff.

Banquo's dead body: That's like asking me to slit my own throat.

The Porter: I suppose you want to slit mine. You can't. I'm alive. I have to get back to the living.

Banquo's dead body: I never heard anything more perverted in my life. "Get back to living." You're just going to learn to feel guilty, and if you can't feel guilty, then scared.

The Porter: I suppose that's the way of the world. Oh please, ghost, don't hurt me. (*Runs away because he's scared of what he knows, only now he doesn't know anything.*) I don't know anything.

(*In England*)

Siward (*an English general*): I've so many soldiers, Ireland has
    to be decimated. Fuck the IRA!

1. *The Porter talks to the hallucinations.*

A woman is having an abortion. This has to be real. *Her aborted gook
is seen and placed next to children. Red blood is covering the children.
This' the place of desolation.*

The Porter: Since I'm not going to hurt anymore, I'm not going
    to hurt anymore.
The Bloody Children: Die. We're killing you because you aborted
    us. (*While they stick sticks into The Porter's body.*)
The Porter (*dying*): Ireland has to succeed! In accepting the job
    of Prime Minister of Northern Ireland, I do so in and with
    the hope that the British army goes back to England dead.
The Child Who Has No Blood (*appears. This child is crowned
    King and holds nature in his hand*): Die, Porter. When
    Birnam Wood walks to Dunsinane, we're going to murder
    you. The Great Commonwealth of Britain must take over
    because Britain's natural. It's your fault: You Irish by trying
    to go against our good sweet naturalness have forced us to
    be as unnatural to you as we are in your minds. When you
    get killed, you want to be killed. We're freaks in this world
    only cause you are.
The Porter: Being a child's just another hallucination or ploy.
The Child: The only non-hallucination you've got is the fact of
    your own death.
The Porter (*croaking in an old man's voice*): I'll tell you what
    we've got against you: Since from 1921 onwards the Irish
    people freely have not wanted the British to govern them,
    the government of Ireland has been a government without
    consensus. When you have a situation like that, you have
    a situation of permanent instability. Permanent instability

means recurring acts of violence. Ever since 1921. What
does one life matter?

2. *In the middle of war, the English're being murdered too.*

In England.

Malcolm (*to Macduff*): Our soldiers, in Ireland that poor place,
have fallen in the trenches. Flies sit on their lips. Pus comes
out of their nostrils. Those who come back to us alive have
hollow eyes, are zombies, need or are, simply, hooked on
heroin the only substitute for life.

Macduff (*dead now that love's abandoned him*): I've decided to
be dead. Rather: these muscles that no longer work, these
continuously wandering eyes, this throat that stops up rather
than issues forth language, the life now in Ireland, are same
as a war which no soldier can understand. The Irish led by
The Porter have plunged their heads into an all-destroying
dream called self-sovereignty and so make maddening confusion and the deafening music of tanks . . .

Malcolm: Why should I trust you? You ran out on your family
so your family died so you're as perverse and evil as any
Irishman.

Macduff: There's no such thing as purity in these times that shit.
Since I'm as dumb as any Irishman, I have to refuse who I
most desire.

Malcolm: No. (*Thinking.*) . . .

3. *Those who're being murdered become fascists.*

Malcolm: . . . Where am I? Run. Walk. Get away. Hunger. No
matter. Live. Run. Breathe. Survive. My guns. What can
I chew? My ankle. Ragged nerves plunge me into hallucinations. Hallucinations're my perceptions. I look at my life
(I remember). The worst things that've happened to me I
in no way caused: cancer, my mother's hatred of me the
instant I came out of her womb so I have no mother, my

marriage's break-up, my grandmother's desire to die right after her only daughter suicided and her subsequent death. Likewise, the fortunate events. There's only chance. Or else I can't know causes. Good doesn't lead to good, evil doesn't lead to evil. I can't tell the difference between good and evil. What're my categories?

Unfold my dreams:

In a rectangle which is also Africa through which a body of water runs I am traveling and there're snakes. As I rise up from the river, the snakes're after me. When two long snakes resembling broken rubber bands lift up, I grab on to the ropes though attached to the walls I cause them to swing and so climb up to the ceiling. But the growing snakes more ferocious can climb almost as far. An inch from me.

I'm fucking with you:

If the categories are wills and desires, what's fascism?

Macduff: In Nakem-Ziuko the winds of emancipation've brought demands for reform. Our Prime Minister has explained to us that England's main concern at this moment is the headlong political development of its colonies such as Ireland, Scotland, and British Africa. Let war and fascism rage. I love war and fascism.

Malcolm: There'll follow six months of bowing and scraping, of correspondence and council meetings at which the griots'll review the political development of the sorrowful Nakem-Ziuko.

The King of England: If our people nominate half-whitened Pakistani servant sons some who have cocks that are still unreddened, they can't write, the best of them managed to stay in school till age thirteen by controlling their teachers and classrooms, if our people nominate these men: they'll win twice as many votes as anyone expects. The niggers're refusing to go back to their holes unless they are our political candidates.

Macduff (*to Malcolm*): Let's follow him.

The King of England: Right without might's a caricature. Might without right's an abomination. Admit it.

Macduff: The triumph of might is the triumph of its right. We'll have to win out over the IRA.

ACT V. THE ENGLISH AND THE AMERICANS OWN THE WORLD

1.

Mrs. Porter: To bed, to bed. (*Still masturbating.*) Here's someone at my gate. He's bald and his hair's so blond it's almost nothing; his eyes are the pale blue of ghosts. Get him out! Get him out! But I have to do it. Here's a doctor. He's French too. He carries big whips around his waist and tells me I'm sick. I know who I, female, am. And another: A face as screwed-up and old as a bulldog's. You're the foul coke-fiend. Come come come. Don't take eight hours.

2.

In the war-time.

War music: Boom boom boom.

(*Malcolm, Siward, Macduff, the good English, enter with English soldiers.*)

War music: Boom boom boom.

(*Now it's wartime. Only one army's advancing, the only army* (English).)

Menteith: Partition is resented but the present generation knows that if partition is ever to be ended it must be by peaceful arrangements. The few young toughs who make up the tiny remnant that will now lay down its arms uses a grand and famous name for their organization, but the *Irish Republication Army* belongs to history and it belongs to better men in times that are gone. Let's put a wreath of roses, a bloody wreath (*laughs*), and move on.

Caithness: With the English bombing campaign at a dead end by the 1939 autumn, Sean Russell and the other like-minded militarists who comprised IRA's depleted inner circle decided to seek assistance from Nazi Germany.

Lennox: The Irish've driven all the Protestants, whom the Irish call "unbelievers of their faith," like swine into the surrounding seas. By force by knife and by poison. They are trying to cut them down like a farmer hews down a mahogany forest. They use any method of deception in order to destroy all Protestants.

Menteith: They're planning to advance the Priesthood and Catholic faith until the Pope rules the entire world.

Caithness: I've reached the stage where I no longer have any compassion for any nationalist: man, woman or child. After years of destruction murder intimidation I have been driven against my better feelings to this decision: the Irish nationalists or us. Why haven't don't we hit back in the only way these nationalist bastards understand? That is; ruthless indiscriminate killing. I'm going to roast the slimy excreta the Irish that pass for human beings.

3.

Malcolm: Of old time priests of high degree with their hands strained on the rack the limbs of delicate Protestant women; prelates dabbled in the gore of their helpless female victims. The cells of the Pope's prison were paved with the calcined bones of men and cemented with human gore and human hair.

Menteith: We doubt it nothing.

Siward: There's a fuckin' Irishman.

Menteith: An real Irishman cause he's drunk!

(The five men rush at the old man. One soldier beats his hands against a tree. Every time the old poop collapses, the same soldier along with a second soldier beats the insides of his feet at his ankles and his hands

until the old man has to again stand up. This happens numbers of times.)

Menteith: Get up!

(The old man crouches on the earth and weeps. He doesn't know why. They kick him back and forth until he's able, standing, to have his hands again thrust against the tree.)

Siward: How large is the IRA? (*Behind the old man a soldier sticks a knee in his spine and shoves his head back.*) What does it matter? Most of the Catholics we have to murder're innocent of any involvement with the IRA.
The Window Cleaner: I'll murder Catholics as they sleep in their beds.
Malcolm: You just want to run off and kill the first Catholic you find. You're like a roamer looking for a teague. I feel we have to be more selective. Let's kill their heads.
Macduff: They don't have heads.
Siward: We're not trying to have any specific effect on the Catholics. I suppose we just want to tell them they can't force their views on us. The IRA is anti-Protestant most certainly. They're haters of everybody: the British, their own people. They'll have to be stopped.

4.

The Butler (*to The Porter*): Your wife's dead.
The Porter: I'll tell you a story. It used to be the only way a Catholic could enter the middle class here in the North was by running a pub.

Owen McMahon was my father. He did just that.

In those days the Ulster Defence Regiment was partly coming from the B-Specials. The B-Specials were a group of men who helped out the Belfast cops by murdering and spreading anti-Catholic bigotry as much as possible. The Catholics had just gotten their shit together in those days,

1922, and started to off the pigs who were decimating them.
No one else. They weren't killing civilians. I want the Irish
to survive. They had to off two B-Special murderers. They
did so. As reprisal, the next day, the B's broke into my father's
house on Antrim Road. Gray early morning. They line him,
my five brothers, and the barman who was working at my
father's place up against his living room wall. They then
shot them in the front. Two of us didn't die. I didn't die
because I had been hiding under the couch. Hiding under
the couch, peering up to where the only light was. In the
light a bullet enters my father's chest. He falls to the floor.
I hear the sound of the body as it hits the floor. The next
bullet goes into one of my brothers. Blood bursts out of a
hole in his right cheek. His eyes are wide open. Simultaneously there's the noise of my youngest brother's body hitting the floor. Suddenly one of my brother's screams, the
first scream, runs forward as a pig-cop catches my brother
in his arms his knee goes up to my brother's tiny delicate
cock. At the same time, the rifle turned, the rifle butt smashes
in my brother's head. I see white worms quivering come
out of this skull. I'm screaming now. Who can fight my
egotism? The barman, stunned, lets them kill him and dies.

The Butler (*interrupting*): Your wife's dead.

The Porter: There'd be time to react to this if I lived in another
world.

5.

Macduff: There must be a change in security tactics. The army
and the local security forces must be released from their
present low-profile: we're finally on the offensive again. I'll
kill The Porter. Both the Northern Irish Protestants and the
Catholics're supporting our determined anti-terrorist campaign. The time is ripe to kill The Porter.

Malcolm (*entering*): Due to the IRA's terrorism, the Irish have
turned against the IRA.

6.

Malcolm: Sixty-six per cent of the Catholics in Ulster are un-
employed. That's not enough.

Siward: It took Bobby Sands sixty-six days to starve himself to
death. We should have starved him more quickly.

Malcolm: We killed Constable Victor Arbuckle in 1969: the first
man in our security forces to die.

Ross: We now control and'll always control Ireland cause it's the
port to Europe. We'll give up any of our other colonies
before we give up this port.

Siward: Are the Catholics dead?

Ross: Aye, in Belfast in February 1982 we arrested so many creeps
and confiscated so many of their arms, we neutralized the
Irish National Liberation Party. When the Sinn Fein and
Irish Republican Socialist Party ran for election in all twenty-
six counties the next month, none of them became TDs.

Siward: Is it a crime to be Catholic?

Ross: What does it matter? They can't win.

(*Macduff, holding The Porter's cut-off head, enters the battlefield.*)

The Porter's cut-off head: What O'Connell gave us is hard to
tell . . .

(*Dedicated to Sean O'Faolain's book on Daniel O'Connell.*)

The Porter's cut-off head: . . . he taught me to have pride. He
taught me the one word (world) I have is *no* and that word
isn't a negative but allows the world. He almost killed truth
back in the early nineteenth century. He exposed the life of
the Empire. He gave the Irish discipline and tolerance. He
accepted duality as the basic fact. (*Blood pours out of his
mouth.*) The Union was a manifest injustice, and continues
to be unjust to this day. If the Union continues, it will make
crime hereditary and English justice perpetual. We've been
robbed, my countrymen, most foully robbed of our birth-

right: our independence. Alas, England that ought to have been to us a sister and a friend—England whom we had loved, and fought and bled for—England at a period when out of the 100,000 seamen in her service 70,000 were Irish—England stole upon us like a thief in the night and robbed us of the precious cherry of our liberty. Here, England: (*He looks up at Macduff who's holding him.*)

All: Hail, King of Ireland!

(*Macduff gives the head to Malcolm.*)

The Porter's cut-off head: While we believe the English, while we believe in this religious dissension, while we're lost in this stupor of insanity: the English have and plunder us of our country. Hammer my brutal reality—my loneliness and hollowness and fear—into an ideal: the struggle of the Irish.

3 ADULT NOW

For Arabia

Preface

The Evil: Shylock R.

Shylock R. on why he's demanding a pound of flesh out of Antonio:

Shylock R.: There's pain in this world. I feel pain. God doesn't feel pain. Considering this: This world's always been this way. This world stinks and always has stunk. Strung up. It must be God doesn't give a shit about human beings.

The Good: Portia

Morning light comes through the curtains. Translucent white curtains, parted as they hang from the high wood bedframe, through which, glimpses of white stain quilts guilts huge white pillows. The laughter of the first morning sun, white, yellow. The flesh is white not because it's white but cause it's ease. Riding light laugh always. See.

Portia: I've seen a vision. It's the vision of freedom or of wild space. "Fuck" rhymes with "stuck." The one nightmare: I'm stuck. I'm stuck in this brain which defines (makes?) the world spatially and temporally. I'm stuck in these returnings. The circles, moving temporally faster, are making me nauseous. I'm stuck in my own world: I can't meet anyone new; I always know what's happening.

 The vision: infinity. Whatever can't be counted or is alive. I saw livingness and it made me laugh and then simultaneously there's no more knowing and this makes me laugh. There's only fucking.

(*All the black people hate all the white people. All the people're black except for Shylock R., the British armies, and Julius Caesar.*)

(*In summer it's so hot that emotions burst out.*)

ACT I. THE SUN

A poor young mercenary named Bassanio falls in love with a woman. Since Portia's beautiful, intelligent and self-independent, the man feels he needs money. He hits up his friend, Antonio. Antonio doesn't know why he's always sad and can lend his friend money only by borrowing cash from Shylock R. who's tight-assed. Since Shylock R. hates everyone who isn't himself or Jewish, he gives Antonio the dough under forfeiture of a pound of Antonio's bloody flesh. All Antonio cares about are his friends.

1.

: You must be mad cause you're in love.

Antonio: I've nothing anymore to do with sex so I can't be in love. I'm sad for another reason.

: You're sad because you're not in love. I guess you're losing all your friends.

Antonio: I guess I am. Bye-bye friends. (*His friends go away. Yells after them.*) Let's have dinner together.

: OK.

(*Two new friends enter.*)

: What's the matter, babes? You look like the pits. You care too much about things—

Antonio: I know nothing's real.

: You're too attached to things of the world. That brings trouble.

Antonio: I am trouble.

: Get a sense of humour. At least you'll live longer or, even if you die, enjoy every moment you live. You're going to die soon the way you're going.

Antonio: So are you. Well, I'll leave you to your dinner. My stomach hurts I'm so hungry all the time.

(*Antonio alone with Bassanio.*)

Antonio: So how're you in love? Who you in love with, boy?

Bassanio: I'll tell you something. Cause I've bought too many clothes, I've no money left and I owe you the most.

Antonio: Don't worry, honey. If you need it, I'll lend you more.

Bassanio: I'm always in need. If you lend me double what I now need, I'll pay your first loan back. I don't want to owe someone.

Antonio: Money's an easy problem. I'm sad.

Bassanio: I'm in love with an uppitty cunt.

Antonio: She must be upper-class. Forget it. That class' women's cunts have teeth.

Bassanio: That's why I need your money in order to get her.

2.

Portia (*who looks exactly like Bassanio*): My father said marriage's a state affair.

The Maid (*the only person who loves her in the world who's still alive*): I thought you've never known your father.

Portia: That's the only thing he ever said to me.

The Maid: Well . . . Anything lasts longer than sex and love: (*Thinking.*) Governments're lasting a long time these days cause they're all becoming one.

Portia: True marriage.

The Maid: This' why you're supposed to get married.

Portia: This' precisely why I don't want to get married. Real men don't exist anymore.

The Maid: Of course they exist. There're still people in the world. The most romantic men're in France.

Portia: Who'd ever know? The French—by "the French" I mean Frenchmen—the French're so provincial, they look down their noses at the rest of us and don't mingle. They're snotty cause their economy's been stable for years and even though they talk all the time and now and then have tiny political revolts nothing never changes in France . . .

The Maid: . . . Stability's good for a marriage. Have you decided to marry France?

Portia: I'd prefer England to France. England looks very proper, but its people're starving to death. Money may not be everything in life, but it certainly buys dresses. As for the English colonies . . .

The Maid: . . . You can go scumming without having to get married. There's only one country left.

Portia: What a description of this world! Who's that?

The Maid: Germany. A solid stolid economic giant.

Portia: What good Hitler did! May we learn all our lessons from politics. The only problem with Germany is their diet . . .

The Maid: . . . The Diet of Worms . . .

Portia: By the end of the day the Germans have so much sausage in them, their guts're red meat. In the nighttime they're little better than beasts.

The Maid: Better animal than human . . .

Portia: . . . red than dead . . .

The Maid: . . . in your bed.

Portia: Except the beast's too drunk on beer to do anything but piss in its sleep.

The Maid: It's more civilized to sleep in separate beds.

Portia: I sleep in my own bed now. Why should I have anything to do with the world?

The Maid: What about Bassanio? He's smart as hell and mercenary. Excuse me, a mercenary.

Portia: He's cute. (*Sighs.*) I wouldn't mind his weight.

Servant (*some old cutthroat*): Excuse me, Miss, another man's knocking on your door.

Portia: I hope he's a locksmith and giving me a chastity belt: I hate men and I don't want their hard world.

3.

Shylock R. has a thick Jewish accent.

Shylock R.: People have been dumping on me all my life and I never had a chance. I'll tell you what it's like to grow up in

The South: If you talked to a black, you were scum you were black! If you liked a black, you were scum you were black! If you dared to read a book, you were scum you were black! If you wanted to go to a play, you were a fag!

Antonio (*pouring himself some of Shylock R.'s wine*): So you had no choice: you were black or a fag.

Shylock R. (*screaming*): I had no chance: there was nothing I could do!

Antonio (*bored*): Why didn't you run away?

Shylock R. (*quietly*): Columbia University accepted me. I came to New York for the first time. A black man on the street spoke to me hostilely. Me; hostilely. My childhood love was a black man shooting me up with junk. It's the first time I tasted junk. And then this black kid on the street speaks to me like I don't know who blacks are.

Antonio: He spoke to you from where he was. That's how people are in New York. It doesn't mean anything.

Shylock R.: How was I to know about New York? I was so freaked-out by the city, I didn't even go to Columbia, I left after two weeks. Do you know how scared I was? (*Screeching.*)

Antonio (*shaking his head cause Shylock R.'s so mad*): Let me get to business for just a minute.

Shylock R.: Who are you?

Antonio: My name's Antonio. I hear you're a coke dealer. I don't mean that. I mean, I hear you dabble, you know, from no one . . .

Shylock R.: I don't deal coke. I just put people in touch with people.

Antonio: It's not my business. I just thought you might be able to lend me money.

Shylock R.: I don't have any money. I have to work for a living.

Antonio: Your girlfriend's rich.

Shylock R.: Are you insulting me? I might be able to lend you what you need.

Antonio: What do I need?

Shylock R.: So what do you need? (*Thicker Jewish accent.*)

Antonio: I need. I need thirty thousand dollars.

Shylock R.: Who has that kind of money? Arafat. Go to Arafat.

Antonio: OK. (*Starts walking away.*)

Shylock R.: Wait a second. I'll be able to borrow the money from a friend, but I'll lose money doing it. I'll do it for you (*staring at Antonio's tits*), because I like you.

Antonio: I'll give you your money back in three months with 300 per cent interest.

Shylock R.: Interest? (*Aside.*) Does this man think the Jews're interested only in interest? Is he so prejudiced? Doesn't he know we have hearts and souls? (*To Antonio.*) I want flesh.

Antonio (*shrinking from fear*): I think you're human.

4.

Roughs on the street.

A Welfare Worker: Here's your new home, ladies. Well, what's the matter with you? Think you have a choice of where to live?

Black Prostitute: As long as we put out.

Welfare Worker: No one lives for free in a democracy. You no longer have one of your brutal pimps above you.

Black Prostitute: You government're so powerful, you don't need to indulge in individual brutality.

Welfare Worker: Me? Do you think I make the rules?

Black Prostitute: No, you live by them.

(*Portia dressed as a leather boy, walking along the street and kicking whatever she sees.*)

Gratiano: Portia!

Portia: What d'you want?

Gratiano: I want to go along with you.

Portia: I don't know. I don't trust you. You don't hold yourself in: you're wild rude unsocial. I have to be with men who adjust to all social classes.

Gratiano: What should I be: a woman?

Portia: I'm sick of men who worship their machoism as the be-
all and end-all.
Gratiano: I want my way as much as you want your way.
Portia: I'm going to get as drunk as possible.

5.

Isabel: Daddy, you want to know about politics. I'll tell you about
politics. The United States' overrunning El Salvador and
Nicaragua. You say you want to devote your whole life to
stopping this inanity but of course you're not going to waste
your time going to Nicaragua. "What can I do?", you pound
your fists tear out your hairs scream desperately, "What can
I do?" First, you say, you need to disseminate information
because when and only when the people receive accurate
info, whatever the hell that is, they'll know how and more
important want to stop the US infiltration of El Salvador
and Nicaragua. "How can I start this first step?" you scream.
"How can I get this information to the people? We need a
large media group. There's no organized group. What can
I do? I'm helpless."
    You're accepting the US government's version of reality:
you say you need a commercially-acceptable organization
or a bureaucracy in order to act functionally. My reality's
mercy.
Shylock R. (*looking at his fingernails*): I told you to get out of
here.
Isabel (*alone*): Even though I'm black, I can fall in love. My father terrorized me because he hated my guts because my
mother whom he adored left him before I was born. Are
we always to be governed by our parents' fucked-up lives?
Rebels're as slavelike as toadies. Me: I hate everyone: rebels
and toadies. But Lorenzo. I'm running away to him! Out
of this hell! He's promised to marry me which means love
me forever even if he doesn't love me. Being without a
mother and my father's hating me's carved bloody ruts un-
able-to-heal below my flesh before I was old enough to have

the power to run away. (*Running down the street.*)
    My father knows nothing about my treachery and'll dis-
own me if he finds out. (*Still running.*)

(*The sun's very bright and almost white. I'd burn up my flesh burn up
so white it turns to black.*)

ACT II. FLESH

*When Antonio can't return the money to Shylock R., Shylock R.
intends to cut out Antonio's flesh.*

1.

*A castle in bright sun. Army enters, flags, horses, approaching
castle. Henry Hereford, Edmund of Langley, the Duke of York,
and the Earl of Northumberland lead the soldiers. Hereford turns
around on his horse to talk to Northumberland. As he does, Northumberland's son, Henry Percy enters from bottom right center.*

Percy: The castle's guards're strong.
Bolingbroke (*quickly turning to Percy*): Against us?
Percy: The King's there. He's established his stronghold. His
    (*pointing to York*) son, Salisbury, Scroop and a non-cock're
    with him.
York: That must be the Bishop.
Bolingbroke: They're all in the same place. Good. This' how
    I'm going to break down the defenses. You all three of you
    (*to Percy, York and Northumberland*) by truce tell the King
    I'll bow to Him if He lets me go free and gives me back my
    ancestral territory. If He does, I'll be faithful to Him. If He
    refuses, I'll kill everyone in sight and turn this summer sun
    and all that its' nudging, red.
Percy: . . . Life 'n society're red . . .
Bolingbroke (*ignoring the younger male*): Tell Richard I don't
    love blood. (*Turns around to the men.*) Shut up on the
    music; walk gently, not with aggression. By giving up, we're
    trying to avoid more blood.
Percy: . . . Life is blood . . .

Bolingbroke: King Richard and I, we are equal powers; neither of us'll be less than the other: I'll play passive and He can play owner because we both have to play something so we'll go to war.

York: Does He know this?

(Martial music blast. King Richard and York's son, Salisbury, Scroop, and the priest on the castle balcony as the white sun blazes around them.)

Bolingbroke: Obviously Richard's scared to death.

Percy: He still owns the power.

King Richard (*to Bolingbroke*): You. Don't you know We're the one power? How dare you approach Us except by crawling? Down. Down, all of you. Down down down.

    The only way a man touches Our dreadful power is illegally. You're less than Us. How dare you try to pretend you're anything else? Crawl, because that's natural. If you at any moment forget to crawl around Us, we'll make you crawl because We're stronger and smarter than you.

    In the past you've gone against Us. Your petty stinky rebellions. Even if no one likes Us even if We've no friend in the world and everyone believes We're a freak, We shine more and more strongly until Our blaze is the only wordly sun who exists. Our power's so strong, We're your only possible seeing light. Try going against Us. Ha.

    And tell that sniveling wivvle-worm Bolingbroke over there: If he dares make one more move that isn't in open adoration of Us, We'll simply step on him as We walk crush him to bloody pulp. His little bit of blood fertilizes Our milk thighs.

Northumberland (*answering King*): Hey, wait a minute. We don't want to touch Your power. We know You're all-powerful. (*Stepping back a few steps.*) Bolingbroke adores You: he's lying around You; he's tonguing Your lavender-colored nipples. He's a faithful slave. Bolingbroke swears, by all he holds dear, which is blood, he's approaching You not with a military intent but just to beg You to let him be near You.

He begs You not to banish him. As long as You don't banish him, he'll give You his arms. As long as You don't banish him, he'll give You his blood and romanticism.

King: Tell him We accept this. (*The couriers leave. Turning to the Duke of York's son.*) If We don't accept these terms, he'll fight and kill Us.

Duke of York's Son: Be hypocritical until You're strong enough to bash in his head.

King: That's a good idea. We're honest. We use hypocrisy honestly. Wartime. Here's that ghost Northumberland again. (*Northumberland enters right, stands in front of castle. Looks like a ghost.*) We're a liar. Because We're social. We've given away purity. Because We're the head of society, We've given away joy. Because We're the head of your society, We've given away Ourselves. We're none. We'll be truthful and become a nun. (*Putting on a nun's habit. In high drag.*) If we fuck again, We'll get AIDS. This girl isn't going to do anything more dirty. Let their feet trample on Our head. Their hands with knives in them're cutting apart Our heart. Rip. Our sex is strips of shredded skin. We can't find where to masturbate. Oh, the habit. Women. We know, We can tell, feel sorry for Us, but We know that tears and sex and all such psychological dramas're unimportant: (*Going back on this.*) Oh We feel sorry for Ourself, that's why We're a poet.

This world stinks and everybody in it stinks.

Northumberland: Especially when it's this hot. (*Turns around and leaves. Faces Bolingbroke.*)

Bolingbroke (*to Northumberland*): Can I stay in England or do we paint our people even redder?

The King (*entering, behind Northumberland, answering Bolingbroke directly*): There's no war.

Bolingbroke: I must remain a man: I have to have rights.

The King: You have Us, Our blood. We'll have war only in those countries we control. (*The Duke of York's son's crying.*) Why cry? Why cry in this world? Why cry for this world?

Cry for another person if you must be human. Or cry because you don't know what else to do. Anything but action's useless and We've no actions left.

The Duke of York's Son (*as Bolingbroke's men're binding him prisoner*): That's not true.

King: We're Bolingbroke's prisoners.

Duke of York's Son: It matters what we do cause it matters what we believe cause this world's belief systems.

King: In jail We'll be able to believe whatever We want. Like women.

Bolingbroke: You've always lived in jail. I act don't moralize. I'm killing you because I, unlike you, am the power.

2.

The Irish criminal and the Slave arrive at The Thames. The Slave is the beautiful slave of the Arabian Nights of Pasolini. The Thames' full of garbage. The female Slave says the Irish Criminal's raped her. She kills him.

She talks of paradise which was her childhood.

Slave: Now paradise to me is war.

(*Modern British soldiers arrive by helicopter to kill her. The British killed Pasolini in order to keep control of their Empire. We always knew the British upper-class're embarrassed of their homosexuality. Caesar and the British Army meet and shake hands.*)

Caesar: We're restoring civilization cause culture 'n' writing are great things and this stinkin' writing's plagiarized.

3. *The scene of my marriage.*

Bassanio (*to Portia*): You're the cause of everything. (*Looking down at her cunt.*)

Portia: Are you going to hurt me? (*Both fright and delight in her eyes.*)

Bassanio: Are you crazy, Portia? What're you talking about?

Portia (*realizing he's not going to get it, lies*): You don't know much yet. I'm evil. (*Has no other way of saying it.*)

Bassanio (*totally ignoring what she's saying cause he has no way of understanding what she's saying*): I want to smell you. (*He thrusts his face into her cunt and smells, hard. Lifts his dripping face, dripping.*) You're wet.

Portia: Let me taste. (*Draws her hand across his face. Then licks her inside. Wrinkling her face, surprised.*) It's not that bad.

Bassanio: I like Camembert.

Portia: I'm always so frightened I taste bad I don't want men to lick me.

Bassanio: I could lick you all night.

Portia: You could? OK boy. (*To herself.*) At least it's something.

Bassanio: Dead fish smell and the desirousness of a cunt're allied just like death and love.

Portia: You want something, but I can't tell what.

Bassanio (*looking at her*): I'm gonna to murder you.

Portia: S & M's unnatural. (*Looking at him closely.*) You're really upset. You don't love me. Did I do something?

Bassanio: Stop talking.

Portia: OK. I did something.

Bassanio: You slept with Tim.

Portia: I haven't fucked Tim.

Bassanio: You shouldn't lie because I'm gonna murder you if you're lying. I own your cunt.

Portia: Then you're not going to kill me. Yet.

Bassanio: In a few minutes. It doesn't matter what you say. For the hell of it tell me everything you've done against me.

Portia: I've always loved and always done everything I could to be good to you. If I've judged badly, please know I've tried.

Bassanio: You hurt me. You wouldn't sleep with me. You slept with other men besides me. I'm going to hurt you forever. I hate your guts.

Portia: I've always wanted to please you and to be however you wanted to be pleased.

Bassanio: You fucked Tim.

Portia: We were always fucking other people. You wanted me
to fuck other men so I wouldn't get too close to you cause
I depended too much on you.
Bassanio: Since I can't say it, I'm going to murder you.
Portia: Divorce me and I'll kill myself. Don't murder me right
now cause I'm scared. I love you.
Bassanio: Get down to the floor.
Portia: Let me spend one last night with you.
Bassanio: Get down.
Portia: Just fuck me once more.
Bassanio: I can't talk. It's the moment. Get down.
Portia: Your kiss' my life. (*Her fingernails're red.*)
Bassanio: I can't talk. No more. (*Sticks a knife across her throat
so there's lots of blood.*) I murdered her.

ACT III. MARRIAGE

*Portia and Bassanio hastily marry. All day it's been hot as hell.
So hot the people are animals. While they walk around, dioxin
sweat pours out of their skins. They don't think anymore. And
now this night, that makes us forget our agony.*

ACT IV

*Portia disguises herself as a boy. She also gets rid of all her feelings
so she can go to Venice to judge the Antonio-Shylock case. She
gets Antonio off by deviousness and trickery and takes all of Shylock R.'s money. She wants in payment only her cunt which smells
of rotting fish.*

1.

Lorenzo: On such a night as this the light of your fingernails ran
over the muffin main. The pirates have left their shore.
Shall we start moving? Now, given the strength of our wills,
we shall not fall into despair again.
I(sabel): On such a night, the music is lullabyes noise the regular

beat that makes us not think voodoo house zebra I can now now. Rowing to their main boat, they could glow at a moon beginning to exist because everything's in consonance with everything else.

Lorenzo: This night which'll never end the night'll never end. Here we dangle our knees over the wooden wharf; there're invisible fishing rods in hands, which stretch over across to that boat for which . . .

I(sabel): . . . We no longer want to go anywhere . . .

Lorenzo: This night here's our ease and our freedom. For light, love, Puerto Ricans throw down, and no tension; we have abandoned your father the Jew.

I(sabel): There're no more parents.

Lorenzo: There'll be no more parents.

I(sabel): Make love to me.

Lorenzo: Make love to you how?

I(sabel): There's only night.

Lorenzo: Or just like when suddenly you've a tiny purple lump at the base of your spine that's growing so fast in size and pain you have to nuisance-like see the doctor and suddenly he tells you you're going to die in a month or when you're lying late at night in a cot plumped in a large hollow living-room and something bursts inside your right hip then in temporal waves keeps bursting and you decide you're hem-orrhaging so you call an ambulance: then, when you find out you're not going to die, since there're no more causes and effects: There're no problems.

I(sabel): I want to give myself away. I'm not what you think. I'm dumb. I've developed myself. I'd give away all I've developed my world, if some man would take me. I'm trying my best to give away everything even though I don't have a boyfriend, because for me giving away's the only life that is. I have to have living life or blood.

Lorenzo: Then your blood's mine.

I(sabel): You're my blood.

Lorenzo: I don't know what's happening anymore. Can this be happening? All I know is life's blood and death's everything else.

(The beginning of sexual desire.)

I(sabel): I haven't been able to want to fuck for a long time.

Puerto Ricans: They want us out of here.

Puerto Rican: Mayor Koch's giving money to the real-estate entrepreneurs to chase us Puerto Ricans out of the Lower East Side so they can buy up all the buildings then make their investments worth as much as possible.

Puerto Ricans: We going bye-bye.

Puerto Rican *(rich from dealing)*: I get rich, boy, so I buy-buy.

White: Thass a lot of scare-talk. I say that cause I'm white.

(On Eldridge Street in New York City.)

Anorectic Prostitute Who Works on the Corner of Forsyth and Houston: I never seen cops come into this neighborhood an' these last three weeks, every other day there's some cop car on the block. I don' know what they think they're doing. They jus' sit on the fuckin' street corner. Then last night around five in the morning I'm lookin' for a John these two fuckin' cops have their cuffs around a bum. A bum! What d'they think they're doing? Cleaning up my neighborhood? They gonna arrest all the bums? Then they just be more bums. Want some bum, mister? *(Lifting her skirt, showing an ass too skinny to be an ass.)*

Prostitute 2 *(slapping her)*: No way. I'm not gonna get your AIDS.

Anorectic Prostitute Who Works On The Corner of Forsyth and Houston: My aid? I got no aid. Sarah 'n' I're just watching these fat farts put their manacles around this has-been; the needle boys're jus' watching; none of us're gonna run; we know the cops can't penetrate our territory. What're they gonna do: blow up the whole Lower East Side? This place's a jungle down to twenty feet down.

Prostitute 2: Money does everything.

Anorectic Prostitute Who Works On The Corner of Forsyth and Houston: Money's made us into graves. (*With a needle in her arm.*) There's no water 'n air anymore.

I(sabel): I don't feel sexual desire anymore. What's going to happen to me? I want to be human.

I'm gonna fight.

Who?

Koch's hirelings.

White Cop 1: You crazy? What you doing that for?

White Cop 2: Everytime I see one, I beat him up.

I(sabel): And meanwhile, this life's so nothing: how can I speak of anything? For how long do I have to scream?

White Cop 1: OK. OK. (*Two more White Cops enter.*) We don't want trouble here.

Bum: I live here.

White Cop 3: No more. This' private land. (*Four White Cops haul off the bum. I(sabel) remains behind.*)

I(sabel): You made little drops in my hair. Sperm within the night.

Another Bum: Don't go yet.

I(sabel): Marry me.

Another Bum: Wait a little while.

I(sabel): I want you to love me. (I(sabel)): a shriveled puppet. My head nods like a doll's. My face's white.)

White Cops (*returning*): We've finally driven her mad.

I(sabel): ha . . . yer.

Why . . . yer . . . yer.

Ha . . . m . . . m . . . b.

T . . . t . . . b . . . w.

B . . . b . . . w . . . w . . .

L . . . l . . .

g . . . g . . .

Were the day come, I should wish it dark

Till I was fucking and stealing against your flesh.

Lorenzo: On such a night as this the light of your fingernails ran over the muffin main. The pirates have left their shore.

Shall we start moving? Now, given the strength of our wills, we shall not fall into despair again.

I(sabel): On such a night, the music is lullabyes noise the regular beat that makes us not think voodoo house zebra I can now now. Rowing to their main boat, they could glow at a moon beginning to exist because everything's in consonance with everything else.

Lorenzo: This night which'll never end the night'll never end. Here we dangle our knees over the wooden wharf; there're invisible fishing rods in hands, which stretch over across to that boat for which . . .

I(sabel): . . . We no longer want to go anywhere . . .

Lorenzo: This night here's our ease and our freedom. For light, love, Puerto Ricans throw down, and no tension; we have abandoned your father the Jew.

I(sabel): There're no more parents.

Lorenzo: There'll be no more parents.

I(sabel): Make love to me.

Lorenzo: Make love to you how?

I(sabel): There's only night:

Lorenzo: Or just like when suddenly you've a tiny purple lump at the base of your spine that's growing so fast in size and pain you have to nuisance-like see the doctor and suddenly he tells you you're going to die in a month or when you're lying late at night in a cot plumped in a large hollow living-room and something bursts inside your right hip then in temporal waves keeps bursting and you decide you're hemorrhaging so you call an ambulance: then, when you find out you're not going to die, since there's no more causes and effects: There're no more problems.

I(sabel): I want to give myself away. I'm not what you think. I'm dumb. I've developed myself. I'd give away all I've developed my world, if some man would take me. I'm trying my best to give away everything even though I don't have a boyfriend, because for me giving away's the only life that is. I have to have living life or blood.

Lorenzo: Then your blood's mine.

I(sabel): You're my blood.

Lorenzo: I don't know what's happening anymore. Can this be happening? All I know is life's blood and death's everything else.

ACT V. TOO MUCH BEGINS TO BE LOVE

When Bassanio returns to Belmont Portia demands to see the ring she gave him:

Portia: I've come home: In arms: In his arms: This is a message to you: This whole book isn't a message to you, but I know that the whole book does revolve around dark red dark brown cerulean the sensuality of your fleshs' our only made value: . . .

Bassanio: Be clearer.

Portia: . . . I refuse: I refuse to give up sensuality for anything: . . .

I(sabel): It's Portia's voice.

Portia: . . . So it's my heart I give to you. It's too soon to say this. It's too soon to say anything. My whole life's changed.

I(sabel): Have our husbands come back?

Portia: I'm not going to marry again.

I(sabel) (*laughing*): Here's your husband, bitch.

Bassanio (*to Portia*): I want to fuck you and I want sensuality cause I love the sun.

Portia: Are you really saying that?

Bassanio: Yes.

Portia: Here's my cunt. Tell me we'll go on forever even in our graves we'll fuck.

Bassanio: I swear our corpses'll fuck to death.

Portia: I'm telling you: you don't even know me.

Bassanio: So I'm giving you nothing and promising you nothing. I don't want to live with someone.

Portia: Where's the ring? The ring I gave you.

Bassanio: What ring? I never phoned you.

Portia: I won't fuck you again unless you get back your ring cause I won't have anything with which to fuck. Because of you, I'll never fuck again.

Bassanio: I gave your flesh to a doctor.

Portia: Just cause I don't want to fuck cause I don't want to get hurt, doesn't mean I need a doctor. Is the doctor cute?

Bassanio: He's civil.

Portia: Who cares about civility in the bed? I want my cunt back.

Bassanio: He's a civil doctor.

Portia: Doctors aren't civil: they're murderers. By inventing penicillin, they've caused AIDS.

Bassanio: This goes to show that doctors heal the soul, cause this society's a sole.

Portia: No. Your flesh, no, more precisely, your wanting me and your real fingertips' touching me 'n' my not sleeping all night're my health and my disease.

Antonio: Then you need a doctor.

Portia: I'm the doctor. Don't you recognize me? I've always made everything myself. I'm self-independent. I don't ask anyone for anything.

Bassanio: And I am my own world.

Portia: I need you like an eye to see needs an object to see. Last night we fucked all night and today I walked through the winding streets of the West Village, blind. So I'll give my cunt to a doctor.

Bassanio: This doctor ain't civil.

Portia: Your wanting to touch me restores my health. For this reason genitals bleed red life.

This book is for Pier Paolo Pasolini

THE END

FLORIDA

MAYBE you're dying and you don't care anymore.
In the nothingness, the gray, islands almost disappear into the water. Black ovals the shape of leaves hide the crumbling of the universe. Key West Islands disappearing into the ocean.

You don't have anything more to say. You don't know what to do. Your whole life has been a mess. Grabbing on to whatever romance came along and holding on to it for dear life until it went so sour you had to vomit and leave. Then you'd recover, just like you recover from a hangover, by grabbing the next piece of tail who came along and wasn't so helpless or so demanding she'd force you to perceive reality.

One cunt's like every other cunt. One ideal's like every other ideal. When one dream goes, another takes its place. You're sick of standing in this shit and so you step out.

At the end of the world. Almost no one living in this perpetual Florida grayness. It may not be paradise, but it doesn't stink of the shit of your dreams. Not much to set you dreaming in this grayness.

There's an old dilapidated hotel on the island. Some old croaker who wheezes instead of talking runs the spa. As far as you know, the croaker won't bother you, no one else's staying at the hotel, and room-and-board are cheap. You decide to stay for a night.

There's nothing else to say. You're a piece of meat among other pieces of meat. It's like when you were at the hospital. The doctor couldn't get the needle in your vein to extract blood. Every time he stuck the needle in your arm, the vein rolled away. You felt like a piece of meat and you didn't care. You saw that the doctor saw living and dying and screaming people and the doctor didn't care if you were dying or screaming. So you didn't care if you were dying or screaming.

You can't tell what matters anymore. Every day you look out

at the ocean and you see a tiny boat going down that grayness.
One dark tiny boat going down the turbulent waters.

You're gonna stick with him, not cause you love him, but you've
gone this far. You've opened yourself to trusting him so deeply
if you turn back now, you'll be throwing everything you've got
away. The only thing you can call your life. You'll be left with
a rotting carcass. Besides, he's not so bad even if he is a gangster.
The dimple in his double chin.

He knows how to handle you. He's cruel to you just up to a
certain point. He knows that point and he knows if he was one
bit crueler to you, you'd leave him. He knows when to press you,
when to be a little bit crueler, and when to leave you alone. He
really cares about you because he bothers to know you so well.
Other people he doesn't bother about, he just kills them. He's
gotten into you and he knows how to manipulate your limbs with
his big naked hands.

He's a killer. O my God, he kills people. You know you've
got to get away from him.

You look up in the car, and there he is. Driving the car, as
usual. Never looking at you.

Johnny's running away from trouble again. He's always more
trouble than the trouble from which he's running away.

You're the big one. The big dingbat. The winner. You're in this
little hick town, this island, and you're gonna take it over until
the boat comes. As usual you've got everything arranged and
under control. You know how to move the little people around
so you can get everything you want.

It's quiet here, and gray. Layers of gray and layers of gray. Like
a numbness you can slice with your hand. When the numbness
separates, there's nothing. This's what you want.

The ocean waves're moving regularly up and down the beach. They leave lines of shells on the beach and sometimes large jellyfish. You can see the shells and the jellyfish only when the light manages to squeeze through the gray layers. Otherwise the shells and jellyfish look like darker gray blobs, then rows, on the gray.

The day gets darker. You see that the beach isn't the sea. The crummy wood boards that lead to the sea look wet. The whole joint's crumbling apart. How many more years does this hotel have? Three? One? One more hurricane? Maybe tomorrow. You can see the bones of the world.

Somewhere behind you, you hear a car stop and voices. You don't believe that you're hearing anything.

So now shitface is gonna take out his little gun. Order everyone around with his little gun, the old fuddy-duddy who doesn't keep up this palsied outhouse, probably pisses in his pants, and the doddering old man who's been the only hotel guest for the last twenty years. Phooey. Isn't Johnny tough? Johnny and his gun. You hope the hotel's got a bar cause you're gonna have to stick with Johnny until you can get out of this grayness.

You need another man. In this grayness it's easier to find a bottle of booze.

What man's gonna want you now? Once upon a time you were really hot stuff. With your blonde hair and big child's eyes, eyes so big and wide they denied the way your nipples got hard under your sweater, men were drooling after you. You could get anyone you wanted. For nothing. Now you get beaten up and shoved around. Every now and then you get a gun shoved in your mouth.

"OK. Everyone get your hands up. I'm taking over here."

You walk into the dark inner space of the hotel. You're gonna show them who's boss. A trembling white-haired guy appears with his hands held up.

You're dreaming that you're wearing your white Givenchy dress and your white and brown shoes. You're wading through about two feet of mud and water. Your dress is getting filthy, but you don't mind. You're trying to reach an old deserted house. Your fiancé's waiting for you there. You lift your eyes and see a large dark structure.

"We're almost there, dear." Your red fingernails carefully flick a cake-crumb off your summer dress.

You're still alone and with the grace of God you'll die alone.

Maybe you'll die soon and it'll all be over. No more fakes.

The ocean's calm. It's almost evening and it looks like dawn with that strange yellow sun, under the dark gray sky, making the lower third of the sky white-yellow-gray. Sending a triangle of yellow-white light out over the ocean.

The air's still and stinks of fish. You realize a storm's coming. One storm more or less don't make any difference to you. You walk into the dark interior of the hotel and see a gun pointed at your face.

"Back against the wall."

I moved back against the wall. I didn't feel frightened, yet.

"All of you, back against the wall."

The geezer who ran the hotel was already rubbing his back so hard against the wall, the wallpaper was crumbling. A dame with booze in her hand who was standing against the hotel register didn't move.

The guy with the gun walked over and slashed her face open with the point of his gun. She looked at him and walked over to the wall.

Lightning.

The hotel door flies open.

"OK Johnny. Men are for fucking and women for friendship. When I'm not fucking you, I'm your enemy."

I ignored what she said. The storm was coming up hard and fast and there was nothing I could do about that. The boat wouldn't come and I'd be stuck with these pawns for days.

"I want you to understand I'm boss here. This storm"

"It's a hurricane."

I gave the old guy a dirty look. "Hurricane. It's gonna be a while and I don't want trouble. As far as I'm concerned, you're pieces on a checkerboard that I'm moving around so everything's easiest for me. You're either on the board or you're off the board." I moved my gun.

The hotel door swung open and shut. When the door swung open again, an old guy in a wheelchair and a tall woman dressed in a lightish dress were standing in the doorway.

I thought I was hallucinating.

"Excuse me. I need help for my grandfather, Senator . . ."

"We're . . ."

You'd think this was Palm Springs at Christmas. "Both of you. Get over here. No, you," I pointed my gun at the hotel clerk. He should be doing his job. "Shove the wheelchair against the wall. No funny business."

I looked at the girl. "You can use your own legs, I presume?"

The girl was a looker. Legs and class. I wouldn't go near her if she was coated with hundred dollar bills. I didn't have to go near her. Johnny, as his drunk girlfriend called him, would be doing all our movements for us.

Hotel lights go out.

Old geezer takes advantage of blackness to try to shove wheelchair with guy in it at me. I laugh and shoot geezer in arm.

"Looks like someone else is going to have to be hotel clerk for a while."

There're no lights and there's this storm, a hurricane I think, and there's this gangster and I'm totally confused. This isn't the way things are back home. Mummy and poppa always kept a quiet home, and now that they're dead,—they must not have loved me as much as I thought cause they died,—grandpa, the senator, takes care of me. I wish we were back home.

Grandpa said that politics was getting so crooked, he had to get away for awhile. He's not running from anyone; he's just trying to figure out how he can fight the crookedness more successfully. I want to be like grandpa: I want to fight for a better world.

I wonder if there are any more men in the world like grandpa.

"All of you. Get to your rooms. Remember that people die when they go out in hurricanes. The phone lines are dead. There's no way you can escape.

"Don't get any funny ideas. Brave pigeons become dead pigeons. Remember: to me you're just pieces of meat."

We were pieces of meat who were still bleeding. The worst was: we might stop bleeding soon.

"In two hours you'll all come down here for dinner. If we can't find any food, we'll live on the booze. I like giving parties. I'll wheel the senator to his room."

"Get upstairs like he says." She looked like an outraged mother hen, only her baby was an old man in a wheelchair and she was probably a virgin. I put my hand on her arm. I didn't want her making more trouble for all of us.

"Wait a second."

"Uh-huh."

"You look like . . . a reasonable man. Is that monster going to hurt my grandfather?"

"I doubt it. Your grandfather's probably too important a person."

"I didn't ask you to be smart. We're in a terrible situation and we have to help each other."

"The kind of help I could give you honey you wouldn't want."

"How do you know what I want?"

"I can tell by looking at your fingers. Your left hand pinky's shorter than the finger next to it. Now will you be a good girl and get upstairs?"

"You're a man! You could overpower this gangster. You wouldn't have to kill him. Just knock him cold."

   "A woman friend once told me the only thing men are good for is fucking. I'm afraid that's true."

"You're not a man. A man would realize that his and other people's lives are in danger. Even if he didn't care about the other people, he'd try to save himself. You're a flea, or some kind of . . . amoeba who just accepts things."

"Listen. I'm not going to do anything. I don't care how I die, honey." I started walking up the stairs.

   I began remembering her long legs and regretting I was walking away from her.

I wanted to kill him. The only thought in my mind was that I wanted to kill him.

I must have fallen asleep, for the next thing I know, I'm hearing these screamings and sounds of beating that make the old hotel seem like a flea-studded whorehouse:

". . . keep your mouth shut."

"Why don't cha beat me up again? Hurting me takes the place of sex these days."
    "I'm a businessman. I want you to remember. I'm a quiet businessman and I like my friends to be quiet about me."

"The only friends you have are dead men.
    "You're just a cheap dice man, Johnny. A cheap dice man who's running from the real crooks, the big crooks, and you think you can be a big guy to these crummy people in this crummy hotel."

"I suppose the takeover of The Flamingo and Virginia Hill's 'suicide' are small-time bits to you?
    "I shouldn't ever talk to you. I weaken myself when I talk to you."

"Johnny, straighten out. You're nothing Johnny, like me."

"You stinkin' whore. I'm gonna kill you one of these days."

"You're nothing like me.
    "Get me another drink, please Johnny"

I wanted to find my grandfather. I left the little room at the end of the hall against which the wild wind was beating and the trees and the telephone poles, the only bit of safety I had left, and I started down the hall. I knew my grandfather was somewhere downstairs.

The hotel was dark, almost black. Walls seemed to drift into more and more corners and walls. Finally I reached the stairs.

Large dark shapes moved in and out of the corners of my eyes. As I walked down the stairs, I saw the walls move, bend and almost crack, as if they were bowing to me. I was walking down the endless stairs in my long white dress. The train of my dress was slowly draped upward behind me. I felt so tall and proud my head was almost touching the ceiling. Soon I would be a new woman.

All the people I had ever known were waiting for me at the bottom of the stairs. My mother was crying and even my father had tears in his eyes. I was so happy I was almost crying. Somewhere in that mass of people, my fiancé, soon: my husband, was waiting for me.

What was I thinking? I had to find my grandfather. I was in a hotel which was being, for some reason, run by a gangster and I had to find my grandfather before the gangster killed him.

I was standing at the bottom of that endless flight of stairs. I could see the hotel door flying open and closed, almost flying off its hinges but not quite, and I could see the winds wiping the panes of glass out of the windows and I could hear the palm trees break and fall against the old hotel. I wanted to run, but I didn't know where I could go.

I realized that I've always wanted to run and never have anywhere to run to. I had to find my grandfather quickly. There were rooms and rooms and most of the rooms were empty and my grandfather was in one room and the gangster was in another room. I could hardly tell the rooms from the doors cause the large dark shapes were moving in front of and away from my eyes.

I couldn't see but I had to keep going. I stuck my hands out in front of me.

I kept on moving. Something clattered to the floor, and I almost tumbled.

A hand grabbed my wrist.

I didn't want to, but I couldn't get those legs out of my mind. I looked outside my room and saw those legs again. I didn't want to, I must have stopped thinking, but I began to follow them.

Long white legs.

They led me through the hall, down the stairs, and into some large room.

I found myself looking into that man's eyes. The one who wouldn't help me. "What do you want with me?"

"I want to talk to you."

"We've done all our talking. I don't want anything to do with men who are cowards.

"Excuse me, I have to find my grandfather."

"You've done all your talking. I still want to talk to you."

She tried to brush by me. I put my two arms around the sides of her body.

"What d'you want?"

"I want to find out who you are."

"I'm in trouble. Or do you want the irrelevant details?"

"Let's say I want the irrelevant details."

"When I was two years old, I refused to drink milk. My parents, they were still alive then, were scared I was going to die. My father started to take a camera apart. Only when he started to break the camera, would I drink the milk."

"That's certainly irrelevant."
    "Is it? I want to stay alive, Mr. Coward. I'm only interested in people who are going to help me stay alive."

"Aren't you being self-centered? Tell me about mom and pops. When did they die on you?"

"When I was eight. Just old enough to start feeling insecure and not old enough to know how to ask someone for help. My grandfather took me into his house and gave me what attention he could."

"Could? You mean you were a lonely child who spent lonely days making up fantasies and living in them?"

"My personal history concerns only those people who love me. Excuse me please."

"Tell me more about your parents. Did they love you a lot when you were a child?"

"I want to find my grandfather." I was begging him to help me. "If you care at all about me, you'll help me find him."

"I didn't know I cared about you."

"Help me."

For some reason I wanted to hear the rest of her words, but I couldn't. I kept hearing that stupid popular song, bits of it, that everyone was singing back where everyone was still living and burning each other out.

> Baby don't give, baby don't get.
> When it's cold, baby gets wet.
> When baby gets wet, baby gets weak.
> Baby don't find, baby don't seek.

> You want to know the story of this song
> It's about a woman who loves to go wrong.
> She gets contented like a big fat cat
> Only when she's lying flat on her back.

> Well, this woman fell in love with a man
> Just like some women unfortunately can.

This man had nuts but was nuts in the head
He refused to take this hot babe to bed.

Baby don't give, baby don't get.
When it's cold, baby gets wet.
When baby gets wet, baby gets weak.
Baby don't find, baby don't seek.

He told her he loved her; he told her he'd give
Anything to her so she'd continue to live.
He'd buy her minks and he'd buy her pearls
He just wouldn't give her cunt a swirl.
Too many women were pursuing him
And he was fucking too many girls.

So she sang him this sad sad song
About how the world was always wrong:
DIE IF I DO, DIE IF I DON'T:
DIE IF I WRITE, DIE IF I DON'T
DIE IF I FALL IN LOVE AND DIE IF I WON'T

He didn't give a shit, he didn't care.
She shouted to the cold winter air;
She slashed her wrists; she shaved her head;
She refused to eat so she'd almost drop dead.

He didn't run to her, he told her he
Was sick of people and their needs.
All he wanted to do was sit alone
In his country house by his telephone.

Baby don't give, baby don't get.
When it's cold, baby gets wet.
When baby gets wet, baby gets weak.
Baby don't find, baby don't seek.

So listen girls, do what you can
To find a horny loving man.
Give him all you've got to give,
Give him more so you can live.